A PITY ABOUT THE GIRL

and Other Stories

A PITY ABOUT THE GIRL

and Other Stories

Michael Gilbert

EDITED AND INTRODUCED
BY JOHN COOPER

ROBERT HALE · LONDON

© The Estate of Michael Gilbert 2008
Introduction © John Cooper 2008
This edition first published in Great Britain 2008

ISBN 978-0-7090-8732-8

Robert Hale Limited
Clerkenwell House
Clerkenwell Green
London EC1R 0HT

www.halebooks.com

2 4 6 8 10 9 7 5 3 1

Typeset in 10/12½pt Sabon
Printed and bound in Great Britain by
Biddles Limited, King's Lynn, Norfolk

CONTENTS

INTRODUCTION

MICHAEL GILBERT (1912-2006) was an extremely talented writer who could produce a variety of styles. He was equally at home writing classic detection e.g. *Close Quarters* (1947), and *Smallbone Deceased* (1950); thrillers e.g. *After The Fine Weather* (1963), and *Trouble* (1987); police procedural e.g. *Blood and Judgement* (1959), and *Death of a Favourite Girl* (1980, US, *The Killing of Katie Steelstock*); espionage e.g. *Game Without Rules* (1967) and *Mr Calder and Mr Behrens* (1982).

His novels and stories are always elegant, credible and entertaining. He wrote thirty novels and 183 short stories, 172 of which have been collected in thirteen volumes. He also wrote plays for radio, television and the stage.

In February 2008, Michael Gilbert was listed in the *Daily Telegraph* article '50 Crime Writers to Read Before You Die'. His skilfully plotted novel, *Smallbone Deceased*, was included by Julian Symons in *The Hundred Best Crime Stories*: (1959) and in H.R.F. Keating's *Crime and Mystery the 100 Best Books* (1987).

The Swedish Academy of Detection appointed him Grand Master in 1981 and The Mystery Writers of America, Grand Master in 1987. In 1994, The Crime Writers Association presented him with its highest award, the Cartier Diamond Dagger, for an outstanding contribution to the genre of crime fiction. Michael Gilbert was appointed CBE in 1980.

Michael Gilbert became a published author in 1947 with his first two novels, *Close Quarters* and *They Never Looked Inside*, (US *He Didn't Mind Danger*). His first short story, 'Weekend at Wapentake', appeared in *Good Housekeeping*, 16 October 1948. In this story, Henry Montacute Bohun, the solicitor and partner in the Lincoln's Inn firm of Horniman, Birley and Craine, hears what happened during that particular weekend: the discovery of a murder, leading to more deaths and a conflagration in which part of a literary heritage is destroyed. Bohun went on to appear in eight more stories and the novel *Smallbone Deceased*.

The second short story, 'Back in Five Years', was featured in *John Bull*, 18 December 1948, (illustrated by A.R. Whitear). In this original form of the story, it is an uncredited Chief Inspector Hazlerigg who explains how a forger of one pound notes is eventually caught. There were three other stories published in *John Bull* in 1949, 'Amateur in Violence', 'Touch of Genius' and 'A Nose in a Million'.

During the 1950s, Michael Gilbert was selling stories to many different magazines such as *Adventure, Good Housekeeping, John Bull, Suspense, Woman's Journal* and *Lilliput*. A long series of stories was published in the *Argosy* and *Ellery Queen's Mystery Magazine*.

At this time, the *London Evening Standard* newspaper regularly featured detective stories, especially written for the paper, by acknowledged leading writers of the genre. In the year 1950, the contributing authors included Margery Allingham, Leo Bruce, Edmund Crispin, Freeman Wills Crofts, Cyril Hare, Michael Innes, E.C.R. Lorac, Gladys Mitchell, John Rhode, Julian Symons, Roy Vickers and Clifford Witting.

Michael Gilbert supplied many stories to the *Evening Standard* right though the fifties and into the early sixties: some illustrated by artists such as Mackenzie and Arthur Wragg. A few of the stories were published under series titles 'A Thriller A Day' and 'Did It Happen?'.

His stories often have tantalizing titles e.g, 'Tea Shop Assassin', 'An Appealing Pair of Legs', 'Scream From a Soundproof Room', (all from 1955). Many of Gilbert's stories were reprinted in a variety of publications with different titles: 'Xinia Florata' has four alternative titles whilst 'Amateur in Violence' has three.

Michael Gilbert had great sophistication in constructing his stories and thankfully many contained his numerous series characters.

Two novels and fifty short stories feature Patrick Petrella. *Petrella at Q* (1977), *Young Petrella* (1988) and *Even Murderers Take Holidays* (2007), between them, contain forty of the stories. Patrick Petrella joined the Metropolitan Police on his twenty-first birthday and his career is carefully followed until he is a superintendent in the story, 'The Spoilers'. These are outstanding examples of the police procedural story and many had their first appearance in *Argosy*. The first published Petrella story seems to be 'Source Seven' in *John Bull* 29 August 1953, illustrated by Zelinski. Petrella uses his skill as a lock picker to save his life as he discovers how heroin is being smuggled from France to Britain. 'Who Has Seen The Wind', published in *Argosy*, November 1956, is stated by Michael Gilbert in *Petrella at Q* to be the first story he wrote about Petrella. In this tale, a poem by Christina Rossetti helps to trap an escaped convict. Working with Sergeant Gwilliam in 'Breach of the Peace', he helps to prove that Mrs Williams is a liar and receiver of stolen goods, which leads to his promotion to Sergeant. Whilst in the story 'Rough Justice', a crooked car repairer is brought to justice and Petrella becomes a Chief Inspector. In 'Old Mr Martin', Petrella eventually finds out how Mr Martin financed his sweet shop.

Chief Inspector (later Chief Superintendent) Hazelrigg of Scotland Yard is another important series character who features in six novels and nineteen stories. He was Gilbert's first series detective. As a superintendent in 'Tea Shop Assassin', he unmasks a political killer whilst having afternoon tea overlooking the Houses of Parliament. During 'Death Money', he states that Miss Hallam's apparently motiveless murder was unique due to 'the fact that her murderers were five in number, ranging in age from a child of thirteen to a middle-age creature of thirty-two.'

Michael Gilbert's twenty-four stories about Daniel Joseph Calder and Mr Samuel Behrens are considered by some crime reviewers to be the best spy stories ever written. These two apparently mild-mannered retired gentlemen are in fact ruthless and efficient, counter-intelligence agents who were recruited by MI6 in the 1930s. Most of the stories had their first publication in *Argosy*. In 'The Headmaster', the hunt for a master spy ends with Calder witnessing death in a London club. 'Trembling's Tours' involves Russian agents and smuggling. Calder believes these are linked to a travel agency. Colonel Mounteagle goes to horrific lengths in 'Signal Tresham' to prevent a new road from being built across his land. Calder is shot but it is Behrens who does the real killing. Commander Elfe makes one of his four appearances in short stories here.

Anything For a Quiet Life (1990) presents nine stories about the solicitor Jonas Pickett, who leaves his busy London office behind and sets up a practice in a sleepy Sussex resort. His intention of having a less eventful life is thwarted, however. All the Pickett chronicles made their first appearance in *Ellery Queen's Mystery Magazine* during the 1980s.

Both the wily solicitor Mr Rumbold and the monocled Hargest Macrea QC, appear in the novel *Death has Deep Roots*, (1951) and also one or other of them appears in four short stories. In the story 'The Blackmailing of Mr Justice Ball', they have to contend with the extrasensory perception of a Siamese cat.

Detective Chief Inspector William Mercer is in charge of the CID at Stoneferry-on-Thames during the investigations in 'The Body of a Girl' (1972). He later operates as an ex-policeman in three linked stories, 'The Man at the Bottom', 'The Man in the Middle' and 'The Man at the Top'. All three originated in *Ellery Queen's Mystery Magazine* during 1979 and were later collected in *The Man Who Hated Banks* (1997).

In 1995, Michael Gilbert started what would be his last series of fourteen stories, centred around the partnership of Fearne and Bracknell, solicitors. Their practice was situated near the northern end of Tower Bridge. Some of the stories had their first appearance in the *Ellery Queen Mystery Magazine*. The title story of the collection 'The Mathematics of Murder' (2000) concerns the catching of a serial killer whose victims are killed on the trains taking commuters home to various towns in Essex. Hugo Bracknell and the firm's managing clerk, Horace Piggin play an important part in catching the killer.

Superintendent Mahood was the investigating officer in two competition stories, 'The Craven Case' in *Suspense* (June 1959) and 'Can You Solve a Murder?' in the *Daily Express* (21–26 May 1956). The stories involve picture clues and have not been collected.

There are forty-eight short stories of Gilbert's, many of them classics, that do not involve a series character. For example, 'Under the Last Scuttleful' features Sam Cotton, who comes to dread collecting coke from the cellar and what he might find under the last heap: with reason! In 'Mrs Haslet's Gone', one never knows what might be used to make the tulips bloom in the garden! Meticulous planning leads to the destruction of an evil blackmailer in 'The Inside Pocket'. Henry Bohun's senior colleague, Mr Birley, recalls in 'The Drop Shot' how he witnessed the perfect murder.

The stories in the present collection span the years 1951–1996. Several of Michael Gilbert's series characters are included such as Henry Bohun, Hargest Macrae QC, Commander Elfe and Noel Anthony Pontarlier Rumbold, a junior partner in his father's firm. The only two stories written about the cunning Colonel Cristobal Ocampos also appear. More exotic locations include France, Austria, Italy, Germany and South America.

There is a rich variety of subjects including a ghost story, a spy story and one featuring Sherlock Holmes and Dr Watson. The crimes range from attempted robberies and drug smuggling to murders by explosives, strangulation, shooting and bludgeoning. A rich menu indeed. Enjoy!

John Cooper
Westcliff-on-Sea

A PITY ABOUT THE GIRL

I T WAS SEVEN o'clock of a lovely summer evening when Andrew
Siward first saw her. He was sitting on the terrace of the Hotel
Dauphin at Cannes, looking across the square of burnt grass and
bent orange trees at the deep blue of the Mediterranean. It was the best
hour of the day. His second aperitif was on the table in front of him. He
was looking forward to a leisurely dinner, not more than two glasses of
marc with his coffee, and an early bed.

The work he had come to the South of France to do was finished. It
was a moment for sitting back and enjoying the scenery; and beautiful
girls were a prominent part of the scenery on the promenade at Cannes.

Not that this particular girl was got up to attract attention. She was
wearing a plain white linen dress cut square across the top of her breasts,
and showing the sunbrowned skin of arms, shoulders, and throat and, as
far as Andrew could judge, nothing else at all. He put her age at nineteen
or twenty.

The man who was with her was a figure as typical of that time and
place as she was. In his middle fifties, but still alert and fit. Frenchmen of
his age seem to grow through middle age more gracefully than the
English or American male. Hair so light it was difficult to see whether it
was grey or not, cut *en brosse*, a bush shirt with half-length sleeves which
showed brown and muscular arms; on one wrist a gold watch, on a metal
strap, and a small gold medallion on a chain around his neck.

Andrew was used to summing people up by their clothes and their
belongings. These were clearly residents, not tourists. In spite of the
informality of their dress, or perhaps because of it, he sensed a background of wealth and position.

He wondered if the man was her father.

He wondered if they were going to come on to the terrace. After a
moment of indecision they climbed the three steps which separated it
from the roadway and settled down two tables from him.

They were so close now that it was difficult to examine them, but their

reflection in the glass front of the hotel dining room gave him an opportunity to do so without seeming rude.

The girl seemed to him as attractive as anyone he could remember.
Maybe a film star? He thought not. She had none of the hardness and
sophistication which encased even the youngest actresses like a protective
shell. It was a shell which might be invisible at ten yards, but was unmistakable at close quarters.

It was possible that she was the man's *petite amie*, but he thought not.
There was nothing in their attitude towards each other to suggest such a
relationship.

Andrew thought, I wish she was sitting here at the table with me,
talking to me, looking at me in that way, or, perhaps, looking at me a
little more intimately than that. We could have dinner together, and after
dinner we would go up to my room. As he put his hand out to pick up
his drink he was shocked to find that desire for a girl he had hardly set
eyes on had made it shake. He put the glass down slowly and said, 'Take
a grip on yourself, Andrew. You're an old man. Well, middle-aged,
anyway. Thirty-five years older than that girl. A whole generation.'

It was a sobering thought, if not a comforting one.

Up to that time his experience of women had been standardised. A few
adventures during and after the war, followed by marriage to an attractive and desirable wife. Twenty years of happiness. Then he had noticed
that she grew easily tired, and curiously weak. She made nothing of it.
She belonged to a stoic generation. A generation that had been brought
up to believe that complaining was something only the lower classes did.
It was the doctors who had spoken the word 'leukaemia' to him. He had
hardly had time to grasp what it meant before she was gone.

When the numbness had worn off he had taken consolation where he
could find it. Not from the professionals who hung around the pave-
ments of Maddox Street and Soho Square but from amateurs,
discontented wives, some of them not much younger than he was. A
sordid, unsatisfactory series of bargains. Pumped-up lust for the price of
a dinner and a theatre. Furtive coupling which left him with nothing but
a bad taste in his mouth.

It had taken one look at this young French girl to show him what he
had been searching for so hungrily and failing so sadly to find.

At this point common sense took charge. It said to him in the flat,
unemotional voice that common sense always uses, 'It's not a young girl
that you're craving for. It's your own lost youth. And that's something
that no amount of wishing is ever going to bring back. If you can't grasp
this simple fact, you're stupider even that I took you for.'

At this point he realised something else.

He had been looking at the reflection of the girl in the glass. The man had been looking at him. It was not a look of hostility. Rather one of dawning recognition. Now that he came to consider it there *was* something in the man that touched a chord of remembrance. The square forehead, the long, straight nose that turned very slightly at the tip giving the face a whimsical look, the set of the chin. And surely he could see – or was his imagination playing tricks? – a zigzag line down the left side of his face, from cheekbone to chin, white against the sunbrowned skin.

None of this had occupied more than a few seconds. The man had made up his mind. He said something to the girl, pushed back his chair, and came across. He was smiling. He said, 'I run the risk of having made a stupid mistake, but is it not the young lieutenant?'

'It is,' said Andrew, 'and you are the young farmer.'

'Neither of us so young now,' said the man. He spoke in French as though he realised that Andrew would answer him in the same tongue.

'It was a long time ago,' said Andrew.

Nearly forty years. Half a lifetime.

By influence of his father, and by virtue of his excellent French, Andrew had infiltrated the army at an illegally young age. He had celebrated his eighteenth birthday on the ship which took him and the rest of the Armoured Reconnaissance Regiment to Algiers for the Torch landings. Their job had been to find the German army. They had found them in the little farm in the hills above Bou Arada.

It was not a strong or well-organised part of that army. Three panzer-grenadiers on a foraging expedition for eggs and wine. The farmer and his seventeen-year-old son had been foolish enough to refuse them and to add some uncomplimentary comments on the German character. The old man had been knocked unconscious. The youngster had been tied to a chair and one of the men was busy with a knife teaching him good manners. He was carving the symbol of his regiment, a lightning flash, on the left-hand side of his face.

They were so preoccupied with what they were doing that they had not heard the armoured car stop in the lane at the far end of the farm. Andrew, standing outside the open window, had drawn the army revolver which he had never used before, and shot one of the Germans in the foot. That was the end of the battle. The three soldiers had surrendered to superior force, and had been taken away. Andrew and his section had been billeted at the farm for a week, and had become friends with the craggy M. Rocaire and his young son Louis. Then the battle had moved on. He had often meant to go back, but had had no chance to do so until after the war, when he was on holiday in Algiers and had driven out to the farm. The Rocaire family was no longer there. Like many

French settlers, they had seen the writing on the wall and returned to their own country.

'This is most evidently the hand of fate,' said Louis Rocaire. 'That out of a thousand tables in Cannes we should have chosen this one. One must never contest the decrees of Providence. You are here yet for some days?'

'My business is finished, and it had been in my mind to spend a little time exploring the countryside.'

'Then you have a car here? Not an armoured car this time.'

'No. A faithful old Humber.'

'A most distinguished vehicle. You will drive out in it, if not tonight then tomorrow morning and will consider yourself our guest for the rest of your visit. I am forgetting myself. I have not introduced my daughter. Marie-Claude. This is the young lieutenant.'

'The man who shot the German in the foot,' said Marie-Claude. 'You are a figure of mystical importance in the history of the Rocaire family. I am delighted to meet you in the flesh.'

'No more delighted than I am,' said Andrew.

'Then all that remains is to give you directions. Our house is in the hills, in the valley of the Loup. You have a map with you. Excellent. An officer of the Reconnaissance Corps, my love, never travels without a map. I will mark the place. So. It is a little isolated but not difficult to find.'

'I can't impose on you for more than a day.'

'It will not be an imposition, I assure you. It will be a pleasure. We see very little company, Marie-Claude and I. We will drink the wine we make ourselves, and will fight old battles. My little girl will be bored, but for her father's sake she will pretend not to be.'

Marie-Claude said, quite seriously, 'You must stay longer than one day, or we will think you do not like us.'

'That would never do,' agreed Andrew. He hoped he did not sound as breathless as he felt.

When, on the following morning, he drove his fifteen-year-old Humber up into the hills, following the course of the Wolf River, he wondered what sort of place he would find. He had pictured something between an old Provençal stone house and a converted farm. As he turned the final corner in the long, winding approach road he dismissed both ideas. This was a very considerable residence. Newly built, on a platform cut into one side of the hill, there was a solidity about it that spoke of money and taste. A solemn dark-haired boy opened the door for him, and took charge of his luggage. A second one led the way to his room. Andrew guessed that they were brothers and might be Corsicans, and this was confirmed by the slurred consonants when the second boy spoke: Mamzelle and her father, he said, were by the pool. He would inform them of monsieur's arrival.

It was the start of a five-day fantasy. Andrew had forgotten that such a life could still be lived. The house staff could not have been less than five, and there was a chauffeur, and a gardener as well. The food and the wine would not have disgraced a three-star hotel. His clothes were washed and ironed daily, and his original intention of staying for a day and a night was neatly thwarted when both his suits were removed and sent down to Cannes for cleaning and pressing.

By day there was riding with Marie-Claude and tennis against her father, who turned out to be a formidable player. All three of them swam in the pool, a cunning piece of engineering, fed by a stream coming in at one end and overflowing into a waterfall at the other. In the evenings, after dinner, they sat on the terrace, the bullfrogs competing with the cicadas, and talked about everything and everybody except themselves.

Only once did Louis touch on their own circumstances. He said, 'You may have noticed that one or other of my boys makes a circuit of our property every evening. They are both armed. It is a necessary precaution. In this part of France we are still fighting a war that most people have forgotten.'

Andrew said, 'I noticed OAS signs on some of the houses. I did wonder.'

'The OAS against the SAC – the Service d'Action Civique. De Gaulle's spies and butchers. There are many of us Pieds Noirs in this area. We have not forgotten. And the SAC has not forgotten. Recently, not many miles from here, a police officer and all of his family were butchered one night.'

This was said when they were sitting by themselves. The arrival of Marie-Claude had switched the conversation to more suitable topics.

It was on the fourth night, when Andrew had at last convinced his host that he must leave, that the suggestion was made.

Louis said, 'You will be proceeding by car to one of the Channel ports?'

'To Dieppe.'

'Which will take you how long?'

'I am not one of your racing drivers. I shall spend at least one night en route. Possibly a second one outside Dieppe, where I have friends.'

'Then may I entrust my little girl to you?' Before Andrew could take in all the implications of this, he added, 'She goes to visit an old friend in England. They were at school in Switzerland together. Normally she would go by train, but in present circumstances I should be much happier—'

The length of this explanation had enabled Andrew to get his breath back. He said, 'I should be delighted to be of service to you. It would be a very small return for the hospitality you have shown me.'

It had been a day of blue skies and hot sun. Andrew had driven steadily, but not fast. The roads had been bad to start with, but after Valence they had improved and as evening was closing in they were in the wooded, hilly country of the Puy-de-Dôme. Marie-Claude, who had been turning the pages of the Michelin guide, had found what sounded like a promising hotel above Châtelguyon in the Vallée de Sans Souci. It was classified as quiet, and possessing a *jardin fleuri*.

'That sounds fine,' said Andrew, 'as long as they're not all booked up.'

There were half a dozen cars in the courtyard outside the hotel. Andrew said, 'Wait whilst I enquire.' He came back to say that they were in luck. There were just two rooms left.

'Lucky indeed,' said Marie-Claude gravely. She had got out of the car and had a holdall in one hand. As she stooped to pick up her suitcase Andrew said, 'Let me,' took a suitcase in either hand, and followed her into the hotel.

The bedrooms were on the first floor, at the back. Looking out of his window, Andrew could see the flowered garden, and, beyond it, a wild stretch of wooded country now fading into the dusk of a late summer evening. There were lights away in the distance towards the southeast. Riom, he guessed. A helicopter buzzed overhead like an angry bumblebee. Andrew went downstairs thoughtfully. Marie-Claude was in the dining room when he got there. She was dressed as she had been when he saw her first, in her simple white dress. Andrew was conscious that every person in the room had observed, analysed, and recorded her, and that every man in the room was envying him.

Marie-Claude was unusually silent at dinner, and when she had finished her coffee, said, 'I am tired. I will go up now.'

Andrew sat over a second cup of coffee, then over a glass of brandy. He knew that if he went up, he would not be able to go to bed and go to sleep. He would be too conscious of the fact that only an intervening door was separating him from a girl he desired more than anything he had ever desired in his whole life.

No doubt the door would be locked.

Doubly locked, in fact, by the trust that Louis Rocaire had placed in him.

'I entrust my little girl to you.'

He was vaguely aware that other people were arriving at the hotel, and thought that they would be unlucky since he and Marie-Claude had secured the last two rooms.

Possibly they had merely called in for dinner, though it was now nearly eleven. He heard voices in the hall, but no one came into the dining room. Ten minutes later he was sitting on the end of his bed. He had taken off his coat, but had made no further move to undress. The window was wide open and he could see the moon riding high over the dark woods, and could hear the owls talking to each other.

Then he heard another sound, closer at hand.

It came from Marie-Claude's room, and was unmistakable. She was crying.

He walked across and tried the door gently. It opened under his hand. The girl had not undressed either. She was sitting on the edge of the bed. He strode across, put an arm round her shoulders, and said, 'What is it, Marie-Claude, what's wrong?'

Marie-Claude said, with a gap between each word, 'I – am – so – frightened.'

At two o'clock that afternoon a car had drawn up at the entrance of the Rocaire house. Two men had gotten out. The driver and another man stayed in the car. It was clear that they were expected. One of the Corsican boys had led them to the business room where Louis was waiting for them, standing.

They shook hands briefly, and without any warmth. The spokesman of the two new arrivals was a thin man, with white hair and a brown face seamed with wrinkles, like the sand when the tide has ebbed. His companion was dark-haired, younger and thicker. He stood a pace behind the other as though to emphasise that he was a subordinate, though no one looking at his heavy, composed face would have doubted that he was a formidable man in his own right.

They all sat down. The white-haired man said, 'We discovered, only this morning, and quite by chance, that you were entertaining an Englishman named Siward.'

'Andrew Siward. That is correct.'

'And he has been staying with you for the last five days.'

'That is also correct.'

'Would it be impertinent to enquire the reason for your hospitality?'

Louis considered the question. Then he said, 'Yes. It would be impertinent. But since you evidently feel it to be important I will answer it. He turned out to be a very old friend of army days. Also, it occurred to me that his arrival might be providential.'

'In what way?'

Louis again considered before answering. Then he said, 'I had certain plans, in which it seemed to me that he might be able to assist me. It has not, in the past, been my custom to discuss details of my plans with you. I have considered our functions as separate. You are the suppliers. I organise the onward transport and the distribution. Is there some particular reason why we should depart from this arrangement? It has worked very well in the past.'

'The reason,' said the white-haired man, 'is that Major Siward – he does not now use his military title, I believe – is an official of the British Narcotics Control Section. A senior inspector in that organisation. He works directly under Colonel Foxwell, who is head of the French liaison branch, with headquarters in Paris. Naturally Siward was followed from the moment he arrived. It seemed to be a routine visit. He called at a number of offices of the Police Judiciare and the Douane along the coast. Six days ago, when he paid his bill and drove off, we assumed that he was on his way back to Paris or London. Apparently we were wrong. I think you will agree that in the circumstances we should be told exactly what use you were planning to make of Major Siward's services.'

There was a long silence, broken by the white-haired man, who said, 'If a mistake has been made, we have not much time to rectify it.'

'But how?' said Andrew. 'And why?'

'You carried my suitcase into the hotel this evening. Because I had a holdall and a smaller bag.'

Andrew thought about it, and said, 'Naturally.'

'Then, naturally, when we arrive at Newhaven, you would carry it through the Customs.'

'Of course.'

'Open it and take a look inside. It's not locked.'

The suitcase was on the second bed. Andrew opened it and stood for a long moment staring down. Then he said, gently, 'Well, you do surprise me.'

The suitcase was full of what certainly looked like his own clothes. He picked out the jacket of a tweed suit. It carried the label of his tailor.

'It will fit you too,' said Marie-Claude. 'That was why they took away your suit on the first day you were with us.'

'Quick work, all the same.'

'They are very quick. And very clever.'

'And the stuff is in a hidden compartment underneath?'

'At the sides.' She put a hand inside the case, feeling for the retaining catch, and drew out, one after the other, four flat cellophane envelopes.

Andrew held them for a moment in his hand, as though estimating their weight, and said, 'Two million francs. A valuable cargo. What did you intend to do with it?'

'It was all arranged, through my school friend and her father. He has connections with the law officers. I was to hand this over, and to give them the names of our contacts in England. The ones who were waiting for this consignment. In return they promised to look after me. Money and papers. A new name and a new life in America. And, at last, freedom from all this.'

'And now?'

'And now it is too late. They must have discovered my plans. They are here already. They would have had no difficulty in tracing your car. They have friends everywhere. You saw the helicopter which watched us as we approached. You heard them arrive at the hotel.'

'I don't think they found out about you,' said Andrew slowly. 'I think it is much simpler. I think, at the last moment, they must have found out about me.'

'What do you mean?'

'Explanations later. What we need now is two minutes on a clear telephone. Not here. The hotel exchange will already be controlled. Somewhere, anywhere outside. Put on a coat.' As he spoke he was pushing the packets down inside his shirt.

'We shall never get away from here.'

'And a pair of shoes. Sandals would be best. We shall have to move quietly.'

'How?'

'Fortunately there is an outhouse roof underneath my window. We shall have to drop on to it, hoping we break no tiles, and slide down it, making as little noise as possible. Then out through the garden, and into the countryside. It would be too risky to try to take the car. It has probably been immobilised. Are you ready?'

Five minutes later they were making their way through the garden among the rose beds. There was a low fence at the bottom to negotiate, and they were in a field. The second crop of hay had been cut, and was lying in swatches.

'It is beautiful,' said Marie-Claude. Her voice had no longer the heavy undertones of defeat. It was singing with the excitement of the night. 'I could go on forever.'

'A mile should be enough,' said Andrew practically. 'We will lie up until first light. Then find a farm with a telephone. We can have enough of our own men here in an hour to deal with all your father's hired bullies.'

They circled the wood ahead of them. At the far side Andrew went down on his knees, scraped a hole between the roots of a massive oak tree, and buried the four envelopes, covering them with leaves. Then they crossed two more fields, waded across a shallow stream, and climbed the slope ahead of them. This time it was stubble, but easy going. At the top was a barn. The door was immovable, evidently barred on the inside, but they found an opening at the back, and wriggled through into the sweet-smelling darkness. Then they climbed on top of the hay, which was piled, not baled, and Andrew took off his jacket and rolled it up for a pillow. They lay down together. He thought, All men wish for their youth back again, and not one man in a thousand is granted his wish. You are lucky. You are the thousandth man. He made love to the girl in the simple way that the situation demanded, and then they both slept, pressed up against each other in the warm hay.

He slept longer than he intended. When he woke, he climbed off the stack, unbolted the door of the barn and looked out. He came back quickly to Marie-Claude, who was blinking the sleep out of her eyes.

He said, 'We are in trouble. Bad trouble. I underestimated them. We should have gone further and faster. There are six men at least in sight. Four of them are beating up the hill towards us. The other two are at the top. There may be more of them.'

Marie-Claude stared at him and said nothing.

'Listen to me, and please listen carefully. We have only one chance. It is not a very good one, but it is better than no chance at all. When the men get close to the barn, you will scream, and run towards them. I do not think you are in any danger. It is me they are after, not you. You will be hysterical. Your story, when you are able to tell it, is that I abducted you by force. They will look after you, but you will not be a prisoner. So you should have an opportunity, sooner or later, of getting to a telephone. Sooner, I hope.' He gave a crooked smile.

Marie-Claude said, 'I understand.'

'Remember this number. It is a Paris number.' He spoke it slowly, and she repeated it after him.

'All you have to do is to ask for Colonel Foxwell. He won't come to the telephone himself. But the fact that you know his name and this particular number will vouch you to them. Tell them where you are telephoning from. The number will be sufficient. Say, very serious. That's all.'

Marie-Claude nodded. He could see her lips move as she repeated the name and the number to herself.

'One more thing.' He felt in his jacket pocket and took out a small black pistol. It was a nine-millimetre Mauser automatic. 'You had better have this. It is no use to me, since they will search me and find it. In certain circumstances it might be useful to you.'

He looked through the opening in the door. Two of the men were quite close to the barn. Two others were behind them, well spread out and covering them. They moved like trained soldiers.

Andrew kissed Marie-Claude gently, and said, 'Run. And scream.'

The men were not gentle with him. They knocked him to the ground and one of them stood on his ankles whilst the other searched him. His arms were twisted behind his back and handcuffed. He was frog-marched across the field, and bundled into the car which was in the lane at the top of the field. Being unable to protect himself in any way, his head made contact with the door handle of the car, and the blood started to run down his face. Through all of this he saw nothing of Marie-Claude, and hoped she was safe.

About half a mile down the lane the car turned off into the courtyard of a prosperous-looking farm. The place had been taken over. There were half a dozen cars parked outside the door, and no sign of the farmer or his family. Andrew was dragged out by his hair, pushed into the front room of the farm, and thrown into an old armchair. The blood had run into his eyes and he wiped it away by rubbing his face on the arm of the chair.

The man who seemed to be in charge was the younger of the two who had visited Louis Rocaire on the previous afternoon. He said, 'You are in trouble, Mr Siward. In bad trouble. There is only one way in which you can help yourself. That is by handing back the property which you stole from us last night.'

Andrew said nothing. He was shaking his head to try and clear it.

'You could be heroic. I hope not. We should start by removing your left eye.'

'I have not the least intention of being heroic. You can certainly have back the packages of which I took temporary charge last night. There is only one difficulty. When one buries something in a wood at night, one can find it again. But it is not possible to explain to someone else where to find it.'

The dark-haired man considered the point. Then he nodded his head towards the two men who had brought Andrew in. Andrew had already begun to think of them as Laurel and Hardy. One was thin and serious, the other was a stout, jolly Marseillais who might have been a sailor.

'Go with him. If he seems to be wasting time, you can do what you like – to encourage him to move more quickly.'

By finding the wrong tree twice Andrew managed to waste a certain amount of time. The second mistake cost him two inches of knife blade in the flesh of his left arm. In less than an hour's time the three of them were back in the farmhouse. Blood from the wound in his arm had soaked Andrew's sleeve and was dripping steadily on to the floor. He felt sick and dizzy and guessed, from the look on the dark-haired man's face, that he had not long to live.

'Just those four packets,' said Laurel.

'Some encouragement was necessary,' said Hardy.

Andrew had no eyes for them. Marie-Claude was there. He could read nothing from the expression on her face, but he thought she nodded fractionally.

Maybe it was his eyes playing tricks.

'I think,' said the black-haired man, 'that we might finish—'

He broke off what he was saying as there was a squeal of tyres, and a car, driven fast, swung into the courtyard and braked. There was interest but no alarm shown by the three men in the room. Some signal must have passed. This was reinforcements, not enemies.

When the door opened and Louis Rocaire came in Andrew felt unsurprised. Louis walked over, and put an arm round his daughter.

'She is safe,' said the black-haired man. 'Everything is now in order. As I was saying, I think we might finish up our business and restore this house to its owners. It is a pity about the blood. Maybe we should buy him a new carpet.'

Marie-Claude had disengaged herself from her father. She was fumbling in her handbag. Andrew knew what was going to happen, and cringed.

He said, 'Please don't do it. One against three. It is hopeless.' This was in a whisper, to himself. If some sort of diversion could be arranged—

The diversion arranged itself. The inner door of the room burst open and a man who must have been posted as a lookout on the far side of the house came in.

He said, speaking so hoarsely in his excitement that the sense of his words could hardly be made out, 'Army helicopters – and police in cars.'

Marie-Claude's hand came out, holding the small gun. She took careful aim at the black-haired man. Andrew thought that she meant to hold him up until the police arrived. Instead she pulled the trigger.

The shot hit the black-haired man in the middle of the face. Before he had dropped, the sailor had shot Marie-Claude.

After these two shots there was a full five seconds of stunned immobility. Then Louis put his hand inside his coat and drew the heavy police special .388 automatic from its shoulder holster, and started to shoot. It was a gun intended to immobilise and to kill.

His first shot slammed the sailor against the wall. The second missed the thin man who had twisted and drawn his own gun. Before he could use it, Louis's third shot tore off his right arm. It was the lookout, standing in the open doorway, who shot Louis before taking to his heels.

Andrew was flat on his face behind the sofa.

'A clean sweep,' said Colonel Foxwell. It was three days later. He and Andrew were alone in the headquarters office of the Anglo-French Narcotics Liaison Section in Paris. 'Excellent.'

'Excellent' was his highest commendation for any operation.

He added, 'A pity about the girl.'

THE BRAVE DON'T TALK

I CAN SEE that it started when 'Spotty' Parsons first pointed out the grey man to me. We were on our way to school and Spotty kicked me on the back of the ankle, which was his way of attracting my attention, and said, in his loud and adenoid-ridden voice:

'See that man? He's a Jerry.'

I said 'Oh?' and went on rubbing the back of my ankle (which is a tender place to be kicked on).

'He was in jug most of the war,' went on Spotty. He was talking, I felt, quite loudly enough to be overheard by the object of his remarks, who was standing patiently in the doorway of the greengrocer's waiting to have his string bag filled with onions. 'He's a profiteer, too, my dad says. He was making money while my dad was fighting.'

Spotty's father had been a sergeant in the R.A.S.C. and, according to Spotty, had had some very exciting war experiences, in Cairo and Alexandria chiefly.

My unfortunate sense of logic came suddenly to the surface.

'How could he be a profiteer,' I said, 'if he was in prison? That doesn't seem to make sense to me.'

'Look here,' said Spotty, 'are you calling me a liar?'

No, certainly not, I wasn't calling Spotty a liar.

'Anyway, he's a dirty Jerry. My brother Patsy said so.'

If Spotty's brother Patsy said so, then, so far as I was concerned, that closed the argument. Patsy was Spotty's elder brother. Already, at the age of eighteen, he had the kudos which attached to three appearances before a juvenile court and two years at an approved school.

I don't want you to start off with any false ideas about me. I was no lone supporter of unpopular causes. If Spotty said that the grey man was a dirty Jerry then, so far as I was concerned, he was a dirty Jerry.

'He's a sissy, too,' said Spotty. 'Look at those fancy gloves he wears. Patsy and the boys are going to bust his windows some day.'

Serve him right, I agreed, for being a profiteer and a sissy. My horizon, at that time, was rather overshadowed by Patsy and the Boys.

Anyway, one evening my mother had sent me out for some cigarettes. It was quite late, but Mr Ferrari sold sweets as well as cigarettes and ran a little lending library, and he didn't often close up before nine o'clock, sometimes later. When I'd bought the cigarettes, I didn't go home at once but started browsing through the books on the shelves and turning over the comics – a form of free reading to which I was very much addicted at that time. Mr Ferrari didn't mind. He was half blind anyway, and the shop was so badly lighted that I doubt if he saw me.

I'd read three complete weeks of Dan Dare when I noticed we had company. Two men had come in – I call them men, because that's how they seemed to me then; but I think they were only seventeen or eighteen. They had come in very quietly. I didn't hear them at all, and I'm sure they didn't see me. They went right up to the counter. Mr Ferrari said in his usual polite way: 'Yes gentlemen, what can I do for you?' and then gave a little squeak because I imagine, he'd seen that they had white silk scarves pulled up over their faces.

They said something which sounded like 'Hand over the takings,' Mr Ferrari dithered a bit. Then the bigger one leaned over the counter, caught the front of Mr Ferrari's shirt in his left hand and pulled him forward, twice, on to his right fist. He didn't hit him – he just pulled his face on to his clenched fist. There was a lot of blood. Mr Ferrari was whimpering. He pushed across the old cash box he kept the money in and the two men went out. As soon as they had gone, I slipped behind the book counter and ran out of the shop.

I wanted no part of it. I knew both of them. One was Andy Harris who was a sort of leader of the boys. He was said to have broken a policeman's jaw in a street fight. The other was his cousin, Roper Harris. They were both friends of Patsy Parsons.

At that time, which was just after the war, there was a lot of that sort of thing in our district. There weren't enough policemen to stop it. Later we got a new superintendent and he got more help and things got better. It was so open at that time that the kids at school knew all about the Boys and used to hero-worship and copy them. They even had a sort of gang in the school, in which Spotty was a leading light. They did a lot of daring exploits like breaking up telephone kiosks in back streets and dropping lighted matches into post boxes. I wanted to belong, but I wasn't tough.

It wasn't until some time after Spotty had first pointed him out to me that I realised that the grey man was our neighbour. I don't mean that he had the house on one side of us, or I should have known about it sooner, but he had the house with the garden at the end of our garden – if you see what I mean. His front door wasn't in our road at all. It was in the next road up.

I happened to catch sight of him mowing his lawn, and I was so full of it that I went straight in to tell my mother.

'Did you know that we've got a Jerry at the bottom of our garden?' I asked her.

'A what?' said my mother.

'A Jerry,' I said. 'A German. He's a profiteer, too.'

'What's he doing in our garden?' said my mother.

'He's not in our garden,' I explained. 'He's in his own garden, and that's at the end of our garden. He's mowing his lawn.'

'Well, that's all right then,' she said, 'and who told you he was a prof-iteer?'

'He wears gloves all the time and doesn't go out to work,' I said. 'He must be a profiteer.'

'That's true, anyway,' my mother admitted. 'He doesn't work. He's not old enough to have retired. He must have money put by.'

'He's a profiteer,' I said. 'He earned his money during the war while people like Spotty's father were fighting.'

I ought to have known better than to mention Spotty. It set my mother off at once. 'You keep away from that Parsons boy,' she said. 'He's no good. Him and his gang. If I catch you with them I'll wallop you—'

She didn't mean it. She never walloped me. No one ever walloped me, for that matter. My father was always talking about walloping me, too, but he was killed at the beginning of the war.

Some time after this, the grey man got talking to me. I was sitting under the apple tree at the end of the garden, putting out a chess problem. I had just got the board ready when a voice over my head said: 'It looks like an exercise in cross-checking.'

It was, too. As soon as I found that he was a chess enthusiast my dislike for the grey man disappeared rapidly.

I have been a chess maniac since that first day when I was taught the moves and wasted sixpence on a book which gave you an incorrect description of the Lopez opening and little else. By the age of ten I was a bit of an expert and had come out winner in the County Schools Individual, which wasn't bad, as it was open to boys up to eighteen.

A week later we arranged our first game. 'You can come over the wall,' he said – with what I see, now, to have been uncommon tact. 'But ask your mother first.'

After that we played a lot, chiefly in the evenings.

I wasn't allowed to go across until I had finished my homework, but after that we went on till almost any hour. I found my host very easy to get on with – there was nothing remarkable about him at all, if you except the fact that he never took his gloves off, even in the house.

We didn't only play chess. Between games, or after a game, we used to talk. It would mostly be me who did the talking, and I imagine the man in grey must have been a good listener. Occasionally he would say something, and it may have been because he said so little that his remarks usually stayed in my mind. One thing in particular I shall never forget, because he said it to me on the night that it all happened – the thing I started out to tell you about.

I was talking about one of the boys – I can't even remember his name now, which is odd, because he was the leading light of the school at that time: captain of football, and the best footballer we had had for years. The League talent scouts were already after him. When I was talking about him I called him a hero.

The grey man took me up at once. 'Don't use words loosely,' he said. 'It's a bad habit. He may be courageous, but that doesn't make him a hero. The things are quite different. Courage is physical. Heroism is in the character – it is spiritual.'

'Have you known a lot of heroes?' I inquired, rather snappily.

'Oh, yes,' he said. 'Half a dozen, at least. They were most of them women.'

After that we got on with our game of chess.

It was at the end of that game – or it may have been the next – that I realized two things: that it had got extremely late while we were playing, and that we were not alone in the house.

There was a quiet movement outside in the passage – not very quiet, but quiet enough to suggest something unpleasant – and then the door opened and the two men came in. It was the same two who had beaten up Mr Ferrari.

I felt cold and powerless with fear. I was sitting on the sofa, and I remember I lifted my legs up under me, as if the mere fact of getting my feet off the floor would somehow dissociate me from the horrible things I knew were going to happen.

Both men looked at me, and I realized at once that they were surprised and annoyed at seeing me there.

They must have been watching the front of the house all the evening, but, of course, I had come over the back wall, and they hadn't known about that. However, I was only a badly frightened schoolboy, so I wouldn't make much difference to their plans, unless – and the thought turned me colder still – unless they realized that I had recognized them behind their silk scarves.

All this takes time to explain, but it happened very quickly. Roper Harris stood by the door, and Andy walked over to the grey man, who had got to his feet but had made no other move. Andy was wearing, on his right hand, quite the most horrible weapon I have ever seen. It was a knuckleduster made out of a thick strap, with a piece of bicycle chain wired on to the outside of it.

'Well, Jerry,' said Andy. 'Where do you keep it?'

'Keep what?' said the grey man.

At this point I got my second shock of the evening, and I'm not sure it wasn't the bigger shock of the two. I saw that the grey man was actually smiling. He was standing, balanced on the balls of his feet, in the way that I have seen a good tennis player stand, when he is waiting to receive a service. And, as I have said, he was smiling.

'The money,' said Andy, and he swung his right hand a little. 'All the beautiful nickers and jack-alives you pay your bills with, you dirty little profiteering Jerry.'

Even I could see that he was working himself up into the sort of rage he had to be in to hit a defenceless man.

'Most of it's in the bank,' said the grey man, 'but now you mention it, I do keep a little here – for emergencies.'

'This is one of them,' said Andy. 'Hand it across.'

The grey man half turned and walked towards the fireplace. Andy followed close behind him. On the mantelpiece stood an old trinket box, and it was for this that the grey man seemed to be reaching, and I could see from the greedy look in Andy's eyes that he had the same idea as I did – that out of the box would come a wad of crisp banknotes.

At the last second the grey man seemed to change his mind. His hand caught hold of a heavy brass candlestick that stood beside the box. Then he turned on his heel with a snap and hit Andy once, back-handed, with the candlestick across the side of the throat. It was a beautifully economical blow. Andy gasped once, as if he was trying to get his breath back, then fell sideways on to the carpet and lay still. The one blow had been enough. He wasn't shamming; he was out.

In the few seconds this took to happen Roper hadn't moved. Then he came forward, half a pace, rather uncertainly. He was swinging a cosh of some sort. The grey man had put back the candlestick very carefully on the mantelpiece, and now he walked forward with his hands empty; nevertheless, I realized with complete certainty that Roper had about as much chance in a stand-up fight with the grey man as a fat, lazy snake faced by a mongoose. He was scared and the grey man wasn't, and that was the simple truth, which I have never forgotten since.

When he had come forward about six paces, and was just outside Roper's reach, the grey man did one more surprising thing. He held out his gloved left hand, put his right hand up to it, and very slowly pulled at the glove, finger by finger, until he had it loose. Then, with a quick jerk, he pulled it off.

While he was doing this, he said, weighing his words: 'When next you and your friend try something of this sort – if there is a next time – be careful to pick someone your own weight.' I can't get anywhere near the contempt in his voice. 'Rob a child's money box, or scare some old woman who'll scream and throw her skirts over her head at the sight of you. But don't pick on a man. And above all, avoid a man like me. Did you think I should be afraid of two ungrown boys, after working for three years in Germany during the war, and after suffering the attentions of the Gestapo?'

He had been holding out his left hand palm upwards. Now he turned it over, and we both saw that there were no nails on the fingers. The ends were white and wrinkled like blanched almonds.

Personally, I had no eyes for anything else, and I don't imagine Roper had, either, because at that moment the grey man's right arm whipped up from his side like a snake, and was round Roper's neck.

They reeled, and stamped, and threshed round a bit, but it didn't last long, because the edge of the grey man's right wrist was locked against Roper's throat, and Roper was quite unable to breathe.

Some time later, after the police had come and gone, and we had cleared up the mess, we sat on the sofa, drinking cocoa.

'Was it really true – were you—' I boggled at the word 'spy' – 'were you in the Secret Service, like you said, in Germany?'

'Yes,' said the grey man. 'I was. Your Government was not ungrateful. I live now on the pension I was awarded.'

'Golly,' I said.

'And,' he went on, accurately reading my thoughts, 'you will not say a single word to anyone about it. Not a single word to anyone at all. It was an error on my part that I mentioned it. In the circumstances I thought that it was justified. Nevertheless, it was an indiscretion. I must have your promise.'

'Oh, I won't breathe a word,' I said.

Three days later, on my way to school, Spotty and I again passed the grey man. This time he was waiting for his meat ration.

'There's that Jerry again,' said Spotty. 'My brother Patsy's going to fix him some day.'

It was a considerable effort, but I said nothing. Nothing at all. I felt that the grey man would have approved.

THE MAN WHO WAS
RECONSTITUTED

MRS MANISTY HEARD the car coming when it was a quarter of a mile away.

The road she was walking along was a narrow one, serving Sibthorpe Village. At the point she had reached a much larger road came in on the right. The car was moving fast. Rather too fast, she thought, for that particular road, but the driver, who was evidently expecting the turning, slowed in good time and changed down before swinging round. At that moment there was a sharp detonation, not much louder than the noise her ancient Morris used to make when it back-fired. The car made no attempt to correct its right-hand turn, but continued its swing, hit the telegraph post at the corner of the road and burst into flames.

Mrs Manisty, who was not lacking in courage, started to run towards it, but was driven back by the heat. There was a telephone box at the exit from Sibthorpe Village. She started back to it, as fast as her middle-aged legs would carry her.

'Yes,' said Elfe. 'I remember reading the account of the inquest. They were referred to as scientists in the employment of the Ministry of Defence. Salmundsen and Prescott. Two of your men, Michael?'

'Yes.'

'That would be Dr Olaf Salmundsen. I know about him, of course. Who was Prescott?'

'Fred Prescott. Head of our Documents Section.'

'I see. Yes. I thought the coroner was being a shade tactful. I suppose you'd warned him not to dig too deep.'

'I did have a word with him,' said Michael Harriman. 'He promised to co-operate as far as he could. The trouble was that the only witness, a Mrs Manisty, had a mind of her own. He tried to get her to say that the car swung out of control, hit the telegraph post, exploded and caught on fire. She wouldn't be bullied. She was quite firm. She said the explosion came first.'

'Which of them was right?'

'The woman. When we took the car down we saw exactly what had happened. Someone had planted one of our latest incendiary devices underneath the petrol tank. Small, but immensely powerful. We call it Tiny Tim. It locks on magnetically. Also, the connecting rod in the steering linkage had been partly cut through. The first swing to the right activated the bomb *and* finished off the connecting rod.'

'I see,' said Elfe. 'Yes, I'm sorry.'

He said it sincerely, but a lot of things were puzzling him. He was not surprised that the discussion was taking place at his office. That was in accordance with protocol. Chief Inspector Harriman was head of the anti-terrorist section of MI5. Elfe, as an Assistant Commissioner, and head of the Special Branch, was greatly senior to him in rank and appointment. No. What was odd was that they should be seeking to involve him in a matter which, on the face of it, lay exclusively in their own field.

'Do you suppose,' he said, 'that this was an IRA riposte for the killing of Dr Quilty?'

Dr Quilty, as everyone knew, but no one could prove, was the main IRA explosives expert. His last exploit had been the blowing up of an SAS leave bus. When, some months later, the car Dr Quilty was in had swung out of control and met a lorry head on, his death had been brought in as an accident. Harriman, who seemed to be reading Elfe's mind, said, 'That's right. He was killed in the same way as Salmundsen and Prescott. Tiny Tim under the petrol tank and the brake rod half cut.'

'On your orders?'

'Certainly not. We were glad to see the last of him, but we didn't organise it. It was a solo effort by one of our men. Frank Oadby. His brother had been in that SAS bus.'

'He admitted it?'

'He was proud of it. We had to get rid of him. But somehow the truth got out, so he became target number one for the opposition. Even though he was no longer one of our men, we had to protect him.'

'Of course. You arranged for him to disappear.'

'Right. You'll understand that when we destabilise an agent the details are handled by as few men as possible. In this case two men only. Dr Salmundsen, who built his new face for him, and Fred Prescott, who did all the paperwork himself, personally. Made out his new passport and driving licence, set up the bank accounts and organised the insurance side. I knew what was being done, but none of the details.'

'After the accident, you examined their offices?'

'Of course. We went through Dr Salmundsen's records – against strenuous opposition from his lady secretary who knew nothing about the work he did for the Department. And we took Prescott's desk and office to pieces. We found nothing. Any relevant papers must have been in Salmundsen's briefcase.'

'Which was in the car?'

'We found the remains of one and some charred remnants of papers in it. Our lab boys have been working on them for the last month, but they're not hopeful.'

'So,' said Elfe thoughtfully. 'Old Oadby has vanished. New Oadby exists. Somewhere. And you know nothing about him. Why not let him rest?'

'And get away with the murder of two of our men?'

Elfe stared at him.

'We'd lodged him in a safe house at Sibthorpe while Prescott did the preliminary paper work. Then he and the doctor went down to finish the job. They were there for a week. Plastic surgery can't be rushed. Whilst they were there, their car was in the garage. Oadby kept his motor-bike there and had the only key. So the car was wholly at his disposal. Quite clearly he rigged up the same trap as he had for Quilty. The job had his signature all over it.'

'I see,' said Elfe slowly. The complications were beginning to dawn on him. 'So he got rid of the only two men who knew the actual details of his new identity?'

'That's right. When he got on to his motor-bike and rode away from Sibthorpe, he was riding into limbo.'

'But why?'

'Limbo's a useful state to be in, if you're planning to blackmail the government, wouldn't you say?'

Elfe, for once in his life, was past saying anything.

'He'd been voted ten thousand pounds – against Treasury opposition – to help him find his feet in his new life. He thought it totally inadequate. And said so. Now he's asking for more. His first suggestion is fifty thousand pounds.'

'Then he's been in touch with you?'

'Yes. By letter. On unidentifiable paper. Posted in central London.'

'And if you refused?'

'All he said was that he would make his presence felt.'

'You took his threat seriously?'

'When you realise that he not only knows a great deal about explosives – I wonder how many Tiny Tims he managed to help himself to? –

but also possesses the most intimate knowledge of our organisation, why, certainly we took him seriously.'

'And you want Special Branch to find him?'

'It seemed to us that you were best equipped to do so.'

Elfe thought about it. He said, doubtfully, 'It's true that we have some experience in tracking down terrorists and cranks. But in those cases we usually have *some* lead. Something to start on.'

'We can give you all details of Oadby's past existence.'

'Details which have been efficiently and carefully rubbed out by your own experts. Correct?'

Noting the expression on Harriman's face he added, 'We'll do our best.'

Guy Horsey had recently been posted as second-in-command to Harriman. Don Mainprice, who was then heading MI5, had recommended him warmly. He said, 'He's a brainy chap, Michael. Full of ideas. Ex-RN.'

Harriman, who was sceptical about recruits, had a word with a naval friend, who had laughed immoderately. When he could speak he had said, 'Guy Horsey? He's a freak. Of course, you might find him useful. After all, most of your boys are mad. He should fit in well.'

Ignoring this, Harriman said, 'What's his particular form of insanity?'

'There were a lot of stories about him. The only one I know for certain is that when he was a junior sub-lieutenant he invented an improved quick-firing mechanism and sold it, through a third party, to the Admiralty. When they discovered that the money had gone to a serving officer they nearly had a fit. And tried to get the money back. They're still trying. It was about then that Horsey decided to quit. I wish you luck of him.'

In the short time he had been working with him, Harriman had discovered two things about Guy Horsey. That he talked a lot; and that he was constitutionally lazy. In spite of this he liked him and found him refreshing.

His first assignment had been to keep an eye on the Oadby investigation and to report progress, if any.

'Elfe and all the little elves,' he said, 'have been working their fingers to the bone trying to solve the problem you've set them. It's like a mad crossword puzzle with lots of clues, but none that lead to any actual words. They know his height and his weight and his age and the size of his feet and the length of his legs and where he was vaccinated and how many teeth he's had out—'

'How about his new bank account?'

'No luck there. He was paid off in cash. If it went into the bank, it probably went into accounts he'd already set up under different names. Oh, they found his motor-bike. Fifty miles away, in a pond. Another dead end.'

'Suppose we stop looking at the negative side and approach the problem positively.'

'Good thinking, Chief,' said Horsey insubordinately. 'But what exactly had you in mind?'

'He said he'd make his presence felt. I read that as a threat. The place he's most likely to attack is this office. He used to work here and knows all about our security measures. We'll have to change them and tighten them up. Have a word with Oliphant.'

Oliphant was head of office staff. With his red-cheeked face he looked, thought Horsey, more like Father Christmas without his beard than an ex-sergeant major in the Guards. He had already had one or two stately rebukes from him over papers left lying about and doors left unlocked. He said, 'Can I tell him what it's all about?'

'Yes. But no one else. If anyone else asks, blame the IRA. One other thing. Have you made anything out of that paper?'

The laboratory, after two months of patient work with screens and colour photography had produced one page from Dr Salmundsen's notebook which had been protected by its central position in that book. On the page, on separate lines, was what appeared to be:

Gee hct/mit m/br con t/3ogr wx eacb/Haem/Tight mass/New Lst.

'Pretty cryptic,' said Horsey. 'And not helped by the fact that like all doctors his handwriting was almost illegible anyway. Would it be all right if I showed it to a friend of mine?'

'What sort of friend?'

'He's an American I met when I was in the Navy. His name's Freund. Otto Freund. A most interesting man. As a matter of fact he used to do the same job for the CIA that Salmundsen did for us. He'd be just the chap to tell us what this means, don't you think?'

Slightly comforted by the thought that he'd be dealing with a fellow professional, Harriman said, 'As long as you're sure he can be trusted to keep his mouth shut.'

Fearful that even this qualified permission might be withdrawn Horsey hurried off, pausing on his way out of the office to talk to Oliphant, who listened patronisingly and then explained the additional precautions he had already taken. They seemed more than adequate. Horsey said, 'Excellent, excellent,' and sped out. He was making for the Special Services Club where Dr Freund could usually be found at lunchtime.

Harriman spent an uneasy afternoon regretting that he had allowed one more man to be brought into a secret which, if it became common knowledge, would make his department the laughing-stock of the security services in five continents.

He was still worrying about this when he reached his house in Twickenham, a small house in a street of small houses behind the Rugby Football Ground. It was not a fortress, but it was guarded, with mortice locks on the front and back doors and window locks on all the downstairs windows. The police, who knew about him, kept an eye on it.

He slipped his key into the lock of the front door and, as he opened the door, it came out to meet him, knocking him flat. He felt the impact almost before he registered the explosion. He climbed slowly back on to his knees, more dazed than hurt, as his nearest neighbour, a solid Scotsman, hurdled the intervening fence and came to his help.

He said, 'Would you care to use my house? Yours is in a bit of a mess.'

'Must telephone the police.'

'I've done that. Come along. I'll give you a hand.'

Harriman went gratefully. A crowd was beginning to collect. By the time Superintendent Naylor of the local force arrived, he had downed a glass of the Scotsman's whisky and was feeling better.

'We've alerted your people,' said Naylor. 'They're sending a team along. They warned us not to touch anything until they came.'

When the team had finished taking photographs and samples they gave the house a clean bill. The explosive packet, they calculated, must have been in the post box behind the front door. The door, a stout one, had absorbed most of the force of the explosion. The damage had not been excessive.

'We've talked to your neighbours,' said Naylor. 'One of them says she did notice a man. Just after your daily woman had left. He walked round to the back and used his own key on the back door. He did it all so openly that she thought nothing of it.'

'Did she describe him?'

'Not really. She only saw his back view. She said he was bulky. Incidentally, he seems to have left a note for you. It was on the kitchen table.'

The note said, 'Just a demonstration. One-way activator. Might have been two-way. Think about it.'

'Do you understand it?' said Naylor.

'I'm not a technical expert in the field of explosives,' said Harriman. 'But I can get it translated.'

At the office next morning he showed it to Horsey who grinned and said, 'He wasn't exaggerating, was he?'

'If you understand it, perhaps you could explain it.'

'It's simple enough,' said Horsey. He said it with such ineffable smugness that Harriman understood at once why the Navy had dispensed with his services. 'Activation can be one-way or two-way. In this case it was one-way. The opening of the door was all that was necessary to detonate the explosive. If it had been two-way the opening of the door would have primed it, the closing of the door would have detonated it.'

'By which time I should have been inside and standing over it. Yes. It certainly makes you think.'

'I've been doing a bit of thinking myself,' said Horsey. Noting the look in his superior's eye he added hastily, 'I had a talk with Freund. He was very interested in that piece of paper and took it away to work on it. He telephoned just before you got in to say that he'd reached what he called an arguable solution. He'd be glad to come round and discuss it.'

'The sooner the better.'

Otto Freund had the massive judicial appearance which seems to clothe Americans when they attain eminence in business or the professions. He had brought with him and spread out on the table an enlargement of the original page. Under six times magnification the scribbled letters stood out starkly. It was now evident that, in two places at least, they could have been misread.

'I would offer the supposition that the second group is "mil-m" rather than "mit-m" and if this is correct, then, again, when we substitute "I" for "t", the third group reads "br-con-I". This seems to produce a more logical sequence.'

'I'm glad you find it so,' said Harriman.

'I only assert that it's logical because in our trade, when one is making alterations to a subject's appearance, one always follows the same order, starting at the top of the head, with the hair. Then other hirsute appendages. Next, the eyes. Then the cheeks and general shape and colour of the face. Then the nose. Finally the jaw and lower frontal, always the most difficult feature. Assuming this to be so, "gee hct" will be some form of haircut. Unfortunately I am not acquainted with all the current English styles.'

'Guardee haircut,' said Horsey. 'Short back and sides.'

'Very possibly. In which case the next group calls for a military moustache. One of those short-clipped affairs, I assume, along the upper lip.'

'Then brown contact lenses,' suggested Harriman. 'Oadby had rather prominent light blue eyes.'

'That must be right. The next two groups are most important. They call for an injection of thirty grammes of wax – that's more than an ounce by your measurements – under each cheek bone. The effect would be a rounding out of the cheeks, which would then be coloured with ochre. Haematite, you note, rather than limonite. This would produce a bronzed, open-air effect, with a tinge of redness. The nose they seem to have left alone. Then the last two groups relate to the chin. The tightening of the masseter muscle would bring the jaw forward, an effect which could be heightened by substituting a new and more prominent lower set of false teeth.'

There was a moment of silence. Harriman was trying to visualise the new Oadby. What he had heard was ingenious and almost certainly correct; but not entirely helpful. He said, 'I don't want to seem ungrateful, doctor. I'm sure you've read our riddle for us. But unfortunately the type they suggest – the military or ex-military man – is very common in this country.'

Horsey said, 'You haven't thought it through, sir.' The fact that, unusually, he added 'sir' to this impertinence made Harriman look at him sharply.

'I presume Oadby was photographed when he joined the Department. I know I was.'

'Of course. Front view and both profiles. Colour prints.'

'Then we can reconstruct him. Get a suitable skull from one of the teaching hospitals. We've got his dental records so we can fit in the appropriate teeth and build on that.'

'Bearing in mind,' said Freund, 'that the skin of your model can't be plastic. It will have to be expandable. Might I suggest the material out of an uncoloured child's balloon?'

Both men looked at Harriman. He said, 'All right. I understand what you're getting at. I'll put it in hand. It'll take a little time. Say a fortnight at least.'

Freund, who was consulting a massive pocket diary, said, 'I could manage October 15th. At least, I hope I'm going to be asked to carry out what looks to me like a truly unique experiment.'

'I think you've earned the right,' said Harriman, with a smile.

'By God,' said Harriman. 'It's him. Him, and no one else.'

It was an astonishingly life-like face that looked up at him from the table; the black hair worn rather long framing the pale cheeks, prominent blue eyes, petulant mouth and weak chin.

He decided that what made it so startlingly life-like was the rubber skin which had been painstakingly stretched over the wax base. Under it, the face of Oadby was alive; alive, saturnine and faintly amused.

'There's your patient, Doctor,' he said. 'Carry on.'

Freund, who had put on surgical gloves, was standing behind the table. He had brought with him an assortment of syringes, clips and tweezers. Horsey, like a theatre nurse, had taken post at his side.

'No need to waste time over the hair. We just remove the old wig and substitute the new one. The same with the moustache. That goes straight on.' He adjusted the adhesive strip delicately, without disturbing the lips which were smiling, as at some private joke.

'Then the contact lenses – the smallest tweezer, please. We'll deal with the chin next and leave the cheeks to the last. We can't do anything about the masseter muscle, because he hasn't got one, but a small wedge in the jaw will produce the same effect. The lower set of teeth can be changed now. Fine. This is where we reach the vital part.'

At which point the telephone on Harriman's desk rang. When he ignored it, it went on ringing. He strode across, started to say something brusque and cut it off.

'Sorry, sir. I didn't know it was you.'

Don Mainprice said, 'This is a warning order, Michael. The Prime Minister will be with you in about twenty minutes' time. He's asked to see all our sections.'

The shortness of the notice did not surprise Harriman. For obvious reasons the Prime Minister's movements were not advertised in advance. He said, 'Do you want us lined up outside with sloped microscopes?'

Mainprice laughed. 'No, just carry on. I gather it's some experiment you're doing. He'll be interested in that, I'm sure. A new identikit arrangement, isn't it?'

'Something like that, sir.' Harriman replaced the receiver and said, 'Sorry you were interrupted, Doctor.'

'As I was saying, it's the sub-cutaneous injection of wax that makes the real difference. It alters the whole shape and character of the face. Actors achieve the same effect, temporarily, by wearing pads inside their cheeks.'

He drove in first one and then the other of the large hypodermic syringes and depressed the plunger. As he did so, the hollow gauntness of the face changed into a robust cheerfulness.

'A touch, now, of the ochre paint. The small brush, please.'

Freund was so engrossed in what he was doing that he did not notice the effect which the transformation was having on the other two.

'Father Christmas, without his beard,' whispered Horsey.

'It can't be.'

'It most certainly is. Or his twin brother.'

Harriman grabbed the telephone on his desk and dialled. 'Ronnie?' he said. 'Michael here. Tell me, how long has Oliphant been with us?'

'Not very long, sir. We had to get someone quickly, you remember, when Westcomb died.'

'How long?' It came out almost as a shout.

'Got the file here, sir. If you could hold on a moment. Seven weeks at the end of this week. I hope there's nothing wrong. We got him from Commissionaires Ltd. They're usually very reliable. They'd only had him on their books for a few days, but he had excellent references—'

But Ronnie was talking into a dead telephone. Harriman had rung off and was dialling again.

'Frank? Michael here. Listen. I want two of your heavies and I want them at the double. In my office. Must be here in five minutes.'

'Do my best, sir.'

There was nothing obviously menacing in the appearance of the two men who came in quietly. Both looked and carried themselves like men in high training. One had red hair, the other black. Apart from this, with their similar faces, white, flat and hard, they might have been twins.

Harriman said, 'One of our staff – I've sent for him – has very possibly planted explosives somewhere in this building. Maybe with a device for detonating them. If I give you ten minutes could you persuade him to tell you about it?'

'Depends on the man, sir. Normally five minutes would be enough. Is there somewhere quiet where we could operate?'

'There's a washroom at the end of the passage, through that door.'

'Just the job.'

At that moment Oliphant came in. He said, 'You wanted me, sir,' saw the two men and broke for the door. Black hair was there first, caught him by one wrist and jerked his arm up behind his back. Red hair said, 'Don't break his arm, Charlie. Not yet.'

Then the three men disappeared into the passage and the door was shut.

Horsey, who was at the window, said, 'There's a bit of a crowd beginning to collect. How do they always hear about these things?'

'Bush telegraph.'

'What are you going to do if the PM turns up before Oliphant has started talking?'

'We'll have to evacuate the building.'

'Difficult to explain why.'

'Very,' said Harriman. He had his watch in his hand.

The passage door opened and red hair appeared. He said, 'We've got what you want, sir. He wasn't very brave. The stuff is planted under the platform in the conference room. The switch is outside the door. There's a sixty-second delay after it's been activated. No doubt that was to let your chap get clear. When this function is finished you ought to get one of your experts to dismantle it. Tricky to interfere with it now. Might set it off.'

'But unless someone actually presses the switch, it's safe?'

'That's what he says. No reason to be telling lies about it now.'

Horsey said, 'Here comes the car.'

Harriman took a deep breath. He said, 'We'll have to play this straight down the middle. Look after that chap for us. He's wanted for at least two murders.' And to Freund, 'If the PM comes up here could you spin him some story about the work we're doing. Then we'll all go down and sit round the platform and pray.'

'And don't tell him about Oliphant – I mean Oadby.'

'Certainly not. Poor chap, he's got enough to worry about.'

The Prime Minister advanced to the edge of the platform and switched on a professional smile. He said, 'It has been a pleasure and a privilege to gain, this morning, some idea of the work you are doing. I was particularly gratified to find our American friends co-operating with you.' He smiled at Freund, who smiled back. 'Your work may sometimes seem to you theoretical and dull, but believe me, it contributes most materially to the safety of all of us—'

ONE-TENTH MAN

IT MUST BE remembered, in extenuation, that it started very late at night. Peter Petrell had stepped off the train at Andernach that evening with only one idea in his head: after the long hot day which he had spent, most of it standing, in the crowded train from Baden-Oos, he sought a good supper and an early bed.

The first he had duly obtained at the Zur Kron, where he had found a room. The second, as it happened, was denied to him.

It had really started when he fell into conversation with the insinuating Herr Wesselman and his friend Bazil. Herr Wesselman he put down as ex-army. He had the look of an Afrika-Korps man: indeed, there was something of Rommel in his face. The blunt strong features, the good-tempered eyes, the bleached and sand-blasted appearance of the skin and hair. Bazil was darker, younger, and less responsible.

It was Bazil who had suggested that they visit the Krokodil.

'Everyone in Andernach goes to the Krokodil,' he observed. 'Good drink, good food, pretty girls.'

'Perhaps Herr Petrell is tired?'

'Certainly not,' said Petrell. In fact, he had got his second wind. It was the sort of chance encounter that made a holiday abroad so pleasant.

They walked to the Krokodil through the lighted streets. It was the close of a hot summer's day. On their right winked the lights from the barges, safely moored for the night. Past them the Rhine swept down, smooth and full. On the far bank rose the hills crowned with vineyards. Over them the stars.

Soon they were sitting together on a red-plush settee. Wesselman gave the order.

'I wonder if Lisa will be here tonight,' said Bazil.

'Who is Lisa?' asked Petrell politely. He picked up the very large goblet of white wine that had been placed on the table before him. It had been well cooled and the rim of the glass was misted. It looked like good wine.

'Lisa,' said Bazil, 'is – Lisa.'

'She sings? Dances?'

'No, I have never heard her sing. She dances divinely. She is – oh, she is the reason you always see so many people here.'

'It is said that she is Herr Bittelburg's daughter.' Wesselman indicated the proprietor, who was leaning across the service counter – a big man with jowls like a bulldog's, a white face, and a lightly poached eye. 'Though it passes all imagination how something so gross could produce something so—'

'There,' said Bazil. 'You need not trouble to describe her.'

The girl had come in as he was speaking. She was dressed in something very simple, and black. And her skin was white and her hair dark. And that was all that Petrell's man's eye noticed. But as soon as she came into the room she was the only person in it.

As she passed their table, Wesselman rose and said, 'Lisa, you forget me?'

'But certainly not, Herr Major,' the girl said politely.

'I would like you to know two friends. This is Bazil. And this, I understand, is called Peter.'

Petrell, though somewhat entangled with the sofa, managed to get to his feet and sketch a bow.

He had a feeling that he was being introduced to Royalty.

'Peter,' she said. 'Why, that's a nice name! An Englishman. I'm crazy about Englishmen.'

'Perhaps,' said Wesselman, 'you could join us? Later?'

'Later?' said the girl. 'Perhaps.'

She moved on.

'Those eyes,' said Wesselman. 'That hair.'

'What a lovely little bottom,' said Bazil dreamily.

'You're a lucky man, Peter. She seems to have taken a liking for you. Why, now?'

Bazil said wisely, 'It is always so. Girls, they are all the same. They crave for something different. It is the *goût de l'étranger*. American girls, I have noticed, are particularly so.'

But it must have been almost an hour before Lisa returned. Though it was well after midnight, the room seemed no emptier.

She sat next to Peter, and more wine appeared. Peter decided that he had been right. It was good wine. It improved his German enormously. He found himself talking, and talking well, to Lisa.

He raised his glass to her.

Bazil followed suit.

'To your eyes,' said Bazil.

Lisa picked up her own glass, looked gravely at the cold yellow wine, and said, 'They are not quite the right colour.'

Bazil laughed loudly.

It was at this moment that Petrell, half turning, happened to glance at Wesselman. He was startled by what he saw – without entirely understanding it. The mask of good nature had been lowered for an instant, and an emotion rode in the bleached face that was not pretty to look at. Anger, jealousy, fear – or perhaps a warning of some sort.

It was gone as quickly as it had come.

Soon after this the dancing started.

'They do such things better in Germany,' thought Petrell. There was no formality and it was altogether delightful. The tables and chairs were pushed back, a space was cleared, then a little man like a gnome produced an accordion almost as large as himself and began to finger it. Later a tall thin man got up absent-mindedly and accompanied him on the violin.

It seemed natural and inevitable to Peter that he should dance with Lisa. She danced beautifully; her firm body pressed against his gave him an intoxicating sense of oneness.

'You dance very well,' he said, rather breathlessly. 'Are you—?' He found himself at a loss for the first time that evening.

'Am I a dance hostess?' she said with a smile. 'No. I dance because I love it.'

'You dance beautifully,' he said. 'Beautifully.'

When they had danced enough, they walked out on to a balcony. They could see the town, unrolled before them, down to the river. There were fewer lights now. Just the street lights, and the string of mooring lights on the barges at the jetty.

In the dimness he could just make out the fascinating wedge of her body, fitting so snugly into the fulcrum of her hips. He had one arm round her shoulder, and turned her slowly towards him.

She said, but very quietly, 'No. That is not on the bill of fare.'

He slid his hand down to her waist.

'Come, little Peterkin,' she said. 'Dance. You dance beautifully.'

'Will you walk with me afterwards to my hotel?'

'I will see you safe back to your hotel.' She was laughing at him.

A blaze of light filled the balcony as the curtains swung apart. Wesselman said, rather grimly, 'I thought I had lost you.'

'We were admiring the night,' said Lisa. 'Now we will dance again.'

The streets were quite empty when they walked home, and the light of a new morning was coming to pale the lamps.

How they managed to avoid Wesselman, Peter never knew. One

moment they were all dancing; the next, he and Lisa were in the cool street alone, their footsteps tapping on the cobblestones.

He had no idea where he was going and was surprised when Lisa said, 'There is the Zur Kron. It will be locked. The landlord will be very angry.'

'A fiddlestick for the landlord,' said Peter. 'It has been the most perfect evening I have ever spent in all my life. Come here.'

'You must not do that,' said Lisa calmly. 'Think to yourself. Think of tomorrow. You will go away tomorrow to England.'

'I can wait.'

'Why should you wait?'

He pulled her towards him and suddenly he could feel her hand, warm, on the cold silk of his shirt.

'Lisa,' he said. 'Lisa.'

'*Um gotteswillen*!' said a shrill voice above them. 'Please to conduct your bestialities elsewhere.'

They looked up. A window had opened and a malevolent head, crowned with a tight fringe of curling papers, peered forth. 'Chatter, chatter, chatter – like lecherous monkeys.'

They ran.

When they got to the hotel he saw that Lisa was shaking. But it was laughter.

'Lecherous monkeys,' she said. 'She had the appearance of an old rock-ape herself.'

Then she was gone.

When he reached his room – the keeper of the Zur Kron was more resigned than angry – he sat on his bed. He could still feel, over his heart, the warm pressure of a hand.

Then he got into bed and lay for a long time on his back, thinking, until things got blurred. And suddenly it was quite light and someone was knocking at the door, telling him it was ten o'clock.

After breakfast the proprietor came over and talked to him.

'You are going back to England today,' he said. 'You will want me to find you the time of the trains.'

'Yes,' said Petrell. 'Or rather, no. I have changed my mind. I may be stopping for another two days.'

'You find the town attractive?'

'Very attractive.' He did not want to talk. He wanted to think.

When he had finished his breakfast he made his way slowly to the Krokodil. Midday was striking from the steeples of Andernach, but the restaurant had not yet come to life. It was barred, bolted and blind.

He walked round to the back where there was a little courtyard which served the kitchen doors. This, too, was shut; but he sensed that there was life somewhere in the building.

He had little remembrance of how he spent the rest of the day. The real things were all happening inside him. He sat for a long time that afternoon on a seat by the river. The sun shone; the dimpled river ran in front of him; but he found no peace in them.

At his ear, soft but persistent, was a voice which told him to go away – to the train he had intended to catch for Cologne. *To go back to England.*

In the end, when most of the heat was out of the day, he returned to the town.

The fat proprietor of the Krokodil was still leaning across the service counter. Presumably he had been to bed. He seemed scarcely to have moved from the evening before.

Petrell sat down. A tired waiter brought him a beer. There was no longer any magic about the place.

When he had finished his beer, Peter walked over to the proprietor, who removed his toothpick.

'When I was here last night,' said Petrell – his limited German made him abrupt – 'there was a young lady.'

'Many young ladies.'

'She sat with me and my friends.'

'You have some complaint?'

'Not at all. I must see her again.'

'Perhaps,' said the proprietor politely, 'if you knew her name—?'

'Lisa.'

'Not an uncommon name. My own daughter, for instance—'

'Yes,' said Petrell eagerly. 'Yes. I was told – I did not know. Could I possibly—?'

'Of course,' said the man. He called over his shoulder. 'Donna! Where is Lisa?'

A dried-up old lady put her head through the hatch and muttered, 'In the kitchen.'

'Send her.'

Presently the door opened and a girl came out. Her big arms were bare to the elbows, and she was drying her red hands on her apron.

Petrell blinked.

'Lisa, my dear. The gentleman requests a word with you.'

'Surely—' Petrell began.

The girl grinned. It was a wide grin and showed large strong teeth. 'I hope your head is all right today. You and your friends had much to drink last night.'

Petrell stared. The deep voice was not unlike – but the face, the figure … It was as if some cruel fairy had waved a wand. The body, which had been firm and well-made, was now bloated. The arms – he gazed at them in fascination; they were the forearms of a boxer. The face … It was not Lisa; it was a caricature of Lisa, drawn by a malicious pencil.

'The young man seems tongue-tied,' said the proprietor.

'A mistake,' said Petrell.

The proprietor laughed.

Petrell wheeled on him. 'You find something funny?' he said angrily.

'Life is often amusing.'

'There's something going on here.' Petrell's voice was rising. 'Where is the girl who was with me last night?'

The man's face was blank again, but his eyes were ugly.

'I do not know what you are talking about.'

'Certainly you know! What is the joke? What were you laughing at? You're not laughing now. You're frightened.'

'Please do not raise your voice.'

'Try and stop me.' Petrell hit the zinc counter with his fist so that the glasses danced. 'I will stay here until I get some satisfaction.'

'You will leave at once.'

'I will not!'

'Then,' said the proprietor, 'there are those who can make you.'

Petrell turned. A policeman was standing stolidly behind him.

'I must ask you,' said the proprietor, 'to restrain this young man. He is making a nuisance of himself. You heard him threaten me.'

'It will be better,' said the policeman, 'if you come with me.'

Petrell went.

The fury had drained out of him. He was cold now. On the way to the police station he shivered and the policeman looked at him curiously.

There was an examination room, very much like that in an English police station, and a sergeant of police, in spectacles, waiting at a table.

A small thick man in a belted raincoat was standing with his back to the fire. This man looked up as they came into the room.

'Herr Petrell,' he said. 'A pleasure.'

'Herr Zimmer,' said Petrell.

'You know this man?' said the sergeant.

Herr Zimmer walked over to the sergeant and whispered something.

'Indeed?' said the sergeant, with something like respect. 'That was not understood. I do not think that Herr Bittelburg will press a charge.'

'If,' said Herr Zimmer, 'you will perhaps release him on my undertaking, I am convinced he will behave with the utmost propriety.'

Everyone seemed quite happy about this.

'Now what about a drink?' said Herr Zimmer. 'Not, I should think, at the Krokodil.'

When they were seated at a table in the Kolnischer Kurhaus, Petrell said, 'I made a fool of myself. But thank you very much. You have popped up before, like a good fairy, and rescued me from my indiscretions.'

'In 1946 – or was it 1947?'

'You are still doing the same job?'

'I am still with the Security Police,' said Herr Zimmer. 'It is no longer a military service, you understand.'

'And what is so well-known a policeman doing in the little town of Andernach?'

Zimmer picked up his glass of wine, thought for a moment, cocked his head on one side, and said, 'I am prospecting for diamonds.'

'Diamonds?'

'Not just any diamonds.' He paused. 'Some of the most famous diamonds in the world. The Hapsburg matching yellow diamonds – part of the payment made to Goering for his part in the Dollfuss coup. Lost sight of at the end of the war. Thought to be in the Eastern Zone. Now known to be back in the Western Zone. An American has offered a price for them. On one condition. That they are first transported to America. That is what I am to prevent. If I can.' He paused again, then said soberly, 'If the treasures of Blackbeard and Morgan were stained with the blood of hundreds, these pretty things have been paid for with the tears of whole nations. Stones bought at such a price must not be traded for money.'

'I had no idea,' said Petrell, 'that diamonds could be yellow.'

'Yellow is a crude description. They are of a most beautiful light golden colour. Almost exactly the colour of an old Erbacher Marcobrunner. Indeed, it is believed that they were smuggled across the Iron Curtain in a magnum of Marcobrunner 1947.'

Something stirred in Petrell's mind – a flicker of memory, no more.

'Have you,' he said cautiously, 'any particular lead?'

Zimmer said, 'It was suggested, but no more than suggested, that the Krokodil might be worth watching…. It has been pleasant meeting you after all these years. You are on your way back to London?'

'Yes,' said Petrell. 'I have been delayed.'

After they parted Herr Zimmer spoke on the telephone. 'He should be followed,' he said, 'but not too closely. He is no fool.'

'You suspect him, then? I thought you said he was reliable.'

'He is a very nice young man,' said Zimmer, 'and when I worked with him in Berlin after the war I found him very reliable. But no man is more reliable than his own heart.'

Petrell was sitting on the edge of his bed. It was not his room at the Zur Kron. He had left that in favour of the Pension Nachtigall, a small dirty boarding-house with one feature that outweighed its defects. It overlooked the rear of the Krokodil.

He had paid for the room in advance, and had not even troubled to unpack.

Outside, as dusk turned to dark and as the red neon crocodile winked and blinked, he chased his tormented thoughts in comfortless circles.

When it happened, it happened quickly.

A shaft of light from the kitchen door of the Krokodil. The sound of steps across the courtyard. Then the courtyard door swung back, and she was there. There were two men with her, and their purpose was plain. One held her arm, the other walked to one side and behind her.

Petrell moved fast. As they turned the corner he was no more than twenty yards behind.

The next half-hour was a nightmare. They did not take the direct way through the town but made a wide detour, first away from the river, then – when they were almost out of the town – back to it again. Fortunately the streets were not quite empty. At one time he got the idea that he himself was being followed, but he dismissed it as unlikely.

At last, by their redoubled precautions, he guessed that the men ahead were near their destination. They had turned from the road down a cobbled alley so steep it was almost a flight of stairs. At the bottom he could sense the presence of the river.

It was a quayside tavern, a desperate place at any hour, doubly unattractive at that hour. Petrell hesitated.

To march in and ask to speak to the girl would be courting the worst sort of trouble. On the other hand, if he went for help she might be removed and he would lose her altogether, which was unthinkable.

Was there no chance of turning the enemy's flank?

He moved along, groping in the pitch darkness, until he had reached the corner. Round the corner, down the side of the house, ran an alleyway so narrow that, as he passed, he brushed the walls on each side with his shoulders.

Under his feet the ground was soft – the filth of centuries over cobbles, he guessed. The smell was indescribable.

Then his right hand touched wood. The blank wall was broken by some sort of door. He tried it, hopefully, but it was heavy and immovable.

Nevertheless it had an iron latch, and an iron latch, even if it could not be lifted, might serve as a foothold. He stretched, felt a ledge for his fingertips, got one toe on to the latch, and pulled himself up. From there the top of the wall was in reach. A moment later he was seated astride it.

Behind and below him the alleyway was a pit of darkness. Ahead, a little light filtering from the rear windows of the tavern showed him a small courtyard and a back door. True, he could now drop down into the court; but would that achieve anything? It would not be easy to get back again. And if the house door was fastened he would be trapped.

Another idea came to him. By standing on the wall he could reach over to the sill of one of the first-storey windows. If by any chance the window was open ...

Seconds afterwards he was breathing hard, in pitch darkness, in what smelled like a woman's bedroom. He opened the door and peered out into a hall.

Below him rose the hum and clatter of the tavern.

There was one door with light shining under it. He tiptoed across to listen. There was no sound of movement. On a sudden impulse he pressed down the handle and opened the door.

'Peter!'

She was standing at the other side of the room, looking down through the curtains. As he ran towards her she came to meet him, and then was in his arms.

'Peter!'

'What are you afraid of?' he said gently.

'How did you get in? Did anyone—?'

'Nobody saw me. And if you don't mind a jump, we can get out the same way.'

'Silly Peter,' she said. 'Why should I want to jump out of windows with you?'

'Because you're being kept here against your will. I saw them bringing you.'

'You saw them bringing me?' There was something in her voice he did not understand. 'Did I seem so unwilling?'

'You – yes—'

'So you thought they were kidnapping me. Handsome, romantic, youthful d'Artagnan. Stupid, stupid little boy.'

'I'm not sure what you're trying to talk yourself out of,' said Petrell calmly. 'But it's a waste of time.'

She said, 'I was afraid it might be. You are the sort of person who leaps before he looks, who climbs up drainpipes in the dark to rescue damsels in distress. Are you really as stupid as that? Do you live in a magazine world? Have you no idea where romance ends and reality begins?'

'Here,' he said.

'Yes, here.' Her hands were on him, her warm strong hands. They held his wrists.

The other man must have been in the room all the time, for Petrell heard no door opening, no footsteps, simply a swish, as of a loaded stick. His world dissolved into a hot, blinding burst of light.

His next clear recollection was a smell. The smell of paint. Of painted ironwork. And of bilges. And nausea. He had been sick. He was going to be sick again. He rolled over and closed his eyes.

Surprisingly, he must have fallen asleep.

The next time he opened his eyes he was in the same position, but something was changed. Slowly he got it. Whereas before the floor had been steady it was now, very slowly, moving. Rolling and pitching, not wildly, but steadily.

With an effort he sat up.

He was in a tiny cabin, so small that it was really more of a closet than a cabin. He was lying on the floor, which consisted of duckboards between painted iron ribs. There was no furniture; but two buckets, swinging gently on hooks, and a pile of brooms and scrubbing brushes suggested that it was some sort of glory hole.

He felt the back of his head. It was tender, but nothing was broken. Whoever had hit him knew how to use a cosh.

He took down a bucket, reversed it, and stood on it. This brought his eyes to the level of the single port-hole. He was, as he had suspected, in the middle of the Rhine. At first sight one thing puzzled him. The boat, or barge, seemed to be going upstream, but if that was so the rising sun should have been ahead of him, behind the hills to the east. Unaccountably it had got into the wrong place; it was throwing long shadows from the west.

In the state he was in, this simple problem took him a long time to work out. Then, with a startled exclamation he looked down at his watch. It was still going, and registered half past eight.

'Good God,' he said. 'It's evening. I've been here all day.' Maybe two days? No, that was impossible. His watch would have stopped. It was Sunday evening. He had been unconscious for nearly twenty-four hours.

Petrell sat down on the bucket and tried to think.

The people who had knocked him out could easily have dropped him into the river at Andernach. They had not done so. Therefore they were not interested in killing him. They wished merely to keep him out of the way for a few days.

He felt in his pockets. So far as he could see, nothing had been touched. His wallet and his passport were there – even the small change in his trousers pocket.

He turned his attention to the lock on the door, anticipating no great difficulty. Locks were part of his trade. He had served an apprenticeship to a lockmaking firm and the triple lever and sliding gate held no mysteries for him.

From the pocket in his waistband he took out the innocent-looking tool, which had the appearance of a lady's manicure instrument and was in fact pliers and file in one. He looked round for material and, for want of anything better, he twisted off the handle of one of the buckets. It took him an hour to cut and shape it to his needs. Then, using both hands, confidently, he opened the lock.

There was no need for caution. He was alone, in a lazaret, at the extreme end of one of the longest barges he had ever set eyes on. Dimly ahead was the tug. There seemed to be no one on the barge.

What Petrell wanted next was a decent bit of rope. In the end he had to cut one off the hatch cover. Twenty feet would do. The barge was low in the water.

As an afterthought he bundled up his wallet and passport in his big handkerchief and tied them on his head in a rough turban.

Then he fastened one end of the rope to the barge, grasped the other, and lowered himself away.

As soon as he could feel the pull of the water on his legs he let go his grip, kicked hard two or three times to get out of the wash, then settled down to a slow, steady swim.

'I think,' said Herr Zimmer, 'that there were misunderstandings on both sides.'

'Yes,' said Petrell. He was wearing an old German Army greatcoat, lent to him by the hotelkeeper in whose garden he had finally climbed ashore; and he was nearly asleep because he had waited up in front of a fire for Zimmer to arrive.

'If they had known that you were an inspector in the Criminal Investigation Department of Scotland Yard I cannot believe that they would have selected you in the first place. Your youthful appearance deceived them – as it has deceived so many others in the past.'

'Never mind my youth. What did they want?'

'First I shall have to tell you something of the people who have been playing with you—'

Petrell made a grimace of distaste which was not lost on the older man.

'They are couriers – smugglers, really, of the highest class. They have been entrusted with the task of taking those diamonds I spoke of to America. They will eventually receive a fifth of the price – which, when one considers what will be paid for the diamonds, is not unhandsome. We know most of their routes and many of their tricks – but not all. A month ago they had bad luck. One of their best couriers, a young man, who travels with English papers, was stopped. His passport was not in order.'

'That seems clumsy.'

'Not really. It was the merest slip. You know, of course, that your Foreign Office changes the paper and the watermark of its passports in small but significant particulars almost every year. This man had a passport dated 1954, but on paper which ceased to be used in 1953.'

'I see,' said Petrell grimly. 'So all they wanted from me was a look at my passport.' He took it out of his pocket and examined it. 'Very neat. I wonder if anyone would ever have noticed it.'

Two of the blank end pages had been removed. It had been so cleverly done and so meticulously repaired, that it was only the break in the numbering of the pages that caught the eye.

Petrell seemed to feel again the pressure of a small, strong, warm hand over his heart.

'They are, superficially, very nice people,' said Zimmer thoughtfully.

'Yes,' said Petrell, hesitantly.

'Some of the bluest blood in the land —'

'She held my wrists,' said Petrell savagely. 'Do you understand? She held my wrists, while her boyfriend knocked me out from behind!'

'You will be better for a night's sleep,' said Zimmer.

Late that night the telephone to London was busy, and in the morning Peter Petrell travelled to Hamburg with Herr Zimmer.

'How do you know that it will be today?' he asked wearily. He had slept little, and his mind was full of the wildest fancies.

'It is, of course, only a guess. But the steps they took to keep you out of the way – a little voyage up the Rhine – that argues that they were only worried about the next forty-eight hours. Since, as it falls out, the only boat to America in the next seven days leaves from Hamburg this morning, you understand our haste.'

'Yes.' Petrell's heart was beating uncomfortably. 'I wonder exactly how I shall be able to help you.'

'I wonder that, too,' said Herr Zimmer politely....

'Might I suggest,' said the official to whom they were introduced, 'that the gentleman seats himself here? He can command the only approach to the boat but remains himself unseen. There is a bell-push by his hand. So. If he should see anyone he recognises, would he wait until they proffer their passport? – then press the bell. We will do the rest.'

They will do the rest, thought Petrell dumbly.

A sudden stir in the crowd. The bustle of porters carrying luggage. A flutter of stewards. Some notability arriving. Heads were turned. The crowd seemed to open and, as she stepped up to the barrier, he saw her for only the third time in his life. Beautiful, confident, endlessly desirable – and now for ever out of his reach.

Being nine-tenths policeman and only one-tenth man, Peter straightway pressed the bell.

WHAT HAPPENED AT
CASTELBONATO?

BOXBOURNE DOES NOT get a lot of visitors: it has no railway station. The second Baron Boxbourne saw to that. He owned all the land himself in those high and far-off days, and said to the railway promoters, 'What, have a stinking, steaming juggernaut run through my land? You'd scare every nesting pheasant out of its few wits. I'll see you dead first. Leathers, show these – er – gentlemen the door.' And young Fred Leathers (who was the son of Barnabas Leathers, who had been agent to the first Baron) showed the discomfited deputation to the door. And that is why, to this present day, a Boxbourner who wants to set out on his travels has to start by taking the bus three miles into Branston, from which point it is thirty minutes' run by the branch line to Chelmsford.

Real visitors, who park their cars and unpack their bags, are rare indeed. So the pair who arrived that autumn morning attracted a certain amount of attention.

Not that there was anything startling about Tom and Lois Brassey. He was a pale man of an age difficult to judge, but less than thirty, one would have said, without a great deal of expression on his face. She was a lovely copper-head, most of ten years younger than him.

Their car, a decent old Morris, was tucked away under the lean-to in the back yard of the *Bear and Staff* Inn, and they themselves wore unstartling clothes, and spent their time pottering about the countryside, trespassing a little on the coverts of the present Lord Boxbourne (Charles, the seventh Baron) and scaring the pheasants whose remote ancestors had kept the railway from the village. In the evening they drank in the saloon bar and played darts. Tom skilfully; Lois indifferently.

'Then, you couldn't exactly expect a furren lady to play darts, could you?' said Mr Farrow, the landlord.

'She 'ent a furrener, Barney,' said Jim Crow, who was the Boxbourne poacher and captain of the Boxbourne darts team. 'Furreners live in Yurrup. She's a Yank. I met 'em in the war. They all talk like that.'

It was on the sixth evening of their stay that they met Captain Roye. He came into the saloon bar in the easy way of a man who is sure of his welcome, ordered a double whisky and drank it standing whilst he cast an eye round the room.

Tom was playing a foursome, partnering Jim Crow against two of the regulars. Lois was sipping her gin and listening to Barney talk about his hens.

'I only kept hens but once,' she said, 'and for me, you can have them. Stupid, dirty creatures. If I want eggs, I buy them in a nice, clean store.'

'Shop, we should say,' said Captain Roye, with a smile calculated to rob the words of offence. 'You're from over the Atlantic?'

'That's so. Do you keep hens?'

'Not hens. Pheasants.'

'That would be the stupid-looking bird like a prairie chicken, only not so fat. They get up with a noise like a cracker when you tread on them.'

'I hope you haven't been treading on them,' said Captain Roye seriously. 'Their feelings are very easily hurt.'

'We've been walking round a good deal,' admitted Lois, 'and I wouldn't say we've always stuck to the roads. Oh, by the way, here's my husband. He's buying the beer, so I guess he's lost his darts match. Hi, Tom. Meet the gentleman who owns the land we've been trespassing over.'

This remark caught one of those little silences which sometimes fall over a room full of people.

'Not the owner,' said Captain Roye. 'Just the agent. Pleased to meet you. I was telling your wife we don't get many strangers around here.'

'I took a fancy to the place,' said Tom Brassey. 'It looked so restful. Will you have one, as I'm ordering? And a whisky, Barney. I'm sorry to hear we've been trespassing.'

'I'm sure you haven't done any harm,' said the Captain. 'Any time you want to see over the place, why don't you look me up? Farrow will tell you where I live. I'd be delighted to show you – and your wife – around.'

'That's very good of you,' said Tom. 'All right, Jim. I've got the beer. Are we going to have our revenge?'

He went back to the dart-board, leaving Captain Roye looking after him.

Later that evening, as they were getting into bed, Tom Brassey said to his wife: 'So that's the Captain. I'd heard about him.'

'Quite a nice little man,' said Lois.

'Bit smooth for me. And where does all the money come from?'

'What money?'

'Don't tell me you didn't notice his car. It stretched from here to there. A custom-made Jaguar.'

'Perhaps he borrowed it from Lord Boxbourne.'

'In the old days,' said Tom, 'agents went round in pony traps and knew their station. And they didn't make passes at the wives of strangers in saloon bars.'

'Do you think he was making a pass at me?' said Lois, looking at herself complacently in the mirror before she put on her night-gown. 'Now you mention it, he looked a bit of a wolf.'

'As you're last into bed you can turn out the light,' said Tom.

Next morning Tom and Lois called by appointment on Dr Meadows. The doctor was nominally retired: in fact, he was regularly called out of retirement in every emergency. He lived in a Georgian house about half-a-mile out of the village.

He was an old, shrewd, grey badger, with the colouring of a countryman and the peaceful eyes of a man who is controlled by a quiet conscience and a good digestion. He greeted them kindly and took them into his drawing-room, which opened through long French windows directly on to the lawn, and was so full of sunlight and the smell of flowers that you might have thought the room a mere annexe to the garden.

'You know young Leathers?' he said. 'How is the boy?'

'Fine,' said Tom. 'Fine. When I saw him last – that was about six months ago in Winnipeg he was in very good form.'

'Is he married yet?'

'He wasn't when I spoke to him six months ago.'

'We miss him here,' said the doctor.

'I think Boxbourne's on his conscience,' said Tom. 'That's really why he asked me to look you up. Someone said that old Tom Leathers died of a broken heart when young Tom refused to come home. I think that's what was really worrying him.'

The doctor reflected.

'Medically,' he said, 'that's nonsense. Old Tom had a marvellous constitution. Sound as a bell! He'd never had a day's illness in his life. Perhaps that was what was wrong with him: if he'd had a few illnesses he might have built up a few antibodies.'

'What actually happened to him, then?'

'He was out hunting. Took a toss. Got bad-ish concussion. Nothing in that, of course. He'd had concussion so many times from hunting falls that he took very little notice of it. But for some reason he couldn't seem to shake this one off. Then he caught a chill. That turned to gastric trouble. And his heart gave out.'

'I see,' said Tom. 'So that was the way it was.'

'Mind you,' said the doctor, 'I'm not saying he didn't feel it when his son decided to stay in Canada. There's been a Leathers as agent looking after a Boxbourne as landlord since – when?'

'The year of Waterloo,' said the young man softly. And added, 'So Leathers told me.'

The doctor looked at him curiously. 'Did Tom ever talk to you – in Canada – about why he wouldn't come back?' he asked.

The young man shook his head. 'He wasn't a very talkative sort of person,' he said. 'I knew the outline, of course. He was in the tank with young Lord Boxbourne when he got killed – the one who would have had the title if he'd lived.'

'Philip.'

'That's right. Philip. It was a place in Italy called Castelbonato. The tank got two direct hits and was set on fire. Philip Boxbourne was killed – and the rest of the crew, except young Tom. He was badly burnt, but survived. The Fifth Army picked him up and an American surgeon built him a new face. Did a great job.'

'I've never had much experience of plastic surgery,' said the doctor. 'But I'm told that even the most perfect operation leaves marks that can never be removed.'

'There may have been marks,' said the young man doubtfully. 'I never noticed them myself.'

'I interrupted you.'

'I hadn't really much more to add,' said the young man. 'I suppose anyone who has been burned alive and lived to tell the tale must be allowed some ideas of his own. That's about all there was to it. As I understand the matter, Tom Leathers had always wanted to be a mining engineer—'

'Now that's an ambition I can appreciate,' said the doctor. 'Very like gastric surgery. Only your mining engineer digs into the bowels of the earth.'

The young man laughed, and for a moment his impassive, almost mask-like face, took on animation and colour.

'That's it,' he said. 'It's the pleasure of the unknown. To look at the surface of old Mother Earth you'd never dream what went on underneath. But sink a three-foot shaft sideways into the most ordinary-looking hill and, hey presto, you've stepped clean through the looking-glass! You're in Wonderland.'

'You speak,' said the doctor, 'almost as if you were a mining engineer yourself.'

The young man's face slipped back into immobility. It was like a blind coming down.

'It's a trick I must have picked up from Leathers,' he said. 'I'm in real estate myself. We mustn't waste any more of your time.'

'I've enjoyed it,' said the doctor. 'I take it you two are here on holiday?'

'Sort of.'

'And will you be going back to Canada?'

'I – I don't think we've absolutely made up our minds.'

'I was only going to say that if you did go back to Canada, and happened to see young Tom Leathers, would you give him an old man's very good wishes? Twenty years ago I taught him to shoot – and gave him his first gun.'

The young man got awkwardly to his feet; said: 'Surely, doctor. Surely. I'll pass that on to him.'

'I think no worse of anyone,' said the doctor slowly, 'for wanting to live his own life. Science is a marvellous creature, but she hasn't thought out any way of giving us more than one life. So a man must be allowed to do what he wants with it. Good-bye, then. And to you, young lady.'

As they walked down the flagged path, the doctor stood looking after them, a puzzled frown on his face. Then he opened a drawer and pulled out an old photograph album. After a search he found what he was looking for.

It was a picture of two boys, of about the same age: something between fourteen and sixteen; both about five-feet-eight, with more growth to come; both with the long-limbed, balanced look of athletes. There was no particular similarity in the faces, except that they both looked good-tempered.

They were carrying guns and grinning down proudly at three small rabbits displayed on the grass at their feet. Underneath, in faded yellow ink, was written: Philip Boxbourne and young Tom Leathers. First holiday from Eton.

'Either I'm the biggest fool in Christendom,' said Dr Meadows, 'or there's something happening here that I don't understand.'

It was about eight o'clock in the evening of the last day but one of their holiday. Lois was sitting on the bed darning a pair of socks, when her husband came in. She took a quick look at his face, dropped the socks, jumped up and pulled him down beside her.

'You look as if you've been seeing ghosts,' she said. 'I told you we ought never to have come.'

'I haven't been seeing ghosts,' he said. 'I've been listening to one.'

'A ghost in Branston?'

'It doesn't sound likely,' he agreed. 'I finished all your shopping for you – here's the wool, by the way – and I decided I'd got time for a quick one before I caught the Boxbourne bus. Fate led me to the *Five Hedgers*, and there in the saloon bar, was one Ernie Barrow. And he was tight.'

'Quick work by six o'clock.'

'That's what I thought. Apparently he's a type who gets tight at midday and stays that way.'

'He sounds a charmer. Do we know him?'

'As a matter of fact, he's not a bad sort at all – sober. Yes, I knew him. He didn't know me, of course. I was just someone to talk to.'

'So he talked?'

'That's right. He bought me a beer so's I couldn't get away, and he talked.'

'About what?'

'About Boxbourne. Where he used to farm, at Longbarrow Farm. He, and his father before him. They used to make quite a good thing out of it. And about the Boxbourne estates, and the present Lord Boxbourne, who, according to Barrow, knows nothing about running a landed estate.'

'Poor old Charles,' said Lois. 'No one round here seems to have a good word for him. Or his wife.'

'Oh yes. Barrow talked about her, too. How she wears the trousers, up at Boxbourne Hall. But it wasn't the Boxbournes that he really wanted to get off his chest. After the second beer we got down to cases. We discussed Captain Roye.'

'That chap,' said Lois thoughtfully. 'And what did Barrow say about him?'

'To paraphrase Barrow, if Roye, a skunk, a rattlesnake and a pregnant goat were in the room together, it would be almost impossible for a blind man to tell which was which.'

'Picturesque,' said Lois, 'but why should it upset you?'

'There was a little more to it than that. You know that everyone round here's been telling us what a useless landlord old Charles Boxbourne is. How he never makes anything pay, and the farms are all going downhill for want of proper capital expenditure and control, and no one seems to take any interest any more.'

'That's what they say,' agreed Lois.

'They don't exactly blame him. He didn't ask for the title. But first Philip gets killed in Italy, and then his father dies—'

'And they lugged poor old Charles out of his deck-chair at Torquay and told him to be a landed proprietor?'

'That's right.'

'Couldn't he have said no?'

'I suppose he could have refused the estate. I don't think he could have got out of the title. You need an Act of Parliament to do that. Anyway, it didn't arise. His wife fancied the idea of being Lady Boxbourne and having a lot of peasants touching their hats to her.'

'I don't think the English farmer today is a very hat-touching sort of man,' said Lois. 'But you still haven't told me what's worrying *you*.'

'Well, according to Barrow, what we've been hearing is only half the truth. He admits that Charles is no great shakes as a landlord, but he says that the real trouble is our friend Captain Roye.'

'And Barrow was drunk when he said it.'

'Yes, he was drunk when he said it. But it made sense. If Charles knew more about things, Roye couldn't get away with it. Old Hugo would have seen through him in half no time. So would young Philip.'

'H'm,' said Lois. 'I'll confess I didn't go for Roye a lot. Waistcoat too loud and hands too soft. But he's just a type. He's not necessarily a crook.'

'Then where does he get the money to buy a car like that and – says Barrow – add a wing to the old bailiff's house, put up a squash court, entertain big, hunt through the season? I *know* what Boxbourne pays his agent. At least, I know what Hugo used to pay old Tom. It wouldn't stretch to three hunters and a custom-built car.'

'Private means.'

'When he came here – Barrow tells me – his creditors were after him. In the last ten years, as Boxbourne's got poorer, Roye's got richer.'

'Just how do you suggest he does it?'

'Every single dirty way – says Barrow – that a dishonest agent with a complacent landlord can screw money out of tenants and land. Here's one of 'em. Apparently, just after the war, the gallant Captain bought ten acres of land from the Boxbournes – for £700. That's about right for farmland. Only it didn't stay as farmland. Next month a London manu-facturer, who was putting up a factory at Chelmsford, appeared in the market *for this precise plot* for a housing estate for his employees. The only person who knew about the project was Jacob Sindy, who's on the Boxbourne Housing Committee. Sindy is a pal of Roye.'

'Says Barrow.'

'Yes. It might be hearsay. But here's one that directly affected Barrow. And it's the reason he keeps a garage in Branston instead of a farm at Boxbourne. In 1950 soft fruit, especially cherries and plums, were bringing in terrific prices. Essex was almost the only county which had a decent crop. Most of the Boxbourne tenants grow them. They sell to

Chelmsford. Roye said, No. They should sell to him. He offered quite normal prices. Then *he* sold direct to Covent Garden – he's hand in glove with a gang of thugs there. The tenants got the milk. Roye got the cream.'

'Why did they stand for it?'

'Barrow didn't. He kicked up a row. Next thing he knew, his five best men were hurried away by high wage offers and someone put in a complaint about his land to the County Agricultural Committee. He'd been a bit short of labour for some time. The position was hopeless and he had to give up the farm.'

'That doesn't smell good,' admitted Lois. She sat straight up on the bed and looked at her husband. 'You're not planning to get mixed up in all this, are you?'

'Well, I—'

'You know why I agreed to come here. It was to be just a sentimental holiday. To revisit the haunts of your youth. Nothing else. Just a break before we go back and settle down to the collar in Canada.'

'Darn it,' said Tom. 'I can't let it go. Anyone else, perhaps, but not me. I can't stand by and let Boxbourne be milked dry by a crook in a fancy waistcoat. I'd never look myself in the face again. You needn't get mixed up in this, Lois, but I—'

Lois let her breath go in one quick gasp. 'Let's have it. Just what *are* you planning to do?'

'That evening in the saloon bar, remember? Roye said: come out and see me any time you like. Tomorrow I'll take him at his word.'

'And I'll come with you,' said Lois.

'Well, this is a surprise,' said Captain Roye. He seemed surprised, too.

'Nice place you've got here,' said Tom. 'Must take a bit of keeping up.'

The Captain surveyed the smooth grass, the clipped hedges and the walls, of that old, dusty red colour; child of time, which neither skill can hasten nor artifice fake. 'It's not bad,' he said. 'It takes two men all their time to keep it tidy. You don't get lawns like this in America, Mrs Brassey.'

'Canada,' said Lois.

'Oh, my mistake.' The Captain seemed put out for a moment. 'Would you care to come in and have a drink?' Inside there was rather too much furniture, and what was old was badly jostled by what was new.

'Some hide-out,' said Lois.

'It's not bad,' said the Captain. 'I have to entertain a good deal. Business, you know.'

'Is that Lady Boxbourne?' asked Lois, pointing to a big photograph on the mantelshelf. It showed a heavy, grey-haired woman with an obstinate, stupid face. She was sitting squarely in a wicker chair on a sunlit terrace.

'That's her Ladyship,' agreed the Captain. 'You know the family?'

'We see pictures of them,' said Tom. 'In *The Tatler*. Are they nice people to work for?'

'Oh – very.' The Captain managed to side-track the question without actually being rude. The young man took no notice at all.

'I suppose,' he said, 'Old Boxbourne not being an expert really makes your job a lot easier.'

The Captain stiffened. 'I beg your pardon?' he said.

'Sorry if I'm being tactless. Only I couldn't help hearing all the local gossip. The boys seemed to think that the present owner being so clueless about agriculture puts all the real work on you.'

The Captain seemed uncertain how to take this; after an interval, which was just long enough to show that he disapproved of the whole topic, he said, 'There might be some truth in that. The present Lord Boxbourne came to the estate very late in life, when his brother the sixth Baron died. He never expected to inherit. There was a son in the direct line. But he was killed in Italy.'

'A pity. I understand he would have made a good landlord. Knew the job and was keen on it.'

'I never knew Philip personally,' said the Captain. 'I only came here myself towards the end of the war.'

'You knew old Tom Leathers, then?'

'I worked under him for about two years. A fine old chap. I took over from him when he died. If you'll excuse me saying so, you seem to know a lot about this estate.'

'Blame my inquisitiveness. I'm the good-natured type that people talk to. I'm a born listener. I spent an hour in Branston, yesterday, listening to a man called Barrow.'

'Barrow – oh yes. We got rid of Barrow some years ago. Not a good farmer. Was he drunk when you met him?'

'More or less. Not so drunk as to be incoherent. He doesn't seem to like you.'

'The feeling,' said the Captain, showing his teeth, 'is reciprocated. Now if you don't mind, I've got one or two things to do.'

The young man half turned in his chair, and said, 'You know, you ought to be careful about Barrow. He isn't doing the estate much good. If what he says isn't true, there's a law of slander.'

'I can look after myself, thank you.'

'No doubt. But I wasn't thinking of you. I happened to be thinking of the estate.'

'From a complete stranger,' said the Captain, getting to his feet, 'I think that is one of the most impertinent remarks I have ever heard. Now, if you've done—'

'From a complete stranger, it would be. I'm not a complete stranger.'

There was a moment of silence in the room.

'As you knew before, or must have guessed by now, my name isn't Brassey. It's Leathers.'

'Yes,' said the Captain. Now that the word had been spoken, he seemed, curiously, more sure of himself. 'Yes. I think I guessed it as soon as your wife said you came from Canada. And now that you've told me, if you'll excuse my saying so, what of it?'

'That's not a very warm reception from an old friend of my father.'

'I knew and admired your father. I don't have to like his son.'

'True,' said Tom.

'Let's stop pretending. You came here to make trouble.'

'I came here for a lot of reasons,' said Tom, 'but making trouble wasn't among them. I wanted to hear about my father's death. Also I was due a holiday and this seemed an interesting place to have it. Old haunts and so on, which I wanted to show to my wife. Also I had a bet with her – which I've won – that no one would recognize me. And when I got here, the first thing that struck me – since we're being honest – was that the estate looked in pretty poor order. Except your house. That's terrific.'

'Go on.'

'Then people started to talk to me. I didn't ask them to. They just talked. And it built up the picture. A picture of a do-nothing landlord with a vain and stupid wife and a – well, a clever agent.'

'A picture based on gossip in the bar and drunken accusations from a farmer who was sacked for incompetence.'

'Agreed. If it had just been what people said, I might have passed it up. But I got corroboration from one witness that doesn't lie.'

With a perfectly white face the Captain said, 'Perhaps you'll name him.'

'My witness is the fields themselves. They shout to me of mismanagement every time I look at them.'

'Interesting,' said the Captain, relaxing. 'But difficult to put a hayfield into the witness-box.'

'I agree. As I said, if I'd been a stranger, I'd have let it go.'

'But as you're not a stranger, you're going to do – just what?'

'I'll be absolutely honest with you,' said Tom. 'I don't know. But if I hang about a bit longer I expect I shall see my way clear. You're sitting on a keg of powder at the moment, Captain. It's only a question of finding a match and we'll blow you to where you belong.'

'You're bluffing.' Roye seemed to have recovered his poise. 'You're bluffing on an empty hand. I've no doubt you'd like this job, and I've no doubt you think you could do it better than me. But it doesn't happen to be going.'

'I see what Barrow meant,' said Tom. 'That bit about the rattlesnake. I thought he was exaggerating.'

'Don't let me keep you,' said the Captain.

'And what exactly,' said Lois, as they walked out after tea that day, '*do* you intend to do?'

'I don't know.'

'Well, I know what you ought to do. Come away and forget about it. If he's as bad as you say, he'll hang himself sooner or later.'

'I don't mind if he hangs himself. I don't want him to take Boxbourne with him. Do you know, this was one of the best run and happiest estates in England. The tenants trusted the landlord, and they knew he was on their side. They worked together. I can't describe the difference now. The place is like – it's like a sick animal. Look at that ditch. It wants cleaning and redigging. Do you see how it's got clogged up and made a swamp right across the entrance? When the tractors come in, they churn it up and make it twice as bad. In the old days, if the tenant couldn't afford to have a job like that done, the landlord would do it for him and work out the cost later. Now they probably both ring up their lawyers. Ugh!'

Lois looked speculatively at her husband. 'All right,' she said. 'The problem's there, I agree. But you can't get over what Roye said. At the moment, it happens to be his problem. Not yours.'

'You may be right,' said Tom, miserably, 'I wish I knew.'

The lorry was a big one, and coming fast. But there was plenty of room for it. They got up on to the verge to allow it passage.

The first time Tom realized something was wrong was when Lois screamed.

He jerked his head round. The lorry was coming straight at them.

'Jump!' he shouted, grabbed her arm and hurled himself forward.

They landed together in the ditch. For a moment the lorry seemed to hang, poised above them. Then it swung out, and roared past in a splatter of small stones and dirt.

As they raised their heads, a man, sitting in the back, laughed.

'The filthy swine,' said Tom. 'The murdering lout. Did you get his number?'

'I was too scared,' said Lois.

Tom was still staring after the lorry, which was now fast vanishing in a cloud of its own dust. 'I didn't see the name,' he said, 'but it was a Covent Garden firm. I saw that much. And I can guess who put them up to it.'

Louis looked at him and said, 'There's nothing to grin about. Look at my frock.'

'I was just thinking,' said Tom, 'that it isn't often you get your mind made up for you quite so promptly.'

'What are you going to do?'

'See Lord Boxbourne.'

'It's incredible,' said Charles, seventh Baron Boxbourne, 'quite incredible. My dear fellow, how are you after all these years? Do you mind just turning your face to the light? I wasn't one of your closest friends, but I visited here often enough to suppose that I would recognize you. But there's nothing – nothing. It doesn't embarrass you to talk about it, I hope.'

'Of course not,' said Tom. 'And it's not surprising really, that people don't recognize me. After all, I've not only got an entirely new face, but I've been using it for ten years. It's acquired a few characteristics of its own, now.'

'It must have been a most upsettin' experience,' said her Ladyship.

'Well, it isn't every day of your life that you get burned to death and resuscitated,' agreed Tom. 'In fact, I believe that medically I *was* dead, for about ten minutes.'

'Interestin',' observed her Ladyship.

'But now that you're here,' said Lord Boxbourne, 'what can we do for you? I'm not sure how much you know. You knew that your father—?'

'Yes. I know about him. As long as he was alive he wrote to me regularly. Then I had a letter or two from the doctor. One of the reasons I came here was to call on him and thank him for the trouble he took.'

'You've been stayin' in the village?'

'That's right. At the *Bear and Staff*.'

'My dear fellow,' said Lord Boxbourne. 'Why didn't you let us know before? We'd have been only too pleased to put you up. Wouldn't we, Phyllis?'

'Of course,' said Lady Boxbourne, after a tiny pause which made it clear that the thought would never have entered her head.

'Well,' said Tom. 'I might as well break it to you now. I never did intend to come and see you at all.'

'My dear fellow—'

'The idea was to come and take a little peep, like a spirit from another world. Not to be obtrusive. Just to roam around and feel sentimental about it all. And then go back to Canada and get on with the business of life.'

'Quite understand your feelings,' said Lord Boxbourne. 'Went back to my own prep. school once in holiday time, and wandered around a bit. Nearly made me cry.'

'Mr Leathers hasn't told us,' said Lady Boxbourne, rather sharply, 'why he changed his mind.'

'Here's where I'll have to watch my step,' said Tom, 'or you'll accuse me, and rightly, of interfering in something that doesn't concern me. Or doesn't concern me any longer. But I couldn't be happy about the way things were going.'

Lady Boxbourne raised her head, but said nothing. His Lordship said, 'I'm not quite sure I follow you.'

'I'll put the matter in a nutshell. I don't trust your agent. That's an understatement. I'm practically sure he's a crook.'

Lois found herself holding her breath, but unexpectedly there was no immediate explosion.

Lord Boxbourne said, 'I expect you'd like to go a bit further than that, wouldn't you? I mean, you can't just say that and leave it there.'

'Fair enough,' said Tom. 'I expect it will sound thinnish, but if you'll hear me out – then it's up to you to decide if I'm seeing bogeys where none exist.'

He talked for all of ten minutes. Lord Boxbourne sat looking at him with no expression at all on his handsome, aging face. The signals came from Lady Boxbourne who snorted and hissed like a steam engine under pressure, and tapped the toe of her heavy shoe on the parquet floor.

At the conclusion, and before her husband could open his mouth, she said, 'Is that all? You're *quite* sure you haven't anything else to say about Captain Roye?

'No,' said Tom, quietly. 'That's all.'

'Then permit me to say that I have never heard anything more outrageous in my whole life. I wish to speak no ill of the dead, but you and your father are both of a piece. Anything a Leathers said was right; everything a Boxbourne said was wrong. Of course, we said nothing whilst he was alive; and, anyway, it was his job. But now that we *have* found an agent who happens to fit in with *our* ideas, even if some of the less efficient tenants dislike him, for you, an outsider, to come here and criticize, is worse than impertinent. It's—'

While Lady Boxbourne was searching vainly for some vice worse than impertinence, her husband managed to speak.

'You were in the Army,' he said. 'You'll understand what I mean when I say that a good sergeant-major was never exactly popular with the troops. If he was efficient, he chased them. And they didn't love him.'

'I agree,' said Tom. 'But it's not a true analogy. If Roye harried your bad tenants and kept the slackers up to the mark, he mightn't be popular, but I wouldn't say a word against him. But he doesn't. If he were efficient, the estate would be well run. It isn't. Just imagine your regiment, if the sergeant-major were not only inefficient, but were actually dipping his hand into the canteen funds.'

'Have you any proof?'

'Not yet. But I don't think that would be difficult to find. Who audits Roye's books?'

'Well … in fact – no one. On the contrary, he sees to the audit of our books – the estate books.'

'I see. How long is it since any of your farms has had an efficiency rating?'

'We don't do that now. We stopped it some years ago.'

'Oh yes.'

'Mr Leathers,' said Lady Boxbourne. 'Will you very kindly answer me one question before we go any further?'

'Certainly.'

'Suppose, after you have made every insinuation that malice suggests to you against our agent, we show you the door. And elect to put the kindest construction on your conduct that occurs to us – that your mind has been deranged by your sufferings. What do you propose to do?'

'There are too many "ifs" in that question to allow a straight answer. First of all,' Tom turned to Lord Boxbourne, 'are you going to take any action, or not?'

'I don't think,' said his Lordship slowly, 'that what you have told us is sufficient to warrant any action.'

'Not at the moment, perhaps. But are you going to make any enquiry to find out whether what I have said is true?'

'Certainly not,' said Lady Boxbourne, before her husband could open his mouth.

'You force my hand, then,' said Tom, swinging round. 'If you will take no step to get rid of a man whom I know to be inefficient and believe to be a crook, then I shall have to get rid of him for you.'

'And how do you propose to do that, Mr Leathers?'

'In due course,' said Tom, 'you will find out.'

A week later, at breakfast, Lady Boxbourne said, 'Well, have you heard anything more of that impudent jackanapes?'

'Nothing in the post this morning, my dear.'

'What did I tell you. All bluster and no performance. Yes, Ellen, what is it?'

'It's Constantine and Jerrold, Ma'am. For his Lordship.'

Lord Boxbourne swallowed the last of his coffee, and got to his feet grumbling. He hated being disturbed over his breakfast. 'Did he say what it was about?' he asked.

'It was Mr Constantine himself, sir. He said he wouldn't have troubled you, but it was very important.'

'Yes. I see,' said Bohun.

He tilted his chair back. Out of the corner of his eye he could see the pigeons, prinking in the sun among the shrubs and flowers of New Square, Lincoln's Inn. It was a sight that never failed to soothe him.

Many sorts of clients were attracted to the offices of Horniman, Birley & Craine, Solicitors and Commissioners for Oaths. Many of them were troubled; and some added to their troubles by not telling him the whole truth.

On that score it was as yet too early to judge the young man with the blank, whitish face and the pretty copper-headed girl who sat before him.

'Let me get this Italian business quite clear,' he said, 'because it seems to me that what happened at Castelbonato is the crux of the whole matter. You were in C Squadron of the 16th/21st Lancers. Your armoured division was leading the advance – and your regiment was leading the armoured division. And since you were in the front tank, you were, so to speak, leading the army.'

'That's about it. We knew, of course, that the German winter line was somewhere ahead of us. But we didn't know just where until we bumped head first into it at a place called Castelbonato.'

'And each tank had a crew of four – each crew being more or less a "happy family" on its own. This particular tank had' – Bohun looked down at his notes – 'a driver, Sam Bellingham, formerly the Boxbourne chauffeur; a wireless operator, Carfew, formerly one of the Boxbourne footmen; a sort of spare wireless-operator-gunner-jack-of-all-trades, who acted as second-in-command of the tank: one Tom Leathers; and, finally, a tank commander, the Honourable Philip Boxbourne, next in line for the Barony of Boxbourne.'

'Right,' said the young man.

'Now tell me, again, in your own words, what happened next.'

'Two anti-tank guns hit us at about the same moment. Sam Bellingham, whose heart was as stout as his body, stayed alive long enough to put the nose of the tank into a small gully. If he hadn't done

that the enemy would have chopped us to pieces at leisure. We weren't a
lot better off, but we were out of sight, nose down, more or less on fire.
And there we stayed, until the battle died down and someone had time
to crawl out and take a look at us. When the squadron second-in-
command came up that night, he found a burnt-out tank, with three
bodies inside it and one outside. The one outside was me. They dug a
hole, there and then, and they put all that was left of the other three into
it. I must have shown just enough signs of life to encourage them, so they
loaded me on to a stretcher-jeep and trundled me back. I was so nearly
dead from shock and burns and, incidentally, two broken arms and a
badly cracked skull, that I'm told it's a medical miracle I didn't drag my
foot over the line and walk straight up into the next world. However, I
kept a toe-hold in this life and the long and short of it is that six months
later I was actually on my feet again. Tottery, and with a new face, and
not a lot of use to anybody but, by heaven, I was still alive.'

Bohun said, with deliberate slowness:

'I was in the infantry, myself. Tell me something of how a tank works.
I'll have to understand that bit.'

'Well, the driver was wholly occupied in driving. The wireless operator had two wireless sets to keep him busy. The third man was a sort of
odd-jobber; gunner, and troop-leader's assistant and so on. That left the
tank commander free to do his one job properly: to get his tank to the
right place at the right time. He stands up, with his head out of the top,
and is the only person who can really see where they are going. It takes
a good deal more practice than you'd think. He's got a map balanced on
the ledge by his nose, and he's listening with one ear to what the
squadron-leader is saying to him, and giving orders to the driver at the
same time.'

'Sounds complicated,' agreed Bohun. 'However, as the tank you were
in was leading the Eighth Army, I suppose it was pretty important to get
it right.'

'Exactly. And that was the crux of the whole matter. Boxbourne was
constitutionally incapable of reading a map. It's just one of those things.
Some people can, some can't. He couldn't. Most people improve with
practice: he just got worse. So, after one or two hair-raising experiences
in England – on training at Bovington, he led the whole regiment in a
complete circle and attacked his own Q echelon instead of the enemy –
the "family" arranged a harmless little deception. On any occasion when
his troop was called on to lead, which would be roughly one time in
every four, Tom Leathers, who was an ace at map-reading, used to
change places with Boxbourne. The first time they did it, it was a sort of
joke, but it worked so well that they kept it up and kept quiet about it.

It was really quite serious, you see. One more mess-up like Bovington and Boxbourne would have lost his job. However, this way it worked splendidly. No one ever gets very close to a tank on the move, and anyway there's usually a cloud of dust round it, and you can see only the head and perhaps the shoulders of the man in the turret, and he wears dust-goggles. So all they had to do was swap hats and shoulder-straps. Tom put on the officer's hat and the "sleeve" with the two pips on it, and Boxbourne wore Tom's beret, which is about the only headgear you *can* wear inside a tank – and the result was that they always arrived now more or less at the right destination.'

'What about the voices?'

'All the voices sound the same on the wireless – I mean, provided they are reasonably similar to start with. Young Tom and Boxbourne spoke the same language, if you see what I mean.'

'And did none of the other tank crews—?'

'I think one or two of his own troop may have suspected it. Certainly the squadron-leader didn't know. He'd have been very stuffy about anything like that.'

'I see,' said Bohun again. The most alarming vistas of complication and misunderstanding were opening before him. 'So when only one body out of the four was salvaged, and that one without, if you'll excuse me mentioning it, very much face left, but wearing a lance-jack's stripe on its arm, no doubt was felt that it – that is to say, that you – were Tom Leathers. Whereas, actually it was Tom who had been killed wearing your hat and shoulder-badges and the other one was – or is – that is to say, *you* are Lord Boxbourne.'

'That's right,' said the young man. 'It's muddling till you get used to it,' he added, helpfully.

Silence fell on the room; on its shelves of stored wisdom; its severe judicial pictures; its badly puzzled owner.

It was the young man who broke the silence. 'I don't think anyone ever had any reason to think anything else,' he said. 'I wasn't in any position to help. As far as the burial went, that was carried out by the light of one torch. We neither of us wore identity discs. A lot of soldiers didn't. Our kits were on the carrier at the back. The clothes we wore couldn't have helped: you didn't wear much, inside a tank. In fact, when I eventually came up to the surface, through the drugs and the exhaustion, it took me quite a long time to work it out myself and decide who I was. Then things sorted out a bit. I noticed, of course, that I was being treated as an O.R. and that gave me a clue. So I didn't give myself away the first time I definitely grasped the truth, that in the eyes of the world I was now plain Tom Leathers; and Philip, Lord Boxbourne, was buried in a hill-side, under an olive tree above Castelbonato, with two fine men to keep him company.'

Silence fell again on the room, which had heard many strange stories.

'Why,' said Bohun at last, 'when you realized the truth, did you keep your mouth shut?'

'I can't really answer that. To start with, if you've been burnt to a cinder, and so near dead that you're three-quarters of the way up to the Golden Gates, when you get back again you don't think like a normal person at all. When I was young, the only thing I ever hankered after being was a mining engineer. It started before I went up to Oxford. I was allowed six months off the leash and I spent it in the north of Canada. Even then I had it at the back of my mind to cut adrift and try my hand. Well, quite suddenly, as I lay in bed, I saw what a chance I'd been given. Literally, a chance in a lifetime. If I turned it down now, it was never going to happen again.'

'So you said nothing, took your gratuity and pension and pulled out for Canada.'

'It wasn't quite that simple; but that was what happened in the end. A Canadian I met in hospital asked me to come over for a long visit. I accepted. I had a bit of money saved—'

'You mean,' said Bohun, 'Tom had a bit of money saved.'

'Yes. I had no difficulty about signatures when I drew it, either. I simply explained that I'd broken all the bones in my right hand.'

'Which was true,' said the girl, sharply.

Bohun jumped. It was practically the first time she had spoken.

'Yes. It was true right enough.' He spread his hand on the desk and they could see the network of white scars. 'I had enough money to pay for my preliminary training in metallurgy and engineering. The Veterans' Society of Canada lent a hand. It was a good life. In the open air, most of it. I didn't pine for England. I wrote once or twice to old Tom. He was pretty cut up about his son not coming back, but he never argued. I liked him for that. I used to tap out long letters to him and sign them with my left hand. From his letters back, he seemed happy enough. He wanted to see me, of course, but I managed to stall him off. I think he understood how I felt – I mean, he understood how I would have felt if I had been his son.'

Bohun said, 'It must be confusing, being two people at the same time.' He added, 'It's all going to be terribly difficult to prove. Was there anyone – anyone now alive – who knew about your habit of changing places?'

'I don't think – wait a bit.... Yes.... It did come out once. It wasn't anyone in our regiment. It was the gunners who were in support of us. We worked with an O.P. tank attached to each squadron. The O.P. officer got suspicious one day – something that was said on the wireless – and taxed us with it. We told him that he'd unearthed our guilty secret, but that he must jolly well keep quiet about it.'

'Do you remember his name?'

'I may have known it once. He was a captain. We called him Andy.'

'When did this happen?'

'A week or two before we got blown up. And I think he was in support that day at Castelbonato, too.'

'All right,' said Bohun. He made a note. 'It's better than nothing. I've known good fish caught on a thinner line.'

'There's one thing,' said the young man. 'I don't know how we're going to stand – in law, I mean – but even if we can't prove our story, it's going to be terribly difficult for anyone to disprove it.'

'What makes you say that?'

'The Boxbournes and the Leathers have been much more than master and servant for the last century. It's a sort of tradition that the eldest son of the Leathers – the one who would be agent when his father died – is brought up with young Boxbourne. They share a governess, and go off to preparatory school together. In this case, the family fancied young Tom so much that they sent him to Eton. It was a great success. Tom was slightly the better of the two at work. Boxbourne a little better at games. But there wasn't much in it.'

'I see,' said Bohun. He looked speculatively at the expressionless face in front of him. From behind the mask, two blue eyes stared back unblinking.

'It's the maddest story I've ever heard,' said Roly Craine, Bohun's senior partner, glaring over the gold-rimmed glasses which, in conjunction with a chubby face and button nose, made up a startling likeness to Mr Pickwick.

'There's no doubt it all happened,' said Bohun. 'The only question is, who was who at the end of it all?'

'What are you planning to do?'

'I suppose it will mean an Originating Summons in the Chancery Division, asking for a declaration that the claimant is Philip, Baron Boxbourne. Then it's up to the other side to defend it if they want to.'

'They'll defend it all right,' said Craine. 'I know the present Lady B. She's an absolute stinker. Have you got any security for our costs?'

'Yes. He put down what I suggested. I think he means business.'

'The Tichborne claimant case,' said Craine dreamily, 'lasted seven years and is believed to have cost half a million pounds from first to last. And that was in Queen Victoria's time, when a pound sterling was worth twenty shillings of anyone's money.'

'Oh, I don't think it'll go to quite those lengths,' said Bohun.

'This claimant is a very different kettle of fish. Even if he is Tom Leathers and not Lord Boxbourne – and I'm keeping an open mind on the subject – you won't find him making mistakes in cross-examination. The two boys were at school together, and Tom was, if anything, the brighter of the two.'

'What about motive?'

'His story is that he intended to stay plain Tom Leathers all his life, but he couldn't bear to stand by and see Boxbourne run into the ground by an incompetent swindler.'

'If he takes that line,' said Craine, 'he may have an action for defamation on his hands after this one's over. What are you going to do now?'

'My first job,' said Bohun, 'is to find a gunner officer called Andy.'

After he had dealt with his post, put off an importunate viscount who wanted to borrow money on his expectations in order to discharge arrears of alimony, and dictated about thirty routine letters on behalf of other clients, Bohun found himself free.

He made for Whitehall and was fortunate enough to locate his old friend Colonel Tooth in his office, unoccupied.

The Colonel had been Bohun's company commander in North Africa, and a friendship formed under the desert sun had survived the cooling winds of peace.

After preliminary exchanges, Bohun, because he trusted the Colonel, told him the whole story.

The Colonel said, 'Good heavens. What a story. It isn't going to be too easy to prove, is it?'

'Difficult, not impossible.'

'I can think of one man right here who could give you a start. Tony Phipps-Mundy. He was in the 16th/21st most of the war. He's kicking his heels in an office somewhere up here. Let's see if we can get hold of him.'

He called a series of numbers and in no time at all was talking to Tony Phipps-Mundy, who suggested that they might all go out and have a beer at the *Antelope*.

Bohun was not particularly anxious to repeat his story in a public-house, so when they were all settled at a table he contented himself with saying that he was acting on behalf of a client who was trying to trace the descendants of one Sam Bellingham, believed to have been killed in Italy.

'Believed?' said Phipps-Mundy. 'No question about it, poor chap. I remember it well. A scandalously mismanaged show—' And he proceeded to tell Bohun a great deal that he knew already; to all of which Bohun listened with practised patience.

At the end of it he said, slowly, 'A rather curious legal point has arisen. It may be necessary to determine accurately *when* Bellingham died. The actual time, I mean. Almost to a minute.'

'I see. Some question of succession?'

'Something like that,' said Bohun, quite truthfully. 'There must have been other people who saw the tank hit.'

'Bound to have been,' said Phipps-Mundy. 'Gunners, for instance, see everything. I'd better put you in touch with our depot adjutant at Colchester. If I tip him off, I've no doubt he'd let you have a look at the regimental records. War diary and so on.'

Bohun said he was much obliged and purchased Phipps-Mundy a tankard of beer.

Two days later, the depot adjutant at Colchester, duly forewarned by Major Phipps-Mundy, made Bohun welcome and consulted the records on his behalf. In the end he said, 'It was almost certainly the 15th R.H.A. They were with us regularly. We usually seem to have worked with C Battery. I can't tell you anything about them, but you'd get all you wanted by applying to them direct. They're a London Territorial regiment. Rather a good crowd.'

Back in London next day, Bohun dealt with an accumulation of work and hurried off after lunch to the Finsbury barracks of the 15th (City of London) R.H.A. (T.A.).

The gunner adjutant, a young regular soldier, said, 'As soon as I got your telephone call I did some research. You may be in luck or you may not. It was an F Troop O.P. who supported that action, and the troop commander sent in rather an interesting report. He saw the whole thing.'

'What was his name?' said Bohun, and held his breath.

'Captain Anderson.'

'Andy!' said Bohun.

'I beg your pardon?'

'All Andersons were called Andy. It's in the bag. Can you tell me where I find him?'

'Sorry to disappoint you,' said the adjutant, 'but I'm afraid you won't. He was killed a month later. His own tank got brewed up at Castel del Rio. Only one survivor. A Sergeant Bird.'

'I see,' said Bohun. It was bitter to have the cup so near suddenly dashed from his lips. 'Well, I suppose I ought to have a word with Sergeant Bird, just to make certain.'

'I might be able to help you there. He's not in this regiment now, of course. We're all volunteers and national service men. Surprisingly good mixture, too. Leave me your telephone number and I'll see what I can do.'

Mr Constantine of Constantine & Jerrold, Solicitors, of Norfolk Street, Strand, was a big, round man, washed smooth by the tides of legal practice. He dressed completely in black, rarely smiled and inspired immense confidence in his many clients.

'I am only glad,' he said, 'that it is not I who have the task of advising the claimant.'

Lady Boxbourne said, 'You mean, you are convinced he is an impostor?'

'Not at all,' said Mr Constantine. 'I mean that he will have the more difficult task. The onus will be upon him of proving his case. Strictly, until and unless he proves his case to the satisfaction of the Court, it is not incumbent on you to do anything.'

'We can't just sit still—' said Charles.

'I was not going to suggest it. We shall, of course, prepare ourselves with a body of counter-evidence which we can use, if necessary. The strongest evidence will be that of people who knew both Leathers and Boxbourne, and are prepared to swear that the claimant is the former and not the latter. School friends, neighbours, employees on the estate. Have you perhaps some old family servant still living who knew the boys?'

'There's Gertrude,' Phyllis suggested.

'Gertrude,' said Charles, thoughtfully. 'I really don't think—'

'Of course. She's been mad for years,' agreed Phyllis, 'but that doesn't necessarily mean she can't give evidence – or does it?'

'Certainly not,' said Mr Constantine, blandly. 'I have heard a good deal of excellent evidence given by madmen. It all depends in what direction their madness – er – tends.'

'Then there is old Ames. He's been lodge-keeper for nearly forty years. He knew young Tom, of course. He's a shrewd old man—'

'Splendid,' said Mr Constantine. 'He sounds just the sort of person we want. Might I suggest that we make arrangements to bring these people up to London and place them where they can observe the claimant. 'Meanwhile, there is one other important matter – and that is – costs.'

'I realize this isn't going to be cheap,' said Charles, ' but you mustn't imagine – I mean – what would you think a reasonable sort of sum?'

'I should imagine,' said Mr Constantine, 'that five hundred pounds should be ample to cover the preliminaries. After all, it isn't until we get into court that the expense really mounts.'

'Five hundred pounds,' said Charles.

'Of course,' said Mr Constantine, 'if you are successful, you will recover the greater part of what you have been forced to expend.'

'There's a message for you,' said Bohun's secretary, 'from a Captain Macdonald. He says to tell you that Bird's out of the Army now. The last address Woolwich had for him was a hostel in Culver Street, Limehouse.'

Bohun had to drag his thoughts back from the depths of a death duty saving scheme, and it was some seconds before he realized what she was talking about.

'Limehouse,' he said. 'All right. See if you can find me the telephone number of a public-house called the *Dog and Witch*.'

When Bohun left the office that evening, he got on to a bus going east and stopped it as it passed through the emptying City streets, past Aldgate Pump, and into the Commercial Road. At the end of the Commercial Road he got off.

He found Three Colt Street after a search, walked down it until he sensed that the river was just ahead of him, then swung left into an alley which opened, after a dozen steps, into a tiny court, enclosed on three sides by buildings. The one in front of which he stopped bore a sign-board indicating that it was the *Dog and Witch*, one of dockland's nicest pubs.

'Ah, Mr Boon,' said Alf. 'Nice to see you. I got hold of him for you. He's in there.'

Alf jerked his large thumb towards the private parlour.

'Good for you,' said Bohun. 'If anyone could do it, I knew you could. Was it hard?'

'Not too bad. Gotter friend up the arsenal. He's a sarnt-major. He keeps up with 'em all.'

Bohun thanked Mr Begg again, enquired after his wife (who was well), and daughter (who had just had her fourth, a regular little comic), and entered the parlour.

Sitting on one of the oak settles was a small, spry man who had old soldier written all over. him.

Bohun said, 'You don't know me, but I believe you're Sergeant Bird and were with 15th R.H.A. in the war.'

'Dickie to my friends,' said the little man, hopping up.

'Sit down, Dickie,' said Bohun, 'and have another beer. I've got a lot of questions to ask you. There's no catch to it.'

'Catch,' said the little man, scornfully, 'you won't catch me, not with chaff. That's O.K. Alf says you're O.K. So fire ahead. Well, since you insist—'

He accepted a further pint brought in by Mr Begg.

'Do you remember Captain Anderson?'

'*Remember* him,' said Bird. 'I ought to. I drove his tank for him, didn't I? The Crazy Captain, we called him. He was always pushing ahead to see for himself. Many's the time we'd find ourselves a mile or two in front of everyone else and I'd say to him, over the intercom, "Where to now, sir?" And he'd say, "Straight on, Bird. Straight on. We're bound to hit something soon." Blimey!'

Bird helped himself to a drink of beer and added, 'So we did, in the end. I was the only one got out of *that* mess.'

'I heard about that,' said Bohun. 'You were supporting C Squadron of the 16th/21st Lancers. In fact, you had been in support of them when they bumped the Gothic Line at a place called Castelbonato. That was about a month before you got hit?'

'I can't remember all those Italian names. Would that be the time the Lancers had two tanks brewed up and a troop-leader killed – Lord Someone – or going to be Lord Someone—?'

'That's the one. The Honourable Philip Boxbourne, next in line to be Lord Boxbourne.'

'And he had a tank crew with his butler and chauffeur in it.'

'That's the chap.'

'Remember them well,' said Bird, promptly. 'Very friendly crowd. Very friendly indeed. Give me a naristocrat every time.'

'Here's where I want you to think very hard,' said Bohun slowly. 'Only not *too* hard, if you see what I mean. I don't want you to remember anything that didn't happen, just to please me. But can you recollect anything about Lord Boxbourne changing places with his assistant?'

'Changing places?' said Bird. 'Oh, you mean map-reading?'

Bohun felt like the small boy who casts an idle hook into the water and draws out a record-breaking catch.

'That,' he said, 'is exactly what I mean. Tell me what you remember of it.'

'We had to laugh,' said Bird, 'when we found out. Old Andy tumbled to it. Something he said on the wireless. Didn't get the right answer. Of course, we never told anyone, not about them changing places. Bad for discipline.' He paused for a moment, cocked an eye at Bohun and said, 'One thing I can't see. Of course, it's nothing to do with me. But where do you come in?'

Bohun took a deep breath. 'We think,' he said, 'that Boxbourne and his assistant – whose name was Leathers, by the way – changed places and hats and badges of rank, and so on, that day they got shot up. And that the man who was pulled out wasn't really Leathers at all, but Boxbourne.'

Bird turned this over in his mind. 'Could be,' he said. 'And I take it there's some sort of case about it?'

'There's going to be.'

'In the Courts?'

'Yes. In the High Court.'

'And you want me to stand up and give evidence?'

'That's the idea.'

'I was afraid so,' said Bird.

'Why?' said Bohun, with a sudden sinking of the heart. 'If it's the truth, why shouldn't you get up in the box and say so?'

'Well,' said Bird. 'There's a snag—'

'We sent four more of them up to town yesterday,' said Captain Roye, 'and the results were quite good. Adamson is prepared to swear that the man is Leathers. He had a good look at him coming out of his flat.'

'How could he do that?' said Lord Boxbourne.

'He wasn't going by the face. It was the walk and carriage and general bearing. He knew Leathers well as a young man. That sort of evidence should be valuable, I think. Mrs Adamson – that's his mother – is prepared to support her son.'

'But she's eighty – and nearly blind.'

'Don't exaggerate,' said Lady Boxbourne. 'She's got all her wits about her. A very shrewd old woman.'

'Collins wasn't so satisfactory. At first he thought it might be Leathers and then he thought it might not.'

'It doesn't matter if he isn't Leathers,' said her Ladyship. 'As long as it isn't Philip Boxbourne. What had he got to say about that?'

'He certainly didn't recognize him as that. In fact, he didn't really recognize him at all. He made a statement to Mr Constantine, but I don't think he thought it was very useful. Then there was Connolly—'

'But I gather he wouldn't recognize him?'

'He recognized him all right,' said Captain Roye. 'Said it was the first time he'd ever had a chance of talking to the Duke of Windsor.'

'Clown,' said Lady Boxbourne. 'I never did like that man.'

'Not a very satisfactory tenant,' agreed Captain Roye.

'Look here,' said Lord Boxbourne, 'I don't like the way this is going.'

Lady Boxbourne raised her heavy eyebrows and stared. Captain Roye said, 'It seems to me to be going quite well.'

'I'm afraid I can't agree. I never wanted to go to law to start with.'

'You couldn't refuse to defend yourself.'

'All right. I was forced into it. But whatever Constantine says, it can't be right to take car-loads of our people on jaunts to London to take peeps at him, and then solemnly cook up what they say into legal documents. It's nonsense, and expensive.'

'And how, Charles, would you tackle it?'

'I don't know. But I'm certain that if people like Doctor Meadows and old Farrow at the *Bear and Staff* who really *did* know Tom and Philip, can't recognize him, you're not going to get anything worth while out of Adamson – who hardly knew him at all, or Mrs Adamson, who's almost blind.'

'We have to follow our lawyers' advice.'

'That's the shortest road to ruin.'

'If I might be allowed to say so,' said Captain Roye, 'I think Lady Boxbourne is absolutely right. We must follow our legal advisers. And he'll be getting at these people if we don't.'

'What exactly,' said Lord Boxbourne, a new and dangerous note in his voice, 'do you mean by that?'

'Well, sir—'

'You said, he'll be getting at them if we don't. Do you mean that *we* are getting at them?'

'Don't be silly, Charles.'

'If he didn't mean that, what did he mean? Are we using our influence on these people, most of whom are our tenants and our servants, to make them say what we want?'

'That wasn't what I meant at all, sir.'

'Does it occur to either of you that what we want here is the truth. I want to know the truth. And I don't think we're going about it the right way at all.'

'Really, Charles—' Lady Boxbourne made a slight gesture which Captain Roye interpreted correctly as meaning that she thought she could deal better with her lord and master if left alone. Roye said, 'Well, if you'll excuse me—'

'No, don't go,' said Lord Boxbourne. 'You've been in on this from the beginning. I'd like you to hear what I've got to say now. There's another thing, that may not have occurred to either of you. So far, we've been lucky enough to keep this out of the press. That won't last for ever. And as soon as they hear about it, life isn't going to be worth living. Can you see the headlines? "TWENTIETH-CENTURY TICHBORNE. LONG-LOST HEIR APPEARS FROM CANADA. WHAT HAPPENED AT CASTEL-BONATO?" They'll be round the house like starlings in a thatch.'

Lady Boxbourne spoke slowly and patiently, as to a child. 'We none of us like doing it, dear. But this is the only way.'

'We didn't start it,' said Captain Roye.

'You keep out of this,' said Lord Boxbourne and the agent subsided. He had never known the old boy carry on in that way. Better watch one's step.

'As a matter of fact I *don't* think it is the only way. Perhaps I've got old-fashioned ideas, but it seems to me there is something we could do. And I'm going to do it.'

At what point these matters become known is always a source of conjecture. There are undoubtedly a number of young men, easily distinguishable by their disreputable raincoats, continuous consumption of cigarettes and general air of untidy sagacity, who hang about the neighbourhood of Somerset House, the Companies Registry and the Law Courts, and have an instinct amounting almost to genius for detecting things which the parties concerned would much rather have undetected.

One such young man might have been observed supported by the beer-stained counter of the refreshment room in the dark sub-basement of the Royal Courts of Justice.

He was talking to a middle-aged man in striped trousers and a black coat and a bow tie, who was eating a ham sandwich, and who looked uncommonly like a new litigation clerk just taken on by Horniman, Birley and Craine.

Ten minutes later the younger man said, 'Bye for now,' and toddled off to a telephone.

'Bowles here. It looks as if I may be on to something. I haven't got the details yet, but it's a claimant case. Involving the peerage, blue blood – yes. And rather an odd story about the war. If I were able to slip a pair of fivers in the right direction…?'

The voice at the other end said that, if he had to, Bowles might push out a pair of fivers, but to try to get it for one.

Tom and Lois usually took their midday meals out; and a few days later were strolling back arm in arm to the furnished flat which they had rented off Campden Hill.

Suddenly the young man stopped.

'Good heavens,' he said. 'Am I dreaming, or is it—? Excuse me a moment.'

He dropped Lois's arm and darted back.

Standing on the top step, in the shadow of a doorway, was a little woman in black.

'Why it is,' said the young man. 'It's G! I thought I couldn't mistake that face. Miss Findlayson, or I'm a Dutchman.'

The old woman peered up at him. There was a very odd look on her face, part sentiment, part pride.

'I don't know—' she began.

'You don't know me, G, because I've got quite a new face, but surely you remember me? Don't say you've forgotten the time when you taught us the kings and queens of England and we hid Binkie, the terrier, under the table and tried to make him bite your ankle. You may have forgotten it, but I can assure you I haven't.'

'But—' said the old woman. Her face was a study. 'Who ... which...?'

'Don't worry yourself about that,' said Tom cheerfully. 'Come and meet my young lady. G – oh – steady the Buffs – what's all this?' His face hardened as he spotted a man lurking beside the railings. 'Is this by any chance a put-up job?'

'I don't—'

'Has someone put you here to spy on me?'

The old lady gave a desperate look over her shoulder and burst into tears. The man hurried up to them.

'I think that's enough,' he said.

'It's more than enough,' said Tom hotly. 'How dare you use Miss Findlayson for this sort of thing. It's all right, G, stop crying. It wasn't your fault. As for you' – he turned savagely on the man – 'if you try any more of this sort of thing, I'll pitch you into the nearest area.'

'No sense in violence,' said the man, backing away. 'I'm just doing my job.'

'Then you must accept the risks of your job. Come on, Lois.'

He was still angry when he reached the flat. The porter said, 'There's a gentleman waiting for you, sir. In the lobby.'

His mind on reporters and solicitors' clerks, Tom strode into the lobby and stopped short.

Lord Boxbourne rose to his feet and said, with weary courtesy, 'Sorry to arrive unannounced. Fact is, I fancy if the lawyers got to know about it they'd try to stop me.'

'Come in,' said Tom cautiously.

'I'm not much of a person for talking,' said Lord Boxbourne. 'I leave that to my wife. She does it better than me. But this thing's come to such a pass that I had to do something to try and stop it. It's not only the expense I'm thinking about. It's the publicity. I warned Phyllis and that ass Roye, but they never take any notice of me.'

'The press have got it, have they?'

'Place is swarming with them.'

'I suppose they'll be here next,' Tom said.

'I shouldn't be surprised. I think we ought to stop it.'

'There's a very easy way of stopping it,' said Tom. 'If you sack Roye, I'll withdraw my case tomorrow.'

'It's not as easy as that.' Lord Boxbourne plucked unhappily at his moustache. 'To start with, I've still got no real reason to get rid of him. Then, apparently, he's got a service contract, and if I just turf him out on your say-so – which I'm not prepared to do – I'd have him after me for damages. And that'd be more money and more trouble.'

'That would seem to be that, then. I won't abandon my claim unless you sack Roye. You can't sack Roye. Deadlock.'

'Well,' said Lord Boxbourne, 'that's where my suggestion comes in, actually. When I die – and I'm not what an insurance company would call a very good risk – as I haven't got any children, the title side-steps again. As far as I can work it out, it goes to a second cousin of mine called Carfew. He lives in Morocco and collects *bijouterie*. When I say it goes to him, I mean, of course,' added his Lordship handsomely, 'that it goes to him unless you can prove you're Philip, which I'm sure you can't because I'm sure you're Leathers. If you see what I mean.'

'All right,' said Tom. 'We'll leave that bit for the court to decide. Where does your second cousin from Morocco come in?'

'He doesn't. I mean, he hasn't any interest in the estate at all. He couldn't say no to the title if it fell on him, but he'd sell up the estate at once. He left the country because of Lloyd George's budget, and swore he'd never come back.'

'I see,' said Tom. 'But I'm still not quite—'

'What I plan to do,' said Lord Boxbourne simply, 'is to leave you the estate. Not the title. I can't do that. But the estate itself.' Tom sat silent for a minute.

'Can you do it?' he said.

'As a matter of fact, I can. It was entailed, of course, but Philip wasn't of age when he went to the war, so they couldn't get him to resettle. When it came to me, it came absolutely. I can do what I like with it. I had a word with Constantine before I came down here. He's quite clear about it. I didn't tell him what was in my mind, of course. He'd have had a fit.'

'And you'd do this, believing me to be Tom Leathers?'

'That's the whole idea. Can't think of a better chap to have it, really. It's no job for an amateur, running a landed estate these days. I should think it'd be right up your street. You'd have to wait for me to die, but between you and me I don't think I can last much more than five years. And think of the money and bother we'll save if we don't litigate. The only people who are going to be sick about *that* are the lawyers.'

'Look here,' said Tom, 'I – I've got to think about this. I'll have to have a word with Lois, to start with. I'll let you know by tonight.'

*

'He said *what*?' said Lois.

Tom told it all to her again.

'For heaven's sake,' said Lois. 'Would you have thought he had it in him?'

'It would mean we couldn't settle permanently in Canada. It might mean giving up the new job.'

'I don't mind,' said Lois. 'I think this would be a job worth doing.'

'It would mean something else, too. It would mean Roye gets away with it for another five years – or more. In that time he can probably wreck the estate.'

'I think,' said Lois sensibly, 'that you've put a spoke in his wheel any old way. They may *say* they don't believe you, and that a man's innocent until he's proved guilty, but I think they'll check his accounts from now on.'

'You may be right. I hope you are. I wish I knew what to do. Until this morning, I had no doubts about the matter. I was prepared to go through with it, come hell, come high water. Now I'm not sure.'

'What happened this morning?'

'It was old G – or Gertrude. Miss Findlayson. She was governess to both of us boys. As nice an old Scotswoman as ever came across the border to rap sense into the knuckles of young English aristocrats. She's over seventy now, and must be getting very shaky. If this ruddy case is going to entail dragging people like G up to court and putting them in the box, then I'm not so sure that I *do* want to go on with it. Hullo, Whatcott. What's the trouble?'

The porter edged into the room and said, 'I've got three gentlemen downstairs, sir, asking for you.'

'Ah, so the press has arrived.'

'I hope we shan't have any trouble, sir. The management are very particular.'

'It's quite all right, Whatcott. You can tell the management that I'm engaged in a respectable law suit to reclaim my title.'

'I shouldn't think that would do us any harm, would it, sir?'

'On the contrary. It'll be an excellent advertisement for your flats.'

'I was going to say, sir, that if you did happen to want to go out without being seen, Mr Partridge on the ground floor east has a kitchen door that leads out into the court.'

'Excellent,' said Tom. 'Lead on. The press shall cool its heels.'

Half an hour later he was talking to Bohun.

'I wish I could make up my mind,' said Tom. 'If it were anyone but

Boxbourne, I should be inclined to suspect a manoeuvre. But whatever one may think of his capabilities as a landlord, Charles is certainly honest."

Bohun said, 'We should have to look carefully at the family settlements, but it's quite feasible. It wouldn't make you Lord Boxbourne, you understand that.'

'Yes,' said Tom. His voice was as expressionless as his face. 'And that doesn't bother me. I made up my mind ten years ago that I didn't want the title.'

'Quite so,' said Bohun.

'I've reached a point where I look on this as a personal battle between Roye and myself. That's the only aspect of it that's really important. If I agree to this scheme, it leaves Roye in possession. Maybe only for a short time. That depends on Charles's health—'

'If I might advise you,' said Bohun, 'I should accept. I don't think we've got much of a chance of proving your case.'

Tom looked at him thoughtfully.

Bohun went on, 'The law says that he who asserts must prove. The other party is under no obligation to disprove. If you fail to prove, you lose your case. This is a case in which, in my view, it would be quite impossible for either side to prove the other a liar.'

'I see,' said Tom.

'We've had a piece of bad luck already. The one thing that might have turned the scale in your favour would have been if we could have produced someone who knew about your habit of changing places. By a series of flukes I did get on to a possible witness. His name's Bird, and he was the driver of the gunner tank that not only saw your brew-up at Castelbonato, but remembered you and your peculiar habits.'

'I think I remember him,' said Tom. 'A little chap with a face like a marmoset? If you've found him, what's the snag?'

'The trouble is,' said Bohun, 'that he's had one or two stormy passages since he left the army. In fact, not to mince matters, he's served two sentences for receiving stolen goods. If that came out, and I've no doubt Constantine would unearth it, I'm afraid his evidence wouldn't carry a great deal of weight. Perhaps the contrary.'

Suddenly the telephone rang.

Bohun picked it up and said, 'Who? Oh, it's for you. Your wife, I think. She sounds upset about something.'

Tom listened quietly to the telephone for a moment and said, 'I'll be right over. Sit back and take a few deep breaths.' And to Bohun, as he ran out: 'I'll ring you back. If my guess is correct, this case goes on.'

He paid off his taxi a hundred yards short of the flat, and walked in the back way. Mr Partridge was on the look-out and opened the door for him.

Tom found Whatcott on guard in the passage.

'What the devil is all this about?'

'I'm not quite sure, sir,' said the porter. 'Two men broke in and upset your wife.'

'Broke in?'

'Well, they knocked on the door, and when she opened it they pushed in. Upset her, a lot.'

'But what did they want?'

'They said they were police officers. Had a warrant to search the flat.'

'Do you think they were reporters?'

'No, sir, I don't. Reporters get up to lots of tricks, but they don't behave like that.'

'Thank you for helping,' said Tom. He pressed a pound note into his hand.

The porter said that it was very kind of him, and Tom went in. Lois came running.

'It was horrible,' she said. 'They were so – oh dear.'

When she had had a good cry, Tom said, 'Now tell me exactly what happened.'

'I opened the door, and these two men pushed in. They slammed the door open so hard, it knocked me against the wall. I naturally thought they'd apologize, but they didn't. They backed me into this room, and one of them stood over me whilst the other looked round the other rooms.'

'Did you ask who they were?'

'Yes. They showed me a sort of card, and said, "Police".'

'I said, "But what's it all about?" One of them said, "You know that as well as we do. Better not give us any trouble," and they started to ransack the room. If they couldn't open a cupboard, they just broke it.'

The room looked as if a small and malicious hurricane had hit it.

'We haven't done anything,' said Lois. 'How dare the police behave like that.'

'They weren't police,' said Tom. 'Put the idea out of your head. That was just for the sake of saying something.'

'But what's it all about?'

'Do you remember a gentleman driving a vegetable lorry, who hustled us into a ditch?'

'Yes, but—'

'This is the same technique, brought up to date. It's Roye's idea of a hint to us to drop the case. Well, some people never learn.'

'What shall we do?'

'First thing is to change our base. Too many people know we live here. Didn't you tell me you had an aunt in Scotland you had to visit? Well, now's the time. We'll telephone her, and if she's agreeable, I'll put you on the train tonight.'

'Put me? What about you?'

'I'm not quite sure yet,' said Tom. 'But I'll tell you what I'm *not* going to do. I'm not going to sit still.'

'Well, there now,' said Ernie Barrow. 'I can't say I'm surprised, I always had my own ideas about that Captain Roye; and what he was Captain in is one thing I've never been able to discover, and why should he go on calling himself Captain now the war's over? I don't call myself Sergeant Barrow—'

'My idea was,' said Tom, 'to lie low, and see if I can't ferret out something definite and get Roye sacked, or run in. If I can do that, you see, I'd drop this case like a shot.'

'Where were you aiming to stay whilst you did your ferreting? Would you like a room in my place?'

Tom thought for a moment.

'That would suit me down to the ground,' he said. 'And it's very kind of you.'

'And any ferreting I can do,' added Barrow, 'count me in. I'd give a year's takings to put that swine behind bars.'

The weeks which followed were enjoyable, if not exactly productive of results. Tom, who had an aptitude for motors, spent a few mornings working in Ernie Barrow's garage and repair-shop. And in the afternoons and evenings he loafed around Branston and talked to a multitude of people.

What he heard confirmed his opinion that Roye was a crook, but made it equally clear that it was going to be very difficult to prove.

''E's got too many frens,' said a small man with a bulbous nose and the wistful eyes of a frustrated drinker, in the back room of a pub behind the railway. 'Frens on the council, and the Agricultural Committee and up at Coffen' Garden and everywhere. They're not his frens because they love him, but they make money for each other, see?'

Tom said he saw.

He came back to his lodgings that evening in a thoughtful frame of mind and had a talk with Barrow.

'I've had an idea,' said Barrow. 'Why don't you have a word with that doctor?'

'Doctor Meadows?'

'That's the chap. He's got his head screwed on the right way. And another thing: he's got no use for Roye.'

The next evening Tom bicycled out towards Boxbourne, and found the doctor waiting for him in his garden.

'Well, my boy,' said Doctor Meadows. 'And what do I call you, Philip or Tom?'

'Tom will do, for the moment.'

The doctor looked at him hard, grunted and said, 'If you want my honest opinion, you're such a mixture of the two, that no one's ever going to get you sorted out now.'

The young man said, quite seriously, 'You mean that when that tank went up in flame and destruction, Tom and Philip both took refuge in the one remaining body?'

'That's right,' said the doctor. 'You may find it difficult to believe. A Chinaman would treat it as commonplace. Now, what can I do for you?'

Tom told him.

'I see,' said the doctor. 'I agree with you over one thing. I'm sure Roye's a bad 'un. I'm equally sure it's going to be difficult to prove.' He thought for a moment, and said, 'Did you ever study the tactics of the Oscar Wilde case?'

'I can't say I did.'

'Queensberry hadn't got a great deal on Oscar, not when the case started. So his advisers arranged the case, I think, with one object: to get Oscar in the box, where he could be thoroughly cross-examined. It's wonderful how a rogue can come apart, stitch by stitch, once Counsel gets him in the box.'

'But how do we get Roye in the box?'

'He's agent of the estate. Just call him as a material witness.'

'We could do that, but we must have *some* ammunition to shoot at him.'

The doctor said thoughtfully, 'The only person likely to supply any real information against Roye is Roye himself. Rascals never trust anyone else with their secrets. But if, as I should suspect, he is the sort of rogue who makes his money from a multitude of small swindles rather than one big one, he must keep *some* sort of accounts.'

'I don't doubt it,' said Tom. 'But I don't imagine that he will invite me to inspect them.'

'I should hardly imagine that he would *invite* you,' agreed the doctor.

That evening, Tom said to Barrow, 'Are you willing to help me commit a burglary? I want to look at Roye's account books.'

'Oh, him,' said Barrow. 'That's not robbery. That's self-defence. Do you know where he keeps them?'

'I can guess,' said Tom. 'When old Tom was agent, he had a fine old drum-shaped table – a rent table I believe is the technical name. It's got six drawers in it, one for each day of the week.'

'You're quite right. And Roye still uses it. I remember him sitting behind it, telling me what a bad farmer I was.'

'The account books are kept in the drawers. They're probably locked, but a table-drawer isn't difficult to force. If you could make me a couple of thin, flat levers—'

'I'll knock 'em up for you in the shop tomorrow. How are we going to get in?'

'That's where local knowledge comes in handy,' said Tom. 'When I was a boy I knew six different ways into that house.'

They set out at eleven o'clock on bicycles. It took them half an hour of quiet pedalling to reach the walls of Boxbourne.

'We can leave the bicycles here,' said Tom. 'And, unless someone's been round altering things, there ought to be a short cut – yes. This is it. Jump and catch the coping with one hand. There's a toe-hold in the brick. Up and over.'

A minute later, and the two men were walking across the rough grass of Boxbourne Park. In the distance, the big house gleamed, white and cold and dead.

A low iron railing to be climbed, and they were in the garden of the bailiff's house.

'Better be careful,' said Barrow. 'I've just remembered. He's got two dogs. Enormous Alsatians. Keeps 'em in the stable.'

'The stable's the other side,' said Tom. 'Here's where it gets tricky. Watch what I do. When I'm up, I'll give you a hand.'

They had reached a block of one-storey outbuildings, formerly laundry and game larder, now used for coke and coal.

Tom got his foot on the window-sill, and started to worm his way up on to the roof of the little building.

As soon as he was safe, he lay down flat, and reached an arm down to help Barrow up.

'All right,' said Tom. 'Now we do a little roof walking.'

They went the length of the outhouses, scaling the last one by means of a buttress. They were two storeys up now, and Barrow looked apprehensively at the pit of darkness which represented the drop on to the flagstones of the back yard.

'Window just here,' breathed Tom. 'Won't be shut.' Nor was it. They climbed in and stood for a minute in the darkness.

Tom switched on his torch for an instant, and they saw that the room was unused. There was a pile of junk in the corner.

'That's all right, then,' said Tom. He shut the window, and then latched it. 'We shan't be coming back this way.'

'You disappoint me,' said Barrow. 'I could just see myself going down those tiles with Roye shooting at me from the window and one of his dogs waiting down below.'

'Better put gloves on now,' said Tom. 'There's a back stairway leading straight down to the kitchen passage. Then there's a swing-door into the hall. The office is on the other side.'

Ten breathless minutes later, they were in Captain Roye's office. Tom said, 'Well open one of the windows wide, at the bottom, in case we have to get away quick. Then draw the curtains. I'll have to use my torch.'

The big rent table stood in the middle of the room, a solid circle of wood, set on a thick, central pedestal with spreading claw feet. It had, as Tom had said, six drawers, three in each semicircle.

Tom got out the thin, strong lever that Barrow had forged for him, and slid it into the crack above a drawer. Then he stopped.

'What's up?' said Barrow.

Tom put out his hand and pulled the drawer. It came quite freely.

'It's not locked,' he said. He went round and tried the other drawers. 'They're none of them locked. I don't like that.'

'Save us the trouble of busting them.'

'A man like Roye wouldn't keep anything damaging in an unlocked drawer.'

'Might as well look at them now we're here.'

After a frustrating quarter of an hour Tom said, 'We're not going to get anything out of these. They're too open and above board. If you ask me, this is the public set of books. The ones he keeps to show people. His private ledger's somewhere quite different.'

'Wall safe,' Barrow suggested.

'Not unless it's been put in since old Tom's day. He never had much use for safes. He used to tell us – hey – wait a moment. I've remembered something.'

'Keep your voice down,' said Barrow.

'Shine your torch on the pedestal of the table. There's a drawer there, somewhere. It's a sort of secret drawer. Those other six drawers are Monday to Saturday, but he used to call this his Sunday drawer.' He knelt beside the squat pedestal and ran his fingers over the wood.

'Better hurry. I think someone's moving.' In the silence, some way off upstairs, they heard a door slam.

'Come on,' said Barrow.

'Hold hard,' said Tom. 'I'll have it in a minute.'

'They'll have us in a minute,' growled Barrow. He got up and moved into position behind the door. Tom put his torch down on the carpet so that he could use both hands. His fingers fumbled, slipped, found the cunning catch. Pressed, then pulled.

A section of the pedestal moved out.

At that moment a number of things happened.

The door of the room burst open, and Captain Roye, dressing-gown clad, appeared framed in the lighted doorway. His hand was fumbling for the switch when Barrow hit him. It was a solid blow, and Roye went down; as he fell, the gun he was holding in his right hand went off with an ear-splitting crack.

Tom thrust his hand into the pedestal drawer, grabbed the small book and bundle of papers which were all it seemed to contain, and jumped for the window.

Barrow was there ahead of him.

As they tumbled out on to the lawn, lights were going on all over the house.

'Front gate,' gasped Tom. 'Not the way we came. Those dogs are too fast for us.'

They reached the wall. 'Give you a leg up,' said Tom. 'Then you pull me.'

In the moonlight they could see the two big Alsatians crossing the lawn, running mute.

For a moment, before he dropped down into the road, Tom hung, balanced across the top of the high wall. In the background, the house was blazing with light and clamorous with voices. Below him, the two big dogs stood, heads on one side, staring. They seemed less excited than their human masters.

'Good boys,' said Tom. Both animals lifted their lips and showed their teeth. Tom dropped down into the road and padded off into the darkness.

'It's weeks now since I heard from him,' said Bohun, 'and months since I saw him.'

'Do you think he's going to let us down?' asked Roly Craine.

'No, I don't. He's paid us handsomely and his instructions are quite definite. He wants Roye put in the box. We've had to subpoena him, of course. And he's laid down the exact topics he wants put to him. Then we're calling Doctor Meadows and Sergeant Bird if we have to. After that he'll give evidence himself.'

'A bit different from the Tichborne case,' said Craine wistfully. 'The claimant called a hundred and fifteen witnesses and took affidavits from ninety-five more.'

'I can't help thinking that the whole thing will really turn on whether Boxbourne's witnesses stand up under cross-examination.'

'What counsel have we got?'

'Hargest Macrea.'

'He should be all right,' agreed Craine. 'He doesn't know a great deal of law, but when he really gets going he could make a dog admit it was a cat. Well, I wish you luck.'

'In the result,' said Hargest Macrea, raking the jury with his celebrated horn monocle, 'we have a situation of the greatest difficulty. We are used to superlatives in this court, but I do not think I shall be accused of exaggeration if I say that this is one of the strangest stories to come out of the war. Four men are wiped out. Indeed, practically speaking, you could say they *were* all of them dead. But a single spark of life remains: almost extinguished, but not quite. By the skill and perseverance of the doctors, it is fanned back into flame. The flame grows, increases, burns steadily at last. But in which body?'

He paused, and looked at the jury and its twelve members looked back at him, in a state of agreeable hypnosis. 'It is therefore your duty, members of the jury, to exercise your judgement on the question, which I noticed propounded in the newspaper headlines this morning: what happened at Castelbonato?'

Mr Macrea added, 'If your Lordship is agreeable, I think we have just time to start on the first witness.'

Mr Justice Breerley consulted his watch and signified his agreement.

'Captain Roye,' said Macrea.

The Captain still had the remains of a beautiful black eye. He was not in a good temper; but there was something more than ill temper. An element of uneasiness. Something deeper than mere irritation with his present predicament.

'I want to protest,' he said in a hard, high voice. 'I am here against my will.'

The Judge said, 'It is noted on the record that you are here subpoena. I think you had better confine yourself to answering Counsel's questions.'

'Your name is Alistair Manfred Roye, and you are the agent at Boxbourne Park?'

'Yes.'

'At Boxbourne you are, I believe, known as Captain Roye.'

'That may be so.'

'*Do* people call you Captain Roye?'

'Sometimes.'

'And you do not object?'

'Why should I object?'

'Because,' said Macrea, 'so far as my information goes, you quitted the R.A.S.C. in 1944 with the rank of lieutenant.'

'You seem very well informed.'

'Is my information correct?'

'Yes.'

'Then your use of the title "Captain" was a piece of vanity?'

'I didn't call myself Captain. Other people did.'

'But you did not stop them?'

'Really. I couldn't go round putting them right the whole time—'

Macrea, who knew when to leave a good point, said smoothly, 'Very well. Can we pass on, Mr Roye, to the date of your arrival at Boxbourne. You were employed, I believe, as assistant to the existing agent, Tom Leathers.'

'Yes.'

'You were learning your job from him?'

'I was assisting him.'

'But since you knew nothing about it, I assume that he was teaching you.'

'If you choose to be offensive, I can't prevent you.'

'Really, Mr Roye,' said the Judge. 'I can't see anything offensive in Counsel's suggestion. We all have to learn our jobs. I have been twenty years learning mine.'

The Court gave a dutiful guffaw, and Macrea said, 'I should like to turn – I think we have just time to deal with the subject – to the circumstances in which you became agent of the Boxbourne estate, Mr Roye.'

'I.... Yes ... if you like.'

'You succeeded Mr Leathers in nineteen-forty-six?'

'Yes.'

'On his death?'

'Yes.'

'Perhaps you could just tell the Court about that.'

There was a short silence. Then the witness said, 'Tell the Court about what?'

'The circumstances,' said Macrea, with deadly patience, 'in which Mr Leathers died and you succeeded to his job.'

'Well, he had a fall. Out hunting.'

'Yes?'

'Which gave him concussion.'

'Yes? But that did not kill him?'

'Then he got a chill.'

'Which affected his stomach?'

'I'm not sure. I believe so. I'm not a doctor.'

'You are not a doctor,' agreed Macrea, 'but I have no doubt you can give evidence on the matter. After all, you were in constant attendance on Mr Leathers.'

Macrea appeared to consult a book which he held in his hand. The crowded press bench looked up, stirred to sudden interest by something in Macrea's voice.

'Come now, it's a perfectly simple question. I believe you yourself attended to Mr Leathers on the last afternoon of his life.'

'I – yes, I think I did.'

'Four o'clock,' said the Judge. 'I shall adjourn the Court.'

'I hope,' said Mr Justice Breerley, 'that there is some adequate explanation for this delay. The witness was informed that the hearing would begin again at eleven o'clock this morning?'

Counsel whispered to solicitor and a solicitor's clerk scurried from the courtroom.

'Yes, my Lord. The witness knew that he was expected to be here.'

'He didn't imagine, perhaps, that his examination was concluded?'

'I hardly think so, my Lord.'

'Well, if there is not some adequate explanation – it is now ten minutes past eleven – this delay may have to be reflected in any order I make for costs.'

Further agitated conferences. Then a small, square man, with an expressionless face came quietly into Court and said something to Macrea, who listened, and then rose to his feet with a rustle of his silk gown.

'I am informed, my Lord,' he said, 'that the witness has met with an accident.'

'I am sorry to hear that,' said the Judge, courteously. 'I felt certain he would not have kept us waiting without reason. Was the accident serious, Mr Macrea?'

'Very serious. In fact, fatal.'

'I see. In that case I shall adjourn the Court until after luncheon.'

'So the case is over,' said Lois.

'That's right,' said Bohun, 'almost before it had begun. When the Court reassembled after lunch today, Macrea got up and told the judge that the parties had agreed on a settlement. Tom is to take on the agent's job now, and the estates are to go to him and you and your children on the death of the present Lord Boxbourne – subject to an annuity for his wife if she survives him.'

'She'll survive him all right,' said Lois. 'Do you think that what happened to Roye was an accident?'

'I don't know,' said Bohun, 'I really don't know, and I don't suppose anyone will ever know. He walked out of his hotel this morning and practically straight under a lorry. The newspapers have got it as an accident.'

'I saw the evening papers at Euston,' said Lois. 'Tom doesn't know I'm back yet.'

'He's due here any moment,' said Bohun. 'I've got a few questions I'd like to ask him myself. This sounds like him.'

Tom came in. He looked fit and happy. He kissed Lois, and said, ' I thought I told you to stay in Scotland.'

'Now,' said Bohun, 'perhaps you'll explain what you've been up to.'

'Up to?' said Tom, innocently.

'For a start,' said Bohun, 'perhaps you would explain why you gave instructions that Roye was to be called as witness late on the first day, so that Macrea could cross-examine him for a quarter of an hour and no more.'

'Well, it needed rather nice timing,' said Tom. 'But the fact of the matter was that I wanted to stop at a point which would give him a really bad night.'

'Why?'

'It's a long story,' said Tom. 'And it starts with me and a sportsman called Barrow committing a burglary.'

He told them about it.

'I still don't see,' said Bohun. 'What did you find in that secret drawer?'

'I found old Tom's diary. Kept right up to the last days of his life. You know he had a bed made up for him in that room – and was there until, at the very end, they took him off to hospital. Here it is. I'd like you to look at two entries. The first one is on the day he had his hunting accident.'

Bohun and Lois peered over his shoulder. It was the writing of an old man, but firm and clear and full of character.

'The Mastertons brought me home in their car. I was really very shaky. They were most kind and Mrs Masterton helped Ada get my bed made up down here, and hot-water-bottles and so on. If I'm laid up I like to be down here. It's less trouble for Ada. Roye was here and pressed me to drink some brandy from his own flask. Fortunately I've had enough tumbles in my life to know that brandy is almost the worst possible thing for concussion. I was strong-minded enough to say "No." Had to be very insistent. He practically forced the stuff down my throat.'

'How horrible,' said Lois.

'Read on,' said Tom. 'Look at the last entry.'

'Roye very attentive. Again fetched my medicine himself. Have I misjudged him?'

Then, in very straggly handwriting: 'They are taking me off to hospital this afternoon. Too late, I fear.'

There was silence in the room as they finished reading. It was Bohun who broke it.

'However certain you felt that Roye was responsible for old Tom's death, you could never have founded a charge on this evidence.'

'I know,' said Tom. 'But that's not the point. Roye had a guilty conscience. When he saw the secret drawer open, in that room where old Tom spent his last days – a few feet from old Tom's bed – and empty! – he realized that something had gone. Some record, or paper, of some sort. But he didn't know what it was. For all he knew, it was a full and damning accusation. I don't know what he thought we'd taken, but I do know one thing: he thought it was important.'

'How do you know that?'

'He and his friends have made three attempts to get it back.'

'I see,' said Bohun. 'And the final straw was when he saw which way Macrea's examination was going.'

'And this morning,' said Tom, 'either he walked under the lorry, or he really was so worried that he didn't look where he was going. For myself, I don't care which way it was. He was an evil man. I expect that my first job at Boxbourne will be to try to disentangle the webs he has been weaving.'

As they rose to go, Bohun said, 'Now that it's all over, I suppose you wouldn't like to satisfy my curiosity. Are you really Tom Leathers, or are you Philip Boxbourne?'

'The way things have come out,' said the young man, 'it's not of the least importance, is it?'

CAMFORD COTTAGE

'HEN I KNOW it,' said Miss Symondson, 'I'm certain I know it. It's at the top of a cliff. Hardly a cliff, more a headland. It's in a little garden of its own, with fields all round it. And there's a long flight of steps leading down from it to a private landing stage.'

'The same place, without doubt,' said Miss Melchior. 'It's some distance from any village. How did you come to be familiar with it?'

'I'd hardly call it familiar, since I had tea there, once only. But it was an exceptionally fine tea. That was thirty years ago. I cannot have been more than five or six at the time.'

'It must have been in the days of "Prince" Camford, the artist. He had no use for architects, you know. The house, we were told, was built by local builders from a sketch he made on the back of a drawing pad. And very well built, too, in local brick.'

'I didn't realize, of course, that he was a famous artist. To me he was just a funny man with a beard. He'd come on my older brother and sister and me, playing some game in the bushes at the top of the headland, Pirates or Indians. We were dressed in holiday rags and he got us to pose for nearly an hour while he made sketches of us. Then he took us down to the house for tea. Cornish butter and cream, on scones baked by his wife, a dumpy little woman with grey hair.'

'Also an artist,' said Miss Melchior. 'A water-colourist. You can still see her Cornish seascapes in the galleries.' Miss Melchior was a woman who knew things like that. 'They are both dead now. My brother bought the cottage – it had some other name – I forget it – but he named it "Camford Cottage" after its famous builder and owner. He and Patricia spent their honeymoon there. They were the only people who ever lived in it.'

'What a tragedy,' said Miss Symondson. She was not thinking of the honeymoon, but of what had happened at Camford Cottage some years later. A tragedy which had been widely reported.

Frank Melchior and his wife were keen sailors; Frank possibly a little keener than Patricia, who was apt to be sick if the sea was rough. They had set out one evening intending to sail down to the south-west, with a favouring wind, spend the night at sea, round the point of Land's End, and finish up by beating up to Fowey, where they had friends. It was a trip they had made many times before. On this occasion they ran into rougher weather than they had catered for. Their boat lost its mast, the auxiliary engine failed, and they were driven on to the Pen-Gallion Shoals. Fishermen, who had observed their plight in the early dawn, picked up Frank; Patricia's body was never recovered.

'He shut the cottage up for years after that. No one was allowed into it. He wouldn't listen to any suggestion of selling it. Not that he had to bother about the financial side of it. Patricia was a Dupont, and her money went to him. Poor compensation for a broken heart, but on top of what he was earning already, it left him free to get on with his writing.'

'I read his last one a few weeks ago, when I was in bed. The nursing home got it for me out of the public library. I can't afford to pay nearly four pounds for a detective story.'

'I don't believe anyone can,' said Miss Melchior. 'Have you met my brother?'

'Yes, once, when he came to give a talk at the school. We were all introduced. I thought him rather formidable.'

'It changed him, of course.'

'Has the cottage been closed ever since – ever since it happened?'

'No. In the end I persuaded him that he was being selfish.' Miss Melchior spoke with the firmness of an elder sister. 'We took some of his nephews and nieces, and I went down with him. I told him, "You'll find no ghosts in Camford Cottage. It's a happy place." The holiday was a great success. Pol-en-Perro is a wonderful place for children.'

'I certainly remember it as such,' said Miss Symondson wistfully. 'I suppose that development has spoilt it now.'

'Not a bit. The land round the cottage is farmland, and very good farmland too, I believe. No one can touch it. And, of course, when the weather was fine the children enjoyed the tiny private beach at the bottom of the steps, and the boating. Frank was nervous about letting them use the boat at all, but I told him, "Forget the past, live in the present." '

It had sometimes occurred to Miss Symondson that the reason Miss Melchior, who was handsome and well endowed, was not married might be on account of her firmness with everyone. She was one of the governors of the school where Miss Symondson taught, and ruled the Chairman and other governors with a rod of iron. Nevertheless, she could be kind. She had been very kind to her, when a bout of influenza, coming on top of an exceptionally hard term's work, had nearly carried her away. It was Miss Melchior who had whisked her out of her lodgings and into a private nursing home; and it was Miss Melchior who had dragooned the doctors into taking her case seriously. Now she was proposing a further kindness.

'A week will do you all the good in the world. It will quite set you up for the coming term. I'll order a stack of logs for the sitting-room fire. The cooking is all done by bottled gas. I'll have two cylinders delivered. They'll be outside the front door. I'm afraid you'll have to do your own cleaning. Local people won't go into the cottage – not since the tragedy.'

'Oh, why?'

'They think it's haunted,' said Miss Melchior, in the robust voice in which common-sense people speak of ghosts. 'I'm sure you're not one of these people who believe in ghosts.'

'If there was one, it should be haunting the Pen-Gallion Shoals, not Camford Cottage.'

'*Exactly* what I told my brother. And I can assure you that when we all went down there, there were no psychic manifestations.'

'But on previous occasions,' said Miss Symondson, 'it's only the family who have used the cottage? Are you sure your brother won't mind? Oughtn't we to ask him?'

'To the best of my knowledge, my brother is in Tangiers, gathering material for a new book. He was uncertain of his movements, and left no address. It could take weeks to get an answer.'

'If you're sure he wouldn't mind.'

'I am ab-so-lutely sure.'

When Miss Melchior was ab-so-lutely sure, there was nothing more to be said.

For the first six days it was as agreeable as Miss Melchior had promised. Although it was still early April the summer, as sometimes happens in Cornwall, had seemed to come earlier than it did elsewhere. The days were warm enough for strolling over the headlands and through the deep lanes, already yellow with primrose and white with may-flower. The evenings were cool enough to enjoy the fire of logs which blazed in the wide brick fireplace, set squarely in the middle of the living-room wall.

The nights were a little troublesome at first. Miss Symondson put it down to sleeping in a strange bed, but she was honest enough to admit that it was than this. She was a child of the city, born and brought up among streets of houses full of people. Holidays had been things you took, with others, in camps or hotels or hostels which were even fuller of people.

Here she was conscious of being surrounded by emptiness. On one side, the sea. On the other three sides, fields. The nearest human habitation was the farmhouse which she visited daily for milk and eggs, half a mile inland down a track which was easily negotiable at this time of year by the tradesmen's vans and by the old taxi which had brought her from Pol-en-Perro Station. It must have become difficult in winter. Her only direct connection with the world outside was a telephone line; a single umbilical cord joining her to the world of men and women.

In the times when she lay awake she comforted herself with what Miss Melchior had said. It was *not* an unhappy house. Why should it be? The tragedy had not happened here, in this snug and civilized cell, but out on the wild grey sea, in a driving wind, among mountainous waves. Sometimes she visualized the helpless boat, its mast gone, its engine useless, drifting on to the fangs of the Pen-Gallion rocks.

She had never herself been on the sea in anything smaller than a cross-Channel steamer, and it is possible that she exaggerated its perils. She looked down on it, timidly, from the edge of the cliffs, but had never even ventured to descend the steps down to the beach and the jetty. They seemed to her to be steep and dangerous. Adequate, no doubt, for nimble children in gym shoes, or for active men and women who took care to use the tarred-rope side rail.

It was on the evening of the sixth day, with the taxi ordered for nine o'clock the next morning, and she was standing at the top of these steps, when it happened.

The day had been the warmest so far, more of an autumn than a spring day, the heat no longer fresh, but turned damp and stale. As she looked out to sea, it was as though a veil, thin at first but thickening, was being drawn across her whole field of vision. The effect was so startling that she passed a hand across her eyes to wipe away what seemed to be a blurring of her sight. Then she realized what was happening. A white fog was rolling up towards the mouth of the Bristol Channel.

It came with astonishing speed. One moment she could see. The next she was blind. One moment she was warm. The next she was shivering with cold. Thank goodness, was her first thought, that I wasn't out on the cliffs, miles from home. I shouldn't have known what to do. She turned round, with great care, took six paces up the path which led from the stair-head, found the front gate, and was soon back inside the cottage.

She turned on the lights in the sitting-room, and put a match to the fire, which was neatly laid. Warmth and light soon worked their magic. The fog was outside. She was inside, safe and sound. The next few hours were pleasantly occupied with cooking and eating supper. For this last meal of the holidays she had saved a half-bottle of red wine; and, greatly daring, she drank it all, finishing the last glass with her coffee.

As she sat, pleasantly drowsy, in front of the fire, she found her thoughts going back thirty years. How odd to think that she, the very same person that she was now, changed in body but the same in essence, had sat at almost exactly the same spot that she was sitting at now. Her brother had been on her right, at the top of the tea table, piling the delicious scones with butter and cream and honey, and stuffing them into his mouth one after another. She didn't want to think too much about him. His body was in Northern France, near the spot where his fighter plane had crashed.

Her sister had been sitting beyond him, half scandalized at the amount her brother was eating, half determined not to be left behind. Married now, with children of her own.

And what of herself? If she tried hard, could she summon back the six-year-old child, with pigtails, dressed in shorts, and a grubby aertex shirt, with sandals on the end of brown, scratched legs. She had always been the thoughtful one, the one who noticed things. What had she been thinking about, what had she been looking at, on that summer afternoon, thirty years ago?

There had been a tiny golden clock on the mantelshelf. That had gone, of course, and had been replaced by two vases. To the right of the fireplace, there had been bookshelves. This worried her. Because she was certain that the bookshelf had not been a detached piece of furniture. The shelves, five or six of them, had been fitted into the alcove on the right of the chimney breast. Yes. And in the corresponding alcove on the other side had stood the old grandfather clock. She could remember thinking, how unusual to have two clocks in one room. Big clock and little clock. Grandfather and grandchild.

Why in the world, she said to herself, should anyone have bricked up those two alcoves, so that the wall now stretched, level with the front of the fire, from side to side?

As she asked the question, the room seemed to change. She was looking at it as it had been. The books were back on their shelves on the right, the gold clock winked on the mantelshelf, and old grandfather swung his pendulum solemnly from the recess on the left. She knew that if she could turn her eyes she would see her brother and sister, and their kind host at the other end of the table, but her head was held, as in a vice.

Something was happening to the lights. They were dimming. And the room had grown deadly cold. But it was now, once again, the room of the present, not the past. She was looking at the blank stretch of bricks on the left of the fireplace and at the lady standing in front of them. She felt unsurprised, and unafraid. The lady was smiling. Clearly she meant her no harm. It was not Mrs Camford. This lady was younger, slimmer, and more fashionably dressed than that grey-haired dumpy water-colourist. Surely she knew the face? She had seen it somewhere, in a fashion magazine. Of course, it was Frank Melchior's wife, Patricia.

Who was dead.

Drowned, battered to pieces, her bones washing about on the floor of the sea, under the Pen-Gallion rocks.

What was she doing here? Why was she standing, quietly, patiently. Standing like someone who had been waiting for help, and knew that help was at hand?

All at once Miss Symondson knew the terrible answer. Moreover, she knew what she had to do, and she was locked to the chair; her body shaken with uncontrollable spasms, the sweat cold on her face.

As she struggled to move, and realized that she was helpless, the spell was suddenly broken.

The telephone was ringing.

A male voice said, 'Miss Symondson?'

Scarcely able to speak she gasped out something.

'I can't hear you.'

'Yes. It's Miss Symondson.'

'My sister told me you were using the cottage. Is something wrong?'

'No. Yes.'

'What is it? You're very indistinct.'

Miss Symondson said, in tones of one stating some unimportant but incontrovertible fact. 'I have just seen your wife. She came out from the recess which used to be beside the fireplace in the sitting-room.'

During the long silence which followed, she began to realize what it was she had said. He must think her absolutely mad. Perhaps she was mad. People had sometimes told her she was psychic. Had she passed over the borderline between sanity and insanity?

'I'm sure you'll think I'm raving mad,' she said, with a pathetic attempt at lightness, 'perhaps it was the fog and the general atmosphere and knowing – knowing the story—'

When the man spoke again it was a surprise. Before, his voice, without being rude, had been cold and formal. Now it had reverted to a friendly, conversational level.

He said, 'I was interested in something you said just now. You mentioned that this – this apparition – came from the recess which used to be beside the fireplace. How did you know that there was once a recess there?'

'I came to the cottage many years ago, when I was a child. I had tea here.'

'That would have been in Prince Camford's time.'

'Yes.'

A further silence. Then, 'I don't want to alarm you, Miss Symondson, but I think you may be in some danger. I don't think you ought to spend tonight alone in the cottage.'

'But how—'

'I'm speaking from Plymouth, where I landed earlier today. Is the fog very thick?'

'Yes, very.'

'It usually clears before midnight. It will only take me a couple of hours to get to you. I'll fix a room for you at Truro. Sit tight, and, Miss Symondson—'

'Yes?'

'My advice to you is, keep out of the sitting-room. Light the stove in the kitchen. You should be safe there.'

He rang off.

She had noticed the old black stove in the kitchen, but had not dared to tamper with it. Now she got sticks and paper, and a shovel full of coal, opened the front, and set it going. It showed a tendency to smoke, but this soon cleared, and she was able to put on a few small logs on top of the coal and closed the front. The stove gave out a companionable roar.

To be doing something was a comfort. It helped to keep her mind off the problems of what danger could possibly be lurking in that front room. It helped to pass the time. And that needed help. Only forty minutes since the telephone call. If the mist stayed thick it might take Melchior hours to reach her. He might not be there until morning.

There was a basket full of logs in the front room. They would keep the stove going for an hour or so. The alternative was to fetch a fresh supply from the woodshed, but this would involve making her way out into the fog and crossing the back yard. Surely it could not be dangerous, simply to go back into that room, just for a moment?

When she opened the door she remembered that she had turned out the light, and the switch was on the far side of the room.

She said, out loud, 'Don't be such a goose. *There's nothing in the room that can hurt you.* Just walk across and turn on the light.'

The fire in the grate had burned low, but it gave enough light for her to see, and avoid the furniture. Her hand was on the switch when she stopped.

The sound was definite and unmistakeable.

Someone was coming up the front path.

By the crunch of the footsteps on the gravel it was a man. He was coming cautiously, but was unable to avoid making some sound.

Miss Symondson was so paralysed with fear that she was unable even to raise her hand to the light switch. She stood in the darkness of the sitting-room and watched the figure loom closer through the fog.

Now he was at the door. A hand came out to try the door. Very gently. Thank God she had bolted it, top and bottom.

The man stood still for a moment, his head bowed as though he was listening. Then he turned and marched straight up to the window, and pressed his face against it.

Miss Symondson, cowering inside, recognized him at once.

It was Frank Melchior.

She was filled with unimaginable terror. The first words which came into her head were, 'He's come back for his wife.'

Plymouth? That was nonsense. He must have lied about that, and lied quite deliberately.

Why had he told her to sit in the kitchen? Was it so that no light would shine out from the front room indicating to any chance passer-by that she was in the cottage?

The man was moving now, quietly, away from the window, on the path that would take him round the house and directly to the kitchen door.

Which, she realized with frozen horror, she had left unlocked.

She tiptoed across to the front door and, with fingers which seemed not to belong to her, slid back the top bolt, and stooped to open the bottom one.

At that moment she heard the sound of the kitchen door being opened, and a voice which said, 'Hello, Miss Symondson. Where are you hiding?'

The second bolt slid back. She straightened up and eased the front door open. Gently, gently.

Footsteps crossing the kitchen floor, and the voice again, 'Are you in there? I thought I told you not to go in there.'

Then she was stumbling down the front path. The front door, as she let go of it, swung shut behind her. The noise must have warned the man that she was escaping. As she reached the front gate she heard heavy footsteps on the path. She stepped off the path, just inside the gate, and cowered down like a wild beast. Like a wild beast, she had the sense to realize that if she moved the man would hear her; and if he heard her, he would catch her.

The footsteps crunched past. The man outside the gate now. His steps were moving away, casting uncertainly, to right and left; lunging into the fog at some supposed shadow.

A sudden scratching of nails, on rock. A wild scream, and a series of horrible bumping noises. Then silence.

Miss Symondson got to her feet, and edged her way out of the gate until she felt the ruts of the track which led to the road. Down it she stumbled for an eternity of time, blinded by fog, her heart hammering, choking, kept going only by fear of what might be behind her.

As she reached the main road a light showed through the mist; there was a squeal of brakes and a car slid to a halt almost on top of her. The Cornish voice of Police Constable Greig said, 'Why the hell can't you look where you're going?' And then, 'Why, Miss Symondson. What's to do here?'

'A killer,' said Superintendent Assher to the Chief Constable of Cornwall. 'A careful killer, and a killer for money.'

They were standing in bright sunshine outside the door of the cottage, watching the workmen finish the demolition of the brick wall which concealed the recess behind the fireplace; a recess from which a skeleton, already identified as Patricia Melchior, had been removed and carried to the mortuary.

'You said, a careful killer?'

'Very careful. He must have been planning it for at least a year. He built that little summerhouse with his own hands.' He pointed to a neat construction, in the same brick as the house, which stood at the end of the lawn. 'He ordered a few hundred more bricks than he needed. And he taught himself, carefully and slowly, how to lay them. I expect his wife watched him, and admired his increasing skill. When the time was ripe, he strangled her, put her body inside, and bricked her up. To balance things, and make the wall look natural, he bricked up the other recess as well.'

'Why not just bury her somewhere outside?'

'He was a writer of detective stories, sir. He knew that digging in farm-land leaves traces. And if the body was recovered from the sea, the pathologist would know she'd been strangled. Safer to keep her in the house. No one had ever used it, except the two of them. No one ventured in afterwards. Maybe he spread the story of its being haunted. Later, of course, he didn't mind family parties as long as he was there to keep an eye on things. And then, by one chance in ten million, it was let, behind his back, to a woman who'd known the place as a child.'

'What do you think he'd have done to her?'

'Thrown her down the steps, no doubt. Everyone would have assumed she was out in the fog, and had slipped, and killed herself. As he did.'

The Chief Constable thought about it. He said, 'Did you believe what she told us?'

'Most of it,' said the Superintendent cautiously.

'About Mrs Melchior appearing to her.'

'I saw no reason to disbelieve that.'

'Then you believe in ghosts.'

'Certainly,' said the Superintendent with a smile. 'Good ones and bad ones. This was a good one. She'll sleep easy now, poor soul.'

He was smiling because he knew that ghosts were hard things for a stolid Devonian like the Chief Constable to credit. He himself had been born and bred west of the Tamar, and like all Cornishmen knew everything there was to know about ghosts.

SAFE!

M iss Sennett ran in panic up the front path. She clattered up the outside steps. The front door was open. Pressing down the switch at the foot of the stairs was an unconscious gesture, but she must have done it, because the dim landing light came on.

The hall was full of the fog.

She ran up the stairs. Her breath was coming in little gasps now. As she reached her landing the light went out. The gasp became a stifled scream. It took a moment to remember that it was an automatic switch, the frugal sort, that always went out before you reached your own flat. She felt for her latch key, got it into the keyhole at the third attempt, opened the door and tumbled through it. It was only when she was standing inside the sitting-room, and had bullied her shaking hands into taking off her hat and coat that she began to recover some hold of herself.

'Don't be stupid,' she said out loud. 'You're not a child. You can't solve it by running away.'

Like a full stop to this sentence the door bell buzzed.

Her first reaction was a return of panic. Her second was cold common sense.

'Use your brain,' she said. 'You've learnt to do that, if you've learnt nothing else. Suppose it is him. It's no good just keeping the door shut. He knows where you are. He can make trouble.'

The bell sounded again.

'And if it isn't him, if it's just a tough out for trouble, better take him on there. Mrs Parmesi's home; her kitchen light was on. She's always complaining about the wireless being too loud. She'll hear quickly enough if you shout.'

As she went to the door the bell sounded for the third time. Not a long, demanding ring. Just a reminder that he was still there.

She opened the door.

'When I follow a girl home,' he said, 'I always give her a minute or two to make herself tidy.'

'What do you want?'

'If you'd listened out there in the street you'd have saved me climbing all these stairs.'

'I don't want to talk to you.'

'If you don't want to talk,' said the man, 'no one can make you. But you might as well listen to what I've got to say. It won't take all night.'

'If you don't go away, I shall shout. There are people in the other flats—'

'That's all right,' said the man genially. 'You shout away. I'm not afraid of people.'

For a long moment they looked at each other. Swords crossed, touched, and crossed again.

'Who are you?' said Miss Sennett.

'You know damned well who I am,' said the man. 'Or you'd have called the police ten minutes ago. I'm told it's quite a family likeness. But we don't want to talk about it all out here – or do we?'

'I – no—' She turned, and walked down the passage without another word.

The man smiled again. He came softly in behind her and shut the front door. Then he followed her into the lighted room.

'Now let's be polite. Invite me to sit down. You that side of the fire, me this. Domestic.'

'You're Ted's brother,' she said at last.

'The late Ted.' His teeth showed. They were good teeth, white and strong as Ted's had been once, but a boot had got among them and after that he'd let them go. The more you looked at him the more you saw the likeness. The hard grey eyes. The mouth which seemed to have no upper lip.

'Yes.'

Her voice was cooler. It was under control now. It had been the suddenness which had shocked her. To see the past walk out of the fog and wait for you, under the street lamp. It would shake anyone.

'I could use a drink,' he said.

She went to the cupboard and took out a bottle of gin.

'Glad you keep up some of your bad habits.'

'It's for my friends. I don't drink myself. And it's all I've got. If you want water with it you can get it from the tap.'

The man took the glass, filled it full of gin and drank it smoothly. Then he filled it again, tipped a little into his mouth and sat savouring it.

He looked up suddenly and saw her eyeing him.

'Don't fuss,' he said. 'I won't get violent. Gin's mother's milk to me.'

'I didn't know Ted had a brother.'

'Introduce myself. The name is Les.'

'What do you want?'

'A glass of this gin makes a nice start. We can move on to the rest – later.'

His eyes rested thoughtfully on her. It was uncanny. He had just that cock of the head that used to tell her that Ted was thinking up something wicked.

'You can say what you want and go away.'

'What's the hurry? Ted won't come back. He's safe under three foot of quicklime in the prison yard. Isn't that where they put him? Oh, of course, you wouldn't know. You were inside at the time yourself.'

'Listen,' said Miss Sennett. 'What's past is past. Nothing you can say can bring it back. I don't know why you've waited – nearly six years—'

'Seven years with time off for good behaviour. Violence. They're very hot on violence.'

'I see. Well, that explains why I haven't had the pleasure of seeing you before—'

It was wasted on Les. He had planned the interview in advance. There were certain stages at which certain things were going to be said.

This happened to be one of them.

'Nice job you've got yourself?'

'I—'

'Don't fuss to make anything up. I found where you were working before I came to look you up. Diamond merchants. Hatton Garden. That's right, isn't it? And you're the boss's secretary. His confidential secretary. The one who brings him his hat and fetches the tea and listens to his secrets and says: "Yes, Mr Arkinshaw. No, Mr Arkinshaw." '

He tipped a little more gin into his mouth, and added: 'I've got plenty of friends. They're interested in diamonds.'

'No.'

'No what?'

'You're not going to interfere with my job.'

'Who says I'm not?'

'I do. Try that and I go to the police.'

'And tell them what?'

Once again they looked at each other. Once again it was the uncanny resemblance that shook her nerve.

'Don't bluff,' he said. 'All we want from you is information. Inside information. No one need know about it. If it's the right information, we move in and clean up. It doesn't hurt anyone – except the insurance company. What are you scared of? Losing your job?' He paused.

'Or is Mr Arkinshaw more than a boss to you? One word from me and you lose him and the job. Right?'

With terrifying suddenness he was on his feet beside her.

'On the other hand' – his fingers just brushed the side of her face – 'if you don't do us right, you might lose more than just a job. The prettiest girl goes to the bottom of the class when she's only got one ear.'

He walked back to the table, picked up the gin bottle, corked it carefully and put it in his pocket. Then he was gone.

Miss Sennett sat still for a long time.

'It's an odd set-up,' agreed Inspector Lugarde. 'I don't know when I can remember an odder.'

He sat in the armchair in Philip Arkinshaw's office and stared at his own highly polished toe-caps.

'You're sure of your facts?' said Mr Arkinshaw.

'No doubt at all,' said the Inspector. 'The past is, as you might say, an open book. It's the future that's problematical.'

'She doesn't look like a – what d'you call it?'

'They never do, sir. That's why they're useful. Just imagine you're going in for armed robbery. You're going to hold up a cinema – or a bank – or a post office. If you get caught the chances are you get caught quick. Something goes wrong with your getaway. The car breaks down, or crashes, and the crowd mobs you. That sort of thing. That's when it's going to make seven years of difference whether you've got a gun on you or not, you see.'

'Yes,' said Mr Arkinshaw. 'I can see that.'

'But if this girl's right on the spot, ready to pick up the gun as soon as you've finished with it, that's tidy help. She's just an ordinary girl, an innocent-looking bystander. She can take the gun away, clean the prints off it, drop it in the river or post it to the Archbishop of Canterbury. You're clean. That's the point. Even if we get you sixty seconds later, it's going to be the devil of a job to pin armed robbery on you.'

'And she did that – she was the red-head in the Ted Tarlo case?'

'That's her. Anna the red-head. You remember it now?'

'Certainly I do,' said Mr Arkinshaw. 'Soon after the war, wasn't it? The papers made quite a splash. He came from Liverpool. She was a London girl whom he picked up. She wasn't very old.'

'Seventeen,' said the Inspector. 'Quite a decent family. Her father was a solicitor's clerk. War bust the family up and she was on her own. Living in one room.'

'And she – er – associated with him?'

'She married him,' said the Inspector. 'For better or worse. For crooked or straight. Towards the end we had our eyes on her, too, of course. She was searched three times, but we never found a thing. I don't know to this day what she did with the gun—'

Quite suddenly Mr Arkinshaw laughed. He threw himself back in his chair and abandoned himself to laughter.

'Our Miss Sennett,' he gasped at last. 'The byword in this office for efficiency, reliability, and respectability. The girl who has never been one minute late in the morning in five years. The best secretary I've ever had.'

'Quite,' said the Inspector. 'And of course we don't know that she's anything but straight now.'

'Of course we don't,' said Mr Arkinshaw. 'I mean, of course we do. She's as straight as a die. I'd trust her with my last fiver.'

'Yes?'

'Maybe I've got a simple mind,' said Mr Arkinshaw. 'Of course, I'm not a policeman. But it seems obvious to me. She was only a girl. She may even have had the old-fashioned idea that a wife helps her husband. Then the big bust-up came. Instead of just threatening, Ted used his gun. Shot a post office man, didn't he?'

'That's right.'

'Then there was the big trial. She was involved, of course. Ghastly business. He was found guilty and hanged. She got—?'

'Two years.'

'A light sentence. Youth and mitigating circumstances. All right. So far as she was concerned, an episode was closed. New leaf. Trained herself. Worked hard. Got a job.'

'Yes,' said the Inspector.

Mr Arkinshaw detected the note of reserve. 'What do you mean?' he said indignantly. 'You can't hound the wretched girl because she made a mistake years ago.'

Inspector Lugarde seemed unmoved by this outburst.

'I don't hound people,' he said. 'I'm a policeman. I've got one job that matters. That is to prevent crime before it happens.' There was a moment of silence that Mr Arkinshaw did not seem anxious to break.

It was the Inspector who spoke. 'How do you imagine,' he said, 'that we got on to Miss Sennett?'

'I don't know,' said Mr Arkinshaw. He was still troubled. 'I suppose you keep an eye on people like that.'

'Fssch,' said the Inspector. 'If we watched everybody who had ever been inside we'd need a sizable police force. No, sir. We were watching somebody, but not Miss Sennett. The name is Les Tarlo. That's right. Ted's younger brother. He came out of prison a month ago. A very dangerous person. I'm not sure that I wouldn't say' – the Inspector considered the matter carefully – 'one of the most dangerous young men on our books. And he's got a nice crowd round him. The remains of the Camden Town Barrow Gang. They went into temporary liquidation when we got Peter Pasco, and between you and me they're a rotten crowd who'd cut up their nearest and dearest if they saw a five-pound note in it. But if there's one thing that they get really excited about – it's diamonds.'

'All right,' said Mr Arkinshaw. 'But where does it touch—?'

'Miss Sennett? Until last week it didn't. But in the course of the last seven days, Les Tarlo has seen her three times. Possibly four. I think he made contact that night we had the fog. He slipped us then, so I couldn't be sure.'

'Yes,' said Mr Arkinshaw. 'But what are they after? She doesn't keep the keys of the safe.'

'Do you ever carry diamonds about – loose, I mean?'

'Well – yes.'

'Often?'

'When I have to.' Mr Arkinshaw felt that a word of explanation was called for. 'Real top diamond buyers are few and far between,' he said. 'I make it my business to find out if they're in London. Then, if I think I've got anything which will interest them I nip round and see them. They don't come shopping. I've got to go after them. In fact, just as soon as we've finished, I've got a date with a Greek gentleman at the Dorchester. I thought he might like these—'

Mr Arkinshaw dipped his hand into a fob pocket, fumbled with the concealed opening, and produced a wash-leather bag. The Inspector examined the contents.

'Twelve thousand?' he suggested.

Mr Arkinshaw chuckled. 'I see you know your stones,' he said. Then he became serious again.

'Are you suggesting—?'

'I'm not suggesting anything yet,' said the Inspector. 'But you can easily work out the angles for yourself. How often do you carry valuable stones? Once a fortnight? Less? All right. If the boys attack you blind, they're taking a fifteen to one chance that they'll find nothing on you. Odds like that don't appeal to them. If they're going to stick their necks out they like to be on a certainty. But if they only had someone who could tip them off—'

'I see,' said Mr Arkinshaw. 'Yes. I see.'

Miss Sennett sat at her elegant desk in the little room off Mr Philip Arkinshaw's room and did some thinking. She had had to think hard in her life before, but never as hard as she was thinking now.

Certain facts had not escaped her observant eye.

One was that her chief Philip Arkinshaw had started taking her into his confidence about his movements. Previously, if he had been going out to see a client, he might have told her or he might not. It was a question of whether the matter happened to crop up. Now it was different. Three times in the last three weeks he had gone right out of his way to tell her: 'I'm going round to the Savoy this afternoon. I'm taking those stones we had from Roos. You might get me a taxi for four o'clock.' And so on.

The first time that it happened she thought it might have been chance. The second, she was not so sure. The third time she was quite certain it wasn't.

That was one thing to think about.

Then there was Les Tarlo. She could keep him in play just so long but no longer.

And there were 'the boys,' who, she fancied, were pushing Les a little harder than he wanted to go. The Hogan brothers, and Minelli, the Maltese. She had met them once and had no desire to meet them again in any circumstances whatsoever.

And there was the unobtrusive-looking gentleman with the military moustache and the hard hat who had come twice already to see Mr Arkinshaw. She reflected that if she had been a nice, ordinary girl he might not have meant much to her. As it was, she had placed him with accuracy, the first time she saw him.

The buzzer sounded over her desk.

When she went in Mr Arkinshaw was standing in front of the fireplace. He was just one shade too casual.

'I'd like you,' he said, 'to get Lot Eight out of the safe.'

'Lot Eight?' Her eyes opened a little. 'Have we found a buyer?'

'I don't know yet. There's a man at the Donnington I think may be interested. But he can't see me until this evening.'

'Then that means – you'll be keeping them out all night. Or could you put them in the hotel safe?'

'Hotel safe?' said Mr Arkinshaw. 'I've no great faith in hotel safes, not for packages like Lot Eight. I'll look after them all right. I'm safer than a hotel safe.'

He smiled his slow smile. 'And one other thing, I'd like you to come along.'

'Me?' She tried not to sound surprised.

'If we get down to terms I want a note made of them. They'll be quite complicated. He's buying on a blocked account. And whatever we agree, I want it typed out for signature by both of us, there and then.'

'All right, Mr Arkinshaw.'

'Sorry to spoil your evening. As compensation I'm awarding you the rest of the afternoon off. No, that's all right. I mean it. You buzz along and get yourself kitted up. We shall have to have drinks with the man and be civil to him. It may develop into an evening. Have you got some sort of – er – cocktail dress, or something like that? Good. I'll meet you at seven o'clock in the foyer. You know the place? Turning off Curzon Street, opposite Shepherd Market.'

'Thank you.'

Whether she was being followed home she neither knew nor cared. She got home as fast as she could. There was a lot to be thought about. And a lot to be done. First, the telephone—

'It's been a lovely evening,' said Miss Sennett. 'And thank you again for the dinner.'

'I couldn't send you home starving,' said Mr Arkinshaw. 'Three glasses of sherry and six little biscuits don't constitute an evening meal for a hard-working girl. Anyway, we had something to celebrate, didn't we?'

'You think he'll buy?'

'He'll have an action for breach of contract if he doesn't,' said Mr Arkinshaw, fingering the paper in his pocket.

'All the same,' she said, 'I wish he'd taken over the stones this evening.'

'Still worried? Wait here while I fetch a taxi.'

He walked out into the darkness of Curzon Street, but found that he was being followed.

'I think I'll come with you, if you don't mind,' she said rather breathlessly.

'O.K., bodyguard.'

A lone taxi came cruising by and the driver gave them an exploratory look.

'I may be a mug,' observed Mr Arkinshaw. 'But not as big a mug as that. We'll have a cab off the rank.'

There was only one cab on the rank at the corner, and there was nothing suspicious about it except that it looked so decrepit that it was a wonder it held together.

'I'll drop you at your flat and then go on.'

'That's rather roundabout,' said Miss Sennett. 'Considering that you live a lot nearer than I do. Why don't we drop you and I'll take the cab on?'

'All right,' said Mr Arkinshaw. He gave the driver his instructions.

'I only hope you've got a good safe at home,' she said, as they swung out into Piccadilly.

'You've got an obsession about safes,' said Mr Arkinshaw calmly. 'Very often they're not safes at all. They're unsafes. People break into my house tonight; they're looking for a very valuable parcel of diamonds – which they happen to know I've brought home with me ...'

The taxi was passing a street lamp and the light fell full on him. Miss Sennett took a quick look at him, but his face was unreadable.

'Where do they look for them? If they know I've got a safe in my house their troubles are half over. All they've got to do is bust it open. But if I haven't – well, they've got a lot of searching to do.'

'I suppose that's right,' said Miss Sennett. 'But where *would* you put them?'

The words came out before she had considered their implications, and she felt her face going hot.

Mr Arkinshaw said, without any trace of hesitation: 'I should put them in the refrigerator. Empty the ice-tray, put in more water, drop them in, and refreeze it.'

'That certainly seems safe enough,' said Miss Sennett. 'Unless they get thirsty searching and decide to mix themselves a cool drink. Here we are.'

The taxi drew up.

Mr Arkinshaw got out, had a word with the driver, popped his head in again to say goodnight, then turned and walked up the shallow steps in front of his big house. He was feeling in his pocket for a latchkey. Miss Sennett watched him until the front door shut.

The taxi started slowly and grumbled off.

As it reached the corner Miss Sennett was still looking back. She was frowning. She leaned forward and tapped the glass. 'Stop, please,' she said.

The taxi shuddered to a halt and she jumped out.

'Do I owe you anything?'

'No, that's all right, miss. The gentleman fixed it. But he told me to take you to—'

'I've changed my mind,' she said. 'It's quite all right. Goodnight.'

The driver shrugged his shoulders and chugged off. Miss Sennett started to walk back the way she had come.

When she reached the house she stopped again. Her heart was thumping. The house was absolutely dark. That was what had worried her. No lights at all. Nothing through the hall fanlight. Nothing through either of the front windows. Surely, when a man goes into his own house, he turns on some sort of light? Unless ...

'Thump,' said her heart. 'He may have gone straight through to the kitchen at the back. And he's going to think it pretty odd—'

She pressed the front door bell. She could hear it ringing, far away but clear.

She waited for a full minute, then pressed the bell again. He must have heard it.

She seized the heavy bronze knocker, raised it, and beat it down. Once, twice.

The door opened silently, inward. An arm came out, caught her, and pulled her through. She was dragged, not gently, down the dark hall, where a chink of light showed. A door was opened, she was pushed in, and it snapped shut behind her.

It was a small, book-lined study. The one window was heavily curtained, and further blocked by a blanket which had been pinned over it. The only light came from a table light which stood in the corner.

Mr Arkinshaw sat on the edge of the table. His coat had been torn open and he looked dishevelled, but still cheerful.

There were three other men in the room. Tarlo, the elder Hogan and Minelli. The young Hogan was the driver. He would be outside some-where in the car.

'So you've come back to see the fun,' said Mr Arkinshaw looking at her, his head on one side.

'I didn't—'

'You keep quiet,' said Tarlo. 'Run her over, too.' It was the Maltese who searched her. He did it very thoroughly and she saw Mr Arkinshaw's mouth tightening and hoped he wasn't going to spoil things.

'She's clean,' said Minelli. 'No gun.'

'All right. Go over there and sit beside him. That's right. Make your-self comfortable. Now then, there's something we want, and one of you's got it, or knows where it is. Either you've put it somewhere or it's hidden on you, in one of those clever pockets. We've got all night to find it – but the easiest way would be for you to tell us where it is. Easiest for you, I mean.'

His eye seemed to rest thoughtfully, for a moment, on the electric fire, which was glowing dark red in the hearth.

Miss Sennett was shaking. Or seemed to be. Her whole body was jerking.

'You're wasting your time,' said Mr Arkinshaw. 'I know just what you want. It isn't here. I left it in the safe at the Donnington Hotel.'

'That's a lie,' said Hogan. 'I had my eye on them all the time. Let's get started on him. Or maybe if we roughed her up a bit he'd change his tune.'

Miss Sennett had turned almost sideways on. She was more than touching Mr Arkinshaw now. She was pressed against him. He sat with one hand behind him on the table to steady himself, and at this moment he felt something cold and heavy slide across the back of his knuckles and come to rest, half on his hand, half on the table.

Without moving his body he shifted his fingers until they were curled round it.

'I reckon we can make him sing,' agreed Tarlo.

'Somehow,' said Mr Arkinshaw, 'I doubt it.'

It was the note of confidence in his voice that made them all look up.

'Ten seconds ago I might have believed you. Not now.'

He brought his right hand from behind his back and the three men saw what was in it. They had nothing to say. Nothing at all.

'I warn you,' went on Mr Arkinshaw. 'I'm not one of your crack shots, so I always aim for the middle of the stomach. Then I'm bound to hit something. That's right. Quite still, please. There's a telephone in the hall, Miss Sennett.'

Some time afterwards Miss Sennett said: 'You were taking an awful risk. Suppose I hadn't turned up?'

'I wasn't risking the diamonds, anyway,' said Mr Arkinshaw.

'You weren't—'

'I slipped them to the head waiter half-way through dinner. They were in the night safe in a Piccadilly bank before we'd finished our coffee. Now perhaps you can tell me something. I saw Minelli search you. Why didn't he find the gun?'

'That lout,' said Miss Sennett contemptuously. 'Why, in my day I've had a police searcher, who knew her job, run me over and miss a full-sized thirty-eight. What chance d'you think an amateur would have?'

'No doubt about it,' said Mr Arkinshaw. 'The perfect secretary.' It was hard to say whether he was smiling or not. 'Finish your drink and I'll see if I can find a taxi for you. By the way, I expect you'll want a sleep-in after all this. I'll warn them at the office not to expect you till lunch-time.'

'Really, Mr Arkinshaw, that will be quite unnecessary,' said Miss Sennett.

THE REVENGE OF MARTIN
LUCAS FIELD ON COLONEL
CRISTOBAL OCAMPOS

MAJOR PATINO, CHIEF of Police of the township and Province of Fernando de la Mora, looked like a contented marmoset. He rode an enormous grey horse; and rode it very well, having been, in a manner of speaking, born in the saddle. If he had not, he would have been thrown as the horse reared and bucked in protest at the salvo of 15 explosions.

Martin Lucas Field came running. He helped to soothe the indignant animal.

'I say,' he said. 'I do apologise. If I'd seen you coming, I'd have post-poned the firing.'

'It's nothing.' Major Patino slid down, handed the reins to one of Martin's mestizo labourers, and looked around.

'In the town,' he said, 'it was put about that you were prospecting for oil. I rode out here, expecting to find a huge, an enormous—' he raised one arm up to the sky and grinned '—a contraption for drilling. Instead I find you discharging a sort of firework.'

'It doesn't look very impressive,' agreed Martin.

The encampment comprised his own tent on one side of the track, a tent shared by the mestizos on the other, a parked truck, a table standing in the open with apparatus on it, and a tangle of 15 wires leading out from the apparatus to 15 black boxes, arranged, in groups of five, in a straightish line.

'You must understand that I'm not a driller,' said Martin. 'I'm just a geologist. I try to discover what lies underneath the crust of your abominable countryside.'

'And those little black boxes will tell you?'

'They are geophones. They record the explosions. The sound goes down, until it strikes a layer of hard rock. Then it bounces back again.

By timing it, I can tell just how deep that hard layer lies. When I have made enough soundings, I can plot it. If the layer runs horizontally in a straight line—' Martin held out his brown hand stiffly '—no good. If it runs like this, however—' he bent his hand, with the knuckles sticking upwards '—and forms what we call a dome, or cap, it is very hopeful. And if it is not only a dome, but a double dome – we call it a hat, for it looks like this—' He drew with his stick in the dust. 'It has the appearance of a hat with the brim turned up on either side – you see?'

Major Patino stared down at the marks in the dust. His good-natured face was puckered.

'If you find that,' he said, 'you are certain of oil?'

'Not absolutely certain. But very nearly so. The last time a structure like that was found, it became the Gran' Cosa Field in Venezuela.'

'I hope you discover no caps nor hats,' said the major, 'for if you do, the drillers will come. Drilling camps mean trouble; we have enough trouble here already.'

'My boys were trying to tell me something about it, when we pitched here last night. I don't speak their lingo well enough to make out exactly what the trouble was.'

The major went over and spoke to the nearest of the three. They were Tupi-Guaranis, half-Indian, half-Spanish, black-haired, brown-skinned, with pale grey, almost yellow eyes. When they found that the major understood their language, they grabbed his arm and started to chatter and gesticulate.

'What they say,' said the major, tearing himself away at last, 'is that they hold this to be an unhappy place.'

'Unhappy?'

'It is difficult to render the meaning exactly; all words in Guarani mean more than one thing. They are so poor, you see, they have to economise even with their language. Roughly, it means a place of ill-fortune. A place where bad things can happen.'

'Supernatural things?'

'Partly. Not entirely. They say that your camp was watched all last night.'

'Watched! By humans, do they mean? I heard a couple of mountain foxes barking.'

'They are not sure whether the watchers are of this world or the next. Whichever they are, they wish to leave. They would have run off if it had not been their pay day tomorrow.'

'I'd no notion things were as bad as that. Couldn't you say something to set their minds at rest?'

'But I might find myself agreeing with them,' said the major. 'It may be that their instincts are sound. You have indeed pitched your camp in a very odd spot.'

'I'm astride the only track leading down to the river. But I'm not blocking it.'

'Not actually blocking it. No. But if people wished to come past, at night, shall we say, they would be certain to disturb you. If you did not hear them, your boys would do so.'

'Probably. But who would want to use the track at night? It leads only to the river bank. And there's no crossing place.'

'On the contrary, this is the only place in 40 miles that the River Mora *can* be crossed. That of course is why the track exists. Above, there is a succession of rapids. Below, the Mora runs through crumbling ravines. Here, it sweeps in a circle. The banks on either side are flat. The current is not too strong, and a boat, well handled, can cross.'

'All right,' said Martin. 'Let anyone cross who wishes. I'm not stopping them.'

'The people who habitually use this track are rough and secretive folk. Contrabandists.'

'And I'm not a Customs Officer,' said Martin. 'So if you should happen to meet any smugglers, please assure them that the path is open.'

'Why should you assume,' said the major stiffly, 'that I am on speaking terms with criminals? I am a police officer. I know my duty.'

It took a cup of tea laced with whisky to mollify the major. As dusk approached, he remounted his great horse and turned to leave. 'I will visit you in the morning,' he said. 'Sleep soundly.'

Martin walked out to inspect the results of the afternoon's shot-firing. The nests of geophones covered, altogether, nearly half a mile. Ideally, they should all have been placed at the same level, but in that mountainous country such nicety was impossible, and by the time he had collected the final reading sheet Martin found himself some way away from his camp and above it.

Looking down, he saw exactly what the major had meant. For people carrying loads, or encumbered with transport, the path formed a bottleneck through which they must pass on their way down to the river.

'And I'm the cork in the bottle,' he said.

The orange rim of the sun touched the saw-edge of the mountains. The indigo blue sky turned to sick pearl, and then to steel grey. It was very quiet. Martin shivered and said to himself, 'Someone must have walked over my grave.'

Only, this time, he saw the grave. It had been dug in a small, flat space surrounded by boulders, and was only visible from where he was standing. The red soil freshly excavated was piled in neat heaps at each end.

Martin made his way back to camp. He was very angry and a little frightened. Using his limited vocabulary of Guarani words he asked his boys which of them had been wasting time doing this unnecessary digging. The mestizos stared at him, their yellow eyes blank.

Either they could not or would not understand him, and in the end Martin gave it up.

He spoke the word for supper and strode off to his tent, took off his field boots, put on a pair of slippers, and poured himself a generous whisky, filling the glass with water from the bottle hanging beside the tent pole.

This was the time of day he liked best. The day's work done, and a peaceful hour before supper; an hour to relax, to sip the first drink of the day, to make plans for tomorrow.

What, he thought with a touch of complacency, would an observer see, should he chance to look through the tent opening into its snug and workmanlike interior. He would see a sun-burned, tough, self-reliant person, the only white man in 500 square miles of wild country, the archetypical Anglo-Saxon adventurer. No romantic, however. Simply a man, doing a man's work. Ha!

Even better, he thought, if the admiring gaze through the tent-flap should happen to come from the eyes of a girl. An attractive girl, naturally. Not necessarily pretty. Prettiness did not go with the rugged back-lands inhabited by men like himself. A girl with close-cropped black hair. Black-haired girls had always appealed to him more than colourless blondes. A girl with a warm face, bronzed by the sun and a mouth ready to smile and show small, even teeth. Small breasts – well, not *too* small, but, emphatically, not too big. And the angle was most important; a nicely rounded bottom and long legs.

A psychologist, could he have read Martin's thoughts, would have realised that most of his ideas about girls came from magazines and very few of them from life.

Footsteps on the path outside heralded the arrival of his supper and brought him back to earth. It would be corned-beef stew, fresh potatoes and tinned vegetables.

The flap of the tent opened, and a girl came in. She had a brown face, black hair, and her mouth, half open in an apologetic smile, showed small, even teeth. For a long moment Martin stared at her, saying nothing. Then he scrambled to his feet.

'I'm sorry,' he said. 'That was very rude of me.'

'It was rude of *me*,' said the girl. She spoke the unaccented English of an educated South American. 'I should not have come here unannounced. Had the matter not been urgent, I should not have done so.'

'How did you get here?' said Martin. It was the first thing that came. He was still struggling between fantasy and reality.

'On horseback, of course.' The girl's half-smile broadened. 'Did you think I flew down from the sky?'

'To tell you the truth, I didn't know what to think. Won't you sit down, please? I heard no horse.'

'I left him hobbled at the head of the path. There is no grazing here. Thank you.'

She took the camp-chair he was offering her, and as she lowered herself into it the light coat she was wearing swung open and Martin glimpsed her body. His first impression was more of strength than of beauty. It was not that she was obtrusively muscled. She looked, he thought, like a big, athletic boy, whose arms and legs have not yet hardened into manhood, but show all the signs of strength to come.

He was aware of a feeling of breathlessness, and walked with deliberate slowness to his own chair, and sat down.

'Your business must indeed be urgent,' he said, conscious that he sounded stilted, 'for you to ride out to a desolate spot like this, at this time of night.'

He could see her on a horse, controlling it superbly.

'It is a matter of life and death.' She said it without any hint of dramatic emphasis. As though life and death were kindred spirits, with both of whom she had a nodding acquaintance.

'First, I should introduce myself with a little more formality, I think. I am Marciana de Jara. My father is Doctor Ignacio de Jara. You will have heard of him.'

For a moment, the name escaped him. Then he remembered. Two journalists talking in a bar down in the capital city. 'He is a politician, isn't he?'

'He was a politician. He was one of the founders of the Partido Democrata Cristiano. For two years now he has been a prisoner at the National Penitentiary at Tacumbu. His crime was to be too successful.'

'The General does not welcome competition?'

'Only when it is too weak to succeed. But he will not tolerate an opposition which opposes. At the last so-called free election it was arranged that his own party would win 80 seats, the Liberals 15, and the Christian Democrats 12. In fact, so popular had my father become personally, that his party won 33 seats.'

'How very embarrassing for the General,' said Martin. He was not really interested in politics, but he wanted to keep Marciana talking so that he could go on looking at her. 'What did he do about it?'

'A recount was demanded in 18 cases, and, curiously enough, sufficient spoiled voting papers were found to reverse the result. Then, a month later came the plot.'

'Plot?'

'It was nothing to do with my father. I think it was devised entirely by the Security Police. They got hold of two or three tame plotters, who were very leniently treated when they confessed.'

'Confessed what?' said Martin, genuinely puzzled.

'Confessed that the true leader of the plot was my father, of course. He was at once arrested, and held without trial, under the Law de Defensa de la Democracia. He has been in prison ever since. They have not treated him well.'

Martin, who knew something of South American prisons, said nothing.

'For nearly two months, they kept him in the stocks, the whole time, with his legs stretched out in front of him. When they let him out, he had lost the use of his legs. He could only drag himself along the ground, using his elbows. When he had recovered a little, they put him back in the stocks. This time, they beat him, on the soles of his feet. They beat him so hard that many of the bones in his feet were broken.'

'Don't talk about it, please, if it troubles you,' said Martin. But there was no weakness in her face. Only calm strength and certainty of purpose.

'I am telling you about it,' she said, 'so that you will understand. A week ago they were moving my father from Tacumbu to a prison in the north. It was because Tacumbu was being visited by an American Civil Rights Committee, I think. We were told of the move 24 hours before it took place. We have good friends.'

Certainly she would have good friends.

'We intercepted the car that was taking my father to his new prison. It was not—' she hesitated for a moment over the idiom '—it was not an affair of kid gloves, you understand. Two of our men were wounded, one of them badly. Two of the police were killed. The driver was wounded and disarmed. But we succeeded in what we had set ourselves to do. My father was brought to a farm, some miles from here, by night. He has been hidden there for the past two days. There were arrangements to be made—'

'With the contrabandists?'

'Yes, with the contrabandists. You know of them?' Her eyes were like steel blades.

'Major Patino was speaking of them.'

'Ah, the fat little local Police Chief. All the same, he is not such a fool as he looks. What did he say?'

'He said that I was blocking one of their only through routes.'

'And what did you say?'

'I told him that I wasn't a Customs Officer.'

The girl laughed. 'It was a good answer. All the same, things will not be easy for us. My father cannot walk. He will have to be carried, in a sort of litter, down to the river. It will take four men to do it. There he will be placed in a boat, and ferried across. Once in Argentina he will be safe. His friends have transport waiting for him.'

'It sounds to me like a piece of cake.'

When she looked puzzled, he said, 'It's a stupid expression we have in England. It means that it should be easy. And if you were afraid that I should try to stop you – then think again. Now that I understand what you are doing, please believe me when I say that you can count on all possible help.'

'You are kind, Mr Field. You see – I found out your name.'

'Then you found it out wrong. My name, to my friends, is Martin.'

'Thank you, Martin. But you must not help me. You must not become involved in this affair, not in any way. I forbid it.' The smile which accompanied these words robbed them of their sting.

She said, 'I think you do not quite realise the dangers of what we are doing. You spoke of a piece of cake. We have here a cake which is served on the First Day of the Year. It is soft and white and delicious.' Her little white teeth gleamed. 'But in one of the slices, there is buried a small hard charm. It is meant to be lucky, but if you are careless you can break your teeth on it.'

'I see,' said Martin slowly. 'And who is going to break our teeth in this case?'

'His name is Colonel Cristobal Ocampos. He is head of the Security Police, and he is a devil.'

'Even if he has diabolic powers, can he guard all the frontiers in this country?'

'He does not have to. He knows that my father will try to get to Argentina. There are not above a dozen crossing-places for a man who *can* walk. For a man who has to be carried, this is almost an obvious choice. Also, the car which brought my father here was stopped on its way back, and the driver was questioned. His answers were not entirely satisfactory to Colonel Cristobal Ocampos, and he is still being held. No doubt they will torture him. I do not think he will speak quickly, because he is a brave man. But there are things they can do to him—'

'Yes,' said Martin uncomfortably, 'I suppose even the bravest man—'

She was not listening to him, but to something outside the tent. Martin's words died away into silence. Her hearing must have been better than his. It was a minute before he picked it up, the shuffling of feet, the tiny clink of iron-tipped boots on stone.

One of his mestizo labourers cried out in a harsh, high voice.

'Damned fool,' said Martin. 'He'll wake everyone for miles.'

'Don't go out,' said the girl, urgently.

'Don't worry about me,' said Martin, and flung up the flap of the tent and received a shock. He had been expecting darkness, and it was almost as light as day. Whilst they had been talking, a full moon had swung over the tops of the mountains and was spreading its lime-light over the scene.

Up the track, from the direction of the river, came a covered litter, or palanquin. From the careless way the men were carrying it, it was clearly empty.

His three mestizos were huddled in the entrance of their tent. Martin strode across to them.

'Quiet,' he said. 'All is well, friends.'

Three of the four carriers were squat and dark, men of the mountains, with black shaggy hair, thick lips and dark faces. The fourth was a curious contrast. He was taller by a head than the others, and much thinner, with a head of hair so light that it looked almost silvery in the moonlight.

But it was not only these physical differences which caught and held Martin's attention. It was the face, severe, composed and ascetic; a face which took Martin's mind back to the first colonisers, the Jesuit Fathers who had come with the Spanish conquerors; the secular arm which had out-lasted the military and left a permanent mark across the country.

He was aware that Marciana was standing beside him. He turned, and noted the serious look on her face.

She said, 'We shall be back in a few hours. No doubt you will hear us. Might I beg of you not to come out.'

'Why?'

'I have told you. You are a stranger to this country. You must not become involved in our affairs.'

'I'm involved already,' said Martin, 'and I should not be afraid to become more so.'

'You would not be afraid, no,' said the girl.

She said it almost sadly. 'But I forbid it. And I have the right to forbid it.'

The carriers had gone past now, and had reached a twist in the track. In a moment they would be out of sight.

'Very well,' said Martin. 'But if by any chance you should need it, my offer of help holds good.'

The girl held out her hand, in the English fashion, for him to shake. Martin raised the warm brown hand to his lips and kissed the back of it. The girl turned, and walked off up the path. Martin stood, his mouth dry, his heart beating double time. Would she turn?

As she reached the twist in the track she seemed to hesitate. Please turn, said Martin to himself. Please turn, once more. The next moment she was gone. Martin swung on his heel and went back into his tent.

When the mestizo cook came across with his dinner, Martin looked at him without seeing him, ate the food without being conscious of what it was, sat back in his chair, put his after-dinner cigarillo into his mouth and forgot, for 15 minutes, to light it.

One thing was clear. He had no hope of sleep that night. He looked at his watch. It was 11 o'clock. His eye fell on the neat pile of seismographic records, 60 of them, the results of four successive firings. He would have to tabulate them some time, and draw the graph which would demonstrate the shape of the hidden strata. It was a finnicking piece of drudgery, which he usually left to the draughtsmen at the base office, but this time he thought he would try his hand at it. It would occupy his mind to the exclusion of thoughts more disturbing.

Two hours later, his head swimming, his eyes bleared with the strain of working in a poor light, he was staring down at the result.

The stratum, sloping gently downwards, had apparently cracked, turning up for a short way, then down again, then up in a perfectly shaped dome, or cap rock. The far side lay beyond his survey, but the general shape was beautifully clear. It would have to be re-surveyed, across several different axes, but Martin had no doubt at all that he was looking at the most promising drilling prospect that he had seen in 20 years of search.

It was at this moment that he heard the men coming. He jumped up, switched off the single electric bulb, and stole across, in the darkness, to the door of his tent.

The moon had swung over, and was throwing long shadows among the rocks, and out of a pool of shadow came the palanquin, more slowly now as the carriers took the strain of its loaded weight. There were still four of them. Three were the dark mountaineers, but the fourth was now no longer the tall, thin, light-haired man. It was Marciana.

Martin held his breath. He said, 'If this is the last time I see her, it is the most perfect. Young, strong, brave, in the moonlight. A daughter helping to carry her father out of hell, into heaven.'

The next moment they had turned a corner and were gone. He could hear the soft chink of metal on stone, frequently at first, then less often, as they went away, then not at all. Only the far-off sound of a night bird, the whisper of bats' wings and the silent stars.

One of the few Guarani words that Martin knew was *pygharé*, which meant night. It also meant infinity. As he stood there, straining his ears for a whisper from the river in the valley below, Martin understood this. Day was finite, but night was infinite.

The first shot sounded like a desecration, as if someone had screamed in church. A ragged volley followed. Without thinking what he was doing, Martin started to run.

It was a miracle that he did not break a leg. Half a dozen times he stumbled in his headlong descent, saving himself at the last moment. There were men not far ahead of him, shouting; and there was a light, stronger than the moon, a blue-white blaze of incandescence that could only be a searchlight.

As he reached the last corner, he halted. The light was focused on the bank, and on the slow, brown stream of the Mora. The palanquin lay on its side, half in, half out of the water. A few yards out from the bank an upturned boat swung round in a slow eddy.

There was no sign of the carriers.

A line of lights was moving downstream, away from the bank, a steady, purposeful advance. The men who held them were sweeping the ground, like hunters who are confident they have their quarry cornered.

A flurry of motion. A figure sprang up from the rocks near the river bank and started to run uphill towards him. Martin saw two things in consecutive heart-beats. The first was that it was the girl who was being hunted. The second, that there was a man with a rifle crouched behind a rock not five yards below him. He heard the bolt of the rifle click as he jumped. Then he was kneeling on top of the rifleman.

The man had time to give one choked scream. Martin had him by the hair, and had banged his head once on the rock when something hit him on the back of the skull and everything was blotted out in a whirl of fire and pain and darkness.

When consciousness returned, it was not a sudden process, but a succession of slow advances and lapses, like the waves breaking on the sand, each one crawling a little higher, lasting a little longer before it sank back into the dark sea. And each sense as it returned built up a total of awareness and memory and pain.

His first retained impression was the smell of a cigar. Curious to see who could be smoking, he turned his head and opened his eyes. A stabbing pain forced him to close them again.

Minutes, hours, years later he heard a voice speaking in Spanish. A hand grasped his chin and jerked his mouth open, something hard was thrust in, and a burning jet of raw spirit ran down his throat. The next minute, he was being sick, rolling on the ground, vomiting his heart up.

The voice said something else. Hands picked him up again and propped him in a chair. He opened his eyes and, with a conscious effort, held them open. He was in his own tent, but there were things about it that were wrong. It seemed that no fewer than four lights now hung from the ridge pole. It was difficult to count them properly, because of the curtain of grey smoke which hung between him and them.

Slowly the smoke cleared, and as it did so the four lights swung together into two, and the two into one. As eyes and mind focused, movement came back. His head was throbbing, an intolerable pulse which kept time with his heart. But he could see and hear now. And understand; and remember.

The man who had spoken, and whose obese body occupied the other flimsy camp chair to the point of protest and disintegration, was a middle-aged Spanish dandy. The black hair was oiled and curled with a nicety which suggested a wig. The nails of the podgy hand which held the cigar were manicured and tinted, and the creature had sprinkled on itself a scent so assertive that it almost vanquished the smell of the cigar.

He said, 'You must allow me to introduce myself. My name is Ocampos. Colonel Cristobal Ocampos of the Security Police. I would offer you one of my cigars, Mr Field, but it appears to me that your stomach—' the colonel lowered his heavy lids for a moment towards the soiled floor '—is in too delicate a condition to appreciate it.'

'What's happened?' said Martin. His voice came out in a dry croak.

'You were stupid enough, although I acquit you of any great malice in the heat of the moment – nevertheless, it was a stupidity – to attack one of my men. Fortunately Sergeant Rovera has a hard head, otherwise you might have found yourself in a very delicate situation indeed. As it was, you got a crack on the head yourself, which might be described as poetic justice.'

There was a question which Martin wanted to ask, but which he dared not ask, for fear of the answer. The colonel took a pull at his cigar, held the smoke for a moment in his pursed cheeks, and then exhaled it. He knew, too, what Martin wanted to ask, and he had no intention of helping him.

'What,' said Martin, controlling his voice with an effort, 'what happened to the men?'

'They took to the river. These Argentinos swim like fish. One was almost certainly killed. His body was observed to go under. Two reached the other bank. One, I think, was wounded.'

'And the old man?'

'The old man.' said Colonel Ocampos thoughtfully.

'Dr Ignacio de Jara.'

The colonel appeared to hesitate. Then he said, 'Ah, yes,' as if something previously obscure had suddenly become comprehensible to him. 'Dr Ignacio is – unharmed.'

'Unharmed,' said Martin. 'Crippled by your torturers!' Fear and uncertainty were working on him.

The colonel said, 'Crippled. I see. By the brutality of his gaolers, or of the police, I suppose?'

A tiny smile appeared for a fleeting moment at the corners of his mouth; appeared, and was gone.

Then there was the question that had to be asked, 'And the girl?' Martin said.

'The girl, I fear, is dead.'

Martin fought against understanding. It was not true. It could not be true. The man was a perverted sadist. He had said it deliberately. He had said it to get pleasure out of Martin's pain.

'She was killed,' said the colonel, 'by a burst from a machine pistol, at medium range. Two, at least, of the bullets hit her in the head. Others – in the body.'

Martin stared at him. His mouth was thick with bile.

'I see that I do not entirely convince you. Unfortunately the plainest method of proof is no longer open to me.'

'What do you mean?' Martin whispered.

'I cannot ask you to inspect the body for yourself. It has already been buried.'

'Buried?'

'My men found an open grave. It seemed convenient. Normally, I should have had to take the body back with me to headquarters, but as I had business here first, it would not have been convenient.'

'Business?' said Martin. 'More torturing, more killing?'

The colonel looked at him calmly. 'Much can be forgiven,' he said, 'to a man who has had a knock on the head.' He pulled again at his cigar, which was now drawing nicely. 'No. Not killing. Just watching. There is a very dangerous man, who *must* be prevented from crossing. His name, which is Rafael Asilvera, would mean nothing to you. No?'

Martin shook his head.

'In case you should encounter him, you will please inform the police at once. You will recognise him easily. He is very tall and very thin, and has remarkably light hair, almost white.'

'Oh, him,' said Martin. 'He went up with the empty litter earlier this evening.'

At one moment, Colonel Ocampos was lying back in his chair. The next, with a spasm of energy incredible in one so fat, he was on his feet, standing over Martin.

'What!' he shouted. 'Here already? When? Where? Why was I not told?' His face, a few inches from Martin, was engorged with anger.

He raised a fat hand, heavy with rings, and smacked Martin on the side of the face.

Martin tried to get up, but the effort started an engine in his head, accelerating, racing at dizzying speed. As the mist thickened, and blackness folded over him, he heard the colonel shouting for his sergeant ...

When Martin woke up, he was in his own camp bed, with a bandage round his head. The pain had retreated into a dull ache, at the back of his skull, and his cheek burned where the colonel's ring had cut it. But he was himself again. He swung his legs off the bed, got cautiously to his feet and tottered across to the tent opening.

The mestizos were boiling water over a fire of thorn, and grinned cheerfully at him when they saw him. They seemed to have recovered from their apprehensions of the night before. Martin said the word for coffee, and moved back to sit down at his table. The geophone sheets were there, and the calculations and the graphs he had drawn the night before.

One night before? A lifetime before.

He folded up and crammed them into the pocket of his jacket, where they made a solid bulge.

After breakfast he walked, very slowly, up the hill, to where he had found the grave. It was an effort to beat the gradient, and he had to sit down twice. When he got there, he sat down on a rock, in the shade.

The grave had been filled. Someone had even spared the time to place a cross at the head of it, two flat pieces of wood which looked as if they had come from a packing case, lashed together with flex.

On the cross-piece, in pencil, was written: *Marciana de Jara*, followed by the date. Nothing more.

Martin sat there for a long time. It was the sun, moving over the edge of the rock and beating down on his head, which finally forced him to move.

First, he took the slab of papers out of his jacket pocket, and tore them, slowly, into small pieces. He was tearing up a hundred million pounds. Maybe a thousand million. Maybe even more. But it was money which would go to the country which had murdered the girl; money which would go to the country of Colonel Ocampos.

Martin grinned crookedly to himself as he got out his lighter, set fire to the tattered pile of paper scraps, and sat back on his heels to watch them burn. When they were a pile of grey and black ashes, he scooped a hole in the loose earth on top of the grave, buried the ashes in it, and covered them again with the earth.

'Money for your journey,' he said to Marciana, and started to laugh.

The massacre in the Plaza Talavera was not reported in the papers as a massacre, but as an untoward incident. It occurred when the General was opening the new Farmers Co-operative Building.

The car, flying the Pennant of State, drew to a halt. The band struck up the National Anthem, the guard of honour presented arms and a figure in general's uniform stepped from the car. Two shots were fired from a first storey window on the other side of the square, and both hit their target. As the figure in general's uniform swung round and crumpled, someone shouted, 'There! There he is. He is running.' Certainly a man was running. Several men were running. Women and children too. The machine pistols of the guards opened up.

The casualties were four men, one woman and two children killed. A further four men, two women and one child seriously injured. Forty people sustained less serious injuries. None of this affected the assassin. It was plain clothes policemen, already stationed at the rear of the building, who caught him emerging, and cut him to pieces with their carbines.

It later transpired that the original victim, whose killing had triggered off the massacre, was not the general at all, but one of his aides. The General, who had been travelling in the second car, without a pennant, was unhurt, and later completed the opening ceremony.

On the morning after the shooting, Martin was summoned to the Seguridad building in the Avenue Diaz. He went to that place of evil reputation with a fairly easy conscience. It was six months since the episode on the river Mora, and since then he had led a quiet life, working mostly in the company office and spending very little time on location.

He gave his name to the sergeant on duty in the reception hall, and after some telephoning was conducted along dim corridors and down uncarpeted steps.

'What happens down here?' he asked. His guide seemed not to understand him.

They stopped at last outside a heavy door, with no handle but with a small window of glass set in the centre. His guide peered through it for a moment, then he put his shoulder to it, and it swung heavily open. He motioned to Martin to enter.

The room was a large one, lit by unwinking fluorescent light. On six slabs lay six bodies, all naked, and all with the signs on them of the violence that had killed them.

Colonel Cristobal Ocampos was standing in the middle of the room. He looked up as Martin came in.

'Over here, Mr Field.'

The body lying on the slab was long and thin. The parts which had not been smashed by the bullets looked sun-burned and healthy. The hair was light, almost white. The face, which was unmarked, was still serene.

'Do you recognise him?'

'Yes.' Martin knew that he was going to be sick. It was not the sights. It was the smell; warm, sweet, fetid, heavy with corruption.

'You're sure you recognise him?'

'Certain. Can I go, please?'

The colonel said, 'You shall come with me to my office.'

By the time they got there, Martin had recovered himself a little. He said, 'Were those others the people who were killed in the Plaza yesterday?'

'Some of them,' said the colonel. He had got his cigar out, and was waving a lighted match carefully under the end of it.

'And the long man?'

'He was the assassin. Yes. The man who tried to shoot the General and succeeded only in killing poor Major Villansanti. You recognised him?'

'I saw him once only, for a few seconds, by moonlight, six months ago. But I could not be mistaken. It is a remarkable face. You told me his name, but I have forgotten it.'

'Rafael Asilvera.' Colonel Ocampos intoned the name slowly. It sounded like a private prayer. 'He was a most remarkable man. A professional assassin. A perfect shot with any weapon. He could also use a knife, and could kill with his hands. He was the man who shot President Perez, at the iron mines up at Tequila, and escaped. He placed the bomb which destroyed Pedro Gimenez in Brazilia, two years ago. He cut the throat of Dr Alvarenga, the man they called the "physician of death". Asilvera cut it, with the doctor's own lancet, in his own surgery, and left the house undetected. He was the man who wounded, and nearly killed, our General's predecessor.'

'And he came here, into this country, with the object of killing the General?'

'That was his next commission. Six months he lay here in hiding. I told you he was a professional. But we have learned to be professionals, too, Mr Field. From the moment we knew that he had escaped our net and was inside the country, the General was placed under a special routine. No announcements were made of his public engagements. If he attended a banquet, every guest and every waiter was screened. The platform from which he normally spoke to the Assembly was moved, so that no window commanded it. When he travelled abroad, one of his aides travelled in the official car. He himself travelled in the second or third car. It was a game of cat and mouse.

'In the end, we allowed the news to leak out to Asilvera's employers that the General would be opening the Co-operative Building. We guessed that Asilvera would use a rifle. It is his favourite weapon. We had our men *behind* every building in the Square.'

'And eight people died?'

'Agreed,' said the colonel. 'And if you had told me ten minutes earlier, on that occasion, six months ago, that you had seen Asilvera, we should have caught him then and no-one would have died – except Asilvera.'

'So the whole thing's my fault?'

'We must be fair,' said the colonel. 'You were under strain.' He looked approvingly at the end of his cigar. He said, 'I have often wondered if you had the least idea of what was going on that night. Have you ever considered, for instance, who dug that grave, and for whom?'

'No.'

'Then I will tell you. It was dug by the contrabandists, under the orders of the lady who now lies buried in it. And it was dug, Mr Field, for *you*.'

Martin stared at him.

The colonel said, 'You were an unforeseen, last-minute obstruction to a very carefully worked out plan. Let me explain. Our frontiers are, for the most part, easy to watch. Particularly for such a remarkable, unforgettable, man as Rafael Asilvera. The operation of smuggling him in needed meticulous planning and timing. It was arranged with the contrabandists. They knew the risks. They stipulated payment in minted silver dollars, with six crates of best Scotch whisky thrown in for good measure. Their part was to ferry Asilvera across the Mora and conduct him to a car on the hill road. The empty palanquin they brought with them was to carry back their reward. At the last moment, when all was ready, what happens? A suspicious-looking foreigner places his tents across the very path they are going to use.

'Well, they are simple men. They thought of a simple remedy. Cut his throat, and bury him. His mestizos will run away, too terrified to speak. Your equipment would have been rolled down into the river. No-one had seen you arrive. So no-one would raise the alarm if you disappeared. Or not until it was much too late for the mystery to be solved. It was a very practical solution.'

'Why didn't they do it?'

'Ah, that was Major Patino. He is a clever little man. He had got wind that something was afoot. He rode over, quite openly, to your camp. His actions announced to all concerned that he knew you were there. That saved your life. So another scheme had to be thought of. If you could not be killed, you might be bought.'

'Bought?'

'Not all purchases, Mr Field, are made with money. Some are made by the employment of imagination. By the use of the magic that lies behind a woman's eyes.'

'Do you mean to tell me that her story – the whole thing – was made up?'

'Since I was not privileged to be there, I do not know precisely what story she told you. But certain things you said suggested parts of it. Doctor Ignacio de Jara, for instance, is not her father, and was in moderately good health when I spoke to him last. Nor has any attempt, successful or otherwise, been made to rescue him.'

Martin was still thinking about the girl. He said, 'Who was she?'

'Her name was Marciana Santacruz. She was of the revolutionary party, and high in its councils. If, as I imagine, she painted you a moving picture of the sufferings of the aged Dr Ignacio in prison, she would be well equipped to do so. She has been in prison three times herself, on the first occasion at the age of 15.'

'If this is true,' said Martin slowly, 'if everything you are telling me is fact, and every word she spoke was a lie, you still had no right to shoot her. Asilvera was already in the country. It was too late to stop that.'

'But we did not know it. We imagined that what was going down to the river was a reception committee.'

'But to shoot! Without stopping to question. In cold blood. It was—' Martin stumbled for words. In the end he said, lamely, 'It was completely unjustified.'

'Since you have pronounced it unjustified,' said the colonel, 'I will not attempt to justify it. I will say only this. The General has ruled us now for nearly 20 years. His rule does not appeal to everyone. But it is a great deal better than anarchy. While he rules, it is my job to keep him alive.

'In a country like England, where you have had political stability for 300 years, you may tend to undervalue it. You had your Civil War. A gentlemanly affair of Roundheads and Cavaliers. I have read of it. But have *you* heard of the War of the Triple Alliance, which ravaged this country not so long ago? I thought not. It is not included in the history books of your schools.

'Let me tell you a single fact. At the start of the war, the population of our country was more than half a million. At the finish it was less than a quarter of a million. And of those left alive, only 28,000 were men. That is what anarchy and civil war mean in a country like this. That is why many people are in prison today who would not have been imprisoned in your country, and why people have been killed who might still be alive. And if the same situation arose again tomorrow, I would act in the same way.'

The colonel knocked the ash off his cigar, and added, 'That is enough of lecturing. Goodbye, Mr Field.'

It was not until a long time afterwards that it dawned on Martin Field that he had met a remarkable man.

BASILIO

SERGEANT TORRERO, WHO was in charge of the in-lying picquet at the San Stefano Military Academy, made his final rounds at five o'clock in the morning.

The two previous rounds, at midnight and at three o'clock, had encompassed the buildings and courtyards. On this occasion, he and his four-man escort made a detour around the inside of the walls which surrounded the sports ground.

A single light showed from one of the small rooms at the back of the pavilion. It was instinct which sent the Sergeant's hand to the butt of his revolver before he kicked open the door. He stood staring into the room for a long moment. He was a veteran of the wars of the Liberation. When he turned round at last his face, seamed and scarred like a stump of old oak, betrayed no hint of his feelings. He said, indicating each member of the patrol in turn, 'You will stay here, outside the door. Allow no one to enter. You will fetch the Commandante. You two will come back with me to the guard-room. At the double.'

The telephone buzzed softly in the office of Colonel Cristobal Ocampos, in the Seguridad building, on the Avenue Diaz. Ocampos, who appeared to be expecting the call, put down the file he was studying, picked up the receiver and said 'Ocampos here. Cardozo? Yes. Where are you speaking from?'

'The guard-room. The telephone is an outside line. It is not connected with the Academy exchange.'

'Excellent. Proceed.'

'The boy has been identified. He was Basilio de Casal. A first year cadet at the Academy.'

'And it was suicide?'

'Our first conclusion was that it could have been suicide. He would appear to have hanged himself by climbing on to a pile of benches, and jumping from the top. The rope he used came from a longer piece, in the corner of the shed.'

'Your *first* conclusion.'

'Then I noticed blood on the boy's shirt, at the back—'

Lieutenant Cardozo continued to speak for nearly two minutes. At the end of it, Ocampos said, 'So then the Commandante arrived. What is his name? General Ramirez. Yes, I know him. And he warned you off, eh?'

'He took charge of the matter.'

'We can be frank with each other, Lieutenant. Did the General order you to stop your investigation?'

'In effect, yes.'

'Did he give any reason?'

'He said that it was clearly suicide. The matter would be fully looked into, by the Police of the Military District.'

'Who could be trusted to act discreetly.'

'That was the impression I obtained. You know that there have been other – incidents at the Academy.'

'Yes,' said the Colonel. 'You say that you are in the guard-room. Who is the Sergeant in charge?'

'His name is Torrero. He seems to be a good man.'

'Where is General Ramirez?'

'Still down at the pavilion, I imagine. There are quite a few men there now. The doctor has come, and there is a Colonel Villagra, of the Military District who seems to be in charge—'

Ocampos was not listening. He said, 'Never mind that. Ask Sergeant Torrero to take you to Cadet de Casal's room.'

'To his room?'

'He will know where it is. Get there quickly and examine it. If you find anything of interest, bring it back here with you.'

'I don't think General Ramirez will like it.'

'The quicker you move,' said Ocampos smoothly, 'the less likely General Ramirez is to know anything about it.'

He rang off, and resumed his study of the file. It was a fat file, labelled 'Siriola'. It had three red stars pasted on its cover.

He was still reading an hour later, when Lieutenant Cardozo was shown in. He was a good-looking young man, with thick black hair and a nose which had an attractive bend in it, the result of a difference of opinion with a drunken *mestizo* during his recruit service.

'How I wish,' said Ocampos, closing the file, 'that we had here a Smersh.'

'A Smersh?'

'You have not heard of the Smersh? It is a famous Russian organisation. It removes traitors who have taken refuge in other countries. Think how useful such an organisation would be to us, if only a poor country like this could afford it. What luxury! How easily it would dispose of our problems. I would summon the Chief of Smersh to my office and I would say to him, "Proceed to such and such a neighbouring country and dispose of General Siriola." And poof!' Ocampos blew a cloud of cigar smoke towards the ceiling. 'No more Siriola. Please be seated, Lieutenant. You were up early. You have had a tiring morning.'

'I managed to get into his room—'

'What is our major problem? It is that we are a small country. We are surrounded, on all sides, by larger countries, hostile to us. So, when he is unmasked, what does a traitor like General Siriola do? He simply drives to one or other of our frontiers. How can poor ignorant soldiers be blamed for not stopping him – a General, in full uniform, flying a flag on the front of his car? He crosses the bridge. He is among our enemies who are, automatically, his friends. But I am interrupting you, Lieutenant.'

'I have here with me—' Cardozo indicated the bulging briefcase.

'Your worms.'

Cardozo looked baffled.

'It is a saying. The early bird catches the worm. You were at the vital point before General Ramirez. You have been rewarded.'

As he spoke Ocampos was plucking out the contents of the briefcase, one by one, and laying them out on his desk, a fat blackbird, picking worms from the lawn.

A white linen robe. A red-covered exercise book with the words 'Field Fortification' written, in purple ink, on the cover. Then half a dozen books, none of them new. Finally, a framed photograph.

'There were other things, of course,' said Cardozo. 'Many other things. Text books of military science, uniforms, under-clothes, personal belongings, of the sort one would expect to find in the room of a cadet.'

'Yes,' said Ocampos. He was examining the books. 'Then why did you select these books in particular?'

'They were not in the shelves with the other books. They were in a cupboard, at the back. Almost, one might say, hidden.'

Ocampos was examining the most battered of the books. It had no front cover or fly-leaf, but the title could still be read, in faded golden lettering along the spine – '*Galizische Geschichten*.'

'Do you speak German?'

'No, Colonel. What does it mean?'

'It means, "Tales from Galicia". It has the date of publication here – see? MDCCCLXXVI.'

'That I *can* translate,' said Cardozo with a smile. '1876, is it not?'

'Correct. Since it has only the one date, it could be a first edition. If it were not in such a deplorable state, it might be valuable.' He was opening the other books as he spoke. Four of them were medical text-books, also in German. The sixth, and last, was in Spanish, and was entitled, 'The Lives of the Martyrs'.

'A curious soldier, young Basilio,' said Ocampos. He opened the red-covered notebook.

'I happened to glance inside it,' said Cardozo. 'It did not appear to be concerned with Field Fortification, or, indeed, with any other branch of military science. It had more the appearance of a private diary, or memorandum book. Did I do rightly to take it?'

'Who can tell?' said the Colonel. He walked across to the big safe, spun the dials, opened it, and placed the book inside. 'Who can tell? Scraps of paper, they can be the most important things in the world. A scrap of paper sent Captain Dreyfus to Devil's Island. Another scrap of paper brought him out again.'

He shut the safe, and returned to the table.

'And this photograph?' It was a framed enlargement of an informal snapshot. It showed a big handsome young man with an arrogant beak of a nose, and rather full lips. He was dressed in riding kit, with polished boots and spurs, and had a riding switch tucked under one arm. 'Why, particularly, did you bring this to me?'

Lieutenant Cardozo said, the embarrassment evident in his voice, 'I recognised it. I thought—'

'You thought – yes?'

'It is the Leader's son, Juvenal Valdez, is it not?'

'Correct. Juvenal is a cadet at the College. In his third year. No doubt he is a friend of Basilio's. Did you find the idea surprising?'

Ocampos was grinning at his Lieutenant's discomfort.

'Basilio de Casal, they told me, came from a poor family. Moreover, it is a Febrerista family. His father was arrested during the Troubles when our Leader came to power. He was kept for some months under house arrest. I believe.'

'Your information is accurate. But youth pays little attention to wealth or politics. The boys could have been friends. However—'

The Colonel re-opened the safe, and put the photograph in beside the red-covered notebook.

It was two hours later and Colonel Ocampos is drinking a cup of coffee, his third of the day, when Colonel Villagra of the Military District Police was shown in. The men being of equal rank, neither wasted effort on ceremony. Ocampos waved Villagra towards a chair. Villagra ignored the gesture, put his broad bottom on the edge of the table, and said. 'I am told that one of your men, Lieutenant Cardozo, visited the room of Cadet de Casal this morning and removed certain items of his property.'

'Indeed?'

'No doubt he was under the impression that he was doing his duty, but I must point out that General Ramirez has entrusted me with the conduct of this case.'

'What case?'

'The case of Cadet de Casal. You are surely aware that he hanged himself last night.'

'I was aware that his body was found suspended from a hook, in a shed behind the sports pavilion. Does that constitute a case? And if so, against whom? Or is it intended that there should be some process against this cadet for the crime of committing suicide?'

'You know very well that a matter like this must be investigated. Particularly since there have been other incidents.'

'Two other incidents. Three years ago Cadet Ruffio was shot in the armoury. A Court of Inquiry decided that it was an accident. Twelve months ago Cadet Under-Officer Perez, a very promising young man, jumped from the roof of the drill hall, fell sixty feet and broke his neck. There was a suggestion, I believe, that he might have been engaged in some sky-larking escapade. Incidentally, *how* long ago did General Ramirez assume control of the College? Three years ago, was it? Or four? Time goes so fast.'

'Your remarks,' said Colonel Villagra, his face distorted with anger, 'shall be transmitted to General Ramirez. He may see fit to overlook your innuendoes; or he may not.'

'Innuendoes? You are imagining things: I was pointing out that General Ramirez must naturally investigate every – episode –which occurs under his jurisdiction. Particularly as there have been such a number of them.'

'Very well, then. And since I have been charged with this investiga-tion—'

'I am sure you will carry it out very thoroughly. For instance, you will no doubt come to some decision on the question of whether Cadet de Casal was flogged before or after he was hanged.'

Colonel Villagra said, in a choked voice, 'Who told you – this story?'

'One of my subordinates, Lieutenant Cardozo. He happens to live near the College. When the Sergeant of the Guard telephoned me I alerted him. Thus he was the first on the scene. He noticed some blood on the back of the boy's shirt, and was interested enough to remove the shirt. The weals were very plain. He had been savagely flogged. Incidentally' – Ocampos deposited an inch of ash from his cigar on to the onyx ashtray on his desk – 'the Sergeant and the members of the guard *all* saw the marks.'

Colonel Villagra said, 'Why did he report this to you, and not to me?'

'Two reasons, I imagine. First, because he is my subordinate, and would naturally report to me. Second, because I am in charge of the investigation.'

'Possibly you did not hear me. I told you that General Ramirez had specifically placed me in charge.'

'Do I gather that General Ramirez is questioning the direct order of our Leader?'

'The direct—?'

'Given to me, personally, an hour ago. If you would like to confirm it, my telephone is at your disposal. The red one has a direct line to the Chancellery.'

'I will tell General Ramirez,' said Colonel Villagra in a stifled voice.

'I'm afraid he was angry with me,' said Ocampos to Lieutenant Cardozo ten minutes later. 'General Ramirez will be angry, too. It is a mistake to get angry, particularly at this hot and humid season. It engorges the arteries, and places a strain on the heart.' He considered whether he would light another cigar, and rejected the idea.

'What shall we do now?'

'We have been charged with this investigation. We shall proceed with it. *You* will proceed with it. You will go down to the College and question all concerned. By now General Ramirez will have received confirmation of our Leader's edict, and you will find that you will receive co-operation. It will be a considerable task. You may take what assistance you wish. Two Sergeants, half a dozen men. Shorthand writers. I leave the details to you with every confidence, Lieutenant.'

'I will do my best.'

'I'm sure you will. And, by the way, a suggestion. You should certainly have a word with the boy's term officer. A Captain Hernandez. I believe he has a reputation as a disciplinarian. A very strict disciplinarian.'

It was the custom of Dr Chavez, the benign and be-spectacled editor of the *Corriera Nationale*, personally to sign his more provocative editorials. Some were so provocative that simple-minded readers wondered why the Doctor was not arrested. The more cynical suggested that there was a private telephone line between his office and the Chancellery. Certainly some of his guesses had proved inspired. The *Corriera*, for instance, had been the first and only newspaper to attack General Siriola for misappropriating foreign relief funds, and that was three weeks before the General's hurried departure to a neighbouring state.

Three days after the discovery of Basilio's body, a signed editorial appeared under banner headlines.

Academia De Tragedias

'The discovery, three days ago, of the body of Cadet Basilio de Casal, a young first-year student at the San Stefano Military Academy, hanging in an out-house behind the sports pavilion, has raised in many people's minds serious questions of the administration and discipline at this important national institution. People will surely not have forgotten—'

And in case they had forgotten, Dr Chavez reminded them, in a succession of pungent paragraphs, of the deaths of Cadet Ruffio and Cadet Under-Officer Perez.

'Where a hundred high-spirited young men are congregated together no one need be surprised at an occasional mishap. But three unexplained deaths in less than three years seems to us to be too many. There are two possible explanations. Either the discipline and supervision is too lax, permitting horse-play, bullying and excesses of this sort. Or, as seems more probable, it is too strict. Young officers must be taught the value of military discipline, but to enforce it in a barbaric manner, upon their own bodies, does not seem to us to be a course likely to benefit either the recipients of punishment or its enforcers. Cadets are slow to talk about such matters. Loyalty often blocks criticism. Nevertheless, certain stories are in circulation which are too circumstantial and too often repeated to be completely dismissed. Is it, for instance, a coincidence that all three cadets were in the Squadra commanded by Captain Hernandez? Or that Captain Hernandez should be known to his squadristas – jokingly, no doubt – as the "Slave-driver"—'

Dr Chavez did not think it a coincidence, and did not scruple to say so, on that day and in the days following. Interviews were obtained with members of the staff. Letters were printed from anxious parents of cadets. The name of Captain Hernandez featured in most of them. His background was investigated by Dr Chavez's reporters and the results of their researches were set out in many columns of print. He came of an aristocratic family, linked by direct descent from the Conquistadores, slave owners and autocrats. His father had fought in the War of Liberation and had been a notorious disciplinarian. Photographs of Captain Hernandez appeared in the papers, grim and unsmiling, a slash of black moustache across a tight-lipped mouth.

It was at the end of the first week that the barrage lifted on to a higher target. Doctor Chavez treated his readers to a further signed editorial and a headline in Latin.

'*Quis custodiet ipsos custodes?*'

On the assumption that most of his readers would have neglected their classical studies, this was followed by a translation.

'*Who controls the controllers?*'

'If, as has been widely suggested,' the editorial began, 'there exists in the Military Academy a system of private discipline which differs little from sadistic bullying, must one not cast a critical eye at the head of that institution—'

Ocampos, who got advance copies of all newspapers, read this with his first cup of coffee and smiled. He said to Lieutenant Cardozo, 'I don't think General Ramirez will like this, do you?'

'I'm afraid he won't.'

'How is your investigation proceeding?'

'It would be simpler if it were the only investigation.'

'Explain.'

'I am not being obstructed, you understand. I have been allowed free access to witnesses. As far as I know they have answered my questions frankly. But the fact that I – that we – are investigating the matter has not stopped General Ramirez from continuing a private investigation of his own. We are using our own officers. He is using the resources of the Military Police. It might be described as an investigation in parallel.'

Ocampos considered the matter in silence for some minutes, drawing evenly on his cigar and watching the blue smoke climb into a curtain over his head.

He said, 'Parallel lines never meet. I was taught that at school. Or rather, they meet only at infinity, which is an inconclusive destination. The problem then is, which of you will arrive at the truth first? Tell me frankly, what progress have you made so far?'

'You ask me to speak frankly, I will do so. Very little.'

'I see.'

'A number of cadets visited Basilio in his room that night, at different times, up to nine o'clock. I have spoken to all of them, and all agree on one point. They say that Basilio was undoubtedly worried.'

'Worried about what?'

'It was assumed that he was in some trouble with Captain Hernandez.'

'Why?'

'It was the most usual reason for a cadet of that Squadra looking worried.'

'Tell me, Lieutenant. In talking to these cadets, did you get an impression of what sort of person Basilio was?'

'Reserved, to the point almost of unapproachability. Extremely law-abiding – no one could recollect that he had ever been guilty of the least breach of discipline. Religious in an austere way which is uncommon in these laxer times.'

'And did it not strike you as a curious contradiction?'

'A contradiction?'

'The estimate you have just given me of Basilio's character. And the fact that, on that one evening, a number of different cadets should have dropped in to his room to talk to him. A perfectly normal proceeding, I agree, *if* he had been a popular, easy-going, social-minded youth. But not so easy to explain if he was the latter-day saint you depict.'

Lieutenant Cardozo considered the matter, and then said, with a smile, 'One must remember that he was very good-looking.'

'True,' said Ocampos. 'Much is forgiven to those whom providence has endowed with good looks. Proceed.'

'One of the servants who visited Basilio's room on some errand at about ten o'clock found it empty. When he went back at half-past ten it was still empty.'

'And was Captain Hernandez in the building at this time?'

'Yes. He was working late that night.'

'Was this usual?'

'Quite usual. In term time, when he was busy, he slept more in the Academy than in his flat outside.'

'One assumption is that Basilio visited Captain Hernandez that evening? That something – untoward – occurred? And that the hanging was an effort to cover it up?'

'Those are certainly assumptions.'

'But you have no actual proof?'

'No.'

'And we cannot move without proof?'

'It would be difficult.'

'Difficult,' agreed Ocampos. 'But, so far as our opponents are concerned, not impossible, apparently. Or have they, perhaps, discovered some vital facts which have escaped our notice?'

Cardozo stared at him.

'Just before you arrived, I learned that General Ramirez had ordered the arrest of Captain Hernandez.'

'On what charge?'

'The charge is causing the death of Cadet Basilio, in the course of unauthorised disciplinary proceedings.'

'But—'

'Let us restrain our impatience. I have no doubt we shall read all about it in the *Corriera* tomorrow.'

And not only the *Corriera* on the next day, but all the newspapers of the Capital, for many days, spread themselves on this exciting topic; the background of the accused and of his supposed victim; the constitution of the military tribunal which had been summoned with exemplary speed; the zeal of General Ramirez in seeking out the truth and the earnest desire of their Leader that justice should not only be done but be seen to be done.

During the whole of this time Colonel Cristobal Ocampos hardly left his office. Insofar as he interested himself in the case at all he seemed to be concentrating his attention on the red-covered exercise book which was locked away in his safe labelled in purple ink, 'Field Fortification'. Each of the scribbled names, addresses and telephone numbers had been typed out, by the Colonel's own podgy fingers on to a file card, and each card accumulated, as the days went by, a series of further annotations in the Colonel's sprawling handwriting. On the evening of the seventh day, he sent once more for Lieutenant Cardozo.

The Lieutenant received his orders with evident surprise. He said, 'Certainly I will do it. But I was under the impression—'

He paused.

'Under what impression, Lieutenant?'

'I had imagined that, in effect, the conduct of this case had passed out of our hands. That it was being conducted by General Ramirez.'

'Now I wonder why you should think that,' said Ocampos sleepily. 'True, that I have made no positive move in the matter over the past week. But that was because I could not see that any actual move was called for. You appeared to me to have made all the necessary preliminary investigations in a thorough and painstaking manner—' The Colonel tapped the bulky folder on his desk. 'However, on re-reading your reports I did note one omission. You would not appear to have interrogated Cadet Juvenal Valdez. Why was that?'

The Lieutenant shifted uncomfortably.

'Particularly, Lieutenant, when we have evidence that he was a friend of Basilio's. Had he not a photograph of Juvenal on his mantelshelf?'

'Juvenal Valdez, being our Leader's son, was a popular figure in the Academy. Many Cadets had such a photograph.'

'And were all these photographs personally inscribed to their recipients, in christian name terms?'

'Well – no.'

'I think, Lieutenant, that you had better have a word with this young man, and the sooner the better. In fact, immediately.'

*

It was the veteran Sergeant Torrero who accompanied Lieutenant Cardozo across the gravelled acres of the parade ground, past the old-fashioned cannon with its perimeter of neatly piled shot, up an echoing flight of stone stairs, along a bare corridor. The Military Academy by night was a place of silence, deep shadows and sharp lights.

'It's not very homely,' he said.

'Soldiers must learn to live without luxury,' said the Sergeant. He knocked at a door at the end of the corridor, opened it and stood aside for the Lieutenant to go in.

Juvenal Valdez was seated in a wicker chair in front of the fire, his slippered feet stretched out to the blaze. He waved a friendly hand, and said, 'Come along in, Lieutenant. Sit down. If I'm to be grilled, I insist on being grilled in comfort.'

He was a thickly built, well-muscled young man with the shoulders of a boxer, and a black-haired handsome face which he must have derived, the Lieutenant concluded, from his mother, Juanita. It had little in common with the thin bloodless look of his father, except possibly for the eyes, which had a certain shrewdness behind the curtain of their candour.

'I have no intention of grilling you,' said the Lieutenant, trying to keep the respect out of his voice. 'But I thought – we thought – that you might be able to help us on a few points—'

'Does one gather that Colonel Ocampos is hunting a different line from our respected Commandante?'

The directness of the question took the Lieutenant by surprise. He said, 'Well—'

'No need to answer if it embarrasses you. Speaking personally, I think General Ramirez is after the wrong fox.'

'You do! Who then should he be chasing?'

'It's a difficult question. To answer it, you would have to know something of Academy politics and personalities. Ramirez is an old-style fascist aristocrat. He does not approve of my father's policy of allowing young men to come to this College on a basis of ability only, without regard to family background. In his view our army should be officered by gentlemen and by the sons of gentlemen.'

'And you do not agree?'

'I wasn't giving you *my* ideas. They are the ideas of my father.'

'And as such, entitled to all respect.'

'Within these four walls, Lieutenant, and in the confidence that it will not be repeated, I will tell you something. My father is not the Pope. He is not infallible. Nevertheless, on this point I think he is right. Our country has not enough gentlemen of appropriate military talent to officer its army. But you can appreciate that a boy like Basilio, son of an impoverished family – and a Febrerista family into the bargain – would hardly appeal to our Commandante.'

'I understand that. Yes.'

'And that was why poor Basilio' – there was a glint in Juvenal's eyes as he said it – 'had to walk so circumspectly. Indeed, it was a narrow and thorny path he trod with unshod feet. A path which led through torment to destruction.'

'At the hands of whom?'

The walls of the College were so thick, the silence was so complete, that they might have been isolated in a capsule in space.

'It is not difficult to guess,' said Juvenal at last. The words seemed to be forced out of him by an inner pressure he was unable to resist. 'If not by General Ramirez himself, then by his creatures. The Military Police. It would need only the lightest pretext—'

'Such as—'

'A hint from above that Basilio was engaged in treasonable activities. Rigorous questioning. A faked suicide to conceal the truth.'

'And you do not think that Captain Hernandez had anything to do with it?'

Juvenal laughed. It was a sudden, harsh bray of laughter. 'Hernandez! Of course not. He is a disciplinarian certainly. But not a sadist. Besides, though he might conceivably have beaten him, how could he, single-handed, have arranged the so-called suicide?'

'No doubt the prosecution will have a theory, and witnesses to support it.'

'Certainly they will have witnesses. All of them Villagra's policemen. They will tell a most convincing story. One of them will have seen Basilio going to Captain Hernandez' room. Another will have heard screams. A third will have noticed Captain Hernandez driving his car in the direction of the pavilion. After all, they have two successful precedents. Why should they not follow them? You have read the accounts of the Ruffio and Perez cases.'

'Yes,' said the Lieutenant. 'I have read the accounts.'

He left Juvenal Valdez's room a badly disturbed man. He was pondering deeply on what he had learned. He was still pondering when he realised that he was being followed.

It was the tink of a steel-capped boot against stone. He swung round, but could see nothing. Or was there a darker shadow in the shadows behind the floodlights?

Cardozo hesitated for a moment, then he swung round, and started to walk fast across the great open parade ground. He heard nothing. The sound of his own footsteps crunching on the gravel effectively blocked out other sounds. It was instinct which made him turn his head. Three men were coming after him, and coming fast.

He had a gun, but it was in a shoulder holster, inside his belted top coat. Before he could reach it, his pursuers would be on top of him.

He took to his heels.

The difficulty was that he had no very clear idea where the main gate lay. The parade ground stretched ahead unhelpfully in the darkness.

A building loomed. At the last moment Cardozo realised that it was the sports pavilion, the very one behind which Basilio had been found. He had come too far to the right. But it gave him his bearings. He had only to swing left, on the path behind the pavilion, and it would bring him to the main gate and the guard house.

As his feet touched the path, he realised something else. The men behind him, appreciating his blunder, had spread out on each side and one of them had already reached the path to his left.

He changed his plan, stopped in his tracks, and swung round.

The man behind him was so close, and coming so fast, that he could not conform to the move. As he went past, Cardozo thrust out a foot, and saw his pursuer go sprawling. Then he was racing for the pavilion.

The third man, who had moved out to the right, was waiting for him in the shadow of the building, crouched low, head forward, arms hanging. A professional fighter.

Cardozo ran straight at him. Then, at the very last moment, swerved to one side and sprinted up the pavilion steps.

At the top of the steps there was a broad railing. He put one hand on it, vaulted it and landed, in the comfortable darkness, among a pile of benches.

He had gained the time he needed.

As the dark shape of his pursuer loomed at the foot of the steps, he fired once, aiming carefully above his head. The crack of the shot split open the quietness of the night.

Cardozo smiled happily. He had his back to a solid building. He had seven more shots in his police automatic, and a spare magazine in his pocket. He was quite prepared, if necessary, to wait for daylight.

It did not prove necessary. Five minutes later, Sergeant Torrero, who had come with the picquet to investigate the sound of the shot, accompanied him back to the gate.

At the Seguridad building he found Colonel Ocampos, still engrossed in his study of the red-covered exercise book. He had just deciphered a further name in it. It was in pencil scribble on the inside of the cover, so faint that it looked as though someone had written it and then changed his mind and tried to rub it out. At first sight it had looked like 'Gonzalez'. But careful work with a magnifying glass, under oblique light, had clarified the first few letters. It was Benitez. And the letter in front of it was a capital 'A'.

'Andrea Benitez,' said Ocampos. He said it aloud as Lieutenant Cardozo came into the room. The discovery had excited him. It excited him more than the Lieutenant's story, which seemed only to amuse him.

'They chased you out, did they,' he said. 'It was to be expected. They're very sensitive about poaching on their preserves.'

'It wasn't at all funny,' said Cardozo. 'Or it wouldn't have been, if they'd caught me.'

'You should wear your gun where you can get at it,' said Ocampos unsympathetically. 'Now, to something important. Andrea Benitez. We have a file on him. A silly little man who tried to stir up trouble in the University. He cooled his heels in prison for a few months last year. He's free now. He lives in a block of municipal flats near the airport. The address is in the file. Bring him in.'

'Tonight?'

Ocampos looked at his watch. It was five minutes to midnight.

'Well, first thing tomorrow,' he said grudgingly.

After breakfast on the following day Cadet Under-Officer Juvenal Valdez obtained permission to leave the Academy and drove his neat and inconspicuous American car to the private parking lot at the back of the Chancellory building, where he left it in charge of the one-armed parking attendant, walked through the private entrance, where the door was held open for him by a doorman who had lost most of his face, and took the lift, which went only to the sixth floor, and was operated by a man who perched all day on a stool, because he had only half a leg. All three men were veterans of the War of the Liberation and owed their jobs to this fact.

Juvenal entered an unmarked door at the end of the corridor.

General Rafael Valdez, Chancellor, Minister of Defence, and Leader of his country, was not, at first sight, an impressive figure. He was six inches shorter than his son, a lack of inches which was emphasised by a stoop which brought his shoulders forward, and showed you the top of his head with its yellowish skin and thinning hair. For some years now he had abandoned the habit of wearing uniform, and although the suit which he wore had been cut in London, and fitted him accordingly, it was hardly the expected garb of a South American dictator.

Yet he was formidable. In spite of the greyness and neutrality of his appearance, he seemed to sound a warning. Partly it was in his eyes, partly in the way he held himself. Some of it was in his voice when he spoke.

He greeted his son formally. They shook hands. They settled themselves at a table, in the big bay window, the son holding the chair for his father to be seated before sitting himself.

'Well?' said Valdez.

'I wish that all *were* well, but it is not,' said Juvenal.

He continued for some minutes. Then his father said, speaking slowly, and dispassionately, as a judge might have done, summing up a case which interested but did not concern him, 'So. Your thesis is that my old friend and comrade in arms, General Ramirez, is plotting against me. That he is in touch with that other old comrade of mine, General Siriola, now resident abroad. The plotters, you suggest, come chiefly from the establishment of the Military District Police, under Colonel Villagra – I cannot, for the moment, recall him.'

'You would not know him. Until recently he was a Captain. He has been promoted rapidly under the influence of General Ramirez.'

'Villagra. But yes. I do remember a man of that name. Large, red faced, and with somewhat prominent side teeth – tusks, almost.'

Juvenal smiled. 'Your memory for faces is infallible.'

'Then, you tell me that these plotters have tried to involve you?'

'More than simply involve me,' said Juvenal indifferently. 'They wished me to lead the coup. I was to take your place as head of the State. I should, of course, have been a puppet only.'

'And that was why you refused?'

'I admit an ambition to succeed you,' said Juvenal with a smile. 'But not to replace you.'

'I wonder if you are wise,' said Valdez. 'It is a position with few attractions and many headaches. Was the approach made to you direct?'

'No. They used this boy, Basilio, as a go-between. They knew that he was a particular friend of mine. Possibly, since his father is of the Febrerista party, they considered that he might be on their side. If so, they misjudged him.'

'And having taken him too far into their confidence, and found him loyal, they first flogged him, and then hanged him.'

'Yes.'

'One might conclude, perhaps, that they made similar approaches – and similar mistakes – with the other two cadets, Ruffio and Perez.'

'I think that is a fair assumption.'

'But you have no proof of it.'

'I have no proof at all.'

'Then what do you suggest that we can do?'

Juvenal looked at his father. There were times when he understood him and liked him. Other times when he did not understand him, and feared him.

He said, 'If you do nothing, you realise that this conspiracy may grow.'

'A fish should not be caught until it has attained a certain size.'

'You realise too that injustice will be done. An innocent man will be condemned and shot.'

'Captain Hernandez?'

'Yes.'

'Thin, dark, with a rather large dark moustache?'

'That's the man.'

'And you are certain that he had no hand in this boy's death?'

'Oh, quite certain.'

He said this with such emphasis that his father looked up for a fleeting second, seeing in the big proud young man in front of him a startling reflection of the passionate girl he had married twenty-five years before.

Juvenal became conscious of his father's gaze. He shifted uncomfortably and repeated, 'Quite certain. It would be entirely out of character.'

'Are you telling me all this for my own protection? Or because you respect Captain Hernandez and wish to prevent an injustice? Or because you were fond of Basilio, and desire to avenge his death?'

'Something of all three.'

'Yes. I see.'

His father got up, stepped to the window, and stood staring down at the traffic crawling round the Piazza. He stood so, for a long time, in silence. Then he said, 'When no effective course of action suggests itself, it is better to do nothing. Sometimes a small injustice will result. Sometimes something will happen to prevent it.'

Juvenal realised that the interview was over, and departed by the way he had come.

After he had driven off, the legless liftman said to the faceless doorman, 'He has his father's temper.'

That was on the Friday.

The military tribunal to try Captain Hernandez was convoked for the following Wednesday. On the intervening Sunday Father Domenico Perez, Superior of the Jesuit Order of Our Lady at Quyquyho, preached to a crowded congregation in the Cathedral Church of the Asuncion.

What he said was reported, under banner headlines, in every newspaper in the Capital, for Father Perez was a nationally respected figure, a man of iron integrity and proven courage.

'If the trial of Captain Hernandez proceeds,' he was reported as saying, 'for a crime which his accusers well know that he is innocent, I shall deem it my duty to offer evidence at the hearing. To do so will involve breaking the sacred seal of the confessional. In order to prevent injustice and save an innocent life I should not hesitate to do even that.'

The newspapers then pointed out that Basilio's family came from the neighbourhood of Quyquyho, and that it was reasonable to assume that Father Perez had been the dead boy's confessor.

So great was the excitement over this unexpected development that a number of lesser occurrences escaped notice. A retired Major living alone took his dog for a walk that Sunday night. The dog returned, but the Major did not. On the Monday morning a junior official in the Ministry of the Interior failed to arrive at his office; and an employee at the airport, called Andrea Benitez, did not report for duty.

To Lieutenant Cardozo, and other members of his staff, who had carried out these three arrests, it appeared that Colonel Ocampos had taken root at the Seguridad building. He had a bed in his office, and his meals were brought to him, at his desk. His only excursions into the open air were a walk to the tobacconist's shop on the corner, where he purchased every day a fresh box of cigars.

On the Tuesday morning he left his office and paid a visit to the lower part of the building. Here were the cells in which prisoners were kept in temporary confinement for interrogation, before they were passed on to permanent establishments. Here also were certain interview rooms, sound-proofed, with concrete floors, and tiled walls. The preliminary interrogation of Andrea Benitez was starting as he arrived.

At the end of it, he said to the Sergeant in charge, 'Show him the photographs of the last man who was obstinate. I should like him particularly to see the photographs of his back. Give him plenty of time to study them. I will be down again in an hour.'

When he got back to his office there was a message that Father Perez had arrived. He said, 'Show him in at once,' and lit a cigar.

The Jesuit was six foot tall and his robes hung down over a body that was as thin as a sword. His lips were withdrawn and bloodless, his face carved out of yellowing stone. He refused the offer of a chair and remained standing. The light from the window threw his menacing shadow across the room.

'I come here under compulsion,' he said.

'Then those who brought you shall be reprimanded, Father. My instructions were that you be *invited* to attend.'

'When an armed policeman invites you, it is an order. Now that you have me here, what do you intend to do to me? Subject me to your special interrogation techniques?'

'That would hardly be profitable, I imagine.'

The thin lips cracked into a bitter smile. 'Under the old regime, when I was tortured, it is true that I was not broken. But I am an older man now. Old men are less tolerant of pain. If you were to whip me hard enough, you might whip a few words out of me.'

'The question does not arise,' said Ocampos. 'I repeat, Father, that you are here by invitation. I desire your help. If you do not choose to give it, you are free to depart.'

'What do you wish of me?'

'I want you to tell me, now, what you would tell the military tribunal were you to give evidence at it.'

'With what object?'

'My object, curiously enough, is the same as yours. To prevent injustice. Indeed, if the truth is what I suspect it to be, there can be no injustice. Because there will be no trial.'

The flint-coloured eyes held the Colonel's deep brown ones for a full ten seconds. Then Father Perez said, 'If you can promise me that, Colonel, then this would seem to be one occasion on which Church and State could act together.'

At half past two on that same Tuesday afternoon Cristobal Ocampos rose from his chair. He had already donned the service uniform of a Colonel in the Presidential Guard. Now, opening the wall cupboard, he extracted the dress overcoat from its hanger, and put it on, draping it carefully to conceal the bulge made by the big revolver in its holster on his left hip.

He examined himself critically in the glass. There was no doubt about it. The coat had become too tight around the waist. It would have to be let out. To Lieutenant Cardozo, also in uniform, he said, 'I think everything will be ready for us now.'

The two men left by the entrance at the rear of the building. The courtyard was crammed with soldiers. There were four troop carriers, each with a full complement of steel helmeted infantry men; a section of armoured cars with machine guns mounted fore and aft; a dozen motorcyclists; and an open olive-green command car with a soldier at the wheel and another beside him.

Ocampos and Cardozo climbed into the car, which moved slowly out of the courtyard and into the street. Behind them, they could hear the roar of the other vehicles starting up.

Colonel Villagra was in his office in the headquarters of the Military District Police when the head of the cavalcade arrived. He looked out of the window, and saw the soldiers jumping from the carriers and running to surround the building, saw the machine guns being set up and the armoured cars moving to strategic points. He was still standing, staring out, when Ocampos came into the room.

He said, 'Might I ask what this – this charade – means?'

Files of soldiers were already moving through the building, bringing out policemen and disarming them. There was no resistance. The demonstration of overwhelming force had been sufficient.

Ocampos said, 'Your gun, please.'

Villagra unbuckled his belt without a word. His red face was a mottled grey, and his plump cheeks seemed to have caved in.

Ocampos said, 'You are under arrest.'

'Is it permitted to know the charge?'

'The charge is conspiring against our Leader. The object of the conspiracy being to bring back the traitor, Siriola, from his well-merited exile.'

'I take it that you have some evidence to support this charge?'

'Two of your agents have made full confessions.'

(Of the three, only the retired and solitary Major had refused to speak. His maltreated body had been buried early that morning behind the Seguridad building.)

'I have no doubt,' said Colonel Villagra, attempting a sneer which lifted his lip and exposed his tusk-like side teeth, 'that you can bring perjured testimony against me.'

'You speak as an expert,' said Ocampos. He turned to Lieutenant Cardozo and said, 'It would be more fitting, I think, if we were allowed to continue this conversation alone.'

As he spoke, he was unbuckling the holster strap on Colonel Villagra's belt, and now he held the Colonel's automatic pistol loosely in his gloved right hand.

Lieutenant Cardozo turned on his heel, and went quickly out, shutting the door behind him.

He had got half-way down the passage when he heard the shot. He did not even turn his head.

That evening Colonel Ocampos called on his Leader; not at the Chancellery, but at his Villa in the foothills above the City. The nights were cold at that time of year, and the two men sat in front of a fire of spindle-wood, in deep leather armchairs.

It was the Leader who broke a long silence.

'After Colonel Villagra, by shooting himself, had admitted his treachery,' he said, 'what did you do?'

'I placed his principal officers under arrest, and I spoke to the men. I felt no doubt that they were innocent dupes. I considered that it was sufficient to disarm them, and send each man home, with orders to stay there. We will, of course, examine their records. If any of them appears unreliable, he will be dismissed.'

'And the officers?'

'The decision must be yours,' said Ocampos. 'We could treat them in the same way as the men, or we could stage a mass trial.'

'I dislike propaganda trials. They usually misfire.'

'They harm our public image,' agreed Ocampos, 'and achieve little.'

'Was it while you were making these arrangements, Colonel, that General Ramirez escaped?'

'That is so.'

'The Academy is some little way from the Military Police Headquarters. Your preparations were made in strict secrecy. How did he get the news in time, I wonder?'

Ocampos considered his reply. He had worked with the Leader for a decade, and had been his friend before he came to power. But there was a saying that blood was thicker than water. He realised that he would be taking a considerable risk if he spoke now. And for what?

The silence must have lasted a long time, because it was broken by the Leader who said, 'I asked you a question, Colonel.'

'Yes,' said Ocampos, 'and I will answer it. General Ramirez escaped because I sent him word. I sent it by Sergeant Torrero. He is one of my men. I placed him at the Academy some time ago, to watch over events.'

'Let us forget Sergeant Torrero, who is no doubt an honest policeman, and find out why you, the head of my Security Police, should have taken such a step.'

'If General Ramirez had not fled, it would have been necessary to bring him to trial, and execute him. He would have been more dangerous to us as a martyr than he will be as a pensioner of our neighbours. As a student of English history, I have often thought that the Jacobite cause would have been greatly strengthened had the Young Pretender been executed on Tower Hill. It withered away as its hero grew fat, debauched and ludicrous in the French Court.'

'Even supposing that you are right, was not this a matter of policy, which I should have been asked to decide for myself? Do such matters come within the province of the Police?'

'In the ordinary way,' said Ocampos, 'they would certainly not do so. But there was a further aspect of this matter. At his trial, one of the matters General Ramirez would have been accused of would have been the death of three cadets under his charge. As to that, certain facts are now much clearer. All three, Perez, Ruffio and Basilio de Casal, had become involved, to a greater or lesser extent, in the treacherous schemes of the General and his immediate circle. In the case of the first two, they had been indiscreet, or perhaps had shown an inclination to back out. They were eliminated. The case of Basilio de Casal was somewhat different.'

'Different, how?'

'Father Perez, who was the boy's confessor, has told me some odd facts about him. Facts which seemed to me, in the context of other evidence which I had, to be significant. He had read deeply in the lives of the Saints, particularly the ones who practised extreme forms of self-mortification. He had a white robe, and whenever he convicted himself, before the tribunal of his own conscience, of some sin or peccadillo, he would dress himself in this garment, and kneel, silent and motionless, in the attitude of a penitent.'

'Father Perez told you this?'

'This, and more. Basilio was, it appears, a student of the works of Count von Sacher-Masoch. This was found in his room. It is the Count's best known work.'

He took from his pocket the tattered volume of the *Galiziche Geschichten* and handed it to the Leader who placed it on the arm of his chair without opening it, and said, 'This Count. He was the man who originated the cult of masochism was he not? The idea that you could obtain sexual satisfaction from the infliction of pain on yourself.'

'Spiritual satisfaction also, in certain cases. He makes that plain in his writings.'

'And are you suggesting that when Basilio found himself helplessly enmeshed in treachery, he sentenced himself to death by hanging? And carried out the sentence himself?'

'Not only to death. For a nature like his, a quick and simple death would have been entirely inadequate to the crimes he felt he had committed. It was necessary that he suffer first.'

'He could not have flogged himself, surely?'

'No.'

'Then who did it? General Ramirez? Colonel Villagra and his policemen? Captain Hernandez?'

'None of those appear to me to be at all likely,' said Ocampos. He was picking his words with great care. 'As I understand the cult of masochism, it is an essential element that the pain should be inflicted by a friend. A close friend. One for whom the sufferer has a warm and reciprocated affection. Almost, one might say, one with whom he was in love.'

He was thinking, as he spoke, of the photograph of a big, handsome young man with an arrogant beak of a nose and rather full lips, dressed in riding clothes, with a riding switch tucked under one arm.

What the Leader was thinking was not apparent.

When he broke the long silence he said, in a toneless voice, 'One gets these relationships between young men who are thrown together. They are inevitable, I imagine.'

'Inevitable,' said Ocampos. 'And, usually, quite transient.'

A stick fell from the fire, blazing brightly. The Leader leaned forward, picked it up with his bare fingers and pitched it back into the flames. He said, 'If there is no trial, then there will be no occasion for Father Perez to give evidence?'

'None at all.'

'And you would advise that course?'

'I would advise it.'

'I accept your advice,' said the Leader. And as Ocampos rose to go, he added, 'Thank you, Colonel.'

PRIZE OF SANTENAC

Professor Bickersteth settled himself comfortably in the client's chair. 'And now, my dear Nap,' he said, 'I want you to tell me all about the law of treasure trove.'

Noel Anthony Portarlier Rumbold sighed. 'I am a solicitor,' he said, 'not the Oracle at Delphi.'

'But solicitors know the law.'

'I could give you a very lengthy and complicated reply to that,' said Nap. 'But I won't. My job is to find out the law for you. I should have to go to an expert – probably a barrister – and put certain questions to him on your behalf, and, in course of time, receive his answers. You would have to pay for them. They would not be cheap. Is it the law of treasure trove in this country, or elsewhere?'

'Well, here, I suppose – and in France.'

'You'd pay twice for that.'

'Oh dear,' said the professor. 'Why do you make everything so difficult? I'm not at all sure that it wouldn't be easier to go straight ahead and ignore the law altogether.'

'Now *that*,' said Nap, 'is a much more practical suggestion. But suppose you tell me something about it first.'

'Well,' said the professor, 'it all started when my old friend Carkeith wrote to me about a set of medieval vineyard accounts from Bordeaux. As I expect you remember, Bordeaux came into the possession of the Crown when Henry II married Eleanor of Aquitaine—'

Nap slumped slightly in his chair. Outside it was a warm day. Two pigeons volplaned off the buttress of Guildhall and came to rest on the parapet opposite....

'Let me see,' he said, finally, 'if I have got it straight. The Comte de Sessac, the owner of Château Santenac, surrendered his castle to the English. The French recaptured the castle, and destroyed it. However, nobody ever caught up with de Sessac, nor was the de Sessac treasure, which the count left behind him when he skipped, ever unearthed. And now you think you know where that treasure is.'

'I think I know where it was originally put,' said the professor, mildly. 'The sketch plan in the accounts was quite definite.'

'But whether the treasure still lies there is another question.'

'Seven centuries is a considerable period,' agreed Professor Bickersteth. 'But you must bear in mind that part of the treasure was a collection of papal jewels. If they had been found I think there would have been a record of it.'

'All right,' said Nap. 'Now let me give you some advice. Take the present owner of Château Santenac right into your confidence. You can do nothing behind his back. But don't tell anyone else.... You haven't told anyone, have you?'

'Just one or two close friends,' said the professor uneasily.

'M'm. I hope they'll be discreet. My suggestion is that you go over yourself. Take perhaps a couple of friends you can rely on. Is the château still in the Sessac family?'

'It's been sold quite recently, I believe – by the last of the Sessacs – to a Monsieur Potier, head of a Bordeaux wine syndicate.'

'When, and if, you find any treasure, will be the time for Monsieur Potier and you to worry about the law. If it will help, I'll send someone with you. I've got an articled clerk kicking his heels here. He takes his finals next month. A compulsory break would do him good. And he speaks French well.'

'It's uncommonly kind of you,' said the professor. 'Would that be the young man you told to look after my daughter? Perhaps we could have them both in and tell them.'

Nap rang a bell. His secretary said she thought it was no good sending for Mr D'Este; he had gone out for coffee with the young lady.

'That's all right,' said Nap. 'I can see them. They're on their way back now.'

The professor walked across to the window and stood beside him. 'Indeed, they seem to be quite good friends already,' he observed.

A week later Richard D'Este stood on the deck of the S.S. Honfleur and watched the squat ugliness of Newhaven disappear over the stern. The girl was tucked into a deck chair beside him.

'Are you a good sailor?' asked Emilia.

'I have crossed the Channel many times without any ill-effects,' he replied, turning to her to resume a very private conversation.

They docked at Le Havre at four o'clock. Richard secured a taxi and they went to the hotel where rooms had been booked. The professor announced that he would spend a quiet hour on his bed, and Richard and Emilia went for a walk.

When they got back, rather later than they had intended, they found Professor Bickersteth talking to a bearded gentleman, whom he introduced as Monsieur Plon. 'He is himself an enthusiast for the wines of Bordeaux.' said the professor. 'We have had such an interesting discussion.'

Richard and Emilia looked at each other in quick alarm.

'You go to Bordeaux, I understand,' said Monsieur Plon. 'Where will you go from there? If you are interested in fine wines no doubt you go on through to Haut Medoc?'

The professor seemed enchanted with this idea. 'It is such a pleasure,' he said, 'to meet a fellow enthusiast. Perhaps you would join us at dinner? Splendid.'

During the meal that followed, the professor and Monsieur Plon talked wine while Richard and Emilia listened to the flow of expertise....

'And of the fifth cru,' said the professor, 'there is no doubt Pontet-Canet holds the field.'

'I agree,' said Monsieur Plon, 'that a château-bottled Pontet-Canet of a good year is difficult to beat in any cru.'

The talk switched to the area of Dijon and the two men descended to Côte d'Or in slow and loving pilgrimage.

And then, as he listened lazily, it seemed to Richard that a change had taken place. The professor had ceased to follow the conversation and had started to guide it.

'And of the white Burgundies,' he said. 'If you had the choice of an inexpensive wine of recent vintage, would be Pouilly-Fuissé, or an Aligoté?'

'The first, I think.' said Monsieur Plon.

'You are not then fond of an Aligoté. Is it a wine you know?'

Monsieur Plon hesitated fractionally before he replied. 'I have drunk it, of course,' be said.

'I wonder if you know the place?'

'I have been through it, certainly, but have never had occasion to stop there.'

The professor said: 'It is charming, quite charming. A few miles south of Mâcon. And talking about Mâconnaise wine—'

He talked of them, exhaustively. Coffee followed the cheese, Cognac followed the coffee.

Monsieur Plon at last rose to go. 'I have rarely enjoyed a meal so much,' he said. 'It emboldens me to make a suggestion. I myself have a car. A large and empty car. I am going through Bordeaux to Arcachon. Would it not be more pleasant than going by train if you were to accompany me?'

'It's extremely kind of you,' said the professor, 'I shall certainly not refuse.'

'Then we will meet after breakfast tomorrow.'

When Monsieur Plon had gone they sat in silence for a few minutes. Then the professor said: 'That man is a vulgar impostor.'

'How do you make that out?' Richard asked.

'Well, when he began to praise a château-bottled Pontet-Canet I had my doubts.'

'But I'm sure I've heard of Pontet-Canet.'

'No doubt. It is a well-known claret. It happens never to be bottled at the château. And then – Aligoté is the name of a very well-known white Burgundy. Only Aligoté does not happen to be a place. It is a type of vine.'

'And he actually said that he had been through it.' said Richard.

'I fear that my indiscretions are catching up with me,' said the professor, repentantly. 'The news of my quest has got about. I fear that Monsieur Plon has been put on to trail us.'

'Then we must lose him,' said Emilia. 'Suppose we catch a very early train tomorrow?'

'I don't quite like that,' said Richard. 'He might be able to trace us, if he inquires at the station. I think it would be better and safer to go by road. I can hire a car here, but not at this time of night.

'It will take probably a day to arrange. What I suggest is that you, sir, have a touch of migraine tomorrow which prevents you travelling. Incidentally, that will serve as a check on Monsieur Plon. If he is what we suspect, he will postpone his own departure. We will then leave at crack of dawn on the day following.'

Nearly forty-eight hours later an old green Chevrolet, with Richard at the wheel, turned in at the gateway of Château Santenac. Monsieur Potier, warned by telephone from Libourne, was on the step to greet them.

He was plainly delighted to see them. The reason became apparent over a glass of wine in his shuttered library.

'I am myself,' he said, 'in a small way a student of medieval history. It is the greatest honour imaginable that I should entertain in my house the celebrated author of *Observations On The Tactical Employment Of The Longbow*.'

'I had no idea.' said the professor, 'that my little opus had been translated into French.'

'I read him,' said Monsieur Potier, complacently, 'in the original

English. Most I understand. A few technical expressions escape me. Tomorrow perhaps you will be able to elucidate.'

'Nothing would please me more,' said the professor.

The next morning Richard and Emilia stood looking down over the gentle curve of the vineyards to the Garonne.

'Come on,' said Emilia sharply. 'We shall want a pole at this corner.'

Richard obediently drove in one of the white and black survey poles.

'And then you can take another one and plant it in the middle of the culvert where the drain runs into the river. And perhaps you'd better line two more up between them.'

'Aye, aye, sir,' said Richard.

'And while you're at it, you can pace the distances.'

Richard groaned and departed. The girl set up the theodolite in line with the pole and centred it expertly with a plumb bob.

After breakfast the professor demonstrated on a piece of paper to Monsieur Potier.

'It is really quite simple.' he said. 'The old drain, or water culvert, ran past the front of the original château and emptied into the Garonne at the water gate. When de Sessac wanted a handy place to bury his treasure he sealed off a section of the drain and circumnavigated it with a semi-circular canal: so that, when the surface was restored, all was in order. Water appeared to flow straight down the culvert.

'Nobody was to guess that in fact, a short portion was sealed off and bypassed. The precise spot can be ascertained by triangulation – a surveying term, you understand.'

'It will be an operation of difficulty?' asked Monsieur Potier.

'My daughter, whom I have grounded in survey, has practically completed it. This afternoon we should be in a position to start digging.'

The soil of a vineyard is stony and inhospitable. For an hour now Monsieur Potier's labourers had been at work in shifts.

One of the diggers said something.

'Indeed.' said Monsieur Potier. 'That will be of interest to you. He opines that where he is digging, the soil has been disturbed before. Not very recently but – ah ha!'

There was a clink as the mattock rang on something hard.

'Spades, now!' said Monsieur Potier. 'It should be – yes it is – the roof of the culvert. Professor Bickersteth, I offer my congratulations to your daughter on the superlative accuracy of her survey. We shall need crow-bars and hammers now.'

Again one of the men who was digging spoke. Monsieur Potier and the professor peered down.

'Yes,' said the professor. 'I'm afraid it looks very much as though the top of the brickwork has at some time been removed in three large pieces, and then replaced. The breaks are evident. And they are certainly not seven hundred years old.'

'A crowbar there. Jacques,' said Monsieur Potier. 'And another there! Leverage will do it.'

'The brickwork itself,' said the professor, 'is clearly medieval. Lovely workmanship indeed. Richard, could you lend a hand? That's right. Up she comes! The other pieces will be easier.'

Eight pairs of eyes stared down into the neat, brick-lined cavity. It was absolutely and completely empty except for the workman standing in it.

The professor bent forward, and said: 'But that is amazing.'

Emilia choked. Richard found it difficult to say whether she was going to laugh or cry. His own feelings sat plain on his honest face.

'Extraordinary!' went on the professor. 'Allow me.' He took up one of the crowbars and descended into the hole. 'You observe the brickwork at this end?' he said. 'How do you explain it?'

'Explain what?' said Monsieur Potier, breathlessly.

'It is not more than a few years old. Twenty, perhaps. The bricks are quite new. If you would hand me a hammer, I fancy I could unseat one of them.'

In five minutes the inner wall was down. The professor thrust in a long arm. 'It's too heavy for me,' he said, 'But I can see the end of a wooden case. Perhaps your men could draw it out. But let me beg of you to handle it carefully. If my suspicions should prove correct...!'

Two hours later Monsieur Potier and the professor sat in the shuttered library. Behind them, in the corner, lay the fragments of a packing case. Before them, in a wicker cradle, lay a dusty bottle.

'It would be better. I think,' said Monsieur Potier anxiously, 'to keep it almost flat. If it has been fifteen years or more undisturbed in its present hiding-place it must have thrown a considerable sediment. Shall I draw the cork now?'

'Fifteen years.' said the professor. 'You think—?'

'To my mind, these were concealed in 1940, when the Germans came. The owner then was Guy de Sessac. I knew him slightly.'

'You think that the de Sessacs knew of this hiding-place?'

'Undoubtedly. See, we are in luck. A fine cork, quite unperished.'

'And had removed the treasure, bit by bit?'

'And disposed of it bit by bit. After all, why not? It belonged to them. Then when the Boche arrived, de Sessac had an empty hiding-place all ready. Into it went his finest vintages. He died before the end of the war. The secret might have been lost.'

'To think,' said the professor, 'that this God-like wine might have perished untasted.' He held the thin glass up to the light and looked lovingly into the clear, deep red heart. 'A Château Santenac of the great year 1924. Probably the last dozen bottles left in the world.'

'Six for you and six for me,' said Monsieur Potier. 'It is no use arguing, I insist.'

'Monsieur.' said the professor, 'I am over-rewarded.'

'It is strange,' said Monsieur Potier, looking out of the window to where Richard and Emilia sat beside each other on the terrace, 'that although you found no gold, you have, all three of you, found treasure.'

A servant came in. 'There is a gentleman,' he said. 'who asks for Monsieur Potier. He states that his business is urgent.'

Monsieur Potier looked at the card. 'Monsieur Plon.' he said. 'Have I the pleasure—?'

'I have had that pleasure,' said the professor, with a shudder. 'He comes in search of treasure. I thought we had thrown him off, but evidently he has perseverance. It will do him no harm to keep him waiting before you break the news to him.'

'Very well,' said Monsieur Potier. 'Tell Monsieur Plon that I will be with him – soon.'

The professor picked up his glass again.

'Besides,' he said. 'if you were to ask him up now we should have to share this bottle with him, and I can assure you that he would not really appreciate it…. Monsieur, your health.'

VILLA ALMIRANTE

LUCIFERO, LIEUTENANT OF Carabinieri in charge of police work in the district of Lerici, paused for a moment at the head of the flight of steps which spiralled down to the Villa Almirante.

Where he stood, his heels were at chimney-top level. All the villas along the coast road were like that, set each on its own ledge in the steep, dusty hillside; the garden, a narrow sleeve of olive and orange tree and arbutus, resting one end on the road and the other three hundred feet below where the wine-dark sea complained and hissed over the rocks.

Dusk had fallen. The only sign of life was a chink of light from the kitchen quarters, a separate building to the left of the villa, where the Italian cook-housekeeper, Signora – Signora – Lucifero frowned. It was his boast that he knew all his own people by name.

Signora Telli. Of course. The Signora Telli was a war widow who ran the house for its English owner, helped by her son, the burly Umberto, and a local girl called – well, really, there were so many girls, one could not remember all of them – probably called Maria.

A loud gust of laughter sounded from the terrace on the seaward side of the villa. The house-party was in good form. Interesting people, thought Lucifero, one of whose tasks – one of whose pleasures – it was to get to know the English visitors who came, year by year in spring and autumn, to escape their own fog and mist and drizzle and bask in the warm sunshine of the Ligurian coast.

Lucifero knew those fogs and mists only too well. He had spent an eternity of two years in London in the wine shipper's office of his uncle; two years of cold and wet and flat beer and rock-like food fried into hard indigestible lumps; two miserable years, as far as anyone could be miserable who was twenty and healthy – and handsome.

The lieutenant passed a leather-gloved finger lightly across the top of his mouth, and smiled to himself in the gathering darkness. Perhaps it had not been so bad, after all. There had been consolations.

There had been Anna. There had been Geraldine, a graduate of

Oxford University, but not too proud to be seen about with a young wine shipper's clerk. And his exile had paid one quite unforeseen dividend.

When Italy entered the war – most ill-advisedly Lucifero had thought even at the time – against the Allies, his quick and fluent grasp of English had stood as a barrier between him and the more unpleasant forms of national service. Rapid qualification as an interpreter had been followed by posts in the officer prisoner-of-war camps at Chieti, at Sulmona, and finally at Garvi, where he had proved so sympathetic to his charges that he had narrowly escaped being carried with them into Germany at the time of the Armistice.

To have joined the exclusive Carabinieri, and to have reached the rank of lieutenant in the short time since the war, was itself no mean achievement. But modesty was not among Lucifero's failings. He knew that it had been well earned. There had been no element of favour in his promotion. Hard work, attention to detail, and a facility for psychology had made him a successful policeman. The psychology, in particular, of women.

Few men, thought Lucifero, understood women as he did.

There was a second burst of laughter from the terrace on the seaward side of the villa. At that hour of the evening the party would be sitting out over their drinks as they waited for dinner to be served. Four of them had arrived ten days before. There was Lord Keaough, their host, the owner of the villa in which he spent two months of every year, an austere and craggy nobleman, and precisely Lucifero's idea of what an English peer should be, even to his baffling name. With him had come Mr Colin Sampson, the publisher; Mr Ralph Marley, the poet; and Miss Natalie Merrow.

His hand actually on the brass knocker, Lucifero paused, as a connoisseur will pause in front of a fine but puzzling painting; a gourmet before an intriguing wine. He had observed Miss Natalie for three seasons now. He had been certain, at first, that she was Lord Keaough's mistress. But that idea had died. She was of the Left Bank, cosmopolitan, bohemian. Knowledgeable about love, yes. But as yet disinterested in it.

Lucifero visualised her as he had seen her three evenings before for a few seconds in the Albergo Maritime, her skin browned by the sun to a colour which would have looked vulgar in a blonde but was perfect under her dark, carefully and carelessly arranged mop of black hair. Lucifero corrected himself. Not black. Peasant women had black hair. This was the colour of very old, dark chestnut. Altogether an interesting specimen to a psychologist; a little tightly wrapped up in herself at present. One day she would fall apart deliciously in some lucky man's hands.

It had been a curious scene at the albergo. The four of them at their table with their drinks. At one side Lord Keaough, immobile, cut from a single piece of well-tanned leather. At the other the girl, between the publisher – with his chubby face and horn-rimmed glasses, boyish and bookish – and the poet, dark-haired, bright-eyed, Byronic, and indubitably drunk.

Lucifero had thought for a moment that they were going to do what English people of their class never did in public: that they were going to quarrel. Words had floated from Ralph Marley, high-pitched, emphatic, tumbling over themselves in bitter, eager spite. And Colin Sampson, normally, Lucifero surmised, a man of peace, had said something so sharp that even Lord Keaough had opened his sleepy eyes.

Lucifero had been sitting six tables away, unable to distinguish a word that was spoken but acutely aware of what was happening. He had half expected to see a glass emptied in someone's face. In his native Calabria knives would have been out long since.

Then Ralph Marley had climbed to his feet, turned his back on the party, and walked away. The others had watched him in silence.

The poet, pushing his way between the tables, had passed within a few feet of Lucifero, and Lucifero had observed his face, an odd mixture of petulance and passion. Now, standing with one hand actually on the brass dolphin knocker of the villa, he tried to picture it. He tried to bring it back into his mind, past the very different picture of Ralph Marley that was presently occupying his thoughts.

It was Umberto who answered the knock. He was only eighteen, but as heavy and as chunky as marble from the quarries of Carrara.

'Tenente?'

'Good evening, Umberto. You are well? And your mother, I hope.'

'Very well indeed.' He seemed almost to be standing guard in the hallway. 'Do you wish me to tell – the Lordship – that you are here?'

Lucifero smiled to himself at this evasion. He was aware, none more so, of the difficulties which attended the pronunciation of Lord Keaough's name in any language, but above all in the Italian tongue which tries so conscientiously to separate every vowel from its neighbour.

'Be good enough,' he said, 'to inform Lord Kuff that I would appreciate a word with him, alone, on a matter of importance.'

'They are on the terrace.' Umberto considered. 'The doors to the salon are open. There is no privacy there. Perhaps the dining-room?'

'The dining-room should do well. But warn your mother that her excellent meal may have to wait a little. What we have to discuss will not be done within five minutes.'

Lucifero was standing in front of the empty fireplace in the dining-room when the door opened and Lord Keaough came in.

'Good evening, Tenente. Lucifero, is it not? I seem to remember that you speak excellent English, so I shall not have to inflict my terrible Italian on you. Do sit down.'

'Your Lordship speaks excellent Italian,' said Lucifero, but he made no attempt to move back into his native tongue. Nor did he sit. 'What I have to tell you will not take a great deal of time. I have to start with a question. How long is it since anyone here has seen Signor Ralph Marley?'

He wished that the lighting was better. The single economical central bulb hid more of Lord Keaough's face than it revealed.

'Ralph? Let me think. Today is Friday. It was some time on Wednesday afternoon when he walked out on us.'

'Walked *out*? You imply—?'

'He stood not upon the order of his going. He said no goodbyes. He took no luggage. He went.'

'Yes,' said Lucifero. Curious how much a single word could imply. To walk was one thing. To walk out was another. He must remember the difference. 'Can you tell me any more?'

'All that I know, and that's precious little. But perhaps you will tell me something first. Has he got into trouble?'

'Why do you ask?'

'In most countries,' said Lord Keaough, 'police mean trouble.'

Lucifero showed white teeth under a hairline of black moustache. 'Signor Marley is in no trouble now,' he said. 'He is dead.'

Lord Keaough leaned forward, bending from the waist in a gentle, courteous gesture of interrogation. 'Dead?' he said.

Lucifero stared at him, opened his mouth to speak, and closed it again in resignation. 'Yes. His body was taken from the sea by a fisherman this morning, a half-mile out from Portovenere.'

Lord Keaough stood, looking out through the window, as if he could see the hidden lines of the bay and estimate the currents as they set between the towering headlands.

'If,' agreed Lucifero, reading his thoughts, 'he had entered the sea just here, in twenty-four or thirty-six hours he would have been carried to Portovenere.'

'Yes,' said Lord Keaough. 'I'm afraid that's it. Shall I tell the others, or would you prefer to tell them yourself?'

Lucifero had given thought to this. Two factors influenced him. The first, that the lights in the salon would probably be better; the second that the other two, younger members of the party would hardly have the same unnatural control over their feelings as was being exhibited by this impossible aristocrat.

'Let us go to the salon,' he said. 'Perhaps you will permit *me* to tell your guests the news.'

'Of course, of course.'

Lord Keaough led the way down the short passage and into a large bright, pleasant room.

Natalie Merrow was sitting, upright, on one end of the sofa, an unopened book beside her, and Colin Sampson was standing behind her, talking to her or at her. He stopped in mid sentence when the door opened.

'This is Lieutenant Lucifero, of the Police,' said Lord Keaough. 'He has some bad news for us.'

'Ralph!' said Natalie.

'What's happened to him?' said Colin.

If it was acting – and the possibility had always to be borne in mind – it was very fine acting. Not an amateur or bungled effort. Precisely the right intonation, exactly the correct proportions of realisation, shock, and pity.

'I have to tell you,' he said. 'I have already told his Lordship, the body was recovered from the sea, near Portovenere, early this morning. By a fishing boat returning to harbour.'

'Yes,' said Colin. It was as if he was confirming something which had been hinted at before. A possibility had turned into a probability. That was all.

'You will, I hope, excuse the observation,' said Lucifero. 'But, in some way, this news seems not to surprise you greatly.'

The other two looked at Lord Keaough, who said, 'Ralph was a poet, and a great admirer of Lord Byron.'

'I see,' said Lucifero. 'He had the same idea? To swim across the gulf?'

'Yes. We attempted to dissuade him, of course.'

'Why?'

'Ralph was neither as good a poet as Byron,' said Colin, 'nor as good a swimmer.' Then he blushed, as if conscious that he had been guilty of some impropriety.

Lucifero said, 'The indications are that Mr Marley started his ill-fated swim in the late afternoon of Wednesday. I say late afternoon because he would hardly contemplate such a feat in the dark. This coincides also with what his Lordship has told me. That you last saw Mr Marley on Wednesday afternoon.'

They looked at him warily.

'Yes?' said Lord Keaough.

'If that is so, why was his absence not reported before?'

'Because,' said Lord Keaough, 'we did not know that he had been drowned.'

'But you realised that he was missing.'

'If we brought in the police every time Ralph walked out,' said Mr Sampson, an edge once more perceptible in his voice, 'we should keep you gentlemen pretty busy.'

'Mr Marley,' explained Lord Keaough, 'was a poet.'

'Temperamental?'

'You could call it that,' said Mr Sampson.

'Really, Colin,' said Natalie. 'Ralph is hardly twenty-four hours dead. I think we might refrain from speaking ill of him. Just until he is buried, perhaps?'

Lucifero looked at them curiously. There was something that he did not understand. Something to be docketed for future reference.

'I'm afraid,' said Lord Keaough, 'that Mr Marley had cried "wolf" too often. Last year he walked out on us in Rome, after a little difference of opinion, and reappeared in Venice. In Venice early one morning, for no reason at all, he decided to go to Scotland—'

'He said, afterwards, that he preferred grouse to pigeons,' observed Natalie.

'And on that occasion, too, he took no luggage. Not even a toothbrush. It was – a sort of – affectation.'

'A poet must be free,' recited Mr Sampson. 'Untrammelled by any bonds. Unrestrained by any conventions.'

'And on this occasion, you assumed that he had walked out on you—' Lucifero managed this newly-acquired idiom quite smoothly – 'on account of – what? Some recent difference of opinion?'

'We had a sort of quarrel on Tuesday evening,' said Lord Keaough. 'It started at dinner, and went on over our drinks at the Albergo Maritime. As no doubt you observed, since you were seated a few tables away.'

'Yes,' said Lucifero. 'I did, I think, observe something.' But Lord Keaough, he could have sworn, had sat with his back to him throughout the incident. 'If you feel at liberty to tell me what it was about—?'

'It's not a secret,' said Mr Sampson. 'My firm, Blakelock & Sampson, that is, had decided that we could not publish his latest book of verse. We had lost money heavily on the other three. Besides, we are not really publishers of poetry—'

'Messrs. Blakelock and Sampson,' said Natalie, 'make all their real money out of detective stories.'

Mr Sampson flushed again. Really, thought Lucifero, for a man in his middle thirties he was extraordinarily susceptible. And was the girl teasing him because she liked him or because she hated him? Time would no doubt give him the answer.

'There was the usual talk,' said Mr Sampson. 'That all publishers are philistines who batten on the genius of the artist and squeeze him to death for their own profit.'

'His eminent prototype, Lord Byron, also made many uncomplimentary references to publishers,' observed Lucifero. 'Could any of you tell me more precisely when you last observed Mr Marley on Wednesday?'

'We pretty well live our own lives here,' said Lord Keaough. 'Get up when we like. Do what we like. We usually meet in the evening for a drink, and have dinner together. On Wednesday, actually, we all four of us had luncheon together. Ralph seemed to have got over his sulks, though he didn't eat much. In the afternoon I retired to my room for my siesta.'

'I painted,' said Natalie.

'I went for a walk, towards Tolaro,' said Mr Sampson.

'We three met for our drink – at about six? 'The others agreed. 'At about six. There was no sign of Ralph then or later.'

'You painted, where?' asked Lucifero.

'On the hillside, overlooking Carrara. An hour's walk there. Three-quarters of an hour back, downhill. I was here by six.'

'And you awoke from your siesta—?'

'I call it a siesta,' said Lord Keaough. 'I don't really sleep. I lie on my bed, and read a little, and then do some writing. I came down at half past five.'

'And you heard and saw nothing?'

'I heard Signora Telli calling out once to Maria in the garden. Maria was, I think, putting out the laundry. Or more likely, at that hour, getting it in.'

'I must question the servants afterwards,' agreed Lucifero.

'Is it important?' said Lord Keaough.

Lucifero's head came round slowly. 'Important?' he said.

'I mean, we are agreed what happened. The late afternoon was Ralph's time for bathing. He had often told us that he would try this particular swim. If it was an accident—'

'But it was *not* an accident,' said Lucifero. 'Mr Marley was taken from the sea fully dressed. And there is no seawater in his lungs. His head was crushed. He was dead before he entered the sea.'

Three faces turned towards him. Three pairs of eyes centred on his. The hard lines which fenced Lord Keaough's nose and mouth seemed a little more marked, but he remained implacably impassive. There was a puzzled frown behind Natalie's eyes, and her lips were parted, showing her small white teeth. Mr Sampson was blushing again.

The servants told him little about the dead man, but quite a lot about their patron and his guests; and, without realising it, a good deal about themselves, too.

'Signor Marley was a man of moods, Tenente,' said Signora Telli. 'A great poet, so we were told. But for me, I judge a man by the way he lives not by what he writes. And it is my opinion, and I say it with the proper reserve due when a man has been called unexpectedly to his Maker, that that young man did not live well. He had not a good name. We hear about such things more than you would imagine. Two years ago, there was an Austrian girl who threatened to kill herself – you heard?'

Lucifero had heard. But he was not greatly interested in what had happened two years before. 'On the Wednesday afternoon,' he said, 'did you yourself see Mr Marley?'

'Not in the afternoon at all. I was busy in my kitchen. Umberto was at the market. Maria might have seen him. She was in the garden part of the time, and may have seen him if he went to bathe.'

Maria was summoned. She was seventeen, a dark girl with a pert, peasant face and a budding beauty. She was also, clearly, very nervous. Lucifero thought it better to question her in Signora Telli's presence.

She had been in the garden on three – or perhaps four – occasions. First to collect some of the firewood which Umberto had chopped and left. Then to pick radishes and lettuce for the evening meal. Twice to bring in washing. She had *not* seen Signor Marley. She was positive she had not seen him. If she had seen him, she would have said so. What reason would there be to lie? She had *not* seen him.

'Understood,' said Lucifero dryly. 'Are you affianced to Umberto?'

Both women seemed to be struck dumb by this question. Signora Telli said at last, 'There is nothing finally arranged. It is an understanding. But Umberto is only just eighteen.'

'He is a good boy,' said Lucifero. 'And old for his age. I was affianced before I was eighteen.'

'He is the best of sons,' agreed the Signora. 'And Maria will be a good wife to him – when the time is proper.' She smiled suddenly at the girl, who smiled back. 'You wish to question Umberto?'

'But if he was at the market,' said Lucifero, 'what could he tell me?'

Signora Telli dismissed Maria with a jerk of her head. When the door had closed behind her, she said, 'I have something to tell *you*. It concerns his Lordship.'

'Yes,' said Lucifero.

'What I have to say has, you must understand, nothing to do with the drowning of Signor Marley.'

'Of that I must be the judge.'

'It is something which I have long felt should be said – to someone in authority. He is a kind patron, generous and easy to work for.' She seemed suddenly unsure of herself. 'But—'

'But?'

'I think he is a spy.'

Lucifero prided himself that he was difficult to surprise, but for a moment he felt his mouth falling open. Then he recovered himself.

'It does not seem very likely,' he observed mildly. 'We are not at war.'

'If he is not a spy, why does he sit for hours and hours on the terrace, with a great pair of glasses—' she demonstrated with her hands – 'staring out at the ships?'

'Perhaps it is the birds he watches. Not the ships.'

She looked at him doubtfully, to see if he was laughing at her. He pinched her arm and said, 'Do not worry. If he is a spy, you have discharged your duty by telling me of your suspicions.'

Nevertheless, before he left for the night he walked back to the house to have a further word with Lord Keaough.

'There is much to do,' he said, 'but it cannot be done until morning. We shall have to examine the private beach at the foot of your garden, and the rocks about it. And there is a fuller autopsy to be made.'

'I've been thinking,' said Lord Keaough. 'What seems most probable is that Ralph went down for his swim, tried the short cut to the beach down through the rocks – it is dangerous, but he had done it before – and slipped, hitting his head as he went into the sea. There is only one difficulty. It that was so, he would have dropped his bathing costume, and we should have found it. Unless it fell and floated out to sea with him.'

Lucifero said, 'When found, Signor Marley was wearing an open shirt and linen trousers. Under the trousers, he was wearing bathing shorts.'

'I see,' said Lord Keaough. 'Then my theory may well be correct.'

'Very likely. Meanwhile, I must ask you and your friends to be patient.'

'We are none of us planning to leave,' said Lord Keaough. 'We are at your disposal. I have no doubt you will soon discover the truth.'

'Speriamo,' said Lucifero, and took his leave.

In police work things did not often happen quickly. It was time and hard work that solved most problems. Some facts, a very few facts, emerged. A painstaking, inch-by-inch search of the grassy plateau which crowned the knoll – a hidden place, open only towards the sea, and much used by the inhabitants of the villa for sunbathing – brought to light two hairpins, the lid of a tin of face-cream, a number of old matchsticks, and a 1930 five-lire piece. There were two routes down to the beach: the one cut from the smooth rock, serpentine but safe; the alternative descent over the sheer rocks, a mountaineer's route. Nothing of significance was discovered on either. Nor was this strange.

'If he went to the beach by the path,' said Lucifero to Lord Keaough, 'he would leave no mark. If he fell from here, he would strike one of those rocks. It has been washed too well by the sea to leave clues for us.'

'Has the autopsy been helpful? Or perhaps you are not allowed to tell us?'

'Certainly I can tell you. It shows two things. That Mr Marley entered the sea with little in his stomach—'

'Which agrees with late afternoon.'

'Yes. And that his head was broken by impact on the rocks. A considerable impact, one would say. There are tiny fragments of rock splinter still embedded in the bone.'

'All of which—' began Lord Keaough.

'All of which,' agreed Lucifero, 'points to your solution being the right one.'

That had been on the Saturday. By Wednesday, routine and order and a surface calm had returned to the Villa Almirante. Lucifero had kept his distance. He spent long hours on the hillside above and to one side of the villa with an excellent pair of glasses. He could see the terrace where Lord Keaough sat, similarly equipped. He studied Lord Keaough. Lord Keaough studied – what? He could see most of the steeply-sloped garden, although the knoll and the beach were both hidden, one by trees, the other by the steep, overhanging bluff. They were days of intense heat. The sun emerged coyly from its veil of early morning mist, swung through a cloudless sky, and retired at last in sulky, crimson splendour behind the hills of the Cinque Terre. Lucifero, was content to wait. Given such people, in just such a situation, it was inevitable that something would happen. It *must* happen. If it did not he would make it happen.

Three times already he had sent for Maria, and each time his questions had been shrewder and Maria's protest more voluble. On the final occasion, the young Umberto had escorted her to the police station, and had waited in the outer room, glowering and unapproachable ...

On the late afternoon of that Wednesday, Lucifero, from his vantage point, watched Colin and Natalie walk down the garden together. They disappeared into the trees. Curse the trees, thought Lucifero. They hid too much. No trees, no problems.

The minutes ticked by. The heat-waves danced and shimmered off the rocks. Something moved at the top of the garden slope, a flash of white. Lucifero steadied his binoculars in his sweating hands. It was Umberto, moving with quiet but purposeful deliberation, keeping behind the shelter of the olive trees, making for the knoll. A peeping Tom? Lucifero thought it possible, but unlikely. Umberto's interest in girls, and in Maria in particular, was much too simple and much too direct for him to have to stimulate his passion by spying on others.

Lucifero contained his soul in patience. A flash of colour among the trees. Natalie appeared, walking quickly for such a hot afternoon. It was too far away to read expressions, but Lucifero deduced from her walk that she was angry.

He shut up his glasses, jumped to his feet, and ran down the hill.

Outside the villa, Natalie passed him. Her face was flushed, but that might have been exercise. She said, 'Good afternoon, Lieutenant,' but made no attempt to stop or talk. She had recovered whatever poise she might have lost.

Lucifero saluted gravely, then ran quickly down the steps, and entered the Villa Almirante without knocking.

Lord Keaough was sitting on the balcony in a wicker chair, his glasses to his eyes. He said without looking up, 'You've come in at the right moment, Tenente. Is that chance, or have you been watching, too?'

'I have been watching, too,' said Lucifero.

It had, of course, occurred to him that if the truth was apparent to him, it might well be apparent also to as shrewd an observer as Lord Keaough.

'I would suggest,' Lucifero said, 'that you walk down by the main path, taking time; I will go by the side path. It is possible, by the exercise of agility, to work across from it to the path above the bathing beach. Try to keep in sight, and do not interfere until I give the signal. Whatever happens.'

He paused and added again, 'Whatever happens.' Lord Keaough nodded, and walked down the steps into the garden.

Colin Sampson lay flat on his back, his eyes tightly shut. The strong sun beat down through the trees, and penetrated his screwed-up eyelids. If I was twenty years younger, he thought, I should be crying. This seemed such an odd thought that he sat up abruptly. He had just asked Natalie to marry him. And she had refused. Being totally inexperienced, he had misread this refusal as coyness and had tried to grab hold of her. And he had had his face smacked.

And now he was quite ready to argue himself back into a mood of self-respect. Natalie, he had come to the conclusion, had been more upset by Ralph's death than any of them had suspected. This was a two-edged thought. It meant that she had been fond of Ralph. No. Fond was the wrong word. It meant that she had been emotionally involved with him. But it meant also that if he approached her again, when she was more herself ...

At this point, he found himself staring into the anger-crazed face of Umberto; a face which was, unnervingly, only a few inches above the ground. Umberto had been snaking forward towards Mr Sampson on his elbows and knees. Now, having been discovered, he scrambled to his feet, and it could be seen that he was holding in the hand a wicked-looking malacca stick, an inch thick; a sort of Penang Lawyer which some guest had left behind him.

Mr Sampson got up awkwardly, and was just in time to avoid the first blow which came hissing down and grazed his left arm.

'Stop,' he said. 'Stop it, I say. There is some mistake.'

The next blow cut him about the shoulders with a cracking force which threatened his collar-bone. He flung an arm round Umberto in a frenzied grapple. But the thirty-five-year-old publisher was no match for the eighteen-year-old peasant boy. Umberto tore himself away with contemptuous ease and raised the stick again. Mr Sampson abandoned any shreds of dignity and began to shout.

A shot exploded out of the bushes below the knoll. Lucifero, sweating with haste and exertion, had drawn his police gun from his holster and fired – into the air.

For an instant all movement ceased. Then Umberto twisted about, and ran for the path which led up to the house. He found Lord Keaough blocking it. He hesitated before that frail but indomitable figure, and was lost. Lucifero had reached level ground, and was walking towards him.

'That will be enough,' he said. 'More than enough.' He had returned his gun to its holster. He knew that he would have no cause to use it. The situation was under control.

'Murdering swine,' said Mr Sampson.

'Enough,' said Lucifero again. 'We will go up to the house. All of us.'

When they reached the small paved courtyard which lay between the villa and the servant's annexe, Lucifero called a halt. He said to Mr Sampson, 'Be kind enough to telephone the Carabinieri post and ask for Sergeant Malagodi.'

And to Umberto, 'I shall charge you, formally, with the murder of your English guest, Mr Ralph Marley. For the moment, you may go into the kitchen. If you try to leave it without my permission, you do so at your own peril.'

He said this in a high clear voice, in which Lord Keaough thought he detected an undercurrent of distinct satisfaction.

Half an hour later Lucifero, Lord Keaough, Mr Sampson, and Natalie were seated in the salon, discussing the unexpected events of the morning. Sergeant Malagodi, a dour Sicilian, had arrived, and was in the kitchen, sitting over Umberto, who had so far said nothing at all.

'I've been trying to work things out,' said Mr Sampson. 'Umberto is terrifically jealous. Almost unhinged. If he imagined that Ralph had been – paying attentions – to Maria, that would account for his attacking him, and toppling him into the sea.'

'And his attack on you?'

'Well – I suppose – he might have had the same idea about me.' He was aware that Natalie's eyes were on him.

'If I may be forgiven the observation,' said Lucifero. 'In Mr Marley's case, there might be grounds for such suspicion. In yours, they would be – well – far fetched. So much so, that unless someone had sowed the seed in his mind ...' He paused.

Lord Keaough gave a dry chuckle. 'He means you're not a ladies' man, Colin,' he said. 'Not yet.'

Natalie said sharply, 'And I'm glad he's not. As the only lady present, I can assure you there is no more stomach-turning description—'

She was interrupted by a loud scream.

The three English jumped to their feet. Lucifero sat still, swinging one jackbooted leg over the other.

A second scream. Loud, shrill protests. The clatter of feet, and Maria was there, a Maria with wild, hurt face and dishevelled clothes. A Maria beyond all fear and past all shame.

'Arrest me,' she cried. 'Arrest me, and let Umberto go. I am a wicked girl. Take me away. Put me in your prison cell.'

Signora Telli appeared behind her, ducked nervously to the company, and put a hand on Maria's arm. Maria shook it off.

'I will confess all,' she said.

'Excellent,' said Lucifero. 'No doubt a confession will make much plain.'

His cool voice had its effect. Maria stopped trembling. She said rapidly but clearly, 'Signor Marley professed himself much attracted to me. I was in the garden when he came down to bathe. We went together to the knoll. He – I – I cannot tell you, but we struggled. As I broke away from him he stepped back, and fell. It was a long time before I even dared to look. When I did so, he was most evidently dead. The sea was already carrying him away.'

'Silly girl,' said Lucifero. 'It has, of course, been plain all along that that is what happened. It only needed that you should speak out and speak the truth. Why, instead, did you tell lies to Umberto about poor Signor Sampson here?'

'It was all those questions you asked me, Tenente. Umberto was suspicious. I had to tell him something. So I told him lies – about Signor Sampson, to lead him away from the truth. I was a bad girl.'

'You are a liar,' said Lucifero. 'Like most girls of your age. But you are not a murderess. That is quite evident. The truth is always evident – when people bother to tell it. Mr Marley's death was, as to the larger part, accident, as to a very small part, self-defence. You will have to give evidence at the Inquest tomorrow. That is all. And I hope by that time you will have recovered your self-possession. Take her away now, Signora, and tell Umberto I wish to see him.'

As he left the villa, Lucifero was content. All had come out surprisingly well. Mr Sampson had decided not to prefer any charge against Umberto. Indeed, for the publisher, the auguries were good. His plight had stirred a motherly interest in Natalie, and Lucifero judged that her first refusal of him might be by no means final.

Maria had, of course, behaved stupidly. But as well desire the world to stop in its course, as desire girls of seventeen to behave sensibly. Umberto, as soon as he got her alone, would beat her for lying to him, and would then marry her. Many a successful marriage has been founded on a good beating.

As for Mr Marley – poor Ralph Marley. That twentieth-century Byron, dreaming of who knew what? What conquests, what triumphs, what Isles of Greece? Stumbling to his death, pushed by a serving-maid.

Lucifero had reached the top of the steps. As he opened the gate, he remembered some lines of Byron's which seemed a suitable epitaph for his successor:

> With more capacity for love than earth
> Bestows on most of mortal mould and birth,
> His early dreams of good outstripp'd the truth,
> And troubled manhood followed baffled youth.

Only one question remained unanswered. Was Lord Keaough a spy?

THE TWO FOOTMEN

I N THE AUTUMN of 1894, as you will find recorded in my account of the case of the Norwood Builder, I sold my slender medical practice and rejoined Holmes in our old quarters in Baker Street. His sensational return from supposed death, followed by the trial of Colonel Sebastian Moran for the murder of the Honourable Ronald Adair, had revived and, indeed, increased his practice to such an extent that he was more often away than at home, and I found myself spending long hours in front of the fire in our sitting room.

I did not resent this. On that particular evening the wind was driving the rain in icy spears down the street outside. The wound I had suffered at Maiwand fourteen years before was, of course, fully healed, but when the wind was in a certain quarter I still felt twinges. To pass the time, I had taken down one of the long row of ledgers and books of cuttings that lined the wall beside the fireplace. It turned out to be a hollow case rather than a book and to contain a number of miscellaneous objects. They were not arranged in any methodical way, although no doubt each one of them meant something to Holmes.

A pearl-handled buttonhook, a paper knife broken across the blade, a pack of cards, which proved, on inspection, to be missing the ace of spades, but to have two aces of clubs. None of them meant anything to me until I picked up a small white cardboard box which must, from the dusty crumbs in it, have contained, at one time, a portion of wedding cake. I was able to read, on the outside – 'Mary Macalister and Sergeant Jacob Pearce. The Baptist Chapel, Friary Lane. December 10th 1886.'

I was thinking, 'Good heavens. Was that wedding really eight years ago? It seems like yesterday,' when I heard Holmes's footsteps on the stairs and he burst into the room, seemingly in high spirits. It looked as though his investigation into the papers of ex-President Murillo was going well. He glanced at the box I was holding and said, 'You are savouring, I see, one of your earliest successes.'

'Yours, Holmes. Not mine.'

'On the contrary, my dear fellow. You did all the spadework – Mrs Pearce appreciates that, I'm sure. Has she not appointed you godfather of her eldest boy and named him John in your honour?'

It was on a November day, in 1882, that Mary Macalister had come to our rooms in Baker Street. I said 'had come.' It would have been more accurate if I had said that she had been propelled in, for it was only the support of Mrs Hudson behind her that got her up the stairs and through the door. She was a pretty girl, with a fresh look in her rosy cheeks. I did not need Holmes's deductive powers to see that she came from the country and was of comparatively humble stock. Also that she had been crying.

Holmes ushered her, with every courtesy, to a seat, and since she seemed overcome by the occasion, it was Mrs Hudson who spoke for her.

'Miss Macalister,' she explained, 'is my niece. She works at Corby Manor.'

'The seat of Sir Rigby Bellairs?' said Holmes.

The girl nodded.

'And what has Sir Rigby done to cause you such distress?'

'Oh no, sir. It wasn't Sir Rigby. It was Terence.'

'Terence Black?'

'Yes, sir.'

'I see,' said Holmes. 'He was a friend of yours perhaps?'

The girl, who seemed to be on the point of bursting into tears again, gulped out, 'We were engaged. The marriage was to have been at the end of the month.'

'Then indeed,' said Holmes, 'I am very sorry for you.'

'I told her,' said Mrs Hudson, 'that if anyone could do anything for her it would be you.'

I could read the indecision in Holmes's face. Though considered by some people to be a misogynist and devoid of human feeling, the sight of beauty in distress naturally moved him. At the same time he was, as I knew, engaged in a complex investigation in the City of London. It was not a type of case which he greatly favoured, but at that early point in his career he could not afford to be too selective and this matter, involving as it did a number of members of the peerage and one of the leading City financial firms, could hardly be neglected for the troubles of a servant girl, however appealing.

All these thoughts must have been passing through his mind while the girl and Mrs Hudson watched him anxiously. In the end he said, 'We will help you if we can. I can promise nothing personally. But my colleague, Dr Watson, will make a preliminary investigation to unearth any facts that the national press omitted, and he will keep me informed of everything.'

Before the girl could speak Mrs Hudson said, 'That's very kind of you, sir. And more than we could have hoped for,' and she gently, but firmly, steered her niece to the door and we heard them going downstairs.

I said, 'Our landlady is becoming a tactician. I'm sure Miss Macalister would have preferred your personal attention.'

'You underrate yourself,' said Holmes. He was busy among his press cuttings. 'The Globe has the best account of the Corby affair. We'll discuss it this evening and make up our minds whether any action is possible. Meanwhile, I must get back to the City.'

'*Tragedy at Corby Manor*' was the heading of the extract. It started with a brief summary of the career of Sir Rigby Bellairs and a description of the fine old manor house at Corby. I could not avoid the reflection that these details were considered more important than the fate of the comparatively unimportant victim of the crime. It seemed that Sir Rigby and his wife had been awakened, shortly after one o'clock in the morning of October 7th, by the sound of a pistol shot. Warning his wife not to follow him, he had run out into the long southern corridor which contained a number of guest bedrooms. His house at that time was full for the shooting: his estate was famous for both its partridge and its pheasant drive.

Outside the bedroom door, three along from his own room, he had almost fallen over the body of Terence Black, one of a number of footmen who had been taken on to supplement the regular staff for the occasion. Black had been shot through the heart and must have died instantly.

The room outside which he had fallen was occupied by Mrs Ruyslander, the widow of Jacob Ruyslander and the owner of the famous Ruyslander diamonds. Hearing no sound from inside the room, Sir Rigby had tried the door and found, somewhat to his surprise, that it did not seem to be locked. The first thing he saw when he ventured in was that the window was wide open and that a long ladder had been propped against it. He could see the top of it projecting over the sill. By this time a number of male guests had come into the corridor, together with the butler, an ex-soldier called Peterson. Lady Bellairs was with them. He signalled her in and said, 'See if you can wake Mrs Ruyslander.'

She went over to the bed and found Mrs Ruyslander so deeply asleep that it needed a considerable effort to awaken her. And when, at last, she did sit up, she seemed too dazed to take in what had happened. Sir Rigby acted with commendable decision. Leaving his wife to look after their guest he went out into the corridor, ordered Peterson to guard the bedroom door, cleared the others back to their rooms and sent an outdoor servant hotfoot to Lewes for the police.

The paper then adverted to the Inquest, which had taken place three days later. A number of facts had been elicited, all of which seemed to point in the same direction.

The first question which had to be answered was, what was Black doing in the corridor at all? The indoor staff were segregated in the two wings of the house; the male staff in the west wing, under the surveillance of Peterson, who slept there himself; the female staff in the east wing, under the equally watchful eye of the head housekeeper, Mrs Barnby. To get from his bedroom to the south corridor, Black would have had to go by the back stairs to the ground floor and climb the main staircase. A considerable and, for him, a totally unauthorised journey.

A second point which came out was that the lock on Mrs Ruyslander's bedroom door had been rendered inoperative by the removal of the retaining latch. In other words, though the key had been turned, the door could still be opened.

Finally, the medical evidence showed that a strong sedative must have been administered to Mrs Ruyslander. It was recollected that she had complained of feeling sleepy almost immediately after taking a cup of coffee after dinner. Lady Bellairs gave evidence on this point. She said, 'I do not approve of the habit of gentlemen sitting for a long time over their port. They know that coffee will not be served until they emerge from the dining room, and on this occasion they had joined the ladies within twenty minutes of our retiring from the table. I then gave the signal to the three footmen in attendance to hand round the coffee.'

The Coroner: 'Do you recollect who handed coffee to Mrs Ruyslander?'

Answer: 'I remember very clearly. It was Terence Black.'

The theory which was now very clearly emerging was that Terence Black, assisted by an unidentified accomplice, had planned to steal Mrs Ruyslander's diamonds. He had fixed the lock of the bedroom and slipped a sedative into her coffee. At the last moment there had been some dispute. The accomplice had shot Black, made his way down the ladder and taken himself off.

The jury accordingly found a verdict of murder against some person, or persons unknown. The Lewes police had called in Scotland Yard and their enquiries were continuing under Chief Inspector Leavenworth of the Uniformed Branch and Inspector Blunt of the Criminal Investigation Division.

At the foot of the cutting Holmes had scribbled – 'Leavenworth is a pompous ass. Blunt is quite a good man.'

Twenty-four hours later, at Holmes's suggestion, I was installed at the Kings Arms, a small, but comfortable, hostelry in the main street of Corby. My instructions were to make contact inside the Manor, to see whether I could locate any suspicious character inside or outside the house and to have a further word with Mary Macalister. 'I am sure,' said Holmes, 'that she has not told us everything. If we are to help her to clear the name of her fiancé, she must be frank with us.'

Such suggestions were easy to make, but not so easy to carry out, and I must confess that first fortnight I was there I made very little progress.

I knew from the papers that many of the guests who had been at the original house party in October for the partridge shooting were back now for the first of a series of pheasant battues, which had been planned for the second week in December. It was an even larger assemblage than last time, some forty gentlemen and ladies with their own servants; and I surmised that the house staff would have increased proportionately. I noted that Mrs Ruyslander was still among the guests. Evidently her earlier experience had not alarmed her too much.

The size and importance of the gathering, coupled with his previous alarming experience had led Sir Rigby to take certain precautions. The manor house and park were surrounded by a formidable wall, through which there were only two entrances, the south and the west lodge. By day these were guarded by the lodge keeper and by night the gates were shut and chained. However, if I could not get in, information could get out. The indoor servants might be kept hard at work in the house, but the stable and garden hands had more liberty, and their favourite port of call was the saloon bar of the Kings Arms. As a resident it was quite natural for me to drop in during the evening and listen to their talk, or even to join in. I prided myself that my time in the army had made me at home with all types of men, but with most of them I found it difficult to extract more than a few civil and noncommittal answers.

The one exception was a rat-faced individual, addressed by the others as Len, who had, I gathered, acquired a temporary job in the stables. He did not seem to be over-popular with the permanent hands and was therefore very willing to accept pints of beer from me and give me his views on life in general and Corby Manor in particular.

'A stuck-up lot,' he said, 'who've never done a hand's turn of honest work in their lives. A pal of mine who's got a job as a footman says the women come down in the evening covered with diamonds and pearls enough to keep ten poor families for a lifetime.'

I supplied more beer and agreed that the wealth of this country was very unevenly divided. I don't attempt to reproduce his accent, which was a sort of cockney whine.

'And what do they come down here for? To shoot a lot of birds which never done them any harm. If they want to shoot, they'd be better off in the army.'

I agreed, perhaps over heartily, because he said, 'Would you be an army man yourself, then?'

'I had some army experience,' I agreed, 'but I was a doctor.'

'And what would you be doing down here, if you don't mind me asking?'

I minded very much, but ordered another pint for both of us, which seemed to satisfy him. I was then forced to listen to a stream of socialist clap-trap, but after half an hour I'd had enough and retired to my room. I had considered writing a report to Holmes, but in fact I realised that, as yet, I had nothing to report and went to bed instead.

The next morning, I was sitting on a bench outside the inn smoking my after-breakfast pipe when I heard a clattering of hooves coming down the cobbled street. There was something alarming about the sound, and as I put down my pipe and rose to my feet, a horse came into view. Two things were immediately apparent. The horse was out of control and its rider, a girl of about eleven or twelve, was incapable of doing anything about it.

As the horse came level with me I jumped forward and managed to seize the cheek strap with one hand and the girl with the other. The sudden checking of the horse, who swivelled round, bucking wildly, threw the rider off. The grip I had on her arm broke her fall, but I could not prevent her hitting her head on the railing which ran along the front of the inn. Fortunately, one of the tapsters came running and grabbed the horse, who had quietened down as soon as he was firmly handled, and I was able to attend to the girl. She seemed to have fainted and there was a lot of blood, but I had had enough experience of scalp wounds to be sure that the situation was not serious. I carried her into the inn parlour, put her on the sofa and started, with the help of the landlady, to bandage her and clean her up. Sure enough, after a few minutes, she opened her eyes and tried to sit up. The landlady told her to lie still. 'I've sent a boy for your father,' she said. 'He'll be here soon.'

Almost as she said the words the rattle of a trap being driven at speed announced his arrival. A grizzled man, of about my age, burst into the room. Like all parents, as soon as he saw his daughter was not in danger, he proceeded to give her a piece of his mind.

'Let the poor lamb be, Mr Pearce,' said the landlady. 'This is the gentleman you have to thank that things were not a great deal worse.'

Mr Pearce looked at me for the first time. The frown on his face was replaced by a smile. 'Why, doctor,' he said, 'if that doesn't beat everything.'

'Sergeant Pearce,' I said, 'I've been hoping for years to see you again.'

Sam Pearce had been my medical orderly, and when General

Burrows's force had been routed at Maiwand and I had been severely wounded, he had put me across a horse and led me through the night to Kandahar. I had been so dazed at the time and in the hospital for so long afterwards, that I had lost touch with Sam, who had left the army and gone to Canada. I had not even had an address to write to and, in the end, had given up trying to find him and thank him.

'What are you doing here?' I said. 'Why did you come back?'

'Canada's a fine country for a young man. When you're as old as I am, you feel your own country calling. I've got a nice cottage and a fine job at the Manor. Head gardener, with six men under me. My wife will be longing to meet you.'

During all this, his daughter's plight seemed to have taken second place. After a final scolding for taking out a horse she couldn't manage, we were both packed into the trap and soon bowling along towards the South Lodge.

'This is an old friend of mine,' said Pearce to the lodge keeper. 'Remember his face and don't try to keep him out.' The lodge keeper promised that I should enjoy the freedom of the park. Ten minutes later we were sitting in front of a fire of logs in Sam Pearce's very pleasant abode.

The fortress had fallen.

One thing I decided on at once. I would take Pearce into my confidence. I had total confidence in my one-time medical orderly. I was only afraid that he might be upset at the idea of me playing the spy. I need not have worried. His reaction was indignation, not against me, but against Chief Inspector Leavenworth.

'The man's a fool,' he said, thus echoing Holmes's opinion. 'He can't see farther than the nose on his face. Because there was a ladder propped up against the window – it came from the grape house by the way – he jumped to the conclusion that one of my gardeners must have been involved. I've known them all for years and I told him I'd trust them as far as I'd trust his own policemen – or further.'

'Nor did he like that,' said Mrs Pearce with a smile.

'I said, if these thieves have got the bedroom door fixed, like we've been told, what do they need a ladder for? All they've got to do is walk downstairs and use the back door. It was a blind, of course. The people he ought to be questioning are the house staff. More particularly the ones who've come in during the last week or so. No one knows anything about them. They come with a reference, but that can be forged.'

'Peterson's supposed to keep an eye on them,' said his wife.

'Peterson's a loudmouth and a bully.'

'He's not popular,' agreed his wife. 'Mrs Barnby – she's the house-keeper and a particular friend of mine – had often talked about him.'

'And here's one thing that wasn't mentioned at the Inquest,' said her husband. 'He's got a revolver. Brought it with him when he left the army, I expect.'

'Has he indeed,' I said. New possibilities were opening up every moment. 'Is it your idea, then, that Terence Black's accomplice was one of the other temporary footmen?'

'Speaking for myself,' said Mrs Pearce, 'I never could bring myself to believe that Terence had anything to do with it. As nice a boy as you could meet. It nearly broke poor Mary Macalister's heart.'

'You're friendly with the housekeeper,' I said. 'Do you think you could prevail on her to let Mary come over here to have a talk. I'm sure there are things she hasn't told us.'

'I'll have her here for tea tomorrow,' Mrs Pearce promised.

Before I left, Mr Pearce took me for a conducted tour of the gardens, of which he was justifiably proud. At that time of year there was not much to show in the beds themselves, but there were three hothouses and row upon row of cloches and cold frames. Finally we reached the grape house, which must have been one of the finest in the country, with its own heating system and an amazing framework of vines trained in espalier. Coming out at the far end we were behind the stable block, and I saw a figure I recognised. It was my socialist acquaintance, Len. He was in earnest conversation with a tall, thin footman. Both had their back to us, and it occurred to me that they had stationed themselves in such a way that they could not be seen from the stable yard.

Hearing our footsteps, Len swung round, recognised me and said with a sly grin, 'Inspecting the high and mighty in their native surroundings, doctor?'

'I'm inspecting the gardens,' I said shortly.

The footman had slipped off. When I was saying goodbye to Pearce I commented, 'There seems to be one footman who isn't confined to barracks.'

'That tall streak,' said Pearce. 'He's a recent acquisition here. I think I've seen him round the stables before. Maybe he was getting Len to lay a few bets for him at Ludlow this afternoon.'

'Very likely,' I said.

That evening I sat down to start my first report to Holmes. It was not, I hope, an unduly immodest document, but I could not help feeling a little pleased with the progress I had made.

The morning papers reached Corby at eight o'clock, and over a leisurely breakfast I was able to read that outsiders had won the principal race at the Plumpton and the Ludlow meetings, and I wondered if the tall footman had made a killing at one of these. I also studied a report, on the financial pages, of the matter that was occupying Holmes's attention at that time. It was written with the calculated reserve that journalists employ when they sense that a scandal is imminent, but are afraid, as yet, to attach actual names to it. Reading between the lines I deduced that Mayhews Bank, a small, but respectable banking institution, was in trouble. A consortium of three eminent depositors (no names) owed the bank a considerable sum of money. The loan was a joint one and could not be called in without the consent of all three men. One of them was standing out against the others. The difficulty the bank was in was clear. The last thing it would wish to do was to take action against three important clients. On the other hand, it had to consider the interest, of its other depositors. A decision would have to be taken soon, said the financial editor.

The more that I studied it, the less did it seem to me to be a matter which would engage Holmes's talents. Nor could I spare much sympathy for any of the parties to the dispute. The financiers of the City of London seemed to me to be as irresponsible and as ruthless as the Pathans I had known on the North West Frontier. I switched my mind back to my own problem. Would Mary Macalister be able to throw any light on it when we met?

Mrs Pearce was as good as her word and Mary was there when I arrived. At first I was disappointed. She was ready to talk in a general way about life in the Manor – the kindness of Mrs Barnby, the rudeness of Peterson, the great shoot which was to take place on the following Monday – but this was not what I was after. In the end, I guessed that it was the presence of the Pearces that was inhibiting her. I think they saw this, too, and when tea was cleared they tactfully removed themselves.

As soon as they were out of the room, Miss Macalister turned to me and said, 'If I tell you something – something which may shock you – will you solemnly promise to tell no one else?'

'Except Holmes.'

'Yes,' she agreed, though regretfully I thought, 'you may tell Mr Holmes if you must. My sister, Alice, who also works at the Manor, shares a bedroom with me. Terence and I had much to discuss about our coming wedding. There was no opportunity to talk by day. So he came up to our room that night.'

'I don't find that very shocking,' I said. 'When did he come and, incidentally, how did he get there?'

'He had to wait until midnight, when most people were in their own rooms. Then he crept down from his quarters in the west wing, crossed by main bedroom corridor and up to our room at the top of the east wing. We must have been talking for an hour, because I heard the stable clock strike one as he left.'

'And he would have planned to return by the way he came?'

'I imagine so.'

'Tell me,' I said. 'Did you hear the sound of a shot?'

'No. It's a rambling old house and the walls are very thick. I don't think anyone up in the wings could hear anything much from the main part of the house.'

It was this answer which convinced me that the girl was speaking the truth. Before setting out, I had read up all that I could about Corby Manor, and a book which I had extracted from Holmes's considerable library of reference works had informed me of one important point. The wings had been added at a later date. This would mean that there were, in effect, two walls separating them from the main body of the house. If Miss Macalister had pretended that she *had* heard the shot, a few minutes after her fiancé had left her, in an attempt to absolve him from participation in the robbery, then I should have suspected that she was lying.

At the same time, it did not clear her fiancé. At the Inquest, Sir Rigby had been woken by the shot 'shortly after one o'clock.' That might mean anything up to ten or fifteen minutes. If Black had made his preparations beforehand there was still time for him to have met his accomplice and proceeded with the robbery.

Miss Macalister was clearly distressed. There was not much else she could tell me, and I soon took my leave. I had several paragraphs to add to my report and the last post left Corby at seven o'clock. I therefore accepted Sam Pearce's offer of a lift back to the village and sat down to work.

That same evening my enquiry took a decided step forward. It fell out in this way.

My report was finished and sealed by a quarter to seven, and I hurried out into the main street to post it. It was a clear and frosty night. To reach the pillar box I had to pass the front of an ale house called 'The Fox and Hens.' It was not a very attractive hostelry and I had never been inside it. As I approached, the door of the public bar swung open, and a man stepped out and went off down the street at a swinging stride. I had only seen his back view before, but I recognised the tall footman I had seen in conversation with Len the ostler two days before. I had had a feeling, too, that I had encountered the man before. Now, noting his lean, supple figure and his way of walking, which was almost a prance, I was suddenly able to put a name to him.

Jim the Fly.

When I had been helping Holmes in one of his earliest cases, which resulted in the breaking up of the Camden Town gang, the only member of that unsavoury fraternity who had escaped prison, on a technicality, had been the actual operator of their thefts, the man who climbed into the house and abstracted the diamonds or other precious stones which were their objectives.

As these thoughts were passing through my mind I was, as you may imagine, in hot pursuit. My quarry was moving so fast that I had almost to trot to keep up, and it was a relief when he stopped outside the twelve-foot-high park wall. To my astonishment, he seemed to climb the face of the wall like the fly he was named after. When he reached the top, he pulled himself over, and I heard him drop down on the other side.

When I came up to the place, some of the mystery was solved. I found that three short iron spikes had been driven into the brickwork, one at knee height, one at shoulder height and a third one above. I should have had great difficulty in using this unofficial ladder myself, but to a man like Jim it was as good as an open door.

As I walked thoughtfully back to my hotel, fate dealt me a second card. Glancing through the bar window of 'The Fox and Hens,' I saw Len. No doubt he had been meeting his accomplice there, but at the moment he was engaged in earnest conversation with a florid man, a Central European I guessed, whose London style garb seemed curiously out of place in an ale house.

The plot was thickening, but the outlines were becoming somewhat clearer. I was sorry that I had posted my first report to Holmes. Now I should have to sit down and write a second one as speedily as possible.

When I reached the hotel I found that there was a letter for me in the rack. I recognised Holmes's angular handwriting, but the envelope was unstamped. It was marked: 'By Hand. Urgent.' Before opening it, I asked the hall porter who had brought it. 'A young boy,' he said. He could give me no further description. Evidently, he was a man to whom all small boys looked alike.

I took it up to my room. It contained a single half-sheet of paper on which Holmes had written, 'I advise you to study Peterson's ears.' That was all.

Well, if he had no further news for me, I had plenty for him.

'From observations I have made,' I wrote, 'and deductions from those observations, I have been able to arrive at a firm conclusion as to what took place at Corby Manor in October, and more importantly, as to what is planned to take place there in the near future, unless steps are taken to prevent it. The key in both cases is a temporary stable hand known as Len. He has the foxy face and shifty appearance which immediately suggest that he is a member of the criminal classes. When his real name comes to light it will, I am sure, be discovered that he has a record. His objective was, and is, to purloin Mrs Ruyslander's diamonds. On the first occasion it is possible that his accomplice inside the house was Terence Black. On this occasion there is strong evidence that his new accomplice is one of the temporary footmen. Having seen the latter in action, both moving fast and climbing a wall, I conclude that he is none other than Jim the Fly, a name which will, I am sure, be familiar to you.'

I felt a little malicious when I wrote this. Jim's escape from the net of the law on the previous occasion was a matter which had rankled Holmes.

'A second possible accomplice is a foreign gentleman I observed talking to Len. His function will, no doubt, be to dispose of the diamonds once they have been abstracted. The timing of the attempt is also clear. On Monday occurs the first great pheasant battue. All the men will be taking part, and the ladies traditionally accompany them to a sumptuous open-air luncheon at one of the butts. Apart from the fact that many of the house staff will be assisting at this function, I under-stand that stable and garden hands are invited to act as beaters, being no doubt well paid for their services. In short, the house and grounds will be practically deserted. Your connections with Scotland Yard will, I am sure, enable you to devise a suitable reception committee.'

With my mind on the shooting, I added, 'In this matter I am acting as beater. You and the police are the guns.'

You will appreciate that I felt justifiably proud of this report, and in order that there should be no delay, I got one of the boys from the hotel to take it into Lewes next morning, which was Friday, to catch the early post. Holmes would receive it on Friday evening, which would give him plenty of time to make his preparations. Also, incidentally, time to write to me. On this occasion, I thought, I should certainly get something less terse and unhelpful than his previous communication.

The weekend passed slowly. On Monday morning I was down early. The post had arrived and the letters had been placed in the rack, but there was nothing for me. As I was turning away, the hall porter said, 'This is for you, doctor. I was just going to put it in the rack.'

'How did it get here?'

'By hand, sir. Same boy as before.'

To say that I was surprised would be an understatement. However, I assumed that the letter would clear up the mystery. Instead, it deepened it.

'Most important,' Holmes had written, 'You are to be at the outside door which leads to the kitchen quarters at half past one this afternoon. Please persuade your friend Pearce to come with you. You should both be armed. You, I know, have your service revolver. Pearce will, no doubt, have a sporting gun. Both should be loaded. We are dealing with very dangerous animals. When you arrive at the door, please follow precisely the instructions you will be given.'

Being, by now, totally confused, I thought that the only course open to me was to do what I was told. When I got to the cottage I found the Pearces sitting down to lunch. I showed Sam Pearce the letter. He read it slowly and then said, 'I take it this would be from that friend of yours, Mr Sherlock Holmes?'

'No doubt about that,' I said. 'I don't believe there's a man alive who could imitate his handwriting well enough to deceive me.'

'He seems to know what he wants. We'd better follow our instructions. Will you join us for lunch? It's only a matter of laying an extra plate.' He added, with that grin of his which always appeared when any excitement was in prospect, 'If we're going tiger shooting, we may as well go on a full stomach.'

I found Pearce's confidence in Holmes a comfort and did justice to an excellent pheasant stew prepared by his wife. At half past one he led me, by a back path, to the kitchen door. He had put on a light coat to conceal the shotgun he was carrying. My trusty revolver was in my jacket pocket, as it had been at other times when I had set out with Holmes at the crisis of one of his cases; though I could remember no occasion on which I had no less idea why I was carrying it, or whom it was to be used on.

During the morning, we had heard the sound of distant shooting. That had now stopped, and I assumed that the guests, beaters and servants were together engaged in one of the Lucullan open air repasts which were a feature of these battues. The garden and grounds were deserted, and I could hear no one moving inside the house. We reached the door, and I was about to knock on it when it was opened. I had speculated a number of times as to who might appear to give me instructions. All such speculations proved to be wide of the mark. Standing inside the door, with a finger to his lips enjoining silence, was the stable hand, Len. He said, speaking very softly, 'I hope you are both armed. Then follow me.' Had he not, by saying this, indicated that he knew the contents of Holmes's letter, I must confess that I should have hesitated. As it was, I did what he said.

We travelled a long basement passage, climbed two flights of stairs, and emerged through a green baize-covered door into what I took to be the main bedroom corridor. There were a number of doors on each side, and I could see, halfway along on the left, a door which might have been the one in front of which the body of Terence Black had fallen. The silence was absolute.

Len opened a door at our end of the passage and motioned us through. It was evidently a gentleman's bedroom. When the door was safely shut I turned, rather angrily, to him and said, 'Now, perhaps, you will be good enough to explain.'

He put his finger up again and said, very softly, 'I beg that you will keep silent, doctor. I promise you that it will not be for long.'

For the first time I noticed, in his face, an air of shrewdness and purpose, which had certainly not been there before. I said, 'Very well. Since we seem to be involved in melodrama, let us play it out to the end.' After that silence fell again.

The corridor was carpeted and it was difficult to be certain, but after about ten minutes I thought I heard footsteps – two lots of footsteps – passing our door. Then the sound of a door opening farther down the passage. After that, silence again.

Len now had our door open a fraction and was peering through. Standing over him, I could see down the passage. The door to the room which I had already, tentatively, noted as being Mrs Ruyslander's bedroom swung open and Peterson came out, followed by Sir Rigby Bellairs, who was carrying a small case. I saw them staring in our direction and thought they had noticed our partly open door. However, it was not at us that they were looking, but at the tall footman, who was advancing toward them, at a stately pace, down the corridor.

Sir Rigby said, in tones in which astonishment and fury were mixed, 'What the devil are you doing here, Simpson?'

'I was keeping an eye on Mrs Ruyslander's diamonds,' said the footman. 'I take it that they are in that case?'

It was only when he spoke that I knew for certain who it was.

'I assume,' the footman went on, 'that on the previous occasion when you attempted this theft, you were interrupted by Terence Black. Of course you had to silence him. Yes, I can see that you are both armed. I am only uncertain which of you used your gun on the poor fellow.'

'Does it matter?' said Sir Rigby thickly. 'It seems that history has repeated itself. We find you here, with the diamonds in your possession—'

'No, no,' said Holmes. 'I'm afraid that on this occasion that scenario won't work. You are out-gunned. Allow me to make the introductions. My name is Sherlock Holmes. This is my colleague, Dr Watson. The gentleman with the shotgun you will, of course, recognise as your own head gardener. Finally, this is Detective Inspector Leonard Blunt of the Criminal Investigation Department, Scotland Yard.'

'I am charging you both with robbery,' said Blunt, stepping forward. 'And there will be a further charge against one of you for murder.'

Peterson had already dropped his pistol. Sir Rigby, after one furious glance, first at his accomplice and then at us, reluctantly followed suit.

In the event, Peterson, who was a coward as well as a bully, gave evidence for the Crown against his employer. His insistence that it was Sir Rigby who had shot Black was supported by forensic evidence which matched the bullet in his gun with the one in the murdered footman. Peterson received a short, but salutary sentence of imprisonment. Sir Rigby was hanged.

'It was an interesting case,' said Holmes. 'I had, it is true, one more item of information than you, yet I knew from the very first who the villains were. What I knew, but you did not, was that Sir Rigby was one of the three recalcitrant depositors at Mayhews Bank. I therefore knew that he was desperately short of money and would go to any lengths to obtain it. Really, the rest of the truth was in that newspaper report. It contained three glaring improbabilities. I, like you, had studied the excellent account of Corby Manor in Gillespies "English Manor Houses," and once I had done so I realised how unlikely it was that a single shot – which, incidentally, Miss Macalister, who was wide awake, admits she did not hear – would have woken Peterson, who was sleeping just as far away in the other wing. And if it had woken him, how could he have arrived in the bedroom corridor – a considerable journey – at the same time as the gentlemen who were sleeping there? No, no. I was sure from that moment that he was in the plot. As soon as I encountered him, this suspicion became a certainty. I recognised him from the curious shape of his ears as George Peters, a man with a long criminal record. And if he was involved, surely his employer was as well. The second point was the fixing of the door lock. For a footman, supervised and busy about his duties, it would have been almost impossible. For Sir Rigby and his head butler, very easy. Finally, there was the sleeping draught in the coffee. This totally exculpated Black. There were three footmen handing round, how could he be sure that he was going to be the one to hand the cup to Mrs Ruyslander? Apart from which, have you considered *how*, in the course of taking it to her, the drug was to be added. This was surely done by Lady Bellairs, before the cup was despatched. I fancy, though it will never be proved, that she was involved in the plot. However, justice was served without looking for a third victim. I fancy that clears up the main points.'

I had a number of unanswered questions in my mind, but the only thing I could think of immediately was to say, 'You were surely very fortunate to obtain the job.'

'Not in the least. I offered my services at under the going rate and was able to supply references from a High Court Judge and a Bishop. Blunt followed a similar course. We were both welcomed with open arms.'

'And why did you take the risk of visiting "The Fox and Hens" in Corby village? Surely you could have held any necessary discussions more safely in the grounds.'

'A risk, but a necessary one. I had to identify the foreign gentleman for Blunt. You were quite right. He was a notorious middle man in illicit diamond dealing, named Bernstorff. We would have liked to have included him in the charge, but the evidence against him was too slight.'

I had one final question, and in putting it I tried to keep the reproach out of my voice. I said, 'Could you not have taken me somewhat sooner into your confidence?'

'My dear fellow,' said Holmes, 'your conviction that the villains were a particular footman and a stable hand – a conviction which soon reached Peterson, through Mrs Pearce and her friend Mrs Barnby – was invaluable. It meant that the real criminals could pursue their plans with confidence. Which they did, to their undoing. Incidentally,' he added with a twinkle in his eye, 'I read both of your reports when I got back to Baker Street. I found them most illuminating.'

'Good God,' I said, remembering my description of 'Len', 'I hope you haven't shown them to Inspector Blunt.'

'They shall remain entirely confidential to the two of us,' said Holmes.

There is not much more to record. A cousin inherited Corby Manor and kept on most of the permanent staff, including the Pearces and Mary Macalister. Jacob, the Pearce's eldest son, returning from the wars, wasted no time in seeking Mary's hand, and their marriage was solemnised on a cold December day in 1886. Eight years later, as I have recorded, I was sitting in our Baker Street room looking at the few crumbs of wedding cake in the small white box, when Holmes burst in and found me doing so.

I have a suspicion that he still felt a twinge of regret for the deception he had practised on me in that early case. Maybe at that stage in our collaboration he had not acquired the full confidence which developed through the years. Whether for this reason, or some other, he took the unusual course of explaining to me the background of the relics in that box. They were all fascinating stories, none more so than the case of the pearl-handled buttonhook, which I hope to relate someday.

TRUST LITTLE AL

A CAR STOPPED ahead of me in Bond Street and Sergeant Cator of the Special Branch looked out. 'Hop in,' he said. 'They want you.'

I felt as if the lift had gone down unexpectedly, leaving me on Floor Six and taking my stomach down to the basement with it. I've been doing small jobs for Them for some time – nothing terrifically exciting, errand-boy stuff, really. I ought to have got used to it by now.

When we got there, I was taken straight up to Captain Forestier's office. I know Tony Forestier as well as anyone is allowed to know anyone in that line of business. He is a red-haired, freckled man with light eyes, who stands poised on the balls of his feet as if he's ready to jump out of the window at the drop of a hat. I play quite a lot of squash with him. He's not subtle, but he never stops running.

'We've got something for you,' he said, as soon as the door was shut. 'Have you ever heard of Alex Baker?'

'Plays centre three-quarter for Richmond,' I said, promptly.

'Not this one,' said Forestier. 'Certainly not this Alex. He's about five foot nothing, looks as if the wind would blow him over, wears glasses, seldom has his hair cut, and doesn't always remember to brush his teeth in the morning.'

'Doesn't sound quite my type.'

'Nevertheless, you're going to take a holiday with him. And you'll have to stick to him like a long-lost brother.'

'What's it all about?'

'In fact, you must never let him out of your sight. We don't insist that you share a bed with him, but your bedrooms must have intercommunicating doors.'

'Would you mind telling me why?'

'Since when have you questioned your orders?' I think he saw the light of revolt in my eye, and relented. 'It's like this,' he said. 'That little man is one of the most valuable assets in this country today. Worth – oh, I don't know – a couple of aircraft carriers – the Brigade of Guards – a wing of jet bombers.'

'To be on the safe side, why not add them together and throw in the War Office?'

'I'm being serious,' said Forestier, coldly. 'And unless you're prepared to treat it seriously, I suggest that we're both wasting our time.'

'I'm sorry,' I said. 'But you must admit, it's a tall order. If you say so,' I added hastily, 'I believe it.'

'He's not much to look at, but providence or nature has given him a brain. He's a physicist, and several other things ending with -ist that I can't even spell. Only he's a cut above them all. His mental processes begin where theirs leaves off. Penny says that he understands some of what Baker's saying most of the time, but that's as far as he'll go.'

'And if something more frightful than the hydrogen bomb exists, it's probably inside his head.'

'That's right.'

The big red Captain thought hard for a moment, and added, 'He's an untidy feeder. And he can't keep his hands off a woman.'

'He sounds,' I said, 'the ideal holiday companion. Why the hell can't you keep him at home?'

'We'd like to keep him in the vaults of the Bank of England. There's stuff there worth a good deal less than he is. Unfortunately, he's not inanimate. He's got to be kept healthy and happy, or his mind won't function properly. Now he's decided that he wants to take a holiday. In Austria. He mustn't be frustrated. So off he goes to Austria. You go with him to keep him out of harm.'

'Well ...' I said.

I supposed I could do it. It was the sort of job I was trained to do. And, in a way, it was obviously a compliment that it had been offered to me.

'When do we start? I could be ready by Saturday—'

'You're going today.'

'Hey,' I said, 'today? But I'm playing in the quarter-finals of the Amateur this afternoon.'

'You'll have to scratch.'

'I can't just walk out. Think what Hayman will say.'

'Colonel Bles chose you himself for this job. Do I understand you are saying no to it?'

I swallowed twice. If Captain Forestier is impressive, his Chief, Colonel Bles, is actually terrifying.

'All right,' I said weakly. 'I'll have to ring up and tell them I can't play.'

'On the assumption that you would agree, I have already scratched your entry. There is absolutely no time to waste. Baker's train leaves Victoria in half an hour.'

'Half an hour! I've got to pack—'

'A suitcase with all the stuff you'll need for the next ten days is already in the train, in the rack above your reserved seat.'

'But—'

'I suggest you leave your bowler hat and umbrella here. There is a tweed cap and a raincoat in one of the suitcases. You carry your passport with you, I know.'

I nodded.

'Sensible man. So do I. Now, here's the money. And the travellers' cheques. Ticket. Seat reservation. And a list of codes in case we have to communicate. You know the procedure. And – oh, yes – there's a gun in your sponge-bag. I've tipped off the Customs, so there won't be any trouble. Now, is there anything else you'd like me to do for you?'

Do you know, quite honestly, I couldn't think of anything. Forestier rang his bell, and his girl took charge of me. Cator was still waiting with the car. He'd got rid of the driver and was behind the wheel himself.

'Hop in,' he said. 'We haven't much time.'

He was more right than he knew. We ran into a solid traffic block at Marble Arch, swung into the Park, and got caught behind a procession.

I was sweating a bit by this time. The Office aren't fond of people who miss important trains. 'Drive across the grass,' I said. 'This is special.'

'That's all right,' said Cator, 'we'll make it.'

And we did, with less than a minute to spare. I waved to Cator, who grinned back at me, and then the train was moving and I walked down to find my seat.

At first I thought I must have got the wrong reservation tab. Except that this would have been unlike the efficient Forestier who could conjure up clothes and shoes to fit; no doubt my measurements were down somewhere in his elaborate filing system, together with the names of my tailor and bootmaker and hatter.

Then I recognized Alex Baker. He had a corner seat, facing the engine. Mine should have been opposite; I saw the new suitcase in the rack above it, but there was a girl in the seat.

When they saw me looking, the girl said, 'Looks like the boy-friend, Al,' and they both grinned. Baker said, 'Sorry about this, but Gwen decided she couldn't bear to leave me. She had to come down to Dover and kiss me good-bye.'

All this in front of the four other occupants of the carriage, who looked down their noses and got on with *The Times* crossword.

'Don't move,' I said – Gwen had made no attempt to do so – 'I shall be quite happy in the corridor.'

The girl was obviously an expensive prostitute. Whether she was anything more remained to be seen.

I found time for a word with Baker as we were drawing into Dover. Gwen had disappeared, and he came out and stood in the corridor with me.

'I'm sorry about that,' he said, but would have sounded sorrier if he hadn't been smiling at the same time. 'Fact is, she insisted on coming, and it was too late to book a seat for her. Nice of you to let her have yours.'

'How long have you known her?' I asked.

'Since last night.'

'Did she pick you up, or you her?'

He didn't seem at all put out, but thought the matter over carefully, and said, 'I should say she made most of the running. I did wonder if she was all she pretended to be.'

'What makes you say that?'

'Bit of an amateur in bed. Too willing.'

'I see,' I said. 'Yes, I thought it might be something like that. When you get to the boat, keep her talking. I've got a phone call to make.'

Unfortunately the train nearly spoilt it by running in late. I had just time to dive for a phone box and ask for one of the numbers I keep in my head but never write down. I told the man who answered what had happened. He would know what to do. Then I ran for it, and got aboard as the gang-plank was going up.

Gwen stood on the quay and waved her wispy handkerchief at us. It was quite affecting.

It's an odd thing, that although I've led a rough sort of life, with a certain amount of excitement in it and plenty of opportunities, I've never really been attracted by women as such. I don't mean matrimony. Some day I'll settle down with the nicest little woman in the world and we'll start a family. But not until I've given up my present job. It's no job for a married man. I'd like to win the Amateur Championship, too, if I can, before I marry.'

'Come and have a drink,' said Baker. 'Or are you going to be sick?'

I must have looked surprised. The sea was like a mirror.

'I can be sick crossing the Thames in a punt,' said Baker. 'That's why I carry these.' He produced a dirty screw of paper from his waistcoat pocket. I could see some white tablets in it.

'You'd do much better,' I said, 'not to think about it at all.'

'It's nothing to do with thought,' he said crossly. 'Seasickness starts in your semicircular canals.' He gave me a lecture on this, most of which was Greek to me; but it lasted us safely into Calais.

There's nothing much to report about the next twenty-four hours. We shared a two-berth sleeper on the Arlberg Express. Captain Forestier was quite right; Baker didn't clean his teeth, either going to bed or getting up. Apart from that, he was fairly inoffensive. I think I'm quite an easy chap to get on with. Anyway, all I had to do was listen.

'I'm a thinker,' he said to me after dinner. 'You remember Sherlock Holmes? That's stupid, most of it. None of his analyses holds water, you know. Not if you really examine it.' Then he quoted about three pages of one of the stories verbatim as far as I could tell, and pulled it to pieces. It was quite an amusing performance.

'That's all very well,' I said, 'but could you do any better yourself?'

'Certainly. But it takes time, like all real scientific processes. The mistake is in calling it deduction. It isn't deduction at all. Just trial and error, trial and error, until the error gets less and less. When it finally vanishes altogether, why, you've got a fact.'

He was still at it when we turned the light out in the sleeper that night.

We changed at Schwarzach and got to Velden after tea next day. The hotel, which was on the south shore of the Wörthersee – a big, attractive lake – seemed, to my simple mind, to offer all the heart could desire: bathing, boating, and woods and mountains behind it for walking and climbing.

Baker's idea of fun was to lie in the sun all day and get drunk in the evenings. After that, I've no doubt he would have liked one of the women. There were plenty about.

I kept him on the straight and narrow the first evening by dint of stopping with him the whole time until I had him safely in his bedroom and heard his distinctive snore. It sounded like a circular saw making slow progress through a tough old plank, hitting a knot every now and then.

Next morning I got a long cable. It appeared to come from a firm of wine merchants – that, by the way, is nominally my business – and there was a lot in it about purchases and prices and vintages. It was one of those mechanical codes that you 'set' on a Duplex Rotator: simple enough if you've got the machine and the right keys, but almost unbreakable without.

It directed me to go to Klagenfurt and make the acquaintance of a Franz Gelert, who kept a bookshop and circulating library in the square.

I gave Baker a straight talk before I left, telling him, in his own interests, to avoid strangers and stick to solo sunbathing. 'You're within less than fifty miles,' I said, 'of people who have probably only two ideas about you. The first and better would be to kidnap you. But if they couldn't do that, it would suit them almost as well to knock you on the head.'

'Don't you worry about me,' he said. His nose was bright red from the sun and he looked more than usually pleased with himself. 'Little Al's quite capable of looking after himself. Brains always beat brawn.'

I said nothing to this, but hurried off to catch the bus into Klagenfurt.

I found Gelert. He was a nice little man. He'd been doing his under-cover job ever since the Occupation in 1945, and evidently knew his way about. We discussed a number of plans for coping with Baker, but they all suffered from the same defect.

'It's simply impossible to tell what he's going to do next,' I said. 'I've no doubt he's very clever – scientifically, I mean – but in the affairs of this life he's got about as much sense as a spaniel puppy. Added to which he's got the morals of a rabbit.'

Old Gelert peered at me through his glasses and said, 'I could get you help, of course. Quite a lot of help, if necessary. But we don't want to be obvious. What about Trude? Could she do anything?'

I'd been conscious of Trude in the background for some time. She was blonde, pink and white, and looked as if butter wouldn't melt in her mouth.

'She's quite – quite reliable,' said Gelert. 'And she's older than she looks. Do you think if, perhaps, we could concentrate his roving affec-tions on her, it might make our path smoother?'

I didn't like the idea at all. Damn it, if I'd had a daughter she'd have been about that age. Besides, in my view, women always complicate these transactions. However, the advantages of the plan were too obvious to need underlining.

'Fix her a room at the hotel,' I said. 'There's no harm in trying. We'd better not go back together. Let her turn up in time for dinner this evening.'

I had lunch in Klagenfurt and got back to the hotel about the middle of the afternoon. Baker was not in his room, nor in any of the public rooms. I tackled the manageress.

'Ah, yes,' she said. 'Herr Baker. You will find him, I think, at the bathing-beach. There is an attraction, you understand,' and she posi-tively winked.

My heart sank. 'Who is it?' I said. 'Tell me the worst.'

'Frau Hodinger. She is not, perhaps, everyone's choice. You saw her at dinner last night. The brunette.'

I had, indeed, seen her; her appearance was not designed to escape notice. A woman of thirty-five, dressed to ape twenty-five, with a face – what we could see of it under its coat of make-up – as hard as the crags of the Karawanken mountains, which filled the sky to the south of the hotel.

I made my way down to the private bathing-beach. There was a good deal of human flesh about, anonymous in its nudity; but a bright pink nose and pair of gleaming steel spectacles were nowhere to be seen. Nor the brunette. I cursed under my breath. If the opposition had got hold of him they had moved with extraordinary speed. It was not impossible but—

'Your friend would seem to be enjoying himself,' said a voice in my ear.

I followed the pointing finger, and my blood froze. There were a number of cockleshell boats with outboard motors belonging to the hotel. One of them lay about four hundred yards out, rocking danger-ously. A fight, or a sham fight was being waged on that shaky platform, between England's top scientist and a hard-faced brunette.

Even as I watched, they went over the side, the brunette on top.

Mercifully, at the jetty there was an empty boat, which started at the first tug. By the time the fighters surfaced I was almost half-way there. My concern proved to be absolutely unnecessary. Alex swam like a fish. It was the brunette who needed rescuing. His idea of fun was to swim below her, catch her ankle, and pull her under. She had had enough of this when I came up, and she climbed thankfully into my boat.

Baker made a rude gesture at me. 'Since you've butted in,' he said, 'you can bloody well make yourself useful and bring my boat back.' And he started on a slovenly crawl to the beach, leaving me speechless.

I didn't see him again until dinner that night. I was resigned to an uncomfortable meal; either a blat about my behaviour that afternoon or an interminable lecture on some obscure branch of physics. What I was not prepared for was silence.

I don't mean that he was sulky. He just ate his food and drank his wine in a normal, companionable way. We were drinking our coffee when he said, 'Don't you think she's marvellous? Perhaps she's a film star. I think she must be a star.'

'Who are you talking about?' I said, screwing my head round for I had my back to the room.

'The blonde, of course. I haven't been able to take my eyes off her all dinner. I thought you were making eyes at her in the mirror.'

'Certainly not!' I said indignantly. 'Who?' And then I saw Trude. She'd done something to her face, and in a low-cut evening dress she looked a mile removed from the *ingénue* I had talked to in the shop that morning.

'I thought you were keen on Frau Hodinger,' I said.

'That bag,' said Baker, gracefully. 'Where do you think my eyes are? Now, there *is* a girl. Looks lonely, too. Little Al must remedy that.'

I see from my report that the next seven days were comparatively peaceful.

I had the chance of a word with Trude one morning. Baker had gone into Klagenfurt to do some shopping, and Trude had somehow managed to get out of going with him. It was the first time they had been separated for a week.

'He's a funny little man,' she said. 'I'm not at all sure that he knows what he does want.'

'I'll give you three guesses,' I said.

'Oh, he'd like to sleep with me, yes. And no doubt plans to do so. But he is more complex than you think. He tells you so often what a remarkable brain he has that you naturally come to disregard it. But he really has got a brain, you know.'

'So I'm told. Most of what he says goes over my head. I never got further at school than making smells in test-tubes.'

'I don't mean science. One evening, he suddenly pointed to a fat little man – you know, the one with the daughters, who plays patience in the corner – and said, "That man was in a concentration camp during the war." I said, "Did he tell you?" Al said, "No, I've never spoken to him." He'd got it all worked out from the way the old boy behaved, and what he did and what he didn't do.'

I passed over that one and went back. 'You say he's planning to sleep with you?'

'Of course. That is what he is doing in Klagenfurt. He has extracted from me a promise that I will dine with him at the Haus Lord Byron on Thursday night – that is your last night here. I expect he has booked rooms for us – you know, in case we miss the last bus back. Separate rooms, of course.'

'I see.' It seemed to worry me a good deal more than her.

'Then he will get me drunk. I expect he is now bribing the wine waiter to put some brandy into my white wine at dinner.'

'I'll attend to that,' I said grimly. 'You've done your part well, and we don't want any complications at the end of it.'

'I am certain I can rely on you,' she said. I wished I could have been as certain myself.

I went to Klagenfurt that afternoon and had a word with Gelert. After all, he was one of the people who was going to get hurt if it went wrong. He said, 'I could have friends on hand with a car, in case he gets violent.'

'I think he'll go quietly,' I said. 'I shall be on hand myself. I've taken a room in a pension that overlooks the hotel.'

We chewed it over a bit more; but without knowing exactly what

Baker's plans were, it was difficult to do more than guard against contingencies.

I think I can truthfully say that Thursday night was one of the most baffling and, in its outcome, most extraordinary nights I have ever spent. I watched Baker's preliminary manoeuvres with a good deal of amusement. First he had to get rid of Frau Hodinger, who seemed to have an idea that he'd promised that evening to go dancing with *her*. I saw him in the distance, having a lengthy and rather heated conversation with her. Then he had to sidetrack me. He served me up a carefully modified version of the truth.

'I'm taking Trude out for a meal at the Klub Kondoterei,' he said somewhat truculently, 'and we don't want an armed guard.' I looked doubtful. 'It's the biggest public restaurant in Klagenfurt,' he said, 'and I've hired a car to take us back to the hotel afterwards. So stop worrying.'

Although I already knew the exact position of the table for two that he'd booked at the Haus Lord Byron and the numbers of the rooms he had reserved for the night, I managed to preserve a reasonably straight face. 'You've behaved like a sensible chap so far. Don't go blotting your copybook on your last night.'

'Trust little Al,' he said.

Like hell I trusted him. I gave him a short start that evening and then set out myself. The bus into Klagenfurt was full of the usual evening crowd, who'd been toasting themselves in the sun all day and were now making for the bright lights and music. Nevertheless, something was not quite right.

After a time, in my job, you get an instinct about these things. There were at least two men in the bus who had no particular reason for being there. And they both got out at the same stop as I, and although they walked straight off, I realized that I was under observation.

I did my best, in the next hour, to shake off any watchers, but it's a difficult thing to be sure about in a strange town, particularly when you have no idea how many people are in the game.

I was pretty certain, nevertheless, that there was no one behind me when I got into the pension and went up to the room I had booked. It was ideally situated. I could look down right into the front dining-room of the Haus Lord Byron, and since Alex and Trude had chosen a table in the window, I could follow the meal, bite by bite.

I nibbled a packet of digestive biscuits and watched the poulet au riz follow the côtelettes de saumon Pojarski and the canapés follow the poulet au riz, washed down by first one bottle, and then a second of Schloss Johannisberg. When the third bottle arrived I walked over to the wash-stand and helped myself to a swig from the fine old vintage water in the carafe.

It was a leisurely sort of meal. I am not sure whether Baker had made special arrangements about this, but by the time they had reached their coffee and liqueurs, the dining-room was pretty nearly empty and I saw from my watch that it was eleven.

The last bus out to Velden left at ten-thirty.

Something of the sort seemed to have occurred to Trude. I could follow the pantomime as from the front row of the stalls. Nothing was left out. The waiter summoned to fetch a timetable. The head waiter brought into consultation. *No, it was very difficult indeed to get a car at that time of night.* The manager's arrival on the scene. *Most fortunately, they had got two single rooms.* Great relief all round. A second liqueur.

Any moment now, I thought. I went down softly into the front hall of the pension and looked out into the street.

About fifty yards away, midway between street lights, a large closed car was drawn up to the kerb. I felt a sudden constriction of the throat, a quickening of the pulse. I looked across the street into the uncurtained window of the dining-room.

Alex and Trude had gone.

Their reserved rooms, as I knew, were at the back of the hotel on the first floor. I had to take a chance on being seen. As quickly and as quietly as possible, I stepped across the street and into the alley at the side of the hotel. As I reached it, I had the impression, from a quick backward glimpse, that the closed car had started to move up.

I edged along the alley, turned the corner, and looked up.

That was when I got the surprise of the evening; for the first thing I saw was a pair of legs. They were waving out of an open first-storey window. As I watched, the groping feet found the ledge, and more of the climber came into view.

My first idea, that someone was climbing in at the window, was wrong. On the contrary, someone was coming out.

I must have been so engrossed in watching that I had no attention to spare for anything else. That was a mistake.

The smallest sound behind me; and the impression that the corner-stone of the hotel had fallen on my head.

I came back to life to the noise of thudding. A lot of it was inside my head, but some of it was actually happening, too.

Someone was knocking on a door. On my bedroom door.

I was in my room at the hotel. Just for a moment I thought that the whole of the events of the night before had been a crazy dream. Then I put my hand up and felt the back of my head.

It was no dream. Someone had knocked me cold and had then brought me back to Velden, taken off my coat and shoes, and tucked me nicely up under the coverlet before leaving me.

The only way to stop the knocking was to say, 'Come in.'

The manageress came in. She was normally completely poised, but some of her composure seemed for the moment to have deserted her. 'I trust you will remember,' she said, 'that the bus leaves at three.'

'The bus?'

'The bus for the train. If you miss the four-o'clock train at Klagenfurt you will not catch your connection at Schwarzach.'

I looked at my watch. My God, it was nearly two o'clock. 'Come in,' I said, 'and shut the door.'

I sat up on the bed. 'Who brought me home last night?'

'The police. You fell in Klagenfurt and hit your head.'

I ignored this. 'You must get them at once,' I said. 'It's desperately urgent. It doesn't matter about me. But Herr Baker has disappeared.'

'Disappeared?'

'Kidnapped, I fear.' The woman simply stood there, staring at me. Then I heard it, too. From the next-door room. The unmistakable sound of little Al's snoring.

We caught the train with nothing to spare, and it wasn't until we were alone in our carriage, turning north towards Innsbruck, that I said, 'I think the time has come for some explanations.'

Neither of us was feeling or looking our best. I had to carry my cap, and still found it wiser not to move my head more than necessary. Alex looked as if he was suffering from the hangover of all time. 'There's nothing to explain,' he said sulkily.

'That won't do,' I said. 'I want to know what happened last night. Who coshed me? And who brought me back to the hotel? Where is Trude? And what happened to you?'

I thought for a moment Alex was going to sulk; then a smile broke through. But it wasn't a nice smile. 'Mind over matter,' he said. 'Remember? I suppose it never even occurred to you that Trude was a Russian stooge.'

I swallowed hard, and said, 'What makes you think that?'

'It was pretty obvious, wasn't it? Her opportune appearance the day after we arrived. The way she made a dead set at me.'

'Go on,' I said weakly.

'That's the sort of thing *you* were expected to guard me against, you know. I didn't expect to have to do all the work myself. However, Frau

Hodinger was a help. She's got influence, that woman. Her brother's in the Security Police.'

'I see,' I said. It was beginning to sink in.

'I thought I'd lead Trude up the garden path a bit. It was quite safe. There were squads of police on duty. Some of the other side too, I think. I understand there was a carload of thugs waiting down the street for Trude to give the sign that I was ripe for the picking.'

'I saw them,' I said.

'The only trouble was that when the police spotted you pussyfooting off round the back of the hotel, they jumped to the conclusion that *you* were a member of the opposition. And laid you out. Of course, I put them right, and they brought you home.'

'It was *you* climbing out of the window?'

'That's right. I'd got an urgent date.'

'Who with?' I asked. But I knew.

'Frau Hodinger,' said Al. 'Give me a woman of experience every time.' The train dived into a tunnel and saved me the necessity of answering.

I reported to Captain Forestier when I got back. He seemed amused. 'I hope you were tactful,' he said. 'That's the great thing in these assignments. Tact.'

'I think I behaved as a gentleman should,' I said stiffly.

'You've brought him back safe and sound, anyway. I only hope he gives you a good chitty to Colonel Bles.'

As a matter of fact, Alex was talking to Colonel Bles about me at that very moment. I only discovered this, of course, long afterwards. The Colonel has a long face, looks like a bank manager, and is about the most ruthless man I have ever had anything to do with – and I've known some in my time.

'I'm sorry,' he was saying, 'we always thought him a sound operator. Not much imagination, but reliable.'

'I did wonder,' said Alex. 'I mean, what exactly your opinion of him was. All that business about not giving him any warning that he was coming with me. Was that because you couldn't trust him not to blab?'

'Purely a routine precaution. The later he knew about it all, the less harm he could do if he did happen to be indiscreet.'

'I see. Nothing more to it than that?'

The Colonel looked at him curiously. 'No,' he said. 'No. Should there have been?'

'I've got a peculiar sort of brain-box,' said Alex. 'There were one or two things. The first was at Dover. You know that girl you put on to watch over my last hours in England – Gwen What's-her-name?'

The Colonel smiled. 'Yes,' he said. 'Yes, I know her.'

'Well, your little boy scout was very suspicious of her. Very suspicious indeed. More or less told me she was an enemy agent. And so she could have been. But *if* he suspected her, why didn't he just put the local police on to her? Why nearly miss the boat in an effort to telephone London? Especially as he told me himself he had some foolproof method of communicating with you from Austria. I mean to say, either something had to be done about Gwen quick, in which case get the local boys working; or else it was just something to be checked up on some time, in which case send a code message to your office. Nearly missing the boat telephoning London didn't add up either way.'

'No,' said the Colonel. 'No. What was your idea?'

'First I thought he just wanted an excuse for a last-minute talk to one of his girl-friends, but he doesn't have girl-friends. So it could be that he was passing on something to someone who could use it.'

'Yes,' said the Colonel. 'Yes. Anything else?'

'Well, the second day at Velden he got a long cable and retired to his room to read it. And burnt it as soon as he'd finished with it. *Did* any of your people send him a cable?'

'I can find out,' said the Colonel. 'What next?'

'If you find that they didn't my guess would be that it came from the people he took all that trouble to telephone from Dover. Perhaps they put him on to a contact at Klagenfurt. That would make sense of a good deal that happened afterwards. It's none of my business, but if I were you I should have a thorough security check on that young man. I think he's an enemy agent.'

And the devil of it was, of course, that he was quite right.

BY THE PRICKING OF
MY THUMBS

S TAN MELDRUM, NIGHT duty sergeant at Compton Green Police
Station, was not an inspired performer, but he knew the ropes. After
replacing the receiver he sat for a full ten seconds. Eleven o'clock.
He was balancing the possibilities that Detective Inspector Rayburn was
at home in bed, or playing bridge at his club. He thought that bridge was
more likely; a correct guess.

'I assume,' said Rayburn, 'that you told him to touch nothing.' But for
the disparity in their ranks, Meldrum would have said, 'Of course I did,'
but reduced it to 'Yes.'

'And told him to lock the front door. Not to go into the front hall, but
wait for us in the garden.'

'I don't think he was at all keen to go into the hall,' said Meldrum. 'He
telephoned us from a box in the road. I gave the address to the hospital
so they could get Dr Mornington round there.'

'Right. And get hold of Hart.'

'I done that, sir. She wasn't too pleased. She'd only just got home. Been
out all evening looking for bicycles.' As Rayburn understood, it was not
bicycles that Detective Sergeant Alice Hart had been looking for, but the
gang of youths who'd been stealing them. A long, tiring, house-to-house
enquiry. Well, that was how detective sergeants earned their keep.

He said, 'Who does our photography now?'

'Boone, sir.'

'Is he any good?'

'He passed the course at Hendon.'

'Pity,' said Rayburn. He didn't mean that it was a pity that Detective
Constable Boone had passed the Hendon course, which was a very good
one. He meant that it was a pity that Sergeant Owtram, who had been
taking their photographs for six years, should have been promoted to a
desk job at Central. He disliked changes.

When Rayburn reached the police station the runabout was ready in the forecourt. Sergeant Hart was standing beside it talking to Detective Constable Boone, who had his photographic equipment ready; stacked in the back.

'Come with me, Sergeant, and you can tell me all you know about this Lavender Box – and Mr Goldsworthy.'

'It's a high-class retirement home, sir. Never more than three or four residents, all good class and with money, I guess, or they wouldn't be able to afford the prices. There's a housekeeper – doesn't live in – and a girl. They do the cooking and cleaning. And, of course, the matron, Nurse Minter. She was there if the residents needed help – they're all well up in their eighties – but her main job was looking after Mrs Goldsworthy.'

'Who is, I gather, a cripple.'

'Yes, sir. It's that osteo-something or other. It destroys the bone tissues. She can't get out of bed without help. It's tragic, really, because she's still mentally alert – I see the doctor's just beaten us to it.'

Five men and one woman stood for a moment on the stone-flagged front path, a compact group summoned by death to this very ordinary-looking house. Leonard Goldsworthy's face, in contrast to his black beard, was the colour of parchment. Partly the effect of shock, thought Rayburn, but the overhead street lighting didn't help. Dr Mornington, the county pathologist, was tubby and self-possessed. The inspector placed himself smoothly in charge.

He said, 'Is there a back way in? A door at the other end of the hall? Splendid.' They trooped round to the rear of the house. Goldsworthy unlocked the back door, stepped inside, and switched on the light. The hall ran through from back door to front door. They could now see what lay on the matting-covered floor of the front hall.

Boone, less hardened than the others, found his eyes drawn unwillingly to the shattered head of Nurse Minter and the blood and brains spilled round it. Sergeant Hart, being a woman, had time to spare for the clothing on the crumpled body. The neat blouse and skirt of a middle-aged, middle-class housekeeper and the blue overall, with its white collar and cuffs, which announced that she was also a nurse.

The inspector was thinking neither of the body nor the clothing. He was thinking of the many things he had to do and the order in which they had to be done.

He said to Boone, 'Photography first. Then a measured plan. It's particularly important to note exactly – to the nearest inch – how far the body is from the front door and the foot of the stairs. And Doctor, when you've done what you have to here—'

'Very little.'

'So I should suppose. Then you'll want to remove the body to the mortuary for a proper inspection. Perhaps we could use Mr Goldsworthy's telephone—'

'No need,' said the doctor. 'I arranged for an ambulance before I came. And might I make a suggestion. As soon as we've lifted the body – we'll work as far as possible from this end – cover the whole floor.'

'Right,' said Rayburn. He was prepared to accept suggestions from the doctor, who had seen many more corpses than he had. 'Sergeant, blankets and mats over the whole area. Then – I'll need a statement from you, sir—' Mr Goldsworthy nodded. He had not opened his mouth since the police arrived. 'We'll go into Nurse Minter's room while you are getting on with things out here.' To Alice, 'Go up and have a word with Mrs Goldsworthy. You can tell her that Nurse Minter has had an accident. She won't be able to tell us much, but she may have heard things.' And to Boone, 'When you've finished the photography, you can tackle the residents.'

Since they arrived they had been conscious of the sounds of a television programme coming from the room on the other side of the hall. 'The window of that room overlooks the front garden. They may easily have seen something. Now Mr Goldsworthy, if you'll step this way—'

He had a great many questions to ask him. Not only a full account of what he had been doing that evening, up to the moment he had opened his front door and seen the body of Nurse Minter, but questions about the home, its residents, and its routine. But one thing he had to bear in mind: It was now nearly midnight and the Court of Criminal Appeal had recently criticised policemen who subjected witnesses to interrogations lasting into the small hours.

He decided to compromise. He elicited the important points. That Mr Goldsworthy had departed after supper for the local cinema, getting there at half-past eight. The film ('Italian – interesting if you like that sort of thing.') had finished at about a quarter to eleven. The walk home had taken a little over ten minutes. So it must have been around eleven o'clock when he opened the front door and saw what was lying there.

'A great shock,' suggested the inspector.

It had been a shock, and he was only beginning to recover from it. And it was he who raised the point that had been in the inspector's mind. He said, 'I do realise that there are other things you will have to ask me. Might I suggest that we continue tomorrow afternoon? Tomorrow morning there will be a score of urgent matters I shall have to attend to. I shall have to ask the hospital to lend me a nurse. A temporary replacement for Minter. My wife needs regular attention, to say nothing of the residents – all well over eighty. And no doubt I shall have to placate Mrs Burches and stop her from deserting us.'

The inspector said, 'Very well. Two o'clock tomorrow afternoon.'

He was not displeased. By that time he would have a number of reports from the doctor and his subordinates which would sharpen his interrogation.

Alice had learned nothing useful from Mrs Goldsworthy, drowsing among her pillows. Boone had been more fortunate. As he approached the door he heard the rat-tat-tat of a six-shooter.

Evidently the sheriff had got his man. When he got into the room he realized that little information about the happenings of the evening was to be expected. The three ladies were seated in a circle in front of the television set. For them the real world was not in the house or the garden. It was in the little box. Credits were now following each other down the small screen. The play was over. Time for a return to reality.

Boone switched on the light and applied himself, without much hope, to his task.

When they understood that he was a policeman, and what had brought him there, they seemed more excited than alarmed. Young policemen often featured in their screen existence. They were nearly always good. As this man seemed to be. There was nothing alarming in his questions.

He started by writing down their names and was given a thumbnail sketch of their families and their histories. Gertrude Tabard, daughter of an Anglo-Indian colonel. Beatrice Mountfield, relict of Dr Mountfield, the celebrated neurosurgeon. Florence Marant. Her father had been an inventor. She was beginning to draw a picture of the Marant patent rabbit hutch when Gertrude decided that she had occupied the limelight long enough.

She said, 'He doesn't want to know about rabbit hutches, Florence. He wants to find out who attacked Nurse Minter. That's right, isn't it, young man?'

'Indeed it is, ma'am. And if any of you happened to hear anything during the past two hours—'

Three heads were shaken, decisively.

Decisively, thought Boone, but not regretfully. They were none of them showing any signs of sorrow at the departure of Nurse Minter. Interest, yes. Even a sort of pleasure. He supposed that to people in their eighties the death of a much younger woman was a symbol of their own survival. A sort of triumph.

After he left them, the three old ladies sat in silence for a time. Then Beatrice said, 'Do you think he knows, Gertie?'

'If he doesn't know,' said Florence, 'do you think we ought to say something?'

'Wouldn't that be sneaking?' said Gertrude.

The word took them back to their school days. Sneaking was something only lower-class and despicable girls did.

'They've no real proof,' said Florence. 'But we've all heard him, lots of times, creeping along to her room. And if she wasn't doing what we think she was doing, what was she doing?'

'She wasn't cutting his toenails,' said Gertrude.

This made them all cackle. Nurse Minter had cut their toenails for them once a month.

'I think,' said Gertrude, 'that if he doesn't know, it would be in the interests of justice to drop him a hint.'

The interests of justice. That was what their favourite television character, young Mack, stood for. Mack would have found a way out of their difficulty. He was a great hand at solving difficulties.

Boone, who was not as simple as he looked, had quickly circled the house and come in through the kitchen door. The wall between kitchen and television room was not soundproof. He listened with great interest to what the old ladies had to say.

On the following morning all four members of the investigating team had been busy.

Dr Mornington had submitted a preliminary report. He said that Nurse Minter's skull had been crushed by one powerful blow delivered from behind and above. This suggested that the killer was taller than his victim, or that she might have been stooping forward when she was hit. He added that the fact that the body had been lying in the same place since death, and that he had been called in so promptly, allowed him to be more certain about the time of death than was usual in such cases. He put it at a few minutes one side or another of nine o'clock.

The second report, which had been typed out the night before, was on the inspector's desk when he came in. In it Boone had recorded – as nearly verbatim as he could manage – the conversation that he had overheard. Interesting, thought Rayburn. Too spotty to come to a firm conclusion, but the needle of suspicion was already swinging in one direction.

He himself had a date with the local bank manager. He was only too well aware of the tiresome restrictions which gagged such men, but this particular manager was an old friend and prepared, within limits, to be indiscreet. Rayburn eased himself towards what he wanted to know by pointing out that a search would have to be made for Minter's Will. 'By the way,' he went on, 'I'm not of course asking for any figures, but perhaps you could at least tell me this. Was she a woman of any substance?'

The bank manager had nodded. 'An active account,' he said, 'and recently very well in credit.'

That was satisfactory, as far as it went. If details were required later, an Order of the Court would produce them.

But by far the most promising results of that morning's work had been produced by Sergeant Hart. She had found the manager of the Palace Cinema in an expansive mood.

'Most local cinemas,' he said, 'have been killed by television. We're lucky to be alive and kicking. We've got a very faithful audience and one thing we do to keep their interest alive is to insert a surprise item every now and then. A short general-interest film, or a cartoon. Not Disney, he's much too expensive, but there are quite good cartoons being made in England and Germany.'

'Do you show it at the beginning or the end?'

'We start with advertisements and a trailer, or trailers, of forthcoming attractions. Then we slip in a slide which says, "And now, for your additional entertainment: Pom-de-pom. Pompetty pom." '

'I beg your pardon?'

'Don't you recognise it? Their signature tune. We've managed to get ahold of two or three of their earliest ones.'

Pom-de-pom. Pompetty pom. Of course. Stan Laurel and Oliver Hardy. It took her back to her own youth.

'And you put that in after the trailers and before the main item. I wonder if you could give me some timings—'

'For last night?' The manager cocked a shrewd eye at her. 'Yes. Well. We were a little late in starting. It was just past twenty to nine before the lights went down. There were some advertisements and we showed two trailers that night. Twenty-five minutes for the comedy. I'd say it was almost exactly nine-thirty when the main feature started. My box-office girl, Stella, could confirm the times. She keeps a sharp eye on the clock. She has to stay to the end. And she's keen to get home. Would you care to have a word with her?'

'Very much,' said Alice. And, gently prodded, Stella had produced a promising budget of information. She recognised Mr Goldsworthy. A tall man with a beard. He had arrived in good time. And had his favourite seat. Not that it was anyone else's favourite. On the left-hand end of the back row.

She led the way into the auditorium and indicated the seat. Certainly not a good one. Partly blocked by that pillar. Why would anyone want that one?

Stella looked embarrassed. She said, 'Well, I did think—' She indicated the curtained opening alongside the seat. 'Elderly men do get – you know—'

Looking through the curtain Hart saw the sign Toilets, and spared

Stella further embarrassment by saying, 'Yes, I'm sure you're right. That explains it.'

There was a door at the far end with a shaded light over it. 'Emergency exit,' said Stella. 'Has to be kept open during the performance.'

What a setup, said Alice to herself and, later, to the inspector, who said, 'It's beginning to add up, isn't it?'

He was aware that anything culled by Boone from Mrs Burches had to be treated with caution since the housekeeper disliked the nurse, but it filled out the picture that was emerging.

'Set your teeth on edge, it would, the way she treated those three old dears,' Mrs Burches had said. 'All good family. Twice as good as hers. Maybe that was why she tried to take it out on them – in small ways. However, give her credit – she looked after Mrs G all right. Maybe she was hoping for a handout of all the money Mrs G kept under her bed.'

'Do you mean she really—'

'Not really. No. Just a story. The way people talk. However, as I said, she did that part of her job very regular. Brought her all her meals. Tidied her room. Gave her her sleeping draught each night. She must have been on her way to do that when she was attacked.'

'How do you make that out?' said Boone, trying not to sound too eager. This might be important.

'How do I know?' said Mrs Burches, scornful of the ignorance of young men. 'I know because she'd put on her overall. Only do that when she was going on duty, wouldn't she?'

Later that evening Rayburn summed up for his team. Hart and Boone had both been in attendance when Mr Goldsworthy was interrogated. They had written down his answers. When he was questioned about his visit to the cinema, he seemed to know nothing about the 'surprise item.' The inspector's questions relating to timing were specific, as were Mr Goldsworthy's answers.

The start, he thought, had been somewhat later than 8:40. There had been the trailers and the tiresome advertising items. He reckoned that it must have been well after nine before the main item got going. The inspector took him through it twice. Boone, who added shorthand to his other accomplishments, made a verbatim note of what Mr Goldsworthy said.

'If he was in the cinema at nine o'clock,' the inspector said, 'he couldn't possibly have overlooked the Laurel and Hardy film. So where was he? Easy enough, in the particular seat he was occupying, to slip out and make his way back to the house; knowing Nurse Minter's routine, he plans to get there just before nine o'clock. Listens until he hears her come out of her room, unlocks the front door, and steps in. Nurse is surprised to see him. He says, "Who's been spilling things on the carpet?" Nurse stoops down to see what his left hand is pointing at. Round comes his right hand with a weapon in it. An iron bar, perhaps—'

Boone wrote down, 'Weapon?'

'Back to the cinema. Home by eleven. Sees what's in the hall. Telephones the police station.'

His assistants nodded. It seemed to fit.

'And the motive. That's clear too. He'd had sex with Minter, more than once. The old ladies heard what was going on. The only other person in the house at night was Mrs G, who'd been given a sleeping draught. A pretty powerful one, we may guess, because if she *had* heard anything, even suspected it, there'd have been the devil to pay. Her body may have been weak, but there was nothing wrong with her mind. Divorce the least of it. Her Will remade. The money that helped to keep the household going cut off. Minter knows this. Starts to put on pressure. Successfully. Her account starts to look very healthy. When we get an order opening bank records, the position will be clear. Regular withdrawals of cash from his account, regular payments into hers.'

Alice said, 'Do you think we've got enough to charge him?'

'I do. And in the old days I would have done so. Now I need the backing of the Crown Prosecution Service.'

'Surely you'll get it, sir,' said Boone.

That was on Wednesday.

Every Thursday the three residents went out for a jaunt. This was a popular move. It enabled Mr Goldsworthy to spend a few undisturbed hours in the office of his almost-bankrupt insurance agency, and it gave the nurse an afternoon off. Each week they hired the same car, with a driver who knew their habits. Compton Green being on the outer edge of the metropolitan sprawl, it took only a short time to get out into the countryside. The village they were making for boasted an old-fashioned tea parlour. Their table, kept for them, was tucked away at the back of it. Gertrude presided over the teapot. When they were all served she said, in the manner of a chairman opening the business of the meeting, 'I should have thought they'd have worked it out by now, wouldn't you?'

Beatrice said, 'Nowadays you can't trust anyone to take any sort of independent action.'

'Red tape,' said Florence. 'Always consult someone else before you do anything. Young Mack wouldn't have stood for it.'

'Nor would my father,' said Gertrude. 'The Colonel never asked anyone's advice over anything important. If something had to be done he did it.'

Two heads nodded approval of this masculine firmness.

'I must say,' said Beatrice, 'that I find our new nurse an improvement. Don't you, Gertie?'

'A distinct improvement,' said Gertrude. 'She calls me madam.' She waved to the waitress, who hurried across. She had a great respect for the old ladies. 'Could you bring us another jug of hot water?' And to Florence, 'I don't think you should eat another of those cakes, Florrie. They'll bring you out in spots.'

'I'd rather have cakes and spots than no cakes and no spots,' said Florence defiantly.

Mr Arbuthnot of the Crown Prosecution Service said, 'I'm sorry, but no.'

Too often recently he had suffered humiliation at the hands of defending counsel.

'Your case is ingenious, but it's got two gaping holes in it. Look at the map. There are eight built-up streets, all well lit, between the cinema and the home. By your account, Goldsworthy went through all of them before nine o'clock. How could he hope to do so without being seen? A tall man, with a beard. Produce me one reliable witness who saw him coming or going and you close that gap. Less serious perhaps, but the defense will latch on to it, what about the weapon? Did he make a detour out into the countryside and throw it into a ditch? Double the chance of being seen. Or drop it quietly into a drain on the way back to the cinema. More likely. Have you searched all the drains?'

The unhappy inspector had to admit that he had not searched all of them. Not yet.

Although it would have been out of his place to say so, Mr Arbuthnot nearly added, 'Get on with it. Do some work.'

It was Mrs Burches's daughter, who was walking out with Ernie, one of the police constables, who gave them all the latest news.

'Been at it a week,' she said. 'And they aren't half making themselves unpopular. First it was questions about bicycles. Now it's murderers. Life's not worth living, people say.'

Many of the uniformed branch thought the same. Ten of them had been dragooned into doing work which, they thought, belonged to the detective branch. Rayburn encouraged them as much as he could, but before the end of the week he began to wonder whether his own small contingent was pulling its weight.

He said to Alice, 'Boone seems to spend most of his time out in the country. What's he up to?'

'He's got an idea.'

'What idea?'

'I think he'd better tell you himself.'

Summoned into the presence, Detective Constable Boone launched out into waters which were full of shoals and rocks.

Taking a deep breath, he said, 'It did occur to me to wonder, sir. I mean, the legal boys seem to think that the main drawback to your – to our – theory was that no one had seen Goldsworthy between the cinema and his house. Although they were all on edge about the bicycle thieves, and keeping their eyes open for strangers.'

'So?'

'What I thought was, suppose the killer was another man altogether – living out in the countryside somewhere. He hears the rumour about Mrs Goldsworthy's money. He could reach the back of the house without going through any main streets. He breaks in. Runs into the nurse, hits her harder than he means, sees he's killed her, and bolts. The weapon could be miles away, in a ditch—'

'So what was Goldsworthy doing when he was meant to be in the cinema – but quite clearly wasn't.'

'I think he was paying a visit to the massage parlour – so called – two streets away. A girl who worked there says he was a regular client.'

'And saw him there on the night of the killing?'

Boone looked unhappy.

'No, sir. She'd been sacked a fortnight before. That's why she was willing to talk.'

'Then you've no evidence at all that he was there that night.'

'No, sir.'

'I see. Well, there's no reason why you shouldn't think out any wild and wonderful solutions you like, but when I give orders, I like to have them carried out. I've read the reports from the uniformed branch. They don't seem to cover the ground. For instance, there are two long back streets – just the sort of quiet way he'd have preferred – they don't seem to have been covered at all. So get on with it.'

Mrs Rayburn, when she was told about it that evening, said, 'That young man's got a swollen head.'

When Boone went to Sergeant Hart for sympathy she said, 'What we were taught as recruits was, consider the physical evidence. Right. And that's what I'm going to do. For a start, where are the photographs you took?'

Boone had taken thirty beautiful photographs, showing not only the body but all the surrounding features from different angles. Three prints had been made of each, one for the inspector, one for the Crown prosecutors, one for the files. So far as he knew, no one had looked at them since.

Sergeant Hart took the file copies home, consumed her simple supper, and started to study them. Some of them had been taken after the body had been moved. One seemed to interest her particularly. A slight disturbance of the matting and the surrounding blood and plasma defined precisely the place where the body had fallen. And surely, there – faintly—?

There was an angle-poise lamp with a daylight bulb that she used when she was doing her tapestry. She turned it on and shone it down on the photograph. Yes. There it was. Someone had drawn a cross, in brown chalk, on the matting. Just visible to the naked eye, clearly visible to the eye of the camera.

She didn't sleep much that night. The possible implications of what she had seen were building up. She visualised the front hall and the staircase that went straight up from it for two flights. On the first storey the bedroom of the Goldsworthys and the nurse. On the second the bed-sitting rooms of the residents. Before sleep finally overtook her she had made up her mind. The day now dawning was a Thursday. In the afternoon the house would be empty, with the possible exception of the Burches, mother and daughter. Boone should keep them out of the way. They would be happy talking to him over a cup of tea.

'Certainly I'll do it, if it will help,' said Boone. 'But couldn't you explain what you're up to?'

'One demonstration,' said Alice, 'is worth half a dozen explanations. Or so we were told.'

For all her certainty, when the moment came she found her hand shaking. The idea was so strange, so shocking, so horrible, that it must be incorrect. A tower of surmise built on a single chalk mark.

Standing in the hall she could hear the murmur of voices from the kitchen, interrupted by occasional screams and giggles from young Miss Burches, which indicated that Boone was doing his stuff. Apart from that the house was totally silent.

She climbed the stairs, up to the top, and looked into the three bedrooms that faced her. In each of them, as she went in, she encountered the same faint and elusive smell. Potpourri, lavender. or just old age?

She searched each room in turn, cautious as any burglar, careful to put back everything exactly where she found it.

Beatrice was the artist. She had a handsome box of watercolour paints, a jar of brushes, a pile of canvases, an easel. And a cardboard box of chalks, all colours. Yes. Including brown.

The only item of interest in Florence's room was a length of cord, neatly coiled and tucked away in one of her tidily arranged drawers.

In Gertrude's room there was a collection of Benares brass, a relic, no doubt, of her father's service in India. It was ranged on two shelves: candlesticks, boxes, vases, and pots. Lovingly cleaned and polished, it winked back at her as she selected one very small pot and one very large and heavy one.

Returning to the landing, she stood for a moment looking directly down. The matting that had originally covered the hall floor had been taken up in pieces and sent to the forensic laboratory for examination. The tiles, which it was now Mrs Burches's job to polish, gleamed in the afternoon sun.

Unrolling the cord, she fastened the small pot to it and lowered it until it tinkled against the tiles. Then she tied the end to the banister and walked down. She had the photograph with her. There was no doubt about it. The little pot was resting exactly where the cross had been chalked on the matting.

Upstairs once more, she pulled up the small pot, untied it, and put it and the cord back where they had come from. Then she went down again, poked her head into the kitchen, and said, 'Sorry to interrupt, but I've got a little job for this young man. Won't be a moment.'

When they had left the room, Mrs Burches said that it didn't seem right to her, a man being ordered about by a girl. Her daughter said she could see nothing wrong in it. Girls did all sorts of jobs nowadays.

Back in the hall, Alice pointed to a cross which she had just made with a piece of brown chalk from Beatrice's box. She said, 'Have another look at this photograph. Isn't that exactly where the cross is on the matting?'

'Pretty well,' said Boone.

'Then get a pillow – better, a bolster – from Nurse's room and put it over the mark.'

When he had done this Alice, who had returned upstairs, called down to him, 'Stand back, well back.' As she spoke, the heavy brass pot fell, with a heart-stopping thud, into the middle of the bolster.

'And that,' said Alice, 'is the answer to both the objections raised by the Crown Prosecutors. No one saw anyone approaching the house, at the front or the back, for the simple reason that no one did approach it. And here's your weapon so carefully cleaned that I'm afraid our forensic experts won't find a speck of blood left on it.'

Boone looked at her with mingled admiration and sympathy. He said, 'Are you really going to try this on the inspector? He'll throw something at you, or burst a blood vessel.'

The inspector did neither. He heard her out, made some noncommittal comment, and refrained from laughing until he got home that evening. Then he gave full vent to his feelings.

'Just imagine,' he said, 'instituting proceedings against those three old dears. It wouldn't be laughed out of court, because it wouldn't even get into court.'

'I don't think it's a laughing matter at all,' said his wife. 'Can't you see that that girl is simply trying to queer your pitch? I remember you told me that there was some arrangement in the division for cross-posting. The sooner that young lady's posted away the better.'

'Well,' said Gertrude, as she filled the three teacups, 'it was half a success. We got rid of Nurse Minter, but not, as we had every reason to anticipate, of Mr Goldsworthy as well.'

'If the inspector had had any gumption,' said Beatrice, 'he'd have charged him. Particularly when we presented him with the motive.'

They had all heard Boone coming into the kitchen and had raised their voices slightly for his benefit.

'Young Mack would have done it,' said Florence. 'However, one blessing. From what her young man told Annie Burches, it seems that Detective Sergeant Smarty-pants Hart has been sacked.'

'Sacked?'

'Well, not exactly sacked. Shoved to another division. To concentrate on cases of child abuse.'

The three old ladies cackled at the thought. They none of them had any use for children.

'All the same,' said Gertrude, 'I don't like leaving a job half done. We shall have to move carefully, but in a month or two, when the dust has settled, I wondered whether we might try something with – poison.'

'Arsenic? Belladonna?'

'Atropine? Nicotine?'

'Strychnine,' said Gertrude decisively. 'Naturally we can't buy it ourselves, but if we complained of infestation by rats in the kitchen, Mr Goldsworthy would have to buy it himself.'

'*And* sign the poison book,' said Florence.

'We could get hold of a dead rat,' said Beatrice. 'From my great-nephew. The one who's a farmer.'

'Excellent,' said Beatrice.

The thought of a dead rat seemed to entrance the three witches.

Double, double toil and trouble;

Fire burn and cauldron bubble.

APPENDIX A

For stories collected in this present volume, information is provided on first publication dates and any alternative titles.

'A Pity About the Girl' in *New Black Mask 3*, edited by Matthew J. Bruccoli and Richard Layman, Harcourt Brace Jovanovich, 1985.

'The Brave Don't Talk' in *John Bull*, 1 December 1951.

'The Man Who Was Reconstituted' in the *Man Who ...* edited by H.R.F. Keating, Macmillan, 1992.

'One-tenth Man' in *Ellery Queen's Mystery Magazine*, October 1956.

'What Happened at Castelbonato?' in *Good Housekeeping*, July and August 1956.

'Camford Cottage' in *The After Midnight Ghost Book*, edited by James Hale, Hutchinson, 1980.

'Safe!' in *Woman's Journal*, March 1956.

'The Revenge of Martin Lucas Field on Colonel Cristobal Ocampos' in *Argosy*, April 1968. This story is also known as 'The Cork in the Bottle'.

'Basilio' in *Winter's Crimes 1*, edited by George Hardinge, Macmillan, 1969. This story is also known as 'The Wrong Fox'.

'Prize of Santenac' in *John Bull*, 22 October 1955.

'Villa Almirante' in *Argosy*, December 1959.

'The Two Footmen' in *The New Adventures of Sherlock Holmes*, edited by Martin Harry Greenberg and Carol-Lynn Rössel Waugh, Carroll and Graf, 1987.

'Trust Little Al' in *Argosy*, October 1955. This story is also known as 'The Case of the Purloined Philanderer'.

'By the Pricking of my Thumbs' in *Ellery Queen's Mystery Magazine*, September-October 1996.

APPENDIX B

For stories mentioned in the introduction to this volume, information is provided on the books in which they have been collected.

Game Without Rules. (11 stories). Harper (US) 1967; Hodder and
 Stoughton (UK) 1968
The Spoilers
The Headmaster
Trembling's Tours
Stay of Execution. (13 stories). Hodder and Stoughton 1971
Weekend at Wapentake
Touch of Genius (as Modus Operandi)
Xinia Florata
The Blackmailing of Mr Justice Ball
Amateur in Violence. (11 stories). Davis (US) 1973
Amateur in Violence
Touch of Genius (as Modus Operandi)
Tea Shop Assassin
Petrella at Q. (12 stories). Hodder and Stoughton, 1977; Harper 1977
Rough Justice
Mr Calder and Mr Behrens. (12 stories). Hodder and Stoughton, 1982;
 Harper 1982
Signal Tresham
Young Petrella. (16 stories). Hodder and Stoughton, 1988; Harper 1988
Source Seven
Who Has Seen the Wind
Breach of the Peace
Anything for a Quiet Life. Hodder and Stoughton, 1990; Carroll and
 Graf, 1990
Contains 9 Jonas Pickett stories
The Road to Damascus. (4 stories) Eurographica (Finland), 1990
Trembling's Tours

The Man who Hated Banks. (18 stories). Crippen and Landru (US), 1997
Back in Five Years
An Appealing Pair of Legs
The Mathematics of Murder. (14 stories). Hale, 2000
The Mathematics of Murder
The Curious Conspiracy. (20 stories). Crippen and Landru, 2002; Hale, 2002
Scream from a Soundproof Room (as Scream in a Soundproof Room)
Under the Last Scuttleful
The Inside Pocket
Even Murderers Take Holidays. (27 stories). Hale 2007
A Nose in a Million
Old Mr Martin
Death Money
Mrs Haslet's Gone
The Drop Shot